London-reared of Irish parents, **Morag Prunty** edited several young women's magazines in London including *More!* and *Just Seventeen* before moving to Ireland in 1990 to relaunch *Irish Tatler*. She is now a full-time writer and lives in Dublin with her husband and son. *Disco Daddy* is her second novel.

Also by Morag Prunty in Pan Books

DANCING WITH MULES

MORAG PRUNTY

DiSCO DADDY

A Pan
Original

First published 2002 by Pan Books
an imprint of Pan Macmillan Ltd
Pan Macmillan, 20 New Wharf Road, London N1 9RR
Basingstoke and Oxford
Associated companies throughout the world
www.panmacmillan.com

ISBN 0 330 48609 8

A CIP catalogue record for this book is available from
the British Library.

Typeset by SetSystems Ltd, Saffron Walden, Essex
Printed and bound in Great Britain by
Mackays of Chatham plc, Chatham, Kent

FOR MY SISTER,

CLAIRE

PART ONE

JUNE

1

The offices of *How'ya* were in a last-minute deadline frenzy. Four days to press and Kellie Logan, the famous Irish-American novelist had withdrawn her permission to use her 'Beautiful Kellie Logan Invites *How'ya* to Visit Her in Her Beautiful Holiday Home on the Beautiful Holiday Island of Antigua in the Sunny Caribbean!'

Intoxicated by sunshine and the glory of being followed everywhere by *How'ya* staff photographer, Roddy Coogan (so smooth he could convince the hoariest of dodgy old crumblies that they could make the front cover of *Vogue/GQ*), Kellie forgot herself. Virtually every photograph featured her substantial and mottled limbs draped around the ebony beauty of an awesome variety of local males. All of them young, and none of them an appropriate backdrop to Ms Logan's less than edifying physique. When the text and pictures had been sent to Kellie's office for sign-off on editorial approval, her agent had seized and destroyed them and sent a solicitor's letter demanding that all remaining contacts and film be released.

It was a disaster.

Karin, *How'ya*'s editor was in an emergency meeting with her publisher.

'Did you tell her we'd pay?'

With Eamonn Doyle, middle-aged businessman and all round comb-over golf-playing slack-wearing gobshite, everything came down to money. He truly believed that even dignity had its price. In many cases, this was true – but not with Kellie. Eamonn honestly could not understand why one of Ireland's most high-profile novelists did not want images of her great lardy arse insulted with the briefest of day-glo thongs emblazoned across the windows of the newsagents of Ireland for the future entertainment of every waiting dental patient for years to come. Frankly, the pictures were so deeply unpleasant – they would have *caused* toothache in even the hardiest of begrudgers. To publish them under any circumstances would have crossed the boundaries of the amusingly cynical into downright cruelty.

'Look, she's not interested in the money, Eamonn. She just doesn't want them seen. By anyone. Ever.'

'But sure,' he said, holding up a head shot featuring two vast mammaries, a drunken lopsided smile and matching polka-dot turban-bikini set, 'she looks grand to me. A fine-looking woman, sure what's her problem? Ah, lookit – maybe we'll run with them anyway. She'll love it when it comes out. It'll be great publicity for her, so it will.'

Karin closed her eyes and took a deep breath. Eamonn was just not capable of weeding out the Number One 'international doing-us-a-favour star-status celebrities' from the 'poor sad bastard wannabes who'd ride their grand-mothers for a bit of publicity' and who made up 90 per cent of How'ya's victims.

She'd never had this problem on the Irish Press. Once, Karin was more than tempted to point out to her greedy buffoon of a boss, she had been a proper journalist. A serious-minded young woman, Karin Sheridan had served her time diligently at University College Dublin – studied hard for a post-grad in journalism and won the prize – staff writer on the Irish Press. News and features. Investigative journalism. Cover stories. Throughout the eighties she fought hard to keep herself out of the girlie ghetto of social columns and fashion pages. Her own column turned her into a well-known national figure, commenting each week on serious issues – government scandals, women in politics – high-minded important stuff. None of your 'Twink Opens the New Peter Mark Salon in Stillorgan This Week' or 'This Season's Fashion Shocks as Skirts Go Thigh-High' for our Karin. Oh no. It was 'The Social Democrats Bite Back' and 'In-Depth Interview With the New Minister for Education' for this lady. If she wanted a break from the politics and the social issues, she would cut her creative juices with a historical book critique or an upmarket restaurant review. Not that she was a bore or anything. Karin still hung out at the Pink with her old friends Valerie and Sinead – both confirmed rock-chicks. She was not incapable of donning the odd pair of fishnets, scrunching up the bob into an eighties 'just ridden' do and chewing the face off a visiting rock dignitary in the Library at Lillies when the mood took her. It's just that – all in all – she didn't make a habit out of having too much fun. Sure, she had the subtle low-lights and the groomed bob. She knew how to coordinate shoulder-pads and shoes so as to keep the Scary Lesbian comments at arm's length and keep the beery old journo bosses just sweet enough to put her in line for constant promotion. She was heading to be the first woman editor of a national newspaper. It would take time, but by the early nineties Karin was confident it was on the cards.

Then disaster struck. The *Irish Press* group went wallop.

Of course, everyone was devastated, but once she had got over the shock, Karin felt things would work out. She was well known enough to get a shot at television – perhaps presenting her own social issues discussion pro-gramme? The *Irish Times* – well, that was her spiritual home really – and when the news broke, they were sure to call her up and offer her something. But then – hey! – London was an option too. The *Independent*? Or the *Guardian*? Yes, that was really more her speed. Sure, she should have gone there years ago. Perhaps this was her chance to really make the leap.

Five months later, Karin's big ideas had been reduced to a perfunctory letter from the features editor on the *Guardian* offering her a possible feature on spec; two advertorials in the *Irish Times* and the promise of a job interview 'should anything come up' which was code for 'when one of our staff reporters retires or dies – which-ever comes first', and an assurance from the RTE newsroom that she was on file for the next round of audition tests which would be happening whenever or never – whichever came soonest.

The devastation of losing all the status she had worked so hard to achieve was gradual, and did not have the great glorious shock that sets the healing and resilient process of grief rolling into action. Over those few months it set about Karin's confidence like a kind of a virus. Claws of cynicism tightening over the hopes she'd once had and petrifying them into little bullets of hate. She changed. She got hard. She lost the almost good-schoolgirl attitude to her life. Integrity was a luxury she could no longer afford.

When *Good Woman Yourself*, the mass-market women's magazine (owned by Eamonn Doyle – Leitrim Crystal, woolly jumper and general Irish tourist tat magnate), rang her up and offered her £800 a month to manage their fashion and beauty pages, Karin realized, finally, that she had crossed the line that separates pride and necessity. The nest egg was gone and the mortgage was due. Karin needed the money badly enough to finally sell out.

It was all downhill from there. Ghastly fashion shows with grisly foundation-caked PR 'girls' always overly delighted to see her. In her former life, when Karin Sheridan walked into a room the same women had quaked in their courts for fear she was about to expose some awful financial indiscretion perpetrated by one of their clients. Nowadays they beamed at her effusively because they knew her presence would result in some inoffensive illustrated piece of drivel entitled 'New Year, New You!' or 'Down a Dress Size in Seven Days!'

Karin got on with it. She learned to lick up to advertisers, write a Go-Get-'Em-Girl! coverline, discern between lip-gloss and lip-shine, make up '101 Ways to Change Your Hairstyle in Under Five Minutes' – and other such skills which seem fatuous until you have to actually learn how to master them. As the years passed, her heels got higher, her hair got blonder and her nails got longer. She took on a new brittle glamour to replace the more respectable conservatism of her newspaper demeanour. She came to enjoy the freedom of being outrageous and over the top; of being able to let it all hang out with the girls without fear of being labelled an air-head floozy. Throughout her thirties she learned to drink and disco and double life. She learned about skin-care and socializing. Four years ago when Eamonn had offered her the editorship of Ireland's first celebrity glossy – she threw herself into charming Ireland's 'Big Names' into the pages of *How'ya* with the smug knowledge that she herself was too smart to ever take it too seriously. All in all, she had come to quite enjoy her new life. But somewhere at the back of her mind was the niggling belief that the *really* smart set – the documentary makers, the BBC exports, the 'hairy clever Trinity set' – thought that she had moved over to the other side and pitied Karin the loss of her erudition and her past status. When she had thoughts like that she had Val and Sinead to turn to and as the years had taught her, there was no dark thought that a couple of vodka cocktails and new hand-bag couldn't cure.

'Eamonn,' Karin gave him one of her best testicle-shrinking looks. The kind of assertive 'I have nails and I'm not afraid to use 'em' Power Glowers that set comb-overs the likes of her boss's a couple of millimetres upright.

'Kellie Logan will *sue*, Eamonn – I know *I* would. Now, if you want to run with it, then it's no skin off my nose, but remember, a million dollars wouldn't keep her in nail technicians for the year – and I just feel you need to think about whether it's going to be worth it.'

Sometimes – just sometimes – Karin's ability for political argument came in handy.

Her boss's lips collapsed into a sulking slab, and his lazy eye twitched unattractively. She'd won. Eamonn was not happy, but he knew this was going nowhere. Really and truly, he didn't give a shit one way or the other. He just liked to swoop down every now and again and throw a bit of authority in the direction of this uppity bird whom he'd done the enormous favour of giving a job to when she was on her uppers. In return for his generous patronage Eamonn Doyle had not enjoyed so much as a passing flirt from the hard-nosed cow – never mind the full blown micky-hockey treatment that he felt was his due – *especially* after he had given her the editorship of *How'ya*! I mean – it wasn't expecting too much surely? A bit of gratitude was all he wanted. Surely to God dinner and an overnighter in the Merrion – what was the harm in that? The rooms there were lovely; telly in the bedroom and him sprawled out on the king-size in a fluffy robe. What more could a girl want? And, frankly, she didn't exactly qualify for the title 'girl' any more. I mean, she was pushing, what, forty? No spring chicken anyway! It wasn't like he was running around after a nineteen-year-old model that was out of his league or anything. Seven years the cheeky strap had been working for him – seven years! And she hadn't put out once! And it wasn't for the want of his asking! OK – so she'd done a great job with *How'ya*. It was pulling in the pennies. But Christ, Eamonn thought as he watched Karin's breasts strain against the confines of her tight, tailored jacket, a man cannot live on money alone!

'Sorry Eamonn, but we will just have to find something else.' Karin was not happy with the idea of having to fill six pages at such short notice, but was confident that at least she had averted another disaster.

As Eamonn was musing on the general neglect of his basement playroom, a lascivious image leapt to the front of his mind, with such speed and surety that he chose to interpret it as a flash of genius. Then the triangular eyebrows raised, indicating ominously to Karin that he had had 'one of his little ideas'.

'I've had one of my little ideas!' he said. 'How about getting that friend of yours – what's her name? The ex-model – woman that owns a clothes shop – used to be married to that pop singer?'

'Jack Valentine?'

'Yes – that's her! Veronica . . .'

'Valerie.' Karin knew exactly where he was going – but she'd let the old lech run his course. Poor fecker with his lazy eye and the fuzzy dyed comb-over – loaded with money and he couldn't find even the most temporary placement for his wee lad. He hadn't a clue.

'That's it! Valerie Valentine! Why don't we do a shoot with her . . .'

'An underwear shoot?' Karin had her eyes closed and was running the tips of her fingers along her eyebrows. Not again. Please God not again. Would he not consider going back to the wife. He'd left her as soon as the millions had earned him playboy status – the sad sod never considered that his atrocious appearance would hold him back. Did he not know this generation of models had upped the ante? The Onassis era was gone. These days you had to be rich – *and* good-looking – or at the very least dripping with urbane sophistication – to get laid. She felt for him sometimes. Honest she did.

'Brilliant! Brilliant idea! An underwear shoot with Valerie Valentine in her shop – in underwear. She sells underwear doesn't she? In her shop? Ladies' underwear?'

'Yes, Eamonn, she does.'

'Yes, I thought so. I thought she sold underwear all right. Lovely. Lovely lacy bras and things – what are they called – those things?'

'Thongs, Eamonn.'

'Yes, yes. Thongs. That's settled then, yes?' he pleaded hopefully. 'Valerie Valentine. In a thong. In her shop. And a bra – of course . . . or whatever . . .' He trailed off pathetically, knowing in himself that he had gone too far.

Karin looked at him with something bordering on pity.

'We ran that story a few months ago, Eamonn.'

Something in her tone infuriated him.

He drew himself up to his full five foot four inches and smoothed his chubby little hand along the twelve strings that passed for a hairdo and composed himself back into a state of authority.

'Yes, we did Karin – and it went down very well – the advertisers loved it.'

Karin could feel her power slipping away.

'Yes, but . . .'

'It will be excellent publicity for her shop – and I'm sure Veronic—'

'Valerie.'

'I'm sure Valerie will be delighted for the opportunity to publicize her shop again.'

'Well, perhaps we can do something different this time – than the underwear . . .'

She was making a cod of him – making him talk about thongs and things – and then acting all cool and professional on him. Really! Her days were numbered! Really they were!

'Whatever Karin! You're the editor – you decide. Really girl – you must stop deferring to me on all these things. I'm a busy man! I don't have time for this!' – and he marched out the door.

Karin had won the battle – but it seemed she was losing the war.

She knew that kind-hearted Valerie would do anything

for her to get her out of this hole, but she still hated asking. She always seemed to be the one asking for favours these days, and it was wearing her out. Karin wondered when it would all end. She had a nasty vision of herself at sixty-five – papery hands with thick horny scarlet nails tapping out some retired celebrity's number on the Star Tac trying to talk them onto the pages of Ireland's oldest glossy celebrity magazine.

She had the feeling that time was running out. But time for what? Karin Sheridan didn't know.

2

[faint show-through text visible from previous page]

Sinead had had enough today. Enough hassle, enough hustle, and enough – more than enough – hard core. Frankly, it had been one of those days.

When Sinead O'Sullivan had announced through a small ad in the *Evening Herald* that her company, SOS Music Management, were looking for 'The rave artists of the future' and invited the DJs of Dublin to an open audition at her offices, she had not been banking on every teenage boy in Ireland with a home mixing desk and a shred of ambition to turn up. But word had long since sliced through Ireland's thriving underground dance scene that Sinead O'Sullivan was the woman behind DJ Dodgy's massive club hit, 'Grunt Bunny' – a catchy instrumental number featuring a single 'nyeep' sound repeated several thousand times per minute to a thumping baseline which, to the carefully trained ear, sounded very like a bunny grunting – hence the title. It was in fact the sound of its creator running a wet hand up the plastic handle of his mother's kitchen mop, one of those little musical gems that God had sent out of the blue to inspire him into an immediate sampling session. Mrs Dodgy had objected mightily at the temporary kidnapping of her kitchen equipment but now, seven months after the huge success of *Animal Manners – The Album*, she enjoyed twice weekly visits from her very own char – and had all but forgotten where the mop was kept thanks to her son's elevation to European DJ Star Status and her own recent position as *Woman's Way*'s 'most glamorous rock mum'. Hence also the fact that by ten o'clock on that grim Monday morning, a gang of baggy-trousered pimply back-to-front-baseball-capped youngsters had formed a nervous writhing snake along Baggot Street the head of which was the otherwise unobtrusive basement door of Sinead's swanky office.

First in was an angry man from the posh dry cleaners on the corner complaining that the entrance to his business had been blocked since eight and that the highbrow clientele enjoyed by Stains of Stature was not accustomed to having to elbow their way through a mob of gangly youths in order to get their silk undies treated in the manner to which they had been accustomed. Sinead apologized profusely to him, and to the indignant lady from the sandwich shop who had had three packets of crisps and a blueberry muffin nicked from her entrance fridge, *and* to the flustered guard who had just arrested young Philbert 'Fleabag' Watson for weeing into the gutter, his defence being that he didn't want to lose his place in the queue. 'Sheez Sinead O'Sullivan maa-an! Sheez a Goddezz man! The Queen of da Dance-zeen ma-an! No! You donunnerstan'! Thizziz my lucky bre-he-

he-he-heak!' he wailed as his Nikes scraped a trench in the paving stones and Guard Pat Donnelly, a staunch Thurles man who it might be said was *not* conversant with the nuances of dance-music culture, dragged him by the ponytail to Harcourt Street Station for the severest of ticking offs.

Although indeed, no punishment could have been greater than young Philbert's denial of an audience with the 'Queen of Dance'. Except perhaps the punishment that Sinead was at this moment feeling locked in the windowless soundproofed ante-room of her basement office, as she listened to yet another track, which sounded, as had the dozen tracks before them, like a million frantic DIY fanatics hammering shelves. The records varied of course. Of course they did. A million DIY fanatics hammering shelves and breaking wind at various intervals. Bang-bang-bang-bang-*ba-arf*-bang-bang. A million DIY fanatics hammering shelves and banging their thumbs at various intervals. Bang-bang-bang-bang-*ee-eek*-bang-bang. At one point Sinead was certain she even heard someone say 'Pass me the hammer mate' in the background. When she questioned the creator, a skinny young lad who was so thin he looked like a little head perched on top of a sweatshirt thrown over her Philippe Starck office chair, he ballooned with pride and told her it was in fact his mate yelling 'Piss on the header Mike'. Sinead did not feel that the sentiment behind this piece of Post-Modern contemporary poetry begged further investigation, and sent yet another Stussy-clad teenager shuffling disheartedly out of her office.

By twelve thirty, she was exhausted. Her head felt as if it was inhabited by a dozen ducks, and in the two-minute breaks between interviews, she could hear them quack-quack-quacking even when the music was turned off. She sent Dizzy her assistant out to do a headcount of the remaining Ear Terrorists – and in the five minutes she was gone downed half a bottle of Ballygowan to try and flush out some of that morning's caffeine in the hope it might make her feel slightly less hysterical. How, in the name of God, had she managed to become the pivot around which these mindless and brain-numbing records were spinning?

The truth was that she knew nothing about dance music. Less than nothing. No, that wasn't true. She knew one thing. And that thing was that she didn't like it. Actually, that wasn't entirely true either. She used to enjoy the *luxury* of just 'not liking' it. Now she found herself in a situation where she well and truly *loathed* it.

Sinead O'Sullivan was thirty-nine years of age. A rock-chick at heart, her passion for music had started young – in her bedroom, Radio Luxembourg glued to her ear listening to Slade and Gary Glitter, envying her older brother the five-year margin that permitted him out to the exotic unimaginable excitement of live gigs. The Miami Showband, the Horslips – dishy Rory Gallagher. She couldn't wait to get her hands on them. When she was fifteen, the punk scene was exploding over in the UK and Sinead O'Sullivan rebelled with a capital 'R'. Touching five foot eleven in a pair of robbed vintage stilettos, she discovered that she was simply too big – and with the addition of black lipstick – too scary for her parents to stop her. While Tom and Mary O'Sullivan sat tearfully offering up rosaries for the safe-keeping of their increasingly satanic-looking daughter's soul, Sinead was professing her dislike of Mondays with the steaming wave of Boomtown Rats fans in Moran's Hotel in Talbot Street.

'We'd poor Bridie's funeral tea in Moran's not a year ago,' said Sinead's Aunt Sheila to her mother during one of their fretful Saturday vigil's for her niece's moral safety.

'The world's gone mad,' she said.

'This won't be the end of it . . .' muttered her husband Pat into his tea, 'sure I've heard they're selling condominiums in the toilets at these places and everything.'

The Vipers at McGonigal's. Revolver at the Baggot Inn. A rim of Loving Care 'Blue-Black' hair dye around her parents' bath; customising the collar of her dad's discarded 'funerals' coat with 450 safety pins; twenty Embassy and a Barry M 'Bile Green' lipstick tucked into the breast pocket of her ripped army surplus jacket from the Dandelion Market. They were exciting times.

In the end, Uncle Pat needn't have worried her mother about the free sale of condominiums in the public toilets of Ireland because young Sinead was already on the pill.

The height, the panstick and the attitude placed her a good five years older than she was, and she was, well, let's just say she was a *very* popular young lady with the – as her father called them – 'Guitar Gutties!' of Dublin.

But the Dublin punk scene was altogether a more civilized affair than its UK birthplace. In other words, you could rebel all you liked as long as you finished your degree. And Sinead's fellating skills always remained secondary to her love of the music itself. She turned out to be the best kind of groupie. While she knew she would never tire of the taste of stage-sweat on steaming testicle on recent release from a leather trouser, she was a bright girl and when she shocked her parents by graduating with a first class honours from UCD she decided to move to London and turn her obsession into a day-job. She spent the eighties clawing her way through the publicity department in a big London record company. Armed with a kooky vintage rock-chick wardrobe and a youthful determination to turn the world onto the mind-expanding benefits of genuinely good music, Sinead was about to hit a very steep learning curve. New Romantic Boys In Blouses on the front cover of *Smash Hits*. Climie Fisher. Sam Fox. Chesney Hawkes. Rick Astley. Fellow Irishman Chris de Burgh. Spiritually, they were dark times for musical purists. Sinead caved. It was Musical Integrity: nil points – Thatcher's Britain: ten points.

Eight years later, as Head of Press Sinead was powerful enough to shift groupiedom in her favour, in other words – enough clout to bone-jump an upcoming boy-band member at will. She had shoulder-pads, a list of contacts that would frighten Trump, and just enough of a dream left to move herself back to Dublin to start up SOS Music Management. The early nineties were great. The massive success of U2 had whetted the world's appetite for good-quality Irish rock. Dublin was heaving with ambitious young wannabes, and she had no trouble getting her UK record company chums for showcase gigs in the Rock Garden followed by all-night sessions in the Library at Lillies. Still hung over, she'd whip them up to Dobbin's and pile big dinners into them, and before they knew it, bish-bash-bosh, the contracts were signed. Her bands were supporting major names at the Point, Ireland's biggest music venue, and she was the country's number-one music manager. Actually, Sinead O'Sullivan was the *only* manager in Ireland. She got lazy and complacent – started to spend too much time lording it up in Leeson Street and not enough time looking around for new bands. She took her eye off the ball and in 1996, the other high-flying emigrants started to come home. Two in particular – Chris McCabe and Bernard Williams – who started up Cris & Bern Artists, started to showcase exciting new bands and just like that – overnight – Sinead O'Sullivan went from 'hugely successful' to 'just getting by'.

DJ Dodgy had just been a little sideline to try and update her increasingly middle-aged client list. Until Grunt Bunny, her old friend Jack Valentine had been her biggest client, but his band Sell-Out had broken up in 1989, and after his last solo album had been slated in Q magazine (the words 'Euro' and 'Vision' had featured heavily), he had all but gone into retirement. Supermarket openings and 'Best Hits' albums couldn't keep a girl like Sinead in lingerie, never mind a penthouse in Temple Bar and a BMW convertible. The dance music stuff had paid off the mortgage and more besides. In truth, it had saved SOS management from bankruptcy. She needed to be doing this, but that didn't mean she had to like it.

Dizzy rushed back into the room, flushed with the effort of counting. She really was a lousy PA, but she looked good. More important still, she knew about this kind of music. Sadly, she was too stupid for Sinead to defer to her on anything. Every bit of two-bit tinny garbage was 'awesome' or 'kicking' or 'monster'.

'Seventy-four—'

'Mother of Christ . . .'

'—and a half.'

'Oh Christ, child – make sense . . .'

'One of them's a midget!'

Sinead almost registered slight interest, but her brain had neither the energy or the inclination to advance it beyond making an immediate decision.

'Where is he in the queue?'

'Who?' Dizzy was already dreaming about blond and gorgeous Number 35 who had given her a flirty wink in the hope of being moved up a few bodies.

'The midget! Where is he in the queue?'

'Oh – about a third up.'

'Right, I'll see him last. Tell everyone behind him to go home and, er, look in the papers next week for a new date.'

In truth she had to get something out of today. Sinead was never, *ever* putting herself through this process again.

Dizzy shifted nervously at the door. She didn't give good rejection.

Sinead sighed with the effort of having to bark.

'Well – go on girl! Jump to it. And Dizzy,' she called as the pink pigtails were just disappearing behind door, 'bring me back a coffee! A large one!'

A midget DJ eh? Whatever would this wretched Dublin dance scene throw up next.

3

Bernard Chequers stood at the door of Dublin's exclusive Rouge boutique and gazed with misty eyed admiration at its owner, Valerie, as she wrapped a pair of size sixteen beaded leggings in silver tissue paper, then slid them with perfect French manicured precision into a white bag.

'Damn it, Valerie – you just get better looking as the years roll on!'

His words passed directly over the path of the ambitiously proportioned leggings buyer as she swung out the frosted glass door.

'Spring/Summer evening-wear nearly all gone, Bernie, and I've two of those full-length satin bias-cuts on order. Can you get them to me by the end of next week?'

'What size?'

He wanted to hear 'Size six – long. They're for Naomi and Christy to wear at the *Vogue* charity bash in New York,' but he knew it was too much to hope for.

Rouge was in a small arcade just off Grafton Street. Off the main shopping strip, it was tucked away in the kind of expensive knick-knack arcade that one might go to if you are so rich that you can afford to shop recreationally for antique kilims, seventeenth-century cameos, cosmetics containing seraphim spittle or exquisite blouses woven from the hair of cherubs. Rouge's clientele were, in the main, women so rich and stylish that nobody knew who they were. The kind of constantly-travelling-until-virtually-homeless glitterati that are too busy being fabulous to fit a *Hello!* shoot into their schedules. Valerie's rock-wives and supermodel chums were flying in from Paris and New York for a low-key lunch in Cooke's Café and a trip in to see 'Val' and to pick up 'something pretty' for that after-gig party in Rome. These women gave Valerie Valentine additional social cachet, even though she was already fêted for her rock-wife beauty. Bernard Chequers was Valerie's bread and butter designer. The old faithful with his generously cut evening-wear and classic separates that pulled in the less adventurous clients looking for an established homegrown label they could trust to keep their flabby edges from public scrutiny. The 'Chequers' range was given its own corner at the back of the shop, away from the front rails and cabinets with their tantalizing diaphanous and glittering titbits. Bernard's conventional fare was not to Valerie's personal taste, but it paid the bills. Bernard had no illusions about that, understanding that Valerie's own exquisite looks could cope with, and indeed complement, fashion frivolities. He knew he was not, at this stage of his life, going to be setting the world of international fashion alight and considered himself lucky to have an outlet at all. Especially one run by as glorious and generous a creature as Valerie Valentine. But sometimes, just sometimes, he longed to see his creations on someone a couple of notches up the fashion ladder than the rich barrel wife with gold Visa card to hand.

Valerie pouted her lips into a reserved grimace: 'Fourteen short and eighteen regular.'

Bernard let out a groan.

'Why are all the women who have the money to buy my stuff fat hounds? Why? Why?'

Valerie gave him a sweet shrug. She was far too lovely a person to slag someone off on the grounds of four extra stone and an attitude problem.

'Jesus! All that beading! All that finishing – *wasted* on Big Ain't Beautiful Judges' Wives from Dalkey!'

'Beauty is in the eye of the . . .'

'Oh don't give me all that new-age dingly-dangly hippy shite, Valerie . . .'

Bernard was spiralling into one of his Queen Ego Dramas. The kind where the spotting of an additional wrinkle could send him into a satanic spin that led one to expect him to vomit up a feather boa.

Valerie had two clients due in from Monaco for a private viewing and couldn't afford to shut up shop for an afternoon counselling one of her oldest friends over nothing.

'You're a *wonderful* designer, Bernard. Your clients love you – you *know* they do. So they're a bit older – a bit less – ' she struggled for the politically correct term – 'a bit less *conventionally shaped* than you'd like, but that doesn't mean they don't appreciate your work – that *I* don't appreciate your work.'

Bernard's huge frame collapsed like a punched balloon and he shuffled over to Valerie's glass and mirror serving pulpit.

'Really?'

'Yes *really*, honey.'

'Really and truly?'

'Now Bernard – I couldn't keep the shop going without your collection. You know I couldn't.'

'I'm good then?'

Valerie smiled. He could have stood there dragging compliments out of her all afternoon and they both knew it.

'Bernard' – she checked the time on her gold Gucci watch – 'I've got Mandy Mason and her mother in at two . . .'

'Rightio, love – I know how to take a hint. I've a dozen oysters and some of Uncle Bernard's special lime dip in the fridge if you fancy popping round tonight for the tea?' he said as he backed out the door.

'Oh Bernard, I'd love to but I'm going to a party tonight . . .'

Bernard's face opened for the invite—

'. . . at Jack's.'

—then clouded at the mention of Valerie's ex-husband's name.

'He's having a few of us round and I said I'd . . .'

Valerie trailed off as the look of genuine concern from

her biggest fan seemed to crumble her words of justification en route to her mouth.

'I'll say nothing,' he warned, 'just call me tomorrow. Lunch at Cooke's and . . .'

'. . . a good talking to?'

'Damn straight!'

Valerie didn't really mind Bernard's concern. As a single woman trotting towards the edge of the hill, she was grateful to be cared for that much by a man, but his disapproval of Jack irritated her sometimes, especially as she knew his fears for her around her on-going friendship with Ireland's most high-profile rake were unfounded.

Valerie had first seen Jack when she was seventeen. She was still living out in her parents' three-storey mansion house in Dalkey. Her father was Scottish, but in that British upper middle-class way where everyone gets sent to boarding school and ends up speaking with a haw-haw accent. He was a banker by profession and an imperialist at heart. In his early twenties, George Barton had met and married Valerie's mother. Veronica Mullins had been his air hostess on a trip to Dublin. Possessed of an extraordinary beauty the graceful Veronica had been chosen as 'the face' of Aer Lingus, her hostess smile adorning leaflets and posters enticing those who could afford it to enjoy the unimaginable glamour of air travel in sixties' Ireland. However, George's infatuation, and his egotistical determination in winning the hand of this young woman who had achieved a kind of national recognition for her looks, had a price. The price was that he had to move to Ireland, a country which he considered to be both backward and very much on the periphery of the civilized world. Valerie had, therefore, been raised in the atmosphere of her father's acute intolerance towards all things Irish. He was forever complaining about the 'lazy ignorance' inherent in 'The Arish' – making an exception of his tolerant, soft-voiced wife as if his ownership of her somehow precluded her birth. In any case, she was only a woman and a wife so somehow, that made it all right. Henry the Eighth had married a Spaniard for God's sake! One was entitled to own property that was exotic and away from the norm, just so long as your own moral fibre and firm judgement did not become swayed by pagan papist ideas and ludicrous celtic myths. But it was harder for George Barton to come to terms with the fact of their birthplace seeping into his children's lives. Valerie and George (the second) were, despite their father's best efforts to the contrary – Irish. He had convinced himself they would grow out of the sing-song lilts and the wild manners in time – but then Valerie had started the rebellion proper at the age of seven when she had bawled for two days solid on being told that she wasn't going to be taking First Holy Communion with the other girls in her class. Veronica finally put the foot down and declared her right as a Catholic to bring her children up in her own faith. As a woman, she knew that Valerie's early signs of religious commitment were based largely on her desire to parade around in a lacy white dress and veil; and that later her son George would doubtless display the same level of fervour in the interests of the financial gifts that would be promised from her vast plethora of relatives – each of whom was delighted that Veronica was siding with the Pope against her imperious, snooty husband.

The betrayal hit George Senior hard, and having to concede to his wife on this one important point, made him even more intransigent about asserting his irrepressible Britishness. He was like a man at war with the easy-going nature of the country he was living in; talking down to the 'servants', as he insisted on calling the middle-aged housekeeper and her gardener husband; only taking British newspapers; sending the children to holiday with family in Norfolk every summer – and keeping Veronica's family at arm's length. Veronica bore his petty bullying with tolerance and love, wearing him down with gentle persuasion if she thought he had gone too far. Massaging his ego with small details; mail-ordering English food hampers from Harrod's; befriending the wives of British diplomats and organising excrutiatingly formal dinner parties where pompous dullards talked endlessly about the ghastly Irish weather and gossiped about English aristocrats with a transparent oneupmanship on who knew them best. Veronica kept the cutlery polished and the conversation polite. She glided through the ex-pat community with a grace and elegance that made her husband proud. 'She's Irish you know,' they used to say, 'but she hides it well.' In truth, Vee would have sooner sat down at the kitchen table and lorried into a pile of bacon and cabbage with the staff and kids – one big happy family. But she did all of these other things to distract George from the crippling control she knew he craved over their children. He could have his genteel dinner parties, his *Daily Telegraph* and his right-wing opinions, but he was not sending his children to public schools and he was not going to cut laughter out of their lives in the interests of some half-baked ideal of Victorian decorum. Veronica gathered herself around her children, keeping them largely free from the over-bearing influence of their father. If Veronica hadn't died tragically in a car crash when Valerie was thirteen, George Barton would never have won. George Junior was sent to Harrow and encouraged to holiday abroad with English friends, and Valerie stayed at home to take over her mother's role. With his son away at school, George Barton put a television in the drawing room to create distraction from this mini–version of his dead wife, whose easy laughter and chattering reminded him of all he had lost. And so Valerie first saw Jack in her father's drawing room as his wiry face sneered through the lyrics of 'Shoot Me!' – Sell-Out's first hit single.

'With the greatest of pleasure – pass me my gun,' mumbled George from behind his newspaper, for he was not entirely without a sense of humour. Except that Valerie knew that he probably meant it. Valerie noticed Jack then all right, but she did not disintegrate into fan-dom. Rather the raunchy limb-flinging figure on the screen represented some kind of an escape from the staunch authoritarian figure of her father.

When she did finally escape from Barton House it was not her own decision.

George called her into his study one evening and handed her a brochure for the Lucy Clayton School of Modelling – a respectable 'finishing establishment' in London.

'You're booked in for eight weeks from the first of September,' he stated simply.

Valerie, who to her father's disdain, had never fully learned to keep her feelings in check, blurted out, 'But I don't want to go, Daddy. How will you manage here on your own?'

George paused, and for a second she thought the impervious mask of severity he had worn since her mother's death, might melt. But he had his mind made up. Her brother was going to Oxford to study Law and her father had always assumed that all Valerie was good for was finding a rich husband. She had her mother's good looks all right, but lacked the natural elegance and social grace that separates your standard-issue females from your good prospect catching lady-wives. She needed this introduction to the real world and he needed time off from the constant reminder of Veronica.

'You will stay with your Aunt Philippa in Knights-bridge. It's been arranged.'

However, Mr Barton's plans to turn his daughter into an obedient Sloane backfired. Miss P. Barton turned out not to be the epitome of respectability she presented to her older brother twice a year when she was looking for her allowance. Philippa, or 'The Goddess Phil' as she liked to be called, was a fun-loving alky who had turned her spinster status and generous inheritance into an excuse for wearing beaded floppy hats, mirrored kaftans, and calling herself an 'artist'. Her paintings were as dreadful as her parties were wild. Her Knightsbridge apartment was constantly full of interesting arty types and leftover hippies who were in training for the title 'True Eccentric' as opposed to 'Sixties Casualty'.

Initially, this Aristo-Boho environment had little impact on Valerie who set about this final leg of her education with considerably more success than she had had in the academically challenging Irish education system. Where she had always been bottom of the class in Maths and Gaelic, she found she was well able for Flower Arranging and Table Setting. Within three weeks she was flying ahead of the other girls in Deportment and Personal Styling, she could get in and out of a car without any professional peeping Tom or paparazzo getting the merest glimpse of her knickers and she had the 'Paris Turn' off pat. This surge of academic progress gave Valerie a confidence that she had never had before. She had always been tall for her age and walked with her shoulders hunched so that she would 'fit in' with the smaller gangs of bouncing girls who marched about the Stillorgan shopping centre slagging the local lads and flicking their Farrah Fawcett fringes back in flirtatious defiance. Valerie had been the gawky giant at the back of the pack, hiding her face behind long blonde curtains of hair. Now, here she was in London, the world's capital of nice young ladies, able to hold her own. She had finally found her niche.

Her father had issued Valerie with a clothing allowance, and on her third Saturday in London, armed with her 'Clothing Essentials for Respectable Young Ladies' list, Valerie went shopping for court shoes, sensible skirts and stripy cotton blouses. The fashion riot of late seventies punk London had created something of a war zone in terms of finding Sloane Ranger staples such as velvet hairbands and knee-length tweeds, and Valerie was hard pushed to find anything that didn't have BOLLOCKS TO QUEEN & CUNTRY emblazoned across it, or outsized nappy pins sewn into the crotch. But after several hours, and the relief of discovering the middle-class haven that was the Peter Jones department store, she walked tentatively with her bags up to the reception desk of Neville Daniel hairdressing for her two o'clock appointment, and was somewhat puzzled when a young man with a chewy brown face called Baz introduced himself as her 'Styling Director'. In Dublin, she had always had her hair done by a hairdresser. She thought there must be some kind of mistake. Especially when, as Baz pulled the hair back from her face he suddenly exclaimed, 'Ducky! You ever dunanny modlin'?'

Valerie gave him a glazed smile. She thought he was joking – and shook her head.

'Nev! Shirley! Cumanaffalookat this!'

Within seconds scissors had been dropped and there was a crowd gathered at the back of Valerie's head, scrutinizing her face in the mirror.

'It's a Bardot all right!'

'Nice fick lips – they'd gloss up luffly they would!'

'Look at the ski-iiin! Look at the ski-iin!'

'Try her wiff a scrunch, Baz, and we'll get the Polaroid out.'

'Fuck that – I'll get Jasper on the phone and gettim round to ava look!'

'You gotta coupla hours, luff?'

Valerie nodded automatically at the shock that she was being addressed in person again.

'We're gonna give you some highlights, take off somma this weight at the back and do you up in a nice messy scrunch, yeah?'

Suddenly Valerie realized that, with all the fuss, she hadn't checked how much money she had left.

'How much will all this cost?' she barely mumbled the words out, mortified.

'Cost, luff?' hollered Baz. 'That's funny, that is Shirley! She wansta know how much iss gonna cost!'

Shirley looked over, wrinkled her nose and said, 'Ahhh. Bless!'

Then Baz hunched down beside her and gazed up into, easily, the most perfect, the most *Vogue*-cover face he had seen in his ten years as a hairdressing maestro and part-time model scout.

'It ain't gonna cost you nuffink love. We're gonna make you a star!'

When you're a model, meeting pop singers is easy. When you are on the front cover of *Vogue* within three months of being signed, it is something of an occupational hazard. In reality, Valerie was still nice nervous kid from Dublin – but in front of the camera she was everything from leather licked dominatrix to snooty beauty in country tweeds to semi-clad damp goddess with winking nipples. Even the most streetwise pop star would be hard pushed, in the face of the finest photography and make-up London could provide, not to believe that this new media-storming face was up for a bit of spanking from a wealthy wild boy of rock.

Although Valerie's innocence would have prevented her from as much as suspecting it, Jack Valentine was merely one of many on a very long list of suitors being kept by Jasper, Chief Booker at her agency.

'She's *huge*, Baz – but we really need to crank it up a notch if she's gonna crack New York. Hook her up with a name. Trouble is, I can't get her out there. This kid just won't be *seen*. She's staying with some aunt of hers in Knightsbridge. Won't party. A real clean liver – you know?'

'Leave her to me, Jasp,' Baz assured, always ready to meet the challenge of a spot of social deflowering. 'What's on your mind?'

'*Melody Maker* party at Slave on Saturday.'

'She'll be there.'

And so it was that Valerie Barton of Barton House, Foxrock, Dublin found herself squashed into a simmering, smoky nightclub in London's West End surrounded by a gang of sweating, half-drunk rock stars – none of whom looked nearly as polished and handsome as they did on the telly – and *all* of whom seemed to be displaying an unnatural interest in the contents of her chiffon YSL blouse.

Baz, who had promised to stay by her side all night and facilitate proper and appropriate introductions, had beamed himself off to the gents half an hour ago, and a young man calling himself 'Dangerous Dan' was making a very fine stab at living up to his handle by simultanousely gurgling whisky and sticking his tongue in Valerie's ear. With a sudden sense of self-preservation, Valerie dismounted from her barstool (without, it should be added, giving anything away – just as she'd been taught) and excused herself politely – leaving the boys to fight over who was going to have first go-of-her when she got back.

There were all sorts of strange things going on at that party – even in the Ladies Room. It seemed that whoever had been in the cubicle before Valerie had sprinkled themselves liberally with talcum powder although, strangely, it wasn't on the toilet seat itself, but on the back of the cistern.

In the cubicle next door, she saw three pairs of legs – even though the cubicles either side were empty.

When she came out, there was a girl with her head down over the make-up counter – sniffing. Valerie, who had been taught by her mother that being always mindful of others was the first lesson in social grace, touched the girl's shoulder and said, 'That's a dreadful cold. I have some paracetamol in my bag if you'd like some?'

The girl looked back at her with swimming, puzzled eyes – a big splodge of white powder caked under her left nostril.

The five or so other girls all stopped mid-eyeliner application and gawked – their amusement delayed by amazement at this obvious show of naïvety. Valerie felt the burn of acute mortification fizz across her cheeks, although she didn't quite know why. Then one of the girls recognized her.

'Hey! You're Valerie Barton – the model.'

The group melted instantly into a kind of groupie all-girls-together gang – assuming the 'cold' comment was an in-joke gag.

'Here, Shirley, chop out a line of Charlie there for the New Face.' Then, poking Valerie with a set of jet-black nails, the punk leader of the coven winked her spidery lashes and said, 'You're gonna love this stuff, Val. Takes you up like an angel's kiss – keeps you going till Wednesday!'

The confused smile that Valerie had been wearing dropped like a flasher's pants as she realized what was going on. Charlie wasn't a person at all but the name of something more sinister entirely! Valerie stumbled out of the room marked 'Babes' – and smashed straight into the chest of a tall, slim man in a Hackett three-piece tweed suit.

It would be an hour after he had rescued her into the genteel comfort of the Waldorf Hotel bar that Valerie recognized him as the well-known pop star or 'musician' (as he would later describe himself to her father) – Jack Valentine.

4

Jack Valentine was passed out under the sunbed when the caterers arrived.

His own live-in cook of seven years had left the week before and Jack had been devastated when Tommy had handed in his notice.

'There's no point in my being here, Jack – honestly. Sure I'm doing nothing these days. You're living on take-aways and frozen pizzas!'

Tommy said it like it was a new thing. Like there had once been a time when his duties had included devising a complicated specialized macrobiotic calorie controlled celebrity diet for his employer – and now that time was past. The reality was that Tommy Grady had been doing little more than mixing drinks and peeling the lid off pizza boxes for his wayward boss for years. Virtually from day one – Tommy had been employed as Jack's drinking buddy and confidant. Flinging together a few half-hearted canapés for druggy rock orgies was as much work as he had done. With a liver the size of Guernsey and ten years of alcoholic drinking, Tommy had finally thrown the towel in and gone to AA. Frankly, the ageing rock & roll lifestyle did not suit the clean & sober Tommy. If Jack was honest, a clean & sober housemate/ cook was not exactly conducive to his own spiritual well- being – which generally started with a toxic egg-nog at eleven a.m. But still? He didn't want to be in this fourteen-bedroomed mansion on his own. It might take him *years* to train in another alcoholic. They weren't born overnight and he'd be fifty-five next birthday. He was getting too old for leading people astray. It was hard work. He needed people to lead *him* astray. People who were *committed* to helping him maintain a certain level of debauchery and general mindless rock-star skulduggery. In the old days, it was easier. The Bad Boy stuff came naturally to him then. These days the worn cotton chinos seemed so much more comfy than the leathers. His liver hurt, and he had a pair of sheepskin slippers under his bed upstairs. If Tommy left he might get in the habit of wearing them around the house – then it would be cardigans and cups of tea. If he didn't still have 75 per cent hair growth and the ability to finish off a fashion model in under forty-five minutes – Jack Valentine might have thought he was losing his touch.

'But what about the parties, Tommy. How will I cope with the parties?'

Clean shaven and with the zealous bright-eyed smile of the newly reformed, Tommy said, 'Oh, you'll manage the parties all right, Jack!' Then he left.

Jack watched the taxi disappear down the drive of Courtship Castle and felt the hollow sound of seventeen rooms with nobody in them swallow him up. He hadn't bought this place for living in. He had bought it for parties. Out in the middle of nowhere to keep him away from the fans, and in Ireland because the Irish were great craic and they loved to party. Well fuck them! First Valerie had left him – now Tommy. He'd show them all. He'd have the party to end all parties. Fill the place up with drink and drugs and dollies. He'd show that fucker Tommy that he could still have a good time – that he didn't need him – that he had *never* needed him – the sanctimonious patronizing prick with his 'One Day at a Time' and his 'Twelve-Step Programme' bullshit. Jack Valentine wasn't going down that route, thank you very much. He still had what it would take to show them all. What he hadn't really considered was that Tommy wouldn't come.

What he had stone pure forgotten was that the caterers were delivering the food around lunchtime.

He always had a snooze under the sunbed at about noon. Sometimes the casual snooze might turn into a little kip, or if he'd had a rough night beforehand, a full-blown nap. Jack had been up all of the night before drinking whisky and watching video footage of *Sell-Out: The Final Tour*. As a result he had fallen into a deep sleep, the heat of the Home-U-Tan lulling him into imagining he was dozing under a hot Caribbean sky with a bevy of bikini'd babes frolicking lustfully in the sand.

So when the caterers arrived and found the back kitchen door open, they just assumed that the owner meant them to come on in and set up. Fifteen-year-old

Kylie Kelly was very excited to be helping out that day. She'd heard all about these wild parties at their local pop singer's house, and her dad was a big fan. Maybe Mr Valentine would autograph a napkin for her. She wished she'd thought of bringing one of her dad's tapes – then she could have given it to him as a special present. Maybe she'd ring her brother Joe later and get him to send one up. She wondered what it would be like meeting the man himself. Kylie had never met anyone famous before. Would he be nice – just like an ordinary person? Or would you just sort of *know* that he was a special sort of person which is why he was a pop singer and not a plumber or something? As she was instructed to carry a large covered platter of sausage rolls and put them somewhere 'safe', Kylie was trying to contain her excitement. If she thought about where she was, she might lose her concentration and drop the tray or something disastrous. Then she'd be sent home for sure and she would never get Jack Valentine's autograph for her dad.

There were so many rooms in this place, Kylie nearly got lost. She went through into a utilities room off the kitchen, but she didn't feel right putting down her huge platter in amongst the washing powder and the brooms. She was about to back out into the huge kitchen and irritate her boss, Bridie MacFarlane, when she spotted another door to the left of the washing machine. Balancing said sausage roll platter on one hip, she opened it and entered. The windowless room was in complete darkness apart from a glowing strip of bluish light at the opposite end to where she was standing. Kylie was at once scared and mesmerized by this strange light. Her eyes were still adjusting as she felt herself being drawn towards it, in a half-trance of curiosity. As she got up close to the white coffin from which the light was emerging, her hand slowly, cautiously, but with the automatic thrill of an about-to-be-bride-of-Dracula reached down to pull up the lid.

There lay Jack, his skin bleached with blue light, ropes of jet-black hair curled moistly around his shoulder and neck – wearing nothing but a red bathing thong which was being stretched to the fullest extent of its lycra content by an erection that, frankly, with another half inch could have sprung the sunbed lid open on its own.

'Eeeeeeeeeeeek!'

Kylie had never seen a dead body before. Or an erection.

'Gaaaaaaaaaarh?' Jack leapt to his feet and brought sausage rolls raining down on his head.

'Eeeeeeeeeeeeeek!' He wasn't dead! She'd dropped the sausage rolls!

Kylie ran around the room several times, screaming hysterically, then around the kitchen until finally she locked herself in a downstairs toilet and it took her father, brother and annoyed Bridie MacFarlane nearly two hours to talk her out.

Jack Valentine had enjoyed more pleasant alarm calls in his life, and the experience more or less set an unpleasant tone for the party itself.

At ten p.m. the first ambulance was called. Bridie MacFarlane had dutifully stayed, despite Jack's insistence to the contrary, to serve the guests their spinach and goat's cheese canapé's (bought in) and ensure that her own delicacies (mini-sausages on sticks with a Spicy Mexican dip) were warmed to exactly the right temperature. However, her motives were not entirely pure as she had heard on very good authority that her own pin-up, the sixties crooner and Showband Star Mr 'Hairy' Heffernan might be putting in a guest appearance. It was a small dream of hers to have her hero sample her excellent rich fruit brack in the hope that his head might be turned by his taste buds. She was no looker, and knew it was a long shot, but if good plain cooking could compensate for a stern face then Bridie was willing to give it a shot. The very good authority had been the wife of the brother-in-law to a nephew of the man himself who lived locally – so Bridie had the eyes peeled and was going nowhere until she was certain he wasn't on the premises. Imagine then, Bridie's horror when she walked into the understairs cloakroom only to find the man of her dreams/the muse of her fruit brack sitting astride the toilet seat bouncing a topless teenage girl (a heathen local strap that Bridie recognized) on his lap in a manner that could only be described as carnal unsavouriness!

Bridie's devastation was complete when, after she snapped the door shut as quickly as she had opened it, she heard the girl say, 'Ugly old boot' followed by drunken guffaws from the man whom she had come to love for his emotional rendition of 'The Old Bog Road', her own dear departed mother's favourite song.

Stumbling, broken-hearted, back to the kitchen Bridie

unthinkingly placed the flats of both hands down on the nearest surface to steady herself against the great well of sobbing disappointment that she had not fully known was there until now. Nor indeed did Bridie get the opportunity to indulge said emotions as the nearest surface turned out to be the catering hotplate. How quickly the haunted yearning of love's loneliness passes when several thousand degrees of hot metal is scorching one's palms into rashers.

No sooner had Bridie been delivered into the arms of a caring staff nurse at the nearest hospital than the drivers were back again at the house to pick up a well-known 'boy band' member who had dive-bombed buck-naked into the shallow end of Jack's swimming pool – and quite badly damaged the innocent pebbles of his boyhood before they'd had the chance to grow into the mighty rocks of a fully fledged superstar.

By midnight, virtually every taxi in Co. Wicklow was infused with the bleak atmosphere provided by the maudlin bug-eyed half-drunk. Only the requisite 'Person Who Passes Out In Bathroom' and three close friends were left behind.

These latter gathered in Jack's 'study' – although as he himself would be the first to admit, very little studying took place in there. 'Drugs Locker' might have been a more accurate description, although with two sets of sirens having blistered up his drive that night, most people had flushed and swallowed their gear – doubtless delighting still more casualty workers throughout the night with 'hilarious' drug-induced antics and chilling out a few sewer rats into the bargain. It was therefore the drinks cabinet that was getting a hammering – three of the four lashing back their own brand of poison.

Jack was more sober than he would have liked. In Tommy's absence, he had had to do all of the calling and coordination of ambulances himself. With increasing depression, he realized that his popularity rating had plummeted when the guests had been so easily scared off. Either that, or they were all getting old. Jack poured himself a large whisky, sat back in his leather chair and did a headcount of what felt like his remaining friends in the whole wide world.

Karin – Sad Mag Hag – was into the gin. There was a bit of fussing around looking for a dash of flat tonic, but it was more for show than dilution. He'd been in her pathetic magazine a few times though, having said that, good press wasn't exactly knocking on his door these days. She wasn't a bad looker – but not up for a jab. He'd tried her once a few years ago – to no avail. Karin had said it would be 'too complicated', as she didn't want to mess up her friendship with their mutual friend Valerie. She had said it regretfully, like it meant something. He didn't correct her because it hadn't seemed appropriate to explain the 'whip-it-in, whip-it-out, wipe-it' nature of his intentions in the face of such fine unsullied principles. All the same, Karin had pressed Jack's relationship alert button and he hadn't tried again.

Sinead had her long black nails wrapped around the

neck of a beer bottle. She was one of his closest friends. He'd got to know her in London years ago when she had been Head of Press at his record company. She was a good girl – hard as nails – really helped him along since he'd come to live in Ireland. She didn't approve of the way he treated women, but she didn't judge him for it, and she had more of a stomach for promiscuous laddishness than most women. Perhaps it was because she was the only woman he had ever felt close to without having had the physical lock-on of sex. When he was younger, he'd had a go – naturally enough. But once she'd slapped him away, Sinead had become like one of the lads. A work colleague. A good friend. When things had gone wrong with Valerie – he'd been worried that Sinead would take sides, but she'd managed to balance things out. Even bringing Valerie back into his life – albeit as a friend.

Valerie herself. He never knew what she was drinking. It looked like a Coke – but he liked to think it was just tinting the vodka. A glamorous ex-wife knocking around was kind of cool, but the thought of her being sober at one of his parties made Jack feel uncomfortable. She was still a beautiful woman, although once you've been married to someone – beauty is something that you can see, but somehow it stops affecting you in the same way.

The first time Jack had seen Valerie, on the front cover of a fashion magazine that was lying around the studio, he had been kind of flattened by her image. Sleepy blue jewel eyes set in sculptured satin; lips dripping with glossy sex; messy blonde hair. He had gone to the party that night with the sole purpose of winning her – even going so far as investigating her background and discovering that she was a Lucy Clayton graduate from an Anglo-Irish background, hence the natty three-piece. The idea of Valerie appealed to him for all sorts of reasons – not least of which was fashion. Jack had never been one to run with the pack. When the essence of male cool was big bouncy blouses and war paint, that was the very moment when Jack would take a sideways step into outdated country-gentleman cravat-wear. Drugs and dolls were all very well and good, but Jack sensed they were becoming a bit passé. What better time to shock them all by settling down. A wife was in order, but there was no point in going off the deep end and marrying a sensible nurse. With his kind of money and glamour rating, he might as well reach for the top of the tree and pluck himself off a model. A model with class, mind you. Valerie seemed to fit the bill. How hard could it be? Jack hadn't quite hit his Happy Combination Cocktail of drugs that night, and had been feeling a bit jittery and paranoid. When he spotted Valerie surrounded by all his ponytailed punkish rivals, the young, arrogant love-god had suddenly experienced an attack of the not-good-enoughs and bottled out. He couldn't believe his luck when the Blonde Goddess had literally slapped into his chest just as he was beating his retreat.

From the moment he rescued her from the iniquitous environment of Slave, to the day he saw his radiant bride walk down the aisle on the arm of that uptight old bastard George Barton, Jack Valentine worked hard at his relationship with Valerie. His maternal grandfather had been some kind of a big-wig in the British Army, and he had used the fact to pump up a normal middle-class background to Borderline Toff. Old George Barton had so much wanted to believe that his daughter had what it took to land herself a decent husband that he embraced every bit of brandy-swilling, cravat-tweaking, cigar-smoking, British Empire Old Boys Club bullshit that Jack threw at him.

With Valerie, Jack gave her what he knew she wanted. She was a vulnerable, gentle soul – not like the hard hell-cats he was used to dealing with. Jack didn't frighten her with grand gestures. He stole flowers from suburban gardens and handed them to her wrapped in a sheet of yesterday's newspaper. He sang her old love songs in soft, reluctant whispers; stroked her bare arms while she was pretending to sleep and told her he wanted her so much that he was prepared to wait for ever. He didn't have to wait for long, because playing the hold-out game wasn't Valerie's style. She was an innocent, and capable of a graceful, selfless love. Jack played the role of tender lover, but he also liked the man he became when he was with her. Perhaps he was, after all, the exception to the Rock & Roll Lifestyle. After six years at the height of his fame, the performing and partying was starting to feel like a speeding treadmill. Going nowhere, but moving too fast to jump off. Perhaps Valerie's love would be able to slow it down to a normal pace. Perhaps she would be able to charm the good out of him. In the beginning, that's certainly how it felt.

'You don't deserve her, mate,' friends used to say to him. Jack would smile at them knowingly as if only he held the secret to the specialness she saw in him.

For the first six months, Jack tried really hard to settle down to married life. He sold the penthouse in Chelsea and bought a huge old mansion in Windsor to indicate that his single life was behind him. Valerie decorated the house in old-fashioned muted shades of amber, mossy greens and lavender. They trawled auctions and bought antiques together. Valerie's eyes lit up when she saw a Victorian dressing-table which reminded her of the one her mother used to have, and Jack bought it, and everything she wanted allowing her to recreate the sedate gentility of Barton House so that she would settle easily into her new life. Their only form of entertainment was the weekly dinner parties which Valerie organized. She kept the names of each guest in a velvet-covered diary, recording the vegetarians with a flowery 'v' and indicating who they had sat next to and what had been on the menu so as not to replicate the same theme twice. Valerie was a truly model wife. Perfect. She rejected Jack's suggestion that they get a housekeeper, preferring to do all of the cooking and the housework herself. She cut short her modelling career as she didn't feel it an appropriate profession now that she was married, and spent so little money on clothes that it was embarrassing.

After six months of respectable married life; the life he thought he wanted; the life he had hoped that Valerie would *make* him want, Jack Valentine felt like he was going to explode with boredom. It started with his just staying in London the odd night after a day's recording. He pretended to himself that it was a pain in the arse having to rough it in town when he would much rather be at home with his beautiful wife; that it was a bore being stuck in an anonymous suite until five in the morning getting pissed with the drummer while some cheap chick begged him to let her blow him off. Then the gaps between the nights away grew shorter. Valerie never complained or asked what he was doing, but Jack felt the need to lie to her anyway. He would ring her from the bathroom and pretend he was on his own before taking another line and heading back out to a party full of garish, giggling groupies and hangers on. He felt guilty. He felt so guilty that he had to distract himself by taking his Jack Daniels straight from the neck and clicking his fingers for a consolation blow job.

He tried to make up for his absence from home by spending money. He would buy her a bigger house. He would buy her anything she wanted. Anything. But Valerie said she didn't want anything except him. Jack was willing to change, but his instincts always took over his intent. He booked tickets for charity auctions and black-tie dinners and awards ceremonies. In the early part of the evening he would be astonished again at Valerie's beauty and elegance. Enjoy watching other men's eyes covet her as she glided about the room; the woman herself as delicate and diaphanous as the fifteen-hundred-pound dress on her back. Feel a surge of pride in the way she turned the lucky Valentines from the predictable vulgarity of a rock couple, into an exception. Fashionable *and* refined.

Then at one in the morning, when the car would arrive to take them home, Jack would feel the party in his head starting to take off. Every nerve ending in his body would be craving excitement; the adventure of going on somewhere; disappearing the genteel niceties of the evening into the dark excesses of the night. Not because he wanted to – but because he *could*. They would travel home in the awfulness of Jack's petulant silence. He knew that Valerie thought it must be something that she had said or done to upset him; that her naïvety and his mood led her into the lie that she wasn't good enough, but he was too angry to contradict her. He resented Valerie for interrupting the debauched destiny of his fame. Mostly he resented her for not making the good in him real.

The marriage lasted just under a year. Valerie would not take any money, but Jack sent George Barton a generous cheque, which the old man tore up. The brief covering note from Jack's solicitor had been patronizingly apologetic and implied that his daughter was not able for the pressures of his client's London lifestyle. George understood it as a failure on Valerie's part. She should have worked harder at her elocution lessons to get rid of her trace of Irish accent.

As the years after her failed marriage fell by, Valerie settled back into Dublin life. Her modelling career continued, and she even ran her own agency before finally opening Rouge. Many of the glam wives she had got to know in London kept in touch. Valerie had that rare quality of enviable beauty tempered with genuine friendliness that makes every girl want to be your best friend, so she had a strong network of people around her. By the time she had been reintroduced into Jack's life by her old schoolfriend Sinead, Valerie had developed beyond the stage of falling into a faint at the sight of drugs, and putting all of her eggs into the box marked 'Good Wife & Hostess'.

But as Jack looked across at her now, a perfectly preserved figure lounging across a huge sheepskin rug; smooth honey hair falling into the same exquisite face, etched more with intelligence than age – Jack found he was being jabbed with an old irritation. Whenever Jack saw her these days – always at a party or with other people and generally Sinead and the Mag Hag – there was always a point in the evening when he found himself searching Valerie's face. Not for desire – but perhaps some hint of sadness? Regret? He never found it. All he ever saw was this calm veil of serenity. If she missed him, or had any feelings at all for him, she hid them well. Had he really become that powerless that he couldn't drum up a modicum of emotion in his ex-wife? Frankly – for some reason he had yet to figure out – seeing Valerie Valentine drove Jack fucking mad!

'Well? What are you looking so fucking smug for?'

'Who?' snapped Sinead. She was always the first to

answer him back. Jack was kind of scary when he got like this – but he didn't frighten Sinead. Nobody did. She was too damn tall.

He had meant Valerie specifically but he said, 'You! All fucking three of you! With your expensive little embroidery cardie thingies and your high heels and all that, all dressed up and nowhere to fucking go!'

'I'm leaving . . .' Karin stood up to go – she was too old for nasty maudlin moments at the end of parties.

'Sit down,' Sinead said, 'you won't get a taxi at this time.' Karin didn't know Jack well enough to be taking insults from him, but Sinead loved a good fight. If she could get him wound up enough into some kind of coherent argument, this could turn out to be a fun night.

Jack looked across at Valerie who was studying her nails nervously. That was more fucking like it.

'We've plenty of places to go Mr Valentine, but we *choose* to be here with you because you are such a *charming* host,' said Sinead.

Jack looked directly at Sinead and growled, 'Fuck off!'

'Now, now, is that any way to address your guests?'

'I'll address my guests any fucking way I like and all I'm saying is the *truth* – ' he waved his glass in the air in a dramatic swilling/toasting motion – 'which is that you three are the *leftovers* – the *scrag ends* . . . the . . .'

Karin was on her feet again at this stage, handbag swinging with indignation.

'I'm not sitting around to take insults from some Has-Been Bollocks. Val? You coming?'

Valerie was standing over by the window, flicking

through a book of old *Vogue* photographs. When things got dirty, she had a way of detaching herself off to some other place. Valerie took passive aggressive tactics onto a new plane, disassociating herself utterly from the fact that this ugly display was entirely for her benefit. She recognized both the book and the mahogany table it was on as things she had bought for their house in Windsor.

'I ahh . . .'

Jack started laughing then. Suddenly, the whole thing seemed hilariously funny. God he really was able to wind them up! Really! What a laugh! Hysterical! Brilliant!

Except it wasn't really. Really, Jack didn't want them all to piss off and leave him in the debris of his first party in that house without Tommy. The first party that didn't end with a dawn drinking session. The party that never took off. He was the guy that made parties happen. He couldn't let the night end with the boredom of everyone just going home to their beds. It was too boring. Too middle-aged. Too damn . . . lonely.

'F'fuck's sake, Karin, relax will you?' said Sinead, the only other one who seemed to get the joke. 'He's only messing!'

'*Funny* guy,' Karin twin-set her sarky voice with a spiteful half-smile, and threw her bag back down by the chair, 'what did we do to deserve such wit *and* charm?'

As long as he was playing the villain of the piece, Jack got straight to the point.

'So? You ladies up for a threesome tonight?'

'Wow *really*?' cooed Karin. 'You mean *sex*? With the *lead singer* of Sell-Out? Me? I can hardly believe it! Would you? Really? Really have sex with us? Really and truly? Ohhhhh!' she sighed, feigning a fainting fit. 'Stay still my beating heart!'

'God – it's been that long Jack, I'd nearly be up for it,' said Sinead, 'only I don't think my underwear's up to it tonight . . .' She made a show of checking in her waistband. 'No . . . navy blue nun's flannelette I'm afraid – wouldn't want to sully my filthy old whore image now, would I? Took me *years* to earn that!'

Karin and Jack laughed.

'I'm going to bed,' Valerie said quietly and left. The other three were so absorbed in their slagging session that they didn't notice.

Ten minutes after she'd gone, Sinead looked around for her.

'Where's Val?'

'Gone to bed,' Jack leaned across the coffee table for a refill.

'Jesus – I hope we didn't upset her,' said Karin.

Jack almost said 'fuck her!', but let the words disintegrate in his mouth in an uncharacteristic show of discretion. The others, too, had things they wanted to say; questions they wanted to ask. 'What happened? Why did you let her go? Do you regret it now?' But their loyalty to Valerie held them back. So all three sat in silence for a few minutes while the uninvited ghost of Jack's conscience walked through them. Jack indicated its departure by starting Round Two.

'Why have neither of you two old hags never been married?'

'Never met the right man,' said Sinead.

'Too busy working,' said Karin.

'And too busy working,' added Sinead.

'And never met the right man,' said Karin again.

Stock answer to a boring question.

'That sounds like a stock answer,' Jack was disappointed by their pragmatism. He thought he'd hit a nerve with that one.

'Well, it's a boring question,' snapped Sinead. 'You'll have to do better than that, I'm afraid.'

'Yeah – who cares?' joined in Karin. 'It's the twenty-first century. You sound like my mother. Next question please!'

There was a point in the state of inebriation that Jack hit from time to time which was a kind of heightened intelligence. It was a canny instinctual thing. That point where he knew that standing up was probably beyond him, but it was as if the part of his brain that was normally given over to basic physical actions had rerouted to fuel his emotional intelligence. While the two women opposite him were smoking nonchalantly and looking around the room as if they could not conceive of anything more dull or uninspiring as the subject of why they weren't married, Jack Valentine knew, really *knew* – that there was lashings more mileage to be got out of them yet.

'Bollocks! You're *gutted* – the pair of you.'

Headshaking, fag-smoking boredom.

'Nearly . . . how old?'

'Forty.' Sinead stated simply as if she was merely humouring an irritating child.

'Forty. Fucking hell – nearly forty, both of you, and can't find a man. You must be sick.'

'*Plenty* of men . . .' Sinead reminded him pointing the fag at him.

'But no one who cares enough to marry you!' Jack finished. He was getting somewhere. Definitely. Karin had poured herself another gin and was lashing it back. He'd keep poking around – just to see what would happen.

'Children yeah? I mean – the old tick-tock thing you women have. Me? I'm all right, keep going till I'm sixty. Always some teenage dolly willing to hook up with an old scrote with plenty of money.'

Sinead was cool from the waist up, but the right foot was slipping the Manolo mule off and on at a frantic rate. She was heating up. Jack was no body-language expert, but she was surely getting riled. Karin had lit another fag from the butt of her last.

Mind games. Nothing like them for a bit of late-night fun.

'I mean – you're good-looking women alright, but, I'll be honest. At the end of the day what we men want is a nice feminine bird whose going to look after us. All this career girl shit – all this 'I-Can-Take-Care-Of-Myself Women-of-the-World' – it's all bollocks isn't it really? Eighties nonsense. What'chew want is a nice bloke who can look after you. I mean let's face it? That's what we all want really.'

Karin lost it then. Not standy-up screamy shouty lost-it. But enough to let Jack know he was on the right track.

'How the *fuck* do you know that I – *we* – ' she looked accusingly at Sinead for letting her be the first to leap to their defence – 'haven't got men in our lives that are desperate to marry us? Who the fuck are *you* to say that we couldn't just click our fingers and have half a dozen golf-playing plonkers fall at our feet? Maybe we are more discerning than to get ourself hooked up for life to some arrogant shit-head who doesn't know how to handle a *Real* Woman. I mean – *you're* not exactly a reference are you? Maybe some of us would rather be on our own than be with ... than be with ... than be with...' Karin's cheeks were flaming with fury by now. Gin did that to her. Made her hypersensitive and emotional. Jack had his eyebrows raised in mock-astonishment at her outburst. 'Oh – *fuck off*! Why the fuck am I arguing with you ... you ... you ... oh fuck off again!'

Jack calmly raised his palms to the air in a papal blessing and looked at Sinead in a 'What did I say?' kind of way.

Sinead had had enough now at this stage. How hard was it to suck a bit of defensive anger out of a thirty-nine-year-old woman about the fact that she wasn't married? Too fucking easy. Bring up kids – and you are into cheap tactics. It wasn't something that Sinead ever thought about. Not often, in any case and not *ever* if she could help it. She looked after herself. Always had done and she liked it that way. Great home – decorated how she liked it. Own business, doing what she wanted. Brilliant friends to love and keep her company, and no strange hairs on the pillow or festering socks under the bed. Sex was not a problem. She had long since discovered the secret that getting a man – *any* man – into bed is really not very hard at all once you don't go all googly-eyed and clingy on them. In fact, if you chuck them out pre-dawn with a curt 'make sure the door shuts properly behind you', they will often plague you with flattering phone calls and keep coming back for more. Once or twice younger men had fallen in love with her, and she had enjoyed the attention. But she had never found one that could match her intelligence or ambition. No one who was 'good enough' for her to want to reciprocate. Most of her old friends were married, and once or twice she had felt, watching one of the mild cardigan husbands making the tea while his wife breastfed blissful baby, a twinge of regret – or wanting. Then she made herself remember all those squalling nights her married sister complained of and the separated no-career casualty friends living in faceless suburban estates in small houses their ex-husbands bought them, struggling with two kids and a part-time job. Girls with the same background as her, but their lives a million miles away from the urban glamour she enjoyed. The day before, Sinead had been offered cunnilingus by a brilliant and strangely attractive DJing midget. Which one of those married women could boast of such interesting adventures? Besides, forty these days wasn't old. Maybe one day, she would get married and have kids – but on her own terms and in her own time. She knew that Karin felt the same.

In the meantime, however, she was fucked frigid if she was going to let this scraggly-haired has-been rat's arse get the better of either of them. She settled her swinging foot back down to slow; laid her beer down on the table in front of her, realigned the pack of cigarettes next to it, and settled back in her chair, indicating that she was ready to bring the discussion to a new level.

'All right then, Jack – here it is. Karin and I are both forty in a few months' time. Are you willing to bet that neither of us will be married by the time the bell tolls?'

'Absolutely.' Jack loved when Sinead got like this. All businesslike and blokey. Strangely horny. Even though butch birds weren't normally his fave tipple.

Karin shot out a pokey sideways look, but Sinead ignored her.

'So. Let me get this clear. You are challenging us on our ability to find a man willing to marry us by – when's your birthday Karin?'

'First October.' She wasn't happy, but Sinead's approach to Jack was clearly better than hers. His sneery smile had started to freeze.

'Just over three months away – mine's a month before, on September fourth – Valerie's is the end of August.'

Jack flinched inwardly at the mention of her name.

'How much, Jack?'

'What?'

'You heard. How much? How much are you willing to bet?'

Sinead's mother called it 'putting manners on someone.'

No other person in the whole wide world more deserved to 'have manners' put on them than Jack Valentine. In that moment, Sinead knew that she had shaken him up – and that feeling was worth doing anything for.

Jack could have backed down then, and turned the whole thing into a big joke. Ha-ha'd it all off like he'd only been winding them up. Like what he had said hadn't been important. Except that, by some cruel accident of denial – it had been. In truth, to all three. Still, in the morning they would have forgotten all about it. He could have let it go, and given them the opportunity to leave it at a few drunk words. But Jack was in a nasty mood that night. Tommy leaving; the party being a disaster; and then something in the way Valerie had seemed so indifferent to him – it had all seemed so . . . nothing. So crashingly boringly non-eventful . . . nothing. Jack needed to make something *happen*. Something so that he could look back at tonight and say, 'That was the night *I* did such-and-such.' I. Me. Jack Valentine. Not Tommy left or Valerie blanked me – but *Me-e*! I did something. Made something happen. The Great Jack Valentine, Wild Man of Rock, Superstar, All Round Interesting Exciting Person did something other than just sit around slurping drink in the aftermath of a non-event party.

'One million punts. I bet you and Karin one million punts you can't.'

Sinead was taken aback. Not least because she could

see by the cut of his suddenly sober, serious face that he meant it.

'Don't be a prick, Jack – I don't have that kind of money.'

Karin said nothing. She was reeling from the words 'one million' and 'punts', used in the same sentence as her name; working down her 'If I Won the Lotto' shopping list and already compiling a 'Vile Golfing Bores Who Might Marry Me' one to see if she could find a point where they overlapped.

'I am sure,' Jack said, arching one eyebrow in a dramatic machiavellian comma, 'that we can come to some arrangement.'

He then reached for his mobile phone which would indicate to all present the seriousness of his intention.

As he dialled his solicitor's suburban Dublin number at the ungodly hour of three on a Sunday morning, Jack felt the true depth of his outrageous star-status power tingle through his fingertips.

It reminded him that, some time ago, he used to be in a rock band.

5

When the pregnant Assumpta Tuffy suffered in the summer of 1971 from an elongated bout of 'nerves' and was sent to her older sister in Monaghan – she could hardly have imagined how her trip would have impacted on a group of young lugs from the townland of Crosscarney, the place where she was from. For her sixteen-year-old son Aloysius Moses Tuffy was sent over to London, into the care of his father who was working on the sites. Aloysius was an unfortunate-looking young man, his head shaped like a turnip and decorated with freckles and moles which only further contributed to the cruel nickname 'Veg Head' given to him by the local girls. A thick rug of orange bristle that stuck up from the top of his head like a cruel announcement of his Celtic roots compounded this young man's complete lack of natural cool. Aloysius's only consolation in life was that there were three other outcast unfortunates within the limits of Crosscarney. Bartley Egan, protruding teeth and severe acne; Irvine Evans, effeminate Protestant, and the gloriously ugly Eamonn Doyle, with his sleepy eye and his stumpy little legs. The others always tried to stand next to Eamonn in Mass, because it made them look better. Technically, his sleepy eye made him deformed and it kind of threw the others' lack of natural beauty into perspective. At least, they hoped, in the eyes of the local girls who giggled and gawked at them from their regular Sunday spot under the Fifth Station.

But all that was about to change with the inception of Al Tuffy's London experience. His epiphany came in the form of an ancient (or so he seemed to the sixteen-year-old Irish lad) West Indian record-shop owner called 'Daddy' Wilson. Al's father had rented a room above Devil Daddy Discs on Kilburn High Road, and, having become friendly with its owner passed the son into his care while he was working. Daddy was the ugliest man that Aloysius had ever seen, with a big scary afro that he teased out hourly a good foot and a half from his scalp with a grubby pink comb, and only five teeth in his head – two of them gold. Most days he wore a tight rainbow-striped sweater that showed off the line of his rounded belly, and baggy jeans that he hoicked up with a skull-and-crossbones belt. He smoked fat but strangely pointy roll-ups that made his breath crawl ahead of the 'Howzit boy!' he greeted his young charge with every morning. Despite, no, *because* of all of this, Al immediately took to Daddy, imagining somehow that they were fellow soldiers on the ugly front. Imagine, then, the young lad's surprise when, on day two, three of the most beautiful women he had ever seen – the kind of women he had only ever seen on the television before now; the kind of women his mother called 'Dirty English Straps', with little short skirts on them and long blondy hair and roundy bosoms that bounced around like they weren't even wearing bras! – walked into Devil Daddy's shop and minced right up to the man himself and made a great big giggly fuss of him like he was the handsomest man in the whole wide world. Then something really scary happened. Daddy put on a record, the likes of which young Aloysius had never heard before. It was a kind of thrummy, twanging, song with a man making lots of rude 'Uh' noises and shouting, more than singing, 'You got it! You got it!' Well. Within seconds the three girls were bouncing their bra-less roundy bosoms around the shop and Daddy was right there, in the middle of them spinning and shaking and grinding his groin around in a way that Al's Granny Tuffy would surely have described as Lustful Impiety. When the song was over, one of the girls gave the proprietor a licky wet kiss on the lips and said 'See you tonight Devil-man!'

After they were gone, and over the coming weeks, Daddy explained his manifesto of love to the naïve teenager from that small, Catholic island on the outskirts of Europe. His theory was based around the potent sexual power of music. Not your twee La-la Beatles shite, wanting to 'hold your hand' or any of that lovey-dovey nonsense. But the dark, pagan power of a black music. Soul music – or better still – Funk.

Aloysius Moses returned to Crosscarney a different man. He still had the freckly turnip face and the orange tuft, but he was armed with an arsenal of James Brown and Funkadelic records which he was confident would send the female population of his local townland into a frenzy of raging wantonness. Al, Bartley, Irvine and Eamonn called themselves 'The Funk Masters of Love' and rehearsed their tribal routines every night in Eamonn's uncle's hay shed until they felt confident enough to expose the people of their parish to the new, hormone-heating practice at the monthly 'Our Lady of Dolours Youth Club Dance'. 'Finty' Flaherty, the DJ was sceptical about accepting a record called 'I Feel Good' onto his turntable, and the ensuing spectacle of the four young goons groin-grinding across the wooden floor of the parish hall did nothing to allay his initial fears. The rest of the room collapsed temporarily into a fit of bawdy mirth, before hollering for the return of 'Green Door', so they could get on with their jigging and jiving like normal young people.

The Funk Masters themselves were naturally devastated – but Al would not let them be deterred. Shunned by their peers, the boys had nothing better to do with themselves than meet three times a week and dance together to the sounds that Devil Daddy sent them hot off the presses from London. Over the next three years the Four Ugliest Boys in Leitrim grew close through their love of the music that Al had brought back with him that summer in '71. There were highs: the Bus Stop, the Funky Chicken; simultaneously falling in love with Sister Sledge and arguing over which of them would win the divas' hearts with the title 'Greatest Dancer'; the night Irvine finally mastered the Hustle – three weeks after the rest of them had it off pat. There were lows: evil Lucy Power pretending to fancy Bartley and insinuating herself and two friends into the practice barn one night under false pretences of being interested in learning some disco steps. They had busted their holes laughing, and when they were chucked out ended up spreading nasty rumours about the place that the four lads were up to all manner of unsavoury voodoo-type practices, a story that resulted in all of them (save Protestant Irvine), being marched up by their mortified mothers to a special confessional, during which the Crosscarney branch of the Holy Catholic Church established that while circular movements of the groin were not, in themselves a mortal sin, the motivation *behind them* could almost certainly be decreed as unseemly. But in the thirty years since that fateful summer the four men had always stayed in touch, forming a sort of secret Masonic bond.

Irvine, always attracted to academia (the only sensible place of refuge for an effeminate Protestant living in Leitrim), went to Cambridge where he studied Physics. Had he stayed at home, he would have been described as one of those men who 'Never Married'. As it was, he lived in England. Al took his love to the limit – and ran a mobile disco – peppering the standard wedding music with snippets of James Brown and Rose Royce. On many occasions, he had considered leaving Crosscarney to broaden his horizons, but then realized that his vocation in life was to bring Black Soul to the people of rural Ireland – whether they liked it or not. Bartley Egan became a dentist and moved, eventually to America where he married a pretty hygienist and had his own teeth fixed to a glow-in-the-dark Hollywood standard.

And Eamonn Doyle.

Ah – Eamonn became one of the wealthiest business-men in Ireland.

His empire spanned traditional Irish gee-gaws (minia-ture men playing golf in Leitrim Crystal), and extensive media interests that included the hugely successful *How'ya* magazine and the impending launch of Ireland's first shopping television channel – Doyle TV.

The sleepy eye and the stumpy legs had failed to hold him back in life, and once the money had started rolling in in his late twenties, he had discovered that a bulging wallet was more than enough compensation for a less-than-perfect visage.

Eamonn was getting ready to go out to a 'do' at his golf club. Annual Black-Tie Dinner Dance. Mixed. Very important networking event. Except that Eamonn, as arguably their most successful member was in the unen-viable position of network*ee* rather than network*er*. This meant that dozens of lesser mortals would be lining up for the old 'Grip and Grin' with Mr Eminent Notable in the hope that he might one day give them a job/finance their new e.business idea or photograph their lovely wife in her new state of the art designer kitchen for a feature in *How'ya* magazine, and get the old hag off their back so they could continue riding their secretary or discreet plumber's mate from Ballybrack according to their sexual preference.

But it was not on the fine gentlemen and their lovely lady wives that Eamonn Doyle was musing as he gelled his seven remaining hairs across the ever widening desert of the disappearing middle parting that had plagued him since his late twenties. No. Once again, Bernard found his mind was wandering afresh across the events of that afternoon. Or rather, the non-event that was his utter lack of success in the Karin Sheridan department. Once again, the uppity strap had made a complete cod of him in his own office. Setting about him sideways until he had got himself all lathered up in a heap over that wretched writer woman and making him say thong and talk about underwear and the like, when really he wasn't that sort of a man at all. Really. Granted, it had just been the two of them today. No audience. Not like the time when he had made, what he thought, was a very smart comment about her front cover subject, a retired politician of some note, and how his nose looked rather 'phallic' – a clever word he had picked up a few days beforehand on the golf course and which he had decided needed a suitable outing. Quick as a whip Karin had replied, 'In that case Eamonn – I should hate to see your penis!'

The whole office had erupted and he had shuffled back to his office where he shivered with humiliation all afternoon. He had spent that afternoon plotting her demise, but then, he could hardly sack somebody for making a joke. Besides, frustrating though it was for him, Eamonn liked Karin. She was bright, good at her job, and had a kind of brittle confident beauty that contrasted sharply with his own slobbery, unfortunate demeanour. Even after all these years at the top, Eamonn was still in awe of pretty girls. He often thought how lucky he was to have built his business at a time when all of the main players in Ireland were still men. If he was starting out now, his empire would hardly have got past start. One of these high-powered broads that were seeping into the boardrooms of 2001 Ireland would have surely traded on his Achilles heel and trampled all over him.

Then, by some thorn of fate, the phone rang and it was Eamonn's ex-wife; Irish housewife, turned Dublin solicitor, turned 'Artist in Need of Space', turned Paris-based lesbian – Eileen Doyle, to inform him that his seventeen-year-old daughter, who he had not seen for five years, was coming to live with him while she completed her foundation course in fashion at Dublin's National College of Art and Design.

Eamonn was not impressed, but Eileen had never been a great woman for leaving room for manoeuvre and her lesbian status had done little to mellow her natural talent for self-assertion. In any case, she was one of a small handful of women who had had Knowledge of Eamonn Doyle's basement accoutrement. Although he knew it shouldn't bother him, what with his Chief Executive title and his big-shot status, Eamonn's mighty masculine man handicap was pretty healthy. But in your actual Self-Esteem/I Am a Beautiful Person/Inner Child/ Underneath It All region, Eamonn was still pretty sensitive about what his mother used to refer coyly to as 'That *Type* of Thing'.

So he swallowed whatever objection he was beginning to form and hummed obediently down the phone as his ex sniped, 'After all, *you* paid for her Eamonn – you might as well get the benefit of your investment, before it's too late!'

Eamonn did not like the reminder that as a father, his role had been largely financial, but he wasn't in any position to defend himself. He hadn't exactly been swamping the girl with invitations. He had done a few dutiful trips to Paris over the years, but had grown uncomfortable sitting with a young French teenager whom he barely knew in various burger bars in the Pigale, the area where he financed her mother's artisan lifestyle. When the kid started to wear black-eye makeup and addressed him exclusively in French, he took it as a rejection. Sometimes, when some wealthy business peer complained of a wayward daughter nagging Daddy for *another* skiing trip, Eamonn felt something echo through a hollow in his heart. But such emotive nonsense was easily quashed with the knowledge that he had 'done his bit' with the monthly cheques, and besides, he was a busy man – forward-looking, entrepreneurial. That stuff was all in the past. Eamonn was a man of the future. He had celebrity magazines to finance! Shopping television to launch! Crystal ornaments to sell! A 'lost' or rather 'temporarily mislaid' daughter coming to live with him did not fit into his agenda. He felt swamped by the very fact of it, but there seemed there was nothing he could reasonably say or do to object. He had six bedrooms, and the other apartments he owned in town were all rented out. Fait accompli – as the French say.

'Oh and she's changed her name,' said Eileen as an afterthought, 'to Lativa.'

'*Latvia?*' Eamonn bawled – his first formed word in the conversation.

'Oh yeah – call her that – she'll *love* it!' she said sarcastically and hung up.

For the second time that day, Eamonn felt bruised by the words of a woman who, although he couldn't be sure, he nonetheless suspected was making a gom out of him.

6

Barry Hooker drew back the florid ruched curtains of his rented city centre apartment and saw the same thing he had seen for the last twenty days since he arrived on this small, wet island.

Grey.

Grey buildings, grey pavements, and a grey, grey sky weeping grubby grey droplets of rain.

This was *not* the way it was supposed to be. Ireland was supposed to be green. He had been promised green. But the back arse of George's Street, Dublin 2 was a long way from the butter-churning-colleens-curing-their-own-ham ideal he had been expecting. The only green currently available to him was the day-glo lime lycra 'exercise pants' of the large man living in the apartment opposite as he performed his morning exercise routine on the small iron balcony that was standard in their exclusive inner-city block. The distant shouts of Jane Fonda's cellulite war-cry drifted through his half-open window as the fat man pushed the great mounds of his green buttocks up and down, up and down on an invisible chair in a way that, given Barry's empty stomach was, frankly, a little off-putting.

Had Barry Hooker been a different kind of man he would have groaned aloud at the sheer, unrelenting 'otherness' of it. For the truth was, nothing could have prepared him for how different things were here from the island he had come from.

In Australia, the sky was blue. Not the kind of half-hearted possibly won't rain duck-egg dreary of a good day in Ireland, but a real genuine honest *committed* azure. Like God had got busy with the paint from day one and finished it off properly with three coats. The grateful inhabitants of Sydney rewarded this magnificent backdrop with tall glass skyscrapers to reflect its glory. Big bold buildings – confident, upstanding, proud – symmetrically arranged so as to enhance nature rather than offend. Over here, the buildings were squat and sprawling, snivelling and shying away from the dribbling monochrome weather.

If Barry Hooker had been a different kind of man he might have noted all of this with a heavy heart. This and the other differences between Sydney, the city he had left behind, and Dublin, the city where he had come to live. Pavements that were so clean you could lick 'em 'n' see versus the vomit puddles that littered Dublin's city centre on a Sunday morning after the Saturday night drink rampage. Take-away sushi for $6 versus microwaved pie and chips floating in cabbage water – the fare at his new local lunchtime pub.

For Barry 'Galway' Hooker – forty-something single

guy, Australian television personality, and proud owner of the finest golden-brown feathered flick-fringe hairstyle since David Cassidy – was a grade A optimist.

Barry Hooker noticed all of these things, but he attached to them a kind of mythical charm that only the second-generation Irish who have been marooned from birth in foreign lands can attach to their one, true, spiritual 'homeland'. The Island of Eire. The land of leprechauns and fairies and green, rolling hills. Of course, he knew that there wasn't *really* any such thing as leprechauns and fairies. Nevertheless, he was hopeful that, as soon as his busy working schedule as anchorman for Ireland's first shopping television station had calmed down; as soon as the launch Extravaganza! and the teething problems (no other presenters, half-built cardboard set, non-union cameraman with exclusive experience in wedding videos) were behind him, Barry could get out there amongst his people – the good people of Ireland – and practise the Irish he'd been learning at evening classes in Woolloomooloo Technical College for the past five years. In the meantime, he would continue to struggle through his own assertion that he was, finally 'home'.

Barry had always wanted to come to Ireland. Always. His father had been born here, and moved to Australia as a young man. For the first seven years of Barry's life, old Patrick Hooker had sat his son on his knee and told him stories of Ireland. Sang him songs evoking the appalling images that make one wonder why any self-respecting second-generation emigrant offspring would want to rush back to the homeland. Famine featured large, as did pillaging oppressors, the shooting of innocent saints, bleak punishing boglands and of course, the dead Mammy. It was this latter that caused a turnaround in the Hooker household. After three trips back home in as many years to bury relatives, Patrick Hooker plunged the family into terrible debt when in the summer of 1965 he had to fly back to Ireland – again – to bury his mother. This final tragic visit put the tin-hat on his longing to go home. He had been bleating on to his wife, and anyone who would listen for the last ten years about how wonderful Ireland was. But his mother's funeral had finally made him realize that there was nothing for him to go back to. The joy of a good pint and seeing his old friends had worn off with the pressure of paying out for all those funerals. Ireland had become, to Barry's father, somewhere that you only went to when people died. They only ever seemed to die in winter, when it was cold and wet and miserable. After he came back, he put the head down in the Designer Dunnies – Exclusive Bathroom Fittings' showroom – where he worked as a salesman, paid off his debts, succumbed to the Antipodean accent and identified himself as a full-fledged Australian man.

'Tell me about the Black and Tans, Daddy?'

'G'way sun, an' pa-aaass me over anuther wan 'a those shrimps off the ba-arbie!'

No more bacon and cabbage. No more C'mallya's. No more breaking Lent for sweets on St Paddy's day. The Hookers were Australian now. Just like everybody else.

While his brothers and sister threw themselves happily into being fine upstanding Aussies – surfing on the weekends and trimming their suburban hedges with neighbourly pride – young Barry found it harder to let go of his Irish roots. One day, whilst rummaging under his parents bed for Christmas presents, he found the jacket his father had worn to his mother's funeral, rolled up in a ball. His mother had been reluctant to throw it away, it being new and all. In the pocket Barry found an Aer Lingus leaflet, and on the front of it was a picture of a beautiful woman with a little green hat perched on the side of a blonde bun. She was offering out a cup of tea and a scone with a smile of such magnanimous serenity, that the ten-year-old boy fell instantly in love. That Aer Lingus hostess came to embody everything that Barry believed Ireland would be. Generous, wholesome, friendly, spirited, good-humoured. Barry himself aspired to be such things himself, and the fact that he had the powerful blood of the Irish in him fuelled his success in that, and many other areas.

By twenty-five, Barry Hooker was a household name in Australia. His *G'Day Australia* breakfast TV slot was watched the length and breadth of the continent. What it lacked in wit and hard news was more than made up for by Barry's open-book approach, innocently nudging his guests into singing songs and talking about their latest film/book/business venture with comfortable ease. *G'Day* was interspersed with shopping television insets, where Barry himself would test with genuine interest and be subsequently wildly impressed with some terrifying gadget – the Thermal Nose Hair Tweezer; The Extendable Foot Scratcher; The Multi-Purpose Top To Toe Body Massage System – alongside its sales presenter, generally some sleek lady in her late thirties who was retired from the world of soap operas.

Eamonn Doyle had spotted him in a head-hunters show-reel of possible presenters for his new TV station, and when Barry had got the call from Dublin that in itself had seemed like a mini-miracle. He hardly heard the salary details never mind negotiated himself a business-class ticket for the gruelling twenty-seven-hour journey. His agent had tried to talk him out of it. Warn him about the fact that he was an unknown outside of Australia. That he couldn't expect the same celebrity status abroad, but what did she know? He was going to Ireland! To work! Like a proper real Irishman! He'd be able to drink *real* Guinness – made by the Guinnesses themselves (probably)! He'd be able to not just practise his Irish in some classroom but *use* it! On *real* Irish people! Ones who lived in Ireland! Like him!

After twenty-seven hours crunching his six-foot frame into a narrow seat with only unidentified nuked mashed meat for sustenance, Barry spent four nights in an outrageously expensive trendy hotel, while, by day, he walked around Dublin looking at 'studio apartments' that were in fact bedsits that smelled of wee. Finally, he found the small brand-new rented apartment that he had called home for the past sixteen nights.

Although today, as he turned his back on the lime green bottom and got ready to squeeze himself into the stunted plastic coffin that called itself a bath, but was, to a man of Barry's size and previous lifestyle, little more than a bucket, he was beginning to worry that this little modern flat in this bustling, busy capital city didn't feel much like home at all.

He searched around the positive thinking module of his brain until he felt a little burst of his natural optimism, and then, rooting about in the document drawer of his suitcase, he found the faded Irish Air Hostess picture, in the plastic pocket he had bought some years ago to preserve it. He propped it up on a small shelf in his bedroom and vowed that, come what may over the next few weeks, he would make this grey city live up to the promise of his perfect hostess's beautiful, smiling face.

It was gone ten when Sinead finally tore her eyes open on Tuesday morning. She leapt out of bed, then remembered she had a hangover and crawled into the Smeg fridge for a Diet Coke. Fuck. Ten o'clock. No harm. Dizzy would open the office, and if she relaxed and made it in for eleven thirty, she'd be better able to face the day. No one ever rang her before lunchtime anyway. The rock fraternity rarely emerged before four in the afternoon. The early morning casting session last week being an exercise in keenness as well as anything else.

The phone rang. It was Dizzy. She'd left her keys at home and had been standing outside the office for the past hour like a drenched rabbit too scared to ring Sinead, and too stupid to go to the landlord's office next door and pick up the spare set. Sinead groaned instructions and vowed the child had a month, tops, before she pushed her back out into the world of chain-stores and tills where she belonged.

As she was putting on her mock-croc PVC trousers a slither of flesh got caught in her trouser zip, and Sinead felt suddenly tired with the effort of being alive. She really shouldn't go out drinking early in the week – certainly not after the weekend that had been in it. She was getting too old. Just five years ago, it was just a question of clothes not fitting her. She had always been big – tall and broad. When she had gained weight, it had always been a question of added extras; *more* cleavage, *more* arse – more clothes for a bigger better woman. Now, it was as if her body was competing with her wardrobe. Bits of flesh sneaking through trouser zips; fleshy wings crawling across the tops of her arms; breasts that used to hoick up plump and inviting into a rounded X now had to be cajoled gently into shape like warm Play-Doh. It seemed that the industrial lift and separate engineering of her underwear was no longer in charge of her vast empire. Her body was rebelling like a petulant servant; literally 'revolting'. This morning, the Great Journey South was hitting her hard, and if the normally pragmatic Sinead O'Sullivan had to attribute this uncharacteristically girlie crisis of confidence to anything, it would surely be that vile exchange on Saturday with Jack Valentine re husbands and non-ownership of same. In the face of his stupid mind games, Sinead was a great woman for never rising to the bait. One of the reasons she was a great music manager was that she was able to stomach, sometimes even *nurture* the kind of brawling egotism that she and Karin had witnessed on Saturday night. But in the physical absence of a partner to spar against, and with last night's alcohol downloading her depress tape, Sinead was beginning to feel distinctly shitty about the whole dirty deal. The truth was, of late, they hadn't exactly been queuing twenty deep at the bar. Sinead's sex life had always been, at best, downright adventurous and, at worst, active. Life, in that department had been one great big party – wall to wall wannabes waving at her from the corners of the clubs waiting their turn at getting 'their foot in the door' with a powerful, influential piece, whom, it was rightly rumoured, would take them for a truly delicious and devouring ride.

In the last year or so, however, things had slowed down. It wasn't the lads. It was, as Valerie's ludicrous new-age friend, Tinara, had called it one night – the Vibes.

'You are not sending out the Vibes Sinead – Into The Universe – Your Vibes are not Seeking Out Your Master, Sinead. You must Find your Goddess and you must Send Her Out – *out there* – into the Four Corners of the Cosmos . . .'

Etc.

Tinara was undoubtedly a nonsense mongerer of the highest order – but she had a point.

Frankly, these days, Sinead would prefer to realign her chakras with a half-bottle of Chablis in front of the telly than have some Master of the Universe banging his head off her headboard and leaving grease marks on her imported Conran pillowcases.

Lonely? Not a bit of it. She had the house done exactly as she liked it, and she enjoyed her own company. Sinead still did the party circuit and put a face on it, but truly her heart was more committed to her cashmere covered hot-water bottle and the Cath Kidston fifties floral pyjamas she'd mail ordered in from London.

Frustrated? Not since Anne Summers had launched their website.

It had never really occurred to her that when she turned around to pick one off from the back of the crowd, the men might have got bored waiting and gone elsewhere.

The proposition from the midget last week was, when she thought about it, which in the light of Jack Valentine's sick challenge she did now, about the strength of it for ... she hadn't counted, but she did now ... six months? That male model? When was he? Decent singing voice? Looking for contacts in London? Clarence Hotel? Maple headboard? Mink carpet? Six – no seven – Jesus! *Eight months!* What month was it now? *Nine! Nine months!* Could it really have been that long? Worse – she'd hardly missed it. No wonder her body was starting to fall apart.

Perhaps if Saturday's exchange had happened at a time when she was keenly working her way through a crowd of hungry leather-clad youngsters, Sinead might have been less defensive and Jack less challenging, and she wouldn't have found herself having to rise to the occasion. And perhaps her feeling of depression around it was down to her fear that it seemed, at this moment at least, an unachievable goal. It certainly wasn't because the whole idea of the bet was cheap. Appearing cheap wasn't something that bothered Sinead. Too many one night stands and licking up to odious record company executives under the bridge to worry about that one.

It was just that this kind of cynical game-playing didn't seem as much fun as it used to.

At one time a game of 'bet you can't bed that virtual stranger' felt like power. She had been dared into lesbian 'shows' with aspiring models in New York; taken three-in-a-bed on a whim – always on her terms, often at her own initiation. Sinead's easy promiscuity had always made her feel free, different, powerful. The opposite of all that clean-living Catholic shite she had grown up with. The fact that she had never bought into it made her feel important, enlightened, glamorous – like some kind of an international cosmopolitan chick. The fact that she had started this whole find a husband deal was what really bothered her. She was troubled that she had come up with an idea that had its roots somewhere so damn conventional. That Jack had swallowed the whole thing up and taken it further was indicative of how nasty he could be sometimes. It must have been Tommy leaving him in the lurch like that. Hangers-on were not Sinead's favourite breed of person. She had seen too often how expensive they could be, financially and emotionally. Leeching wannabes clinging on to her clients for the bit of reflected glory. Tommy had always been different in that way. As sad in his drinking and the excessive lifestyle Jack afforded him certainly; but, for all that, in the seven years he had been living with Sell-Out's lead singer, he had proved himself a good, if not always sensible friend.

If Jack had gained anything from witnessing first-hand Tommy's new-found sobriety, it was just a nastier, sharper edge. Sinead had been foolish enough to skirt across its surface on Saturday night. Maybe it served her right for not keeping her mouth shut.

She managed to get dressed and made a half-hearted slap-it-on attempt to reassemble her face into something resembling respectable, all the time trying to pick off shreds of the ludicrous positive thinking jumble that had trickled through her tough edges from just hanging around with Valerie. She was far from committed to the 'Search for Your Inner Goddess' mind-set, but sometimes it helped. New Day, New You. Reject the Negative Energy and Embrace the Positive. It got her out the door anyway. Perhaps Jack will have forgotten the whole thing – they had all been pretty steamed. She'd call him later in the week, and make out like nothing had happened.

When she arrived at the office Dizzy was sitting behind her desk, blithely filing her nails like a character in a bad sit-com.

'A man rang,' she said simply, 'and *this* came.'

The envelope she pushed across the desk with a short purple nail had the stamp of Jack's solicitor on the top left-hand side. Sinead groaned inwardly. Now she would have to figure a way around this without losing face. Now, while she was feeling early-morning flabby and raw was not the best time, and Dizzy with her high performance perky personality and little pointy tits wasn't helping. Best get a day's work in first. Sinead put the envelope straight in her bag for later, saving it until she was on her own. (Dizzy often suffered a sudden attack of intelligence whenever she was in the presence of something she wasn't supposed to know about. 'Oooooh – the clinic rang to say your special cream is in,' she had once blurted out in the middle of an important contracts meeting at which she was meant to be merely taking the minutes.)

'Who was the man?' Sinead asked bluntly, trying to divert Dizzy's eyes from following the envelope into the pocket of her Prada handbag.

The Child giggled in reply.

Sinead wondered if there was a nice sensible girl working in her bank who would take a plummet in salary to get a start in the glamorous world of show business.

'Didn't leave his name – but it *sounded* like it *might* be that little midget man who was in the other day.'

Sinead's hackles rose.

'For God's sake Dizzy – don't call him that. The correct term is . . . is . . .'

'Vertically challenged?'

Sometimes she wasn't as dumb as she made out. Now *that* was a scary thought.

'And besides – *you* were the one who called him a midget.'

It was true. A Midget DJ – not an everyday occurrence even in the circles she moved in. Sinead had just wanted to get a look at him, hoping, in some ghoulish way for a bit of out of the ordinary to break up the tedium of that morning.

Miles, for he had a name, certainly did that. Firstly, he

carried himself with a confident, almost *arrogant* swagger that put Dizzy's misguidedly christian cushion/phone book search-plans right back in their box.

'No need to start getting out the phone books, love,' he smirked at her, 'I'll find somewhere to put myself,' and with that he hopped up on the chair and swung himself onto Sinead's desk, perching himself on the edge like a precariously placed paper weight. Sinead, who was accustomed to a certain amount of reverential heel-kissing from potential clients was temporarily thrown off course by the fact that (a) he was a midget and she was not au fait with the normal seating procedure; (b) he was around her own age which was unexpected and (c) he had the most extraordinary blue eyes which were currently hypnotizing her like a couple of covetable sapphire earrings. These things combined, she never managed to regain her authoritative status throughout the course of the meeting.

He pushed his CD across to her, and she held it over her shoulder for Dizzy to take unable to move herself from his gaze, saying to her loitering assistant, 'Shut the door on your way out.'

Within a few seconds the room was filled with the most extraordinary symphony of electronically produced sounds. It started simply with a cushioned pulse which was gently overlaid with a soft shimmering cymbal that sounded like breathing against the bass's thudding heart-beat. A pretty mewing melody was seamlessly introduced building in power and intensity to a stunning crescendo. She closed her eyes to cut out the additional complication of her guest's gazing at her, and felt the music wander innocently into her body, gradually tightening around her emotions until she thought she was going to burst into tears. She didn't. In fact, the feeling was so powerful that she could barely admit that she had never heard anything so beautiful in her life. In just a few minutes, she had been utterly transported from the flat thumping drone she had been listening to all morning and into the kind of intimate self-containment that only the most extraordinary kind of music can produce.

When the track finished, she opened her eyes, and Miles, still staring at her said, 'Well?'

'No,' she said, as firmly as she could, given her heightened state, 'I'm sorry but no. It's very . . . em . . .'

'Brilliant,' he finished for her.

'*Different*.' Something in this little man's confident manner was unnerving her into not wanting to indulge him. 'And at the moment we're looking for . . .'

'You.'

'Sorry?'

'You. *You're* looking. I assume the other one is your secretary? No need to soften the blow by pretending you're merely representing a consortium.'

Popular musicians, in Sinead's experience, did not usually use words like 'consortium'. They used simple, one and two syllabled words like 'Man' and 'Kickin' and 'Cool'. This guy had managed to confront, flatter and impress in three short sentences. Sinead didn't know whether to feel uncomfortable or interested. Uncomfortable won.

'Exactly. I am looking for straight down-the-line dance music. And this isn't it.' Then with a massive burst of pretend assertiveness, she twirled around in her chair, flicked his CD out of the system, and handed it over with the words, 'Now if you don't mind, I've a busy day and I need to . . .'

And that's when he said it. That outrageous thing.

'Would it help if I gave you head?'

That could have been the end of it then. If Sinead had been a less unshockable person; if she hadn't gone down on half of rock history herself, she might have stood up and ordered this impudent imp out of her office with a scandalized roar.

But she didn't. She laughed. Not a flirty come-on embarrassed giggle. But a great whelp of a 'Ha!' An open door of a laugh, and he walked straight in.

'I thought as much.'

His smile was as charming as his eyes were hypnotic, and then he surprised her again by having the good sense to leave it at that. He slid the CD across to her and said; 'Look. Listen to it again. Have a think about it and I'll call you next week.'

With that he hopped off her desk and walked out the door.

Miles's exit was so abrupt that he left a brief feeling of emptiness behind him. He had somehow known that Sinead wouldn't be offended by his question, and it was that knowing that, five days later, made her slide his CD into the player and decide to call him that afternoon.

8

*One million pounds. Mmmmmmmmm. One. Million. Pounds.
Punts in Irish. Lovely. Lovely lovely million pounds in money!*

*Sitting in a hot tub on the deck in the back garden of her
beautiful house in Killiney, looking out over the bay; stars
overhead, champagne cocktail in hand, Prada mules slung
casually on the steps of the patio as she waits for the house-
maid to call her in for dinner. Slipping into a devastatingly
soft slinky gown, she pads slowly into the house, and as her
eyes adjust to the soft yellow light of the Alessi candelabra on
the magnificent antique mahogany table she recently picked up
on a shopping expedition to Venice, Karin begins to focus on
the figure in the leather armchair by the fire. Her husband.
The man who made all this possible. She floats towards him,
but as she plunges her fingers into the hair of a young and
virile J. F. Kennedy, her hands hit a cold globe and seven
strands of greasy string . . .*

Karin bolted awake.

Eamonn Doyle!

She had been sitting on the sofa of her Ballsbridge
shoebox all night. When Karin was appointed as editor

of *How'ya*, she had decided to stretch herself and get onto the property ladder. The terrifyingly assertive estate agent, (a fake-posh woman in her early fifties whose peach and lilac wardrobe of work-suits made her look like she was permanently en route to a wedding) had introduced her to this 400 square foot of 'bijoux luxury' in 'Dublin's most eggs-glusive address!' with such unequivocal certainty that this was the bargain of the century, that Karin felt that she had no choice but to buy.

'Yew can see that thee bothroom hez been mod-e-fayed op to thee very high-est of standaa-rds, and thee décor has a pink the-eme which *Ai* think is very femi-nine.'

The place came fully furnished with a level of over-bearing flowery flounce that made Karin want to hurl right from the off. But she was desperate for the security of owning her own place and ghastly Gladys seemed so sure. 'For a lay-dee living on her own, there ees twenty-four-har security.'

Four years on, and Karin had never had the money to gut the place back to the Habitat Haven she had once dreamed of. The rose shagpile was littered with ancient red-wine stains covered in a mish-mash of shredded rugs, and the great ruched sofa (which Sinead once commented resembled a whale in a floral Issey Miyake house-coat), was, despite the five cream throws that slid constantly down its wipe-clean poly-nylon surface, on its last legs. Every inch of every surface place was packed with the paraphernalia of her life, not least important of which was a pile of stylish interiors books and magazines, which she devoured on a weekly basis in the hope that she might one day become Japanese and learn how to use her limited space more efficiently. Sadly, no one had yet written *How To Feng Shui A Broom Cupboard*, and Karin was therefore still spending 75 per cent of her salary to keep her in an apartment that she hated. Her lifestyle was therefore chiefly motivated by the ideal of 'Never Coming Home Unless to Shit or Sleep', but there were only so many hours she could while away at press dos or hanging out at Sinead and Valerie's gaffs, before she had to come back to her flowery hovel and face the fact that the greatest thing about her home life was that she had resisted the urge to get a pet, and her home was therefore innocent of the unmistakably spinsterish smell of over-loved cat. She had tried to move; downgrade from this expensive area to a small cottage in artsy Stoneybatter. But the likes of glamorous Gladys the estate agent had buried every single woman over thirty with a reasonable income in these pretty little caskets, and now they were all trying to sell at once. Pay rises and freelance nixers barely kept her wardrobe up to scratch for meeting all these high-flying celebs. Every time she went to interview the likes of 'Bridget and Tom Wilkin-Walkins in Their Beautiful Home Overlooking Killiney Beach' these days she felt like weeping openly. More than once she had considered shoving the wife down the stairs and *flinging* herself on the husband in begging abandon.

Jack's offer had come at a time when Karin was feeling horribly trapped. She didn't want a husband, as such. But she really, *really* wanted a house. Marry, move in, redecorate, divorce. She'd probably have to hand over half of her booty as compo to the abandoned husband, which would leave her with five hundred thou. worst-ways, enabling her to buy a decent semi in this area. Jack's ludicrous bet may only have been a game, but it had inspired Karin to sit up all the following night in her soon-to-be-dispensed-of bijoux box plotting her escape before the mad pop star changed his mind.

Eamonn Doyle was not on her current list. At least, not yet. If he was in the running at all, it would be in the form of barrel scrapings – and despite her twenty-four-hour vigil over Ireland's *Who's Who* – Karin was feeling a little more positive than that. Her current list was divided into three parts; Single Notables; Separated Eminents; Bad-Marriage Gadabouts. The third section was by far the longest, but she didn't know if she had the time, or the willingness, to go to all the trouble of dragging men out of their existing marriages into a new one with her. Several of its members had already had her head opened with offers of dinner – (or worse!) – but then, men always wanted what they couldn't have. For Separated Eminents – the competition was fierce. Once a politician or a high-profile accountant was officially declared single, every blonde hopeful in the country converged upon the Shelbourne Bar on a Friday evening like a plague of Shalimar-sprayed wasps. Assuming they had not left their wives for their secretaries, in which case the new relationship would often take a good six months to come to notice, by which time the hooks had been well and truly embedded, and Mr Separated Eminent was off the market again. Too messy – but with her behind-the-social-scenes contacts, it was worth her keeping an eye out for one that might have got away. In the meantime, no harm in having a crack at the shortlist of Single Notables, which currently numbered four and which Karin had been putting in order of both preference and availability before she nodded off.

At number Four was Rogue Chef, Carlos Zambuki; under thirty, devilishly handsome and a bit of a laddo by all accounts. Pros: good cook, easy on the eye. Cons? Arrogant shithead who had tried to charge *How'ya* £500 for using one of his recipes after he'd said they could have it for free. In at number Three was Fergus Brennan, newsreader and general man-about-town. Pros: she knew him from her Press days as a decent, steady kind of stick, but, big Con here, had once written a vicious column about a female politician who, it later transpired, was his sister. Hadn't spoken to her since. Number Two was Lorcan Smith, big PR man. Lovely sense of humour, gorgeous person and utterly get-at-able and tie-down-able, but he had a ballooning belly and always smelt faintly of port and liver. Wedding night would be a bit of a challenge.

Circled with red pen then, was Number One. Claude Moore. Novelist, poet, full-on Irish intellectual. Forty-odd, handsome in a kind of hirsute, demented-with-his-own-brilliance kind of way. He was no cinch, that was for sure – otherwise he would have been snapped up years ago. But he was, on paper at least, the best of a bad bunch. Karin had never met him, but she had seen him on a book programme the week beforehand and he had been compelling enough to distract her from polishing off the family tub of Haagen Daas which was, these days, her only home comfort.

As she looked down at the page, she wondered was she up to it? Claude was, it was generally agreed, one of Ireland's Cleverest Men. He had a string of letters after his name and more literary awards than you could shake a Thesaurus at. From what little Karin had seen of him, milling around in the background at book launches and the odd charity do, he was a dishevelled disorganized-looking creature who was probably just a bit girl-shy and needed some feisty broad like her to wrestle him into some kind of shape. Remembering his TV appearance only backed up Karin's fantasy. Intense brooding eyes peering out from under a thatch of black, rambling hair, mumbling out meaningful metaphors which appeared to bear no relevance whatsoever to the interviewer's questions, but which left the viewer in no doubt that they were in the presence of a Mighty Intellect.

Great! That was that then! Claude Moore – number one on the list. She'd get right onto it as soon as she got to work. 'Claude Moore relaxing in the Library of His Beautiful Home.' Her job might be trite and boring and not pay enough – but by God it came in handy sometimes. If her greatest perk was networking, she was going to make the most of it now!

As she was elbowing her way through the cosmetic-filled basin that was her bathroom, the post arrived, and in it was a letter from Jack Valentine's solicitor. Karin rush-read the contract through to its end, her hands shaking with excitement. No clause in there for staying married for a certain length of time. No mention of divorce. Nothing. The fool! She grabbed a pen, counter-signed it and would stick it into the post that morning. She was doing Eamonn's wet-dream fantasy shoot with Valerie and her thong that afternoon, and she'd run C. Moore's profile by her – see if she had any added info. Lots of these big shot 'Littry' types hung out with pop stars and their like. Made them a bit more of the people and all that. Maybe she'd be able to fill her in a bit. Whoops though – better not mention the whole 'Marry for a Million' business. Sinead said to keep shtum with Valerie for the time being. She was a bit sensitive like that. The two of them had better meet up first for a bit of a coven on how to handle it. *So* exciting!

As she left her apartment that morning, Karin was walking on air in the sure knowledge that in a year's time she would be out of there. Certainly married, and possibly even intending to stay with the faintly delicious Claude Moore. You never knew your luck, and Karin Sheridan certainly felt that hers had started to change.

9

'You are reee-cheeing out! OWT into the fa-har ca-horners of the Uni–ver-her-herse. The Uni–ver-her-herse is se-hending you messa-gezz of la-haaaave. They are fla-ho-eeeng throoooo ya-hoooo, reee-cheeing intoooo the ca-horners of you ma-hi-ind . . .'

Valerie had Roddy Coogan and Karin arriving to take the *How'ya* shots in less than an hour, but Tinara had insisted that her friend, neighbour and landlady (the plump redhead ran her 'Goddess Within' workshops from Rouge's upstairs office), had clearly misaligned her chakras over the the weekend and so had bullied Val into her magic healing chair so she could reconnect her with 'the mystical spirit that dances with the limitless abandon of the unspoken heart'.

Valerie was more worried about what Karin would say about finding herself in the company of Tinara's whooshing incense wielding presence, than the fact that she hadn't even started on her own hair and make-up for the shoot.

'Keep that dingly-dangly *freak* away from me,' Karin

had said after Tinara had offered to personally guide her 'To-Wards the Mean-ing-full and more Full-fill-ing Life' she was so obviously 'Yearn-ing For'.

The washing machine had flooded Karin's minuscule apartment that day and she was seeking refuge in Valerie's house, when the Goddess had popped in to clap out a few spirits she insisted were still inhabiting Val's fridge after she had turned her vegetarian. Tinara had little trouble convincing the impressionable Valerie that the souls of slaughtered pigs lived on, long after the sausages themselves had been consumed, and had generously waived her normal exorcism fee of £50 in the name of friendship, although it didn't take a psychic to see that she would be in looking for payment in kind at some stage later in the day. Karin hated seeing Val being taken for a ride, and the critical comment on her own spiritual well-being just added insult to injury.

'Can you afford to buy me a house, Tinara?' she had snapped in reply.

'It is not what you have that matters, Kar-een – it is who you are,' she said with an expression of such patronizing pomposity that Karin felt like plaiting her great fuzzy mane of waist-length hair and strangling her with it.

'Yeah right. Nice cardigan . . .' Karin was about to launch into a bitchy comment about Tinara's by-now legendary ability to manipulate free clothes out of Valerie in exchange for her hocus-pocus services, but seeing the openly vulnerable look of hurt on her friend's face shut her up.

When she was gone, Karin huffed, 'That fucking woman!' and could not resist shouting through the soundproof, double-glazed window after her, *'Get a haircut you fat dog!'*

Valerie was not amused, but said nothing. As ever, her quiet disapproval was marked only by the offer of herbal tea. Karin wanted gin, preferably straight and served in a vase, but she felt bad for losing her rag and accepted the cup of strained flower-piss as if it would help.

Karin and Sinead had long ago given up trying to convince Valerie that Tinara's 'Money Is Not Important' method of non-rent payment was bringing her business down, quite apart from the fact that she smelled of patchouli and dressed like a cheap Moroccan hotel – she was an unlicensed looney, jumping on every touchy-feely-healy bandwagon going and talking vulnerable people like Valerie into parting with hard-earned cash in exchange for her kaftan billowing bollocks.

Valerie wasn't sure how much she believed in it all herself, but she *wanted* to believe that there was something more. Something higher than the shallow world of selling clothes and looking nice. Although she *really* did enjoy those things and, actually, they seemed to fulfil her, on the surface at least. But she felt that she *ought* to be trying to reach some higher dimension in her life. And Tinara did see things sometimes. Like today, she was feeling a little tired and not herself after the weekend. She hadn't liked staying in Jack's house on Saturday night, and driving back with Sinead and Karin, the two had been very quiet in the car. She knew she could talk anything through with them, but for some reason, she had felt uncomfortable with the fact that they had stayed up after her talking with Jack. She knew it was silly, but somehow she had the feeling that they might have been talking about her. Valerie knew she shouldn't have gone to the party really. She could have had a nice evening around at Bernard's apartment discussing his sorry love-life instead of being reminded of her own failures. She didn't know what drew her back to being in Jack's company. It was as if each time she went to his house she was looking for clues to what went wrong. Lying in one of the upstairs bedrooms, she had stayed awake for hours wondering why she still felt so uncomfortable after all these years. Other women got divorced and got over it. But for Valerie, it seemed that her marriage to Jack really had been for life. And yet, there she was, feeling like a stranger in his house. Like she had always done, really. She had so wanted to be a wife. But it had been more of a sense of identity than a feeling of intimacy. Valerie understood that a feeling of comfort was something that came after years of living with somebody. Letting them see you without your make-up; squabbling and nagging and knowing they will still be there in the morning; not always having to be well groomed and polite. They hadn't been married for long enough for Valerie to expose herself in that way. And she had never felt confident that Jack would have loved her if he saw the woman behind the 'lady'. In reality, Valerie wasn't sure if she could see it herself. Tinara was a natural woman. All breasts and hair and never a scrap of make-up. When Tinara had her period she wore a huge T-shirt printed with the words 'I MENSTRUATE WITH THE MOON'. Valerie admired that kind of openness and secretly longed to be that free. She had thought that a man might come along one day who would make her feel that way. But Tinara said that men were not the point. You had to connect with your own goddess first before the universe sent you the gift of everlasting love.

Tinara had Valerie's head clamped between her two vast Healing Hands and was shaking it nineteen-to-the-dozen, groaning like a climaxing rhino. The room was moving up and down in coloured stripes and Valerie felt a bit scared. She had seen Tinara go into a trance once before and it wasn't very ... em ... becoming. Lots of frothing and shouts from the womb; she'd lost a couple of clients as a result of the noise in the past, but then, that was the price you paid for the honour of renting a room out to a Goddess. If Karin came in now, she'd break a whole lot more than Tinara's 'Spell'. She wished Karin and Sinead were more understanding about her new friend. She really was helping her get in touch with herself. *Really* she was.

'Gaaaaaaaaaaar! I am *over-whelmed* ...' she shouted, 'with the pos-eee-teeve ener-gee of *la-huv* ...'

Valerie started to feel a bit nervous. Sinead's words, *'fat lesbian from hell after your body, mark my words'* were seeping through one of the negative patches in her subconscious mind – which Tinara had assured her were there.

The Goddess was quivering now from head to toe, like she was really onto something!

'A Ma-an ... I can see A Ma-an ...' Valerie sighed with relief, despite herself. 'The Uni–verse is sending a Ma-an in-to your la-high-F! I can se-ee that heee is a *tall* Ma-an and that he is no-hot from the-ese side of the wa-horld ... I can se-hee ...'

'Fuck's sake!'

It was Karin with a smirking Roddy Coogan peering over her shoulder.

'Lovely cameo girls – hold it right there a minute till I load me camera!'

Tinara removed her hands from Valerie's head in a dramatic snap.

'It is gone! The moment has passed ... the Universe's work is interrupted!' and she pushed past the two Karma terrorists down the stairs, into the shop and off to the McDonald's on Grafton Street to comfort her muse and refuel her spiritual resources with an Egg McMuffin and a chocolate milk shake.

Valerie was a little annoyed, and, for the first time, it occurred to her that she might, in fact, be doing Karin a favour appearing in her magazine – and that she had no right to invade Tinara's space.

Karin saw Valerie was upset, and both she and the photographer sensed that they had probably waded in when they shouldn't have. The editor turned on Roddy like it was all his fault.

'Well? What the fuck are you looking at?'

He was in fact drinking in the sight of arguably, Dublin's most elegant woman, lying in a red satin couch looking mesmerizingly vulnerable and wanting to take a picture of the scene for his own personal use.

'Get downstairs and set up!'

As Roddy scuttled down the stairs, Karin said, 'Sorry, Val.'

But Valerie wasn't listening. She was wondering about this tall, foreign man that Tinara had predicted was coming her way. Nothing would come of it probably, but she certainly felt somehow different than she had earlier that day. Perhaps Tinara's magic would work on her after all.

10

Eamonn Doyle's week had been unusually busy and stressful. What with preparations for the impending launch of the TV station and Karin giving out more than her usual quota of gyp over his decision to replace a feature she had been planning on 'Ireland's Most Eligible Bachelors' with an ad for Television You Can Trust. The offending item featured a photograph of This Winter's Must-Have Essential – the All-In-One Cozee Body Slipper – which was being modelled (in the loosest possible definition of the term) by some smiling and anonymous octogenarian. 'From England,' Karin presumed out loud, 'Irish pensioners have more dignity – and more bloody sense than to spend over a hundred quid on a fucking fur-lined strait-jacket.' Never one to hold back an opinion, Karin had been more than usually lippy over the last few days. But where in lesser employees such insubordination would be intolerable, Eamonn drew some strange comfort from the fact that there was clearly something troubling this usually impenetrable ice maiden. More bizarre still were the nippy shivers of excitement he seemed to feel every time she used an expletive.

'I mean – fucking, *fucking* hell Eamonn! You are ruining *my* magazine with your tacky fucking ads!'

Ignoring the reality that *How'ya* was, in fact, his magazine, and bathed in the sweet confusion of her having used a term for copulation three times in the one sentence, Eamonn crawled through what he thought, inadvisably, might be a window of opportunity.

'I suppose you'll be wanting to put me in?' he said.

'In what? A tartan body bag and bury you up to your neck in all that cheap crap you're trying to flog?'

He should have walked away then, but he seemed powerless over his own hope.

'In Ireland's Most Eligible Bachelors list?'

Karin's incredulous glower and a derogative 'Ha!' was all the answer he needed, and the rejection had more or less occupied his thoughts for the rest of that week, irritating him into forgetting that his estranged daughter was due to arrive from Paris and land on top of him any day now.

He had replied to Lativa's brief letter announcing the date of her arrival by sending her back a set of keys to the Mount Merrion house. He had half-thought that he might be abroad when she arrived, or rather, half-hoped that something would turn up that would prevent them from both being in the same place at the same time. In the true spirit of denial, however, he had not taken the trouble to arrange anything concrete. That would have meant owning up to the fact that he didn't want to see her, and that would make him what? A bad father? A weak man who couldn't face up to his responsibilities? No. Better to just reroute his thoughts away from the treacherous bog of emotional reality and pretend that it wasn't happening until it was time to deny everything and fall back on that old fail-safe, 'It was your mother's fault'.

And so, on rising into this particularly drizzly Saturday, Eamonn decided to put his week behind him and kick his weekend off by indulging in the luxuriant habits that the privacy of his bachelordom would allow. *Not* the 'Eligible With a Speedboat' bachelordom of Karin Sheridan's dreams, but rather the 'Lonely With a Tractor' variety of his own country upbringing, which, Eamonn had discovered in recent years brought its own brand of comfort.

After lying in bed enjoying a particularly satisfying scratch (the kind of leave-no-stone unturned root in all those generally unexplored nooks and crannies in which one can only decently indulge in the presence of an all forgiving God), the mindless quacking of Saturday morning pop TV reminded Eamonn that there was precious little that one could call music in this day and age. This thought propelled him from his pit, and into his living room where he stood perusing his record collection whilst puffing a bit of fresh air through the waistband of his favourite wear-and-tear Y-fronts, openly revelling in the sheer perfection of their yeasty softness. With a 'Ya Boyo Ya!' he selected Rose Royce's Greatest Hits, and placed it carefully on the turntable, meticulously twiddling the volume and bass knobs until it was up to what he defined as full pelt and fuck the neighbours.

The bit of aul disco never failed to lift Eamonn Doyle's spirits, and while he rarely indulged himself in public these days (the Funky Chicken not being generally considered the most dignified of stances for a businessman of his stature to be caught in), he could not but help a couple of modest buttock lunges as he made his way into the kitchen to prepare breakfast.

Ahhhh breakfast.

There was no meal in the world that Eamonn enjoyed more than his Saturday morning fried-egg sandwich. Eaten in the spirit of convenience for which it was invented i.e. over the sink to avoid (a) dribbling and (b) washing up. No greater luxury, he thought, hath no man ever enjoyed than to fire into a great lump of the messiest foodstuff on earth without the disapproving glower of some female telling him to stop showing himself up as a common animal of the lowest order. Of course, one had enough class to put on a show for the punters one did business with. Lap up the fancy fayre in the posh restaurants, learn to tell if the wine was corked, get to grips with your oyster pins and your mathematically aligned cutlery, know to tell your tartar from your béarnaise and to never order chips in front of a woman. But, at the end of the day, if there was an Irishman alive who wouldn't trade it all in – all the glamour and the starched linen and the how-are-you's – to be eating a fried-egg sandwich over the sink in the peace and comfort of his own castle,

Eamonn Doyle would, at this very moment in time, very much have liked to have met him.

Most men, he knew from his own experience of being married, were denied such small delights. Wives, and women generally, drew the line at such culinary atrocities and more especially the manner of their execution. The Fried-Egg Sandwich Over the Sink was one of Eamonn's small compensations for being without a woman in his life, and so he enjoyed it with a vigour that was, frankly, disco.

Pan on ... 'at the car wash' ... lunge two three – egg in pan ... 'come-on now an' sing it to me' ... two slices fresh white ... 'car wash' ... sideways slide to fridge – door open – butter out ... 'lemme tell you it's better than diggin' a ditch' ... air punch, demi turn – butter bread, fish slice, egg on bread ... 'at the car wash yeah!'

Eamonn was halfway through the sandwich, a Limerick From Lovely Laois novelty tea towel tied into a bib around his neck to catch any errant squirts of yolk, before he realized that there was a body standing in his kitchen doorway.

'Hullo, Dad.'

She didn't look too shocked, but Eamonn was transmogrified with the horror of being 'caught'. The bravado of every man's right to eat over the sink in his own castle, semi-nude or otherwise, was speedily sucked up the extractor fan, its electric humm providing small comfort from the dense mortified second of silence of both parties.

That young Lativa did not yelp in bitter horror at the undignified demeanour of her old man was testament to the modern young woman's grip on basic social protocol. For being an aspiring fashion student, and having been raised in Paris, it would have been infinitely more palatable for her to find her father naked, or even lounging about the house in a diaphanous ladies' nightie and furry mules, than wearing a tea-towel kerchief and a pair of voluminous grey pants that you wouldn't dry a dog with. The sad comb-over and the lumps of eggy bread she could handle. But unsightly Y-fronts, even hidden from the world under the Gucci-est of tailored suits were an anathema to this impeccably stylish youngster. A fashion crime par excellence. She was shocked and disgusted.

Her disappointment did not entirely pass Eamonn by either, as he struggled to make up ground by trying to think about an opening line that would somehow dissipate the dreadfulness of the moment. But he was so utterly discombobulated by a barrage of unexpected facts; (a) his daughter was here (b) he hadn't seen her for years (c) he was wearing horrible pants and a tea-towel and holding a congealed egg sandwich which he had rather been looking forward to finishing, that the one vital fact he needed to get hold of seemed to be swimming off somewhere in the back of his subconscious. Without it, he knew he could not continue. Without it he was doomed. The lack of it made him, surely, the worst father in the whole wide world, but worse still than that, it made him a half-naked old man standing in his kitchen unable to talk his way out of an awkward situation. It was fact (d). His daughter's new name. In some nasty quirk of shock, it had even taken her birth name with it. Then with a sudden flash it came to him. Relief surged through his trembling body and in an unnervingly inappropriate gesture of glee Eamonn held his eggy palms aloft in the manner of a welcoming messiah and pronounced, 'Latvia!'

It was only then, in the expectation that this word would somehow make everything else go away, that Eamonn really began to look at his daughter standing there. She was tall, slim too, and wearing a smart black trouser suit. Expensive, well cut. He knew the difference from the women in the office ooh-ing and ahh-ing over the fashion pages in *How'ya*. That much he had noticed about her already, but as he searched her face for some kind of approval, he noticed the extravagant curve of her features. Sculpted into adulthood with the secret female skill of subtle make-up, there was an uncompromising confidence in the straightness of her nose, the heavy arch of her eyebrows, the full pink petals of her mouth. Was it possible that his daughter was a beauty? His mother must have been once, although he scarcely remembered ever having thought it. Eammon felt the horror of his own physicality mirrored in the perfect little lady framed by the arch of his tasteless suburban kitchen. How pathetic he must look with the scrappy excuse of a head on him and the one good eye frozen onto her, begging her to say something to make him feel better. To make everything all right, to make the last ten years melt away and him into a good father.

'I had better get dressed,' he said edging his way past her. Then, and he wished it didn't sound so much like the afterthought it was, 'Make yourself at home.'

What with her parents being separated, being whisked off to Paris aged seven, and her mother bringing home various men of every shape, colour and creed before finally settling for a tattooed performance artist and political lesbian called Francine whom she was asked to refer to as 'Maman deux', the self-christened Lativa was pretty resourceful when it came to organizing her emotions around family. Naturally, she was disappointed by her father's appearance, and he was clearly no great shakes when it came to paternal details like remembering names, but over the years her expectations of him had been more or less pared down to nil. Despite the lack of a welcoming party, she was nonetheless grateful to be out of the grim drizzle and in a house which, despite its unfortunate owner, looked like it had the makings of a home. Her mother's house was cold and studenty. Having more or less failed to become a successful artist, Eileen had concentrated largely on developing the boho lifestyle end of things, leaving her daughter to more or less look after herself. From the age of thirteen, she had learned how to cook and tidy, while her mother pretended to be poor and interesting by eating out of tins and sitting up half the night with hairy French poets and potters discussing how unfair life was that nobody appreciated how brilliant they all were. Looking around her father's living room, Lativa was surprised at how much it was like the normal suburban house she had longed for all those years living with her freaky mother. The house she had left at seven had been smaller than this, in Stillorgan, just before her father made all the money she had heard about and which her mother bitterly resented. ('Three thousand pounds? The tight bastard...' she would hear her mother squall to Francine. 'He's loaded, and he hasn't got an artistic bone in his body. It's so unfair!') She had not thought about that house much since she left. Or Ireland. Or, if truth be told, her father. It had seemed better not to. Having a born-again fruit-cake for a mother had made her sensible and self-contained. It was either that or give in to the patchouli and the bad poetry, in which case she'd have surely been drug-addicted or swinging from a rope by twenty. That's not to say that she didn't resent her father's lack of interest. She did. Deeply. It's just that she had made a decision way back then, at seven, not to squawk and cry. Moving away was a done deal, and she knew by the fact that it was happening at all, that, as a child, she was powerless. Her tantrums in being torn away from her home and her friends and her father, had borne no results. It had happened anyway. And so she left it up to her father to make all the moves over the years. When his attempts were as half-hearted and weak as they were, she tried to accept that her father had chosen to not be a part of her life, probably because he just didn't love her very much. She created her own little life apart from the lack of interest from both her parents. She did well at school, made friends easily, developed a strong sense of style, devoured fashion magazines and diligently pursued life-drawing classes on Sunday mornings, keeping the results away from her mother so that she wouldn't get jealous of her obvious talent. She had applied for her own grant and won the place at the National College of Art and Design in Dublin. She had already been offered a place in Paris, but she was tired of living with her mother, and thought this might make a change. Lativa knew that her optimistic attitude and unshakeable ambition made her different from other seventeen-year-olds. Several kind adults, tutors and 'interested' older male parties had told her she was 'an extraordinary young woman'. But Lativa didn't want to be extraordinary. She wanted to be loved. And if her feelings for this ugly old man and his horrible underpants were locked in a box, in a drawer, in a dresser, in a room, down an unlit corridor in the basement of her subconscious, then looking around this room, with its big squishy sofas and it's cosy rosy carpet, some hopeful seven-year-old had just switched the light on.

When Eamonn returned from the good hour of arduous toilet and neurotic dressing it had taken to compose himself into both mental and physical order, Lativa was sitting on the edge of his leather reading chair. She was cradling an old lacy cushion which she suspected she recognized from the old house in Stillorgan, but was too embarrassed, or just plain petulant to ask about. Her father was wearing an acutely detailed crayzee-patterned sweater, part of his carefully selected 'good' weekend wear, and a pair of gun-metal grey slacks whose sharply creased frontage suggested a mating of the two greatest fashion crimes on earth – Nylon and Golf. The hair was crucified into position with Brylcreem and underneath it his scalp glowed a visible pink. He was a mode monstrosity. A clothing criminal. A makeover in waiting. And yet . . . Lativa sensed there was something. Some little detail, so small, she might have missed it. Something salvageable from the great carnage of bad taste that stood in front of her.

'You like Rose Royce,' she stated more than asked.

'Yes,' Eamonn said. Then, still struggling with the correct format for dealing with unexpected daughters arriving upon one, he decided to dive right in with the lot.

'Would you like a cup of tea? Some breakfast? Will I show you your room? Well, that is *a* room – you see, there's no room in particular, that is, I haven't *prepared* one, as such – but you have any room you like really – I have plenty – ' his voice trailed off into a kind of terrified whisper – 'of rooms, plenty of rooms that is for . . . for you to choose from.'

And so this was her father then. A shambly mumbly social inadequate who couldn't deal with this situation. He didn't want her, but she was here now. They were both stuck. Lativa inhaled a deep breath over her disappointment and held it until she remembered that she didn't need him. She had survived without him this long and if he was a bad parent, well then, so was her mother, and he at least deserved the same level of detached politeness. After all, she was planning to stay in his house.

'I like Rose Royce too,' she said, 'Retro Disco is big in Paris right now. My friends and I listen to it all the time. My friend Fabio is a DJ and he mixes the old with the new, you know? Like Disco Rave and . . .' she was babbling now, but it was better than the crippling, formal silence, and at least her father had sat down on the sofa. 'We tried to get a video of the film? *Car Wash?* I think the clothes then were great. Wild – you know? I want to study it maybe, for my course – I'm going to be studying fashion. Would I be able to get it here do you think? The video? Of *Car Wash?*'

As this elegant young stranger finished her question she looked straight across at him, right in the face. Eamonn felt as if no one had ever looked at him with quite such intensity ever before. Her eyes seemed to grip his in their soft blueness and hold them until he gave them the answer they wanted. Eamonn was adept at not making eye-to-eye contact, and due to his disfigurement, few people challenged his desire to negotiate without it. Lativa wasn't afraid to look, and at first it made him nervous. 'Well, I wouldn't know about that now really, it's just a record that I pulled out, I don't know if . . .'

He pulled his eyes down, but the young woman craned her head down and around until she found them again and locked them into moving his face back onto hers. As she sat, her head tilted, her eyes waiting for an answer to his question, Eamonn suddenly felt it. A recognition so complete that even the shame of having forgotten, it faded into nothing. A knowledge that was so entwined in his own blood that he knew he didn't need to even speak the words.

'Noreen Laura Doyle,' he said silently in his own mind. Little Noreen. Back and babbling away like she'd never been away. It was that easy. Like a spell cast and broken.

Eamonn slapped his knees with his palms and stood up.

'I have the film myself actually, imported from America on DVD. Now young lady, we'll pop that bag of yours in the top-floor en-suite, then, I don't know about you, but I've a date with an egg sandwich to finish. Care to join me?'

PART TWO

JULY

11

Claude Moore, it was generally agreed, was one of the cleverest men in Ireland. Although, clever was, really too small a word to describe him. On this morning, the man himself was preparing to read that day's edition of the *Irish Times*, in which he had written a full page article on the state of contemporary Irish literature. The basic thrust of the piece was that it was no great shakes, excepting, naturally enough his own work. Of course, Claude wasn't crude enough to come right out and say; 'I'm the only living Irish writer worth a shite', but one only had to look at the angular brooding cut of his picture, all pained expression and borderline-unkempt hair to tell that this man was the Real Deal. He was sitting in the kitchen of his Fitzwilliam Square 'attic rooms', as he humbly described his top-floor Georgian habitat with its magnificent view over the civilized patch of park for which only treasured residents had the key. Visitors then, having been led to believe that he lived in a garret, would be doubly impressed by the sedate, gentlemanly décor of artefacts and antiques seeing him as he truly was; not just a great intellect, but also a man of erudite aesthetic tastes.

The *Times* was spread out across the table and his housekeeper, Mrs Morley, had placed his morning croissant and coffee on top of it while he had been performing his day's ablutions. When he returned from the bathroom to find his profound descriptions littered with crumbs and a blob of coffee interrupting the moody linear intensity of his brooding photograph, Claude was irritated anew with the ignorance of the Irish working classes when it came to matters of academic importance. Claude had tried, several times over the years she was in his employ, to share the bottomless extent of his creative genius with Mrs Morley; even giving her a signed copy of his celebrated collection of poems, *The Black Carnage of My Soul*. But she had declared them 'a bit depressin'', entirely missing the point and remaining seemingly impervious to the charms of the great mind for whom she did light housework. On a normal day, the inattention of this homely mother from Ballybrack, and her use of his important cultural contribution to the *Irish Times* readers as a breakfast plate, would have broken a sweat on Claude's irritation and turned it to fury. But he was in a sombre mood that morning, having woken from a most disturbing dream.

In it, he was at a fabulous party in a large house, surrounded by important historic literary and intellectual figures. Cicero was there getting his toga in a twist whilst in heated discussion with Spinoza; Einstein, Van Gogh, Beethoven, Joyce, all standing around in a civilized manner engaging in clever chit-chat. Claude was in his element, knowing that he was in with the 'in' crowd and was working his way around the room indulging himself in the wet-dream fantasy of his own indisputable brilliance. He was in discussion with Karl Jung as to the meaning of this dream (that he was on a par with the finest minds in history), when out of the corner of his eye he saw two chancers stirring up trouble. His first reaction was, 'What are they doing here?' Brendan Behan, a troublemaker whose common prose had done little more than promote the vernacular of the uncivilized, and Dylan Thomas, a sentimentalist alcoholic whose persona was as scary as his poetry. As he turned to express his irritation at their invitation to Jung, things went out of his control. Thomas started up on the piano and Behan shouted 'Conga!'. Then the world's most brilliant minds let out a mighty 'whay-hey!' and joined onto each other to make a hip-hugging, leg-flinging party snake and danced out the door leaving Claude standing alone and confused in an empty room. His dream hijacked by a couple of lesser reprobates. What did it mean?

As Claude began to munch on his lone croissant and sip on his imported Brazilian coffee, Mrs Morley singing away to her daughter Sharon's Boyzone CD on the Walkman she had clipped to the waistband of her pinny as she pushed the Hoover over his antique Moroccan kilim, he began to peruse the meaning of it all. He had won over the cogniscenti, no doubt about that. Sure wasn't he right there? In the *Irish Times*? Pontificating on all-sorts on a regular basis. Literary awards? Don't be talking! Didn't he have to have an Italian craftsman flown in all the way from Italian Italy to construct a special cabinet to fit them all in? And yet his housekeeper and her like, sadly, represented a greater portion of the world's population and they didn't have a clue about him. They thought Einstein was a great man altogether, and Beethoven? They knew who he was all right. Irish people of all classes, even people who lived in the country, knew who James Joyce was, even if they'd never read him – or certainly not had the requisite education to understand him. Joyce even had pubs named after him. In the fullness of time, Claude Moore knew he would surely go down in the annals of history as a great Irish mind. But he didn't want to wait until he was dead. Being famous after you're dead was no good at all. And being admired by other very clever people and people with a third-level education generally was all right but it wasn't really 'Famous'. Not famous enough to impress Mrs Morley in any case. While the admiration of Mrs Morley was not anything much in itself, it was nonetheless representative of his status among the ordinary people. He should not, Claude Moore decided, be so dismissive of the respect of the working classes. They too deserved to revere him; to have a hero in the manner of Joyce they might enjoy and idolize while he was still alive. He would try to find a way of reaching them. He would get onto his agent later and tell him he was to no longer refuse breakfast television interviews and that he would be happy, no, honoured to be asked to judge poetry competitions in popular women's magazines.

The phone rang, and Claude, lifted into a state of something bordering on reverie by the altruism of the Everyman Persona he intended to adopt, picked it up and said;

'Good Morning – I mean – Hi there!' in a manner which made him sound a good deal jollier and more approachable than he actually was.

'Mr Claude Moore?'

'Oh, call me Claude please. That's me yes?' First name terms. Part of the new, friendlier, man-of-the-people-me, he thought. Talking lots was good too. Unnecessary additions to sentences were something that ordinary people did. He should try that. Claude's modus operandi to date had been to not reward stupid questions with an answer. Social silence was his way of not dispersing the intense brilliance of his mind before he had the chance to write it down. Speaking was a dilution of his genius. If someone wanted to know something about him, let them read it in his books and figure it out for themselves. If they wanted to know more, then they should get a commission to interview him for the *Observer* or become Melvyn Bragg. And if they did, even the most highbrow of journalists found him sullen and unforthcoming. It was like Claude Moore was too clever for his own good; so clever it hurt; too clever to be wasting time sitting around talking about how clever he was. Claude believed in thinking carefully before you spoke. That way everything one said would be of great importance and significance. Sadly, the rest of the world appeared to disagree, mindlessly chattering their opinions on radio talk shows and saying obvious things like 'It's raining today' and 'The traffic is bad' instead of holding their tongues and waiting until they had something to say that one mightn't already know. However, if he wanted to reach into the depths of society's dungeons and raise up the minds of lesser mortals, if not to his own level, then at least to a place where they might appreciate his genius, he was going to have to be tolerant, and even move slightly in their direction. He was a long way from slewing back enough brew to inspire the chorus of 'Fields of Athenry' out of him of a Saturday night, but conversing in an affable and friendly manner, even mastering the art of small talk, was at least a start. He would practise with this female on the other end of the phone.

'Oh Mr More, Claude, I am so sorry to trouble you at home. My name is Karin Sheridan and I'm the editor of *How'ya*, Ireland's leading glossy celebrity monthly magazine. I tried to get in touch with you some weeks back, but it seems that you were away on a book tour, and I rang your agent, Paul in London and he said that you wouldn't be back until now, so that's why I'm ringing you now. Anyway . . .'

You see – this was what he meant by utterly mindless. He knew he'd been away, he knew he was back, and he knew his agent was called Paul and that he was in London. Get to the point woman! Remembering his vow, Claude held himself back.

'. . . I was just ringing to see if you might be interested in an interview in *How'ya* magazine.'

Claude's testicles clenched at the mere mention of that

vile forum for Ireland's most fatuous grippers and grinners. He remembered it only because he had been so profoundly horrified by its sugary content during his last trip to the dentist, that his teeth had seemed to hurt more as a result.

'I am sure you are familiar with the magazine, but might I also mention that we have a readership of half a million. Our readers cover a very broad spectrum of the Irish reading public, and well, the thing is, your agent seemed to think that it wouldn't be your thing, but, to be honest, I really think that your audience crosses over all the social boundaries, and with your new novel coming out it could be great publicity and . . .'

Claude's eyes were scanning the kitchen, looking for some kind of an escape from the verbal torture this consummate babbler was inflicting on him, when he saw How'ya's yellow and red logo peeking out from the top of Mrs Morley's shopping trolley.

'I'll do it,' he said.

Mercifully, after a second of silence, the woman got to the point.

'Friday at two?'

'Fine.'

'Your place or would you rather I took you to lunch? A lovely new hotel has just opened up on . . .'

'5 Fitzwilliam Square, 2 o'clock Friday. Don't be late.' And then suddenly remembering, Claude tried to keep the grudging mumble out of his voice as he added, 'Nice talking to you and see you Friday then,' before hanging up.

Relaxing after the effort of his new-found affability, Claude turned to his paper to finish the appreciation of his picture which had been so rudely interrupted by that morning's whim. Under it the caption read; *Claude Moore – Ireland's Greatest Literary Novelist*. Hmmmm – there was something not quite right. 'Ireland's Greatest Literary' – that was true enough – but then? Somehow the title mere 'novelist' seemed to bring the whole sentence down. Surely there must be some other word that would better describe the breadth of his talent. Fictional Philosopher? No 'fiction' was bad. Fiction was what women read on holidays. Scrabbling around in the Thesaurus part of his mind for a word that meant Genius but was less 'obvious', Claude shifted the corner of his croissant so he could get a better view of himself.

And there it was.

Disaster. A veiled insult. Right there in black and white. In the *Irish Times*.

A question mark.

What, a few short moments ago had read; *Claude Moore – Ireland's Greatest Literary Novelist*, croissant crumb, now read *Claude Moore – Ireland's Greatest Literary Novelist?*

Or rather blah blah blah QUESTION MARK! QUESTION MARK! QUESTION MARK!

He had always believed that the *Irish Times* was little more than a parochial pamphlet masquerading as an intelligent broadsheet, and had said as much in a recent interview in the *Guardian* – an altogether superior British publication in his opinion. But he had never imagined that the philistines who ran the rag would be petty enough to betray him in this way. After all, he was an artist. Great artists should have leeway to say anything they bloody well want, and if people don't like it they just have to put it down as part of a cultural contribution to history.

The cheek of them! The nerve! Who the hell did they think they were!

Right. That was it then. Fuck the *Irish Times* and all belonging to them. It was quite good really, Claude decided, because he had already made his mind up that he was going populist *before* he saw the offending article. He was on his way to becoming a man of the people. He was going to be in *How'ya* magazine. Then the ordinary people of Ireland would love him; rise up in his defence; talk about him in taxis and name pubs after him.

As Mrs Morley left that morning he gave her three signed hardback copies of *Illuminati Insurrection* with a gesture of such benign sincerity, 'A few copies for your family – I hope you enjoy it', that she felt almost touched. Until she remembered the last time and realized that she might be expected to actually *read* the wretched thing!

12

Sinead could not even begin to credit how fantastically happy she was feeling on this Friday morning. Life was more or less the same as it had been a month ago. Dizzy was still saying 'Hiya' instead of 'SOS Management how can I help you?' when she answered the phone; Jack Valentine's bet still stood – Karin's determined enthusiasm precluding Sinead from calling it off and neither woman had yet had the courage to tell their friend Valerie that they had thrown her name in the pot with her ex-husband. Business was still quiet enough, aside from one important new signing which was almost in the bag, and she was four weeks closer to her fortieth birthday. In other words, all was as per except for one crucial detail – Sinead was in love.

It was all a question of perspective. Sitting in her office this Friday afternoon, the world was a very different place. Dizzy was a dote. What a joy to have a young pretty dolly about the place when one knows oneself to be a love goddess of extreme loveliness and supreme sexual prowess. Business? Pah! Who needs it when there are songs to be sung, fields to be frolicked in with one's dearest heart. And Jack Valentine? The toad and his insulting bet were enjoying the light of the sweetest of sweet ironies being thrown on them from the vantage-point of Sinead's bursting heart. How *ironic* that Jack should think her unlovable and over the hill. How *ironic* that he should perceive her as being beyond the sugar-coated claws of true romance. And by the way how *ironic*, that the sad, lonely old rock star was sitting out there, in his empty mansion still wallowing in the smug surety that she couldn't possibly win his bet when, in fact, she had a deep and unshakeable instinct that there was every chance she might be able to pull off a double-irony coup by actually being seriously in line for that million-pound cash prize. Not that it mattered, of course. Money was mere piffle next to the grand magnitude of being in love. But still . . . it was amusing to think that, despite herself, Sinead might get one over on him. Life had felt so sweet of late, that Sinead suspected Jack's million might, just might, be her great reward for having to wait until thirty-nine before she experienced true love.

And it was true love. It had to be. Sinead had calculated all of the requiring factors and come out with a full house.

Firstly, the way they had met. It had been too bizarre to not have been kismet. His being part of a crowd of suitors, so to speak, and Dizzy picking him out from the middle of the queue. That kind of random coincidence only happens if really important things are going to happen.

Secondly, the first time she saw him. Her reluctance to take him on as a client despite the extraordinary brilliance of his music. That kind of push-back pull-forward sense-of-danger-but-I-don't-know-why stuff. Very 'Gone With the Wind'. An early signal that this was a 'Love Epic' type scenario. And then there was that thing he said. A sign that he knew her, even though, of course, he couldn't have known her at all. Instinct. Karma. Surely the stuff soul mates are made of.

Thirdly, and this really was the clincher, was the different-ness of it all. Sinead had always believed she was different with a capital D. Not your run-of-the-mill Suburban Dublin Girl. Right from the word go she had gone out of her way to defy convention. Different clothes, different job, different attitude. It only made sense that she should end up being with someone who was as 'different' as Miles was. She didn't know why she hadn't thought of it before. But then that was the key too. Brilliant! – the way love suddenly makes things so *obvious*. If she had said to herself, 'Right – I'm going to go off and find myself a midget', then it would never have happened the way it did. You cannot mess with the natural order of things. It was the very fact that falling in love with Miles was the last thing that Sinead was expecting that made the whole thing so . . . so . . . *real*.

Miles had rung and left a message with Dizzy earlier to say that he couldn't see her tonight because he wanted to stay in his studio and work up a couple of tracks he'd been playing with. That was another thing about their relationship that worked so well. It was mature. They gave each other plenty of space like real adults. Not living in each other's pockets like lovestruck teenagers. Feelings aside, they might both want to stage a twenty-four-seven love-in, but it was important not to lose the run of themselves and keep their own independence. That was the key to staying in love, Miles said. Always keeping a part of yourself separate. Maintain the allure, that's what he said. He said she was alluring. He used words like 'allure' all the time. 'You fascinate me,' he said over dinner after she had described what she thought was a fairly full day's work. 'My temptress' he called her after they had made love for the third time in as many hours. 'Temptress'. So much more classy than 'Sexy Bitch' which had been her best seductive handle before. That was what she loved about Miles. It was a cliché, but he had a way of saying the right thing. And it was never the right thing you were expecting. It was always somehow better, smarter. Like he was compensating for his physique. The knowledge of that made him seem vulnerable, and that only made Sinead love him even more.

Sinead decided that, as she wasn't seeing Miles tonight, she would take a couple of hours off to just sit at her desk and indulge herself in a rewind. A spot of euphoric romantic recall to get her through the next twenty-four hours before she saw him again.

Five days after his initial visit, Sinead had played his demo again. Without the distraction of his sitting staring at her, she was able to listen to it with the trained ear of a professional. Was there a market for this kind of thing? It had an ethereal, almost classical quality that put it out there with the Enyas and the Oldfields, yet it was extremely contemporary. She could see the bang-bang kids doing their spooky swoony dances to it in the clubs, yet it wouldn't feel out of place while Mary Murphy was doing her ironing out there in Ballybunion. Yes. This stuff could cut across the board all right. Could be the real thing. It was clearly the work of a brilliant musical talent, but hey – talent wasn't everything. This was a funny business where a half-wit with a nice haircut could make it big, and she had seen the most brilliant young bands go down the tube because they refused to highlight their hair and wear spandex. So he was a midget, and that wasn't great from a marketing point of view. But after Grunt Bunny, Sinead had enough cutesie teenage wannabes she could use to front this stuff up. Might be a bit tricky negotiating the whole midget/PR issue, but he had seemed like an intelligent chap and she was sure she could pull it off.

He sounded surprised and delighted when she rang, which was a good thing. His arrogance on their first meeting was enough to draw her in, but he had enough sense to temper it with good manners saying that he would 'very much like to' take her for dinner to thank her for even bothering to call him back, adding, rather touchingly, that he wasn't a big fan of pubs on account of – Sinead cut him off with a sympathetic, 'I know'. They arranged to meet at the bar in the Merrion Hotel, where he said he would book a table at Guilbaud's. Sinead was horrified. Guilbaud's was Dublin's most expensive and established restaurant. Far too posh for an upcoming DJ, who had queued in the rain for their last and first brief meeting. He laughed her off when she suggested the same and ended wittily saying that he was confident she would find something suitable to wear. Patrick Guilbaud himself was there to take them to their table, and seemed to know Miles, although Sinead allayed her confusion by reminding herself that the gliding Frenchman always appeared to know all of his customers. Impeccable intimacy was all part of the service here. The meal was superb, and the conversation varied and easy, but as Miles was scanning the wine list for a suitable accompaniment for dessert, Sinead realized that they, notably he, had not once mentioned why they were there. With a rising sense of embarrassment, Sinead realized that she was on a date. OK, she had given herself the full pluck and purify treatment on the way out. Major upholstery was undertaken in the underwear department, fail-safe little black number carefully selected, tights checked for ladders and chin checked for stray hairs, but then she treated every night out like a potential date without really realizing it. 'Just in case' had become a way of behaving unbeknownst. And, with an even more pink-inducing snap, it occurred to her that Miles was, in many ways, a dream date. Guilbaud's – ten out of ten. How many men had the wit, the intelligence, the *confidence* to take a woman they hardly knew to a place like this. Conversation? Same again. Sophisticated without being smarmy. None of your fatuous 'So tell me about *you*' crap, so that they cannot listen to the answer and just stare at your tits, holding out for their 'afters'. They had covered a broad spectrum of topics, without even exchanging surnames. Manners – James Bond get to the back of the queue. He had even managed to pull her chair out himself, despite the hoard of waiters queuing up to do same. Humour – witty but not overbearing guffawing bore. Intelligence level – high to soaring. Features – well structured, fabulous eyes. Hair – opulent and own. Teeth – all in place. Clothes – smart and fashionable. Hygiene – no evidence to suggest the lack of. Height – Nil points! Nil points! Nil points!

'Does my height bother you?'

Sinead coughed into her tarte Tatin.

'No, I mean I . . .'

He laughed. 'Hey. No big deal – pardon the pun.'

Then he launched into the requisite first date life story. Except that it wasn't the usual blah blah two-arms-and-two-legs who gives a shit biog. Mother – fallen Argentinian aristocrat artist; father – world-renowned Scottish architect. An only child, he was conceived on a plane between Brazil and Edinburgh, born on the wind-swept Scottish island of Skye and reared in Paris, Barcelona, New York and, in latter years, London – wherever his father's work and his mother's eccentric whims took them. His body had been neither presented to nor taken by him to be a handicap or disadvantage of any kind. It was just the way he was, and was certainly no more peculiar than his mother's predilection for young English bricklayers or his father's tolerance, or even encouragement, of same. He studied Engineering at Cambridge, and had held every kind of conceivable job, from sign writer on a Greek holiday island, to managing director of an organic food company in Italy. He spoke five languages fluently and seven to 'get-by-and-barter' standard – twelve in total. He had even done a stint as a circus 'gnome' as research for an academic paper on attitudes towards Persons of Restricted Growth for a French university.

'Oh,' Sinead blurted out.

'That's right – Persons of Restricted Growth,' he smiled, 'that *is* the correct term, but you can call me a midget if you like.'

Sinead laughed nervously, although, she wasn't feeling nervous. Not any more. This man wasn't like the self-made artisto types she had met before. Remove the drugs, the fame, the debauchery and you've got your run-of-the-mill three-bed semi suburban bore with a chip. Miles had been *born* interesting. He was a one-off. An exception. His restricted height was no longer a disadvantage. Within twenty minutes, he had managed to turn his four-foot-nothing status into a Unique Selling Point.

By the time the waiter slid the petits fours onto their table Sinead said, 'Shall we skip coffee and move on?'

His apartment was as much of a surprise as the invisibly subtle way he paid the bill. Sinead had been expecting – what? Some kind of a half-baked hippy boy-pit in Rathmines. Certainly nothing to compete with her own stylishly tidy mews. Firstly, it was distinctly Des Res – a penthouse, no less, in trendy Temple Bar.

Then. His apartment itself. Jesus! Where to begin. It was *magnificent*. Art carefully placed in areas appropriated by impeccable lighting. Sinead didn't know much, actually anything, about art, but her acquisitive antennae were twitching. She knew, just by the cut of the place that this was the real thing. None of your Habitat buy-one-get-one-free nonsense here. Furniture? Italian imported – no question. That tan leather sofa could not be bought in Ireland for less than nine grand. She knew, because she'd had a cheap copycat version on order for the last six months from a chi-chi shop in Val's arcade, and almost had to remortgage to pay for it. She gave the floors a subtle tap with her heel. Maple. The genuine article. She was *dying* to know where he got all this money but managed to restrain her gauche nosy-neighbour instinct to stroke the sofa and say, 'This must've cost a few bob?'

She might have been tempted but for one other major oddity, which it took a few seconds for her to absorb. The apartment itself was huge, and notably given its owner's diminutive stature, so was everything in it. Sinead, trying not to look too shell-shocked, wandered over to an African carving of a naked woman in polished ebony and ran a finger down her curved back to the hill of her magnificent buttocks.

'My ex,' Miles said from behind her.

Sinead looked back at him, incredulous, not just by the beauty of the carving, but by the experience of just being there. For half a second she thought she saw a glimpse of satisfaction in his eyes, like he had won. Then it disappeared into a smile of such natural mischief, that she felt certain she had imagined it. 'Only joking,' he said. 'Coffee?'

Sinead watched as he moved about his open-plan kitchen. Nothing there either, was modified to suit his height. He stood on a footstool to reach up into the tall cathedral-inspired presses for the cups, manoeuvred the coffee down from the high worktop with a wooden spoon. And yet, he moved so seamlessly, with such comfort, that this intimidatingly stylish and enormous apartment could not have belonged to anyone else. Somehow, his presence there was so much greater than his body, that he was able to fill the place.

However, less than five minutes after they had arrived in his penthouse such lofty appreciations were far from Ms Sinead Sullivan's mind. The meal, the conversation, the apartment, and some strange notion about being 'different' were conspiring to cause a cacophony of hysterical hormones to run riot through the substantial content of her almost six-foot frame. At the forefront of her mind was the notion that, if Miles could live like a big man, she would very much like to see if he could fuck like one too.

But she didn't say that. With all the confidence of a woman wise to the fact that no man in current use of all his faculties is ever likely to say 'no', Sinead simply let her easy-access black silk Donna Karan shift fall to the floor and asked, 'Shall we?'

There was nothing, in the whole wide world, that annoyed Sinead more than average sex. Bad sex wasn't great, but at least it had the advantage of the anecdotal post-mortem, and many's the night she had amused Karin and embarrassed Valerie with stories of some premature pop star. Good sex, well that was just good. But at the age of thirty-nine, there were few unexplored avenues and few surprises left. Good sex was competing with good television and good company. Frankly, she'd had her first Eve Lom facial a couple of weeks ago and for eighty quid it had brought her to a new level of physical and spiritual satisfaction that made her wonder if sex was ever going to be worth it again. And so, it was not in the virginal spirit of the newly sullied that Sinead announced, after Round One in Miles's emperor-sized bed, 'Wow!'

Not, one could argue, the most erudite of expressions for a mature woman of the world to use with legs splayed in a wide V, a halo of Crimson Vixen lip-gloss mashed across her chin and her stockings wrapped around her ankles, but the purveyor of the most magnificent, the most sublime, the most stupendously fantastic orgasm that Sinead O'Sullivan had ever experienced, did not seem to mind. Far from it but if the adventurous wee monster wasn't wiping his mouth and hopping on board for Round Two before Sinead had time to gather herself out of her exhausted ecstasy.

While Miles was preparing for Cunnilingus 3 – The Sequel, Sinead grabbed his ears and said, 'You've made your point Miles, you get the contract.'

She was going to do it anyway, but after tonight, she

knew; really, really knew, for the first time, that it wasn't the point.

The weeks passed, and she learned more about him. There was little he didn't know about her, because there was little to tell. He wasn't interested in the shallow drivel of the pop world she had inhabited in London. He listened to Mahler and Liszt; took her to art exhibitions. He was, in addition to everything else, a computer whiz and minted in the cash from specialized programming work he was able to do on the same computer with which he created his extraordinary music. But it wasn't the talent, or the intelligence, or the money, or even the sex that interested Sinead any more. Perhaps it had been created out of a winning combination of all four, but it had gone beyond that for her now. She watched him sometimes when he was sleeping and monitored his shallow breathing to see if she could match it with the slow rise and fall of her own heavy breasts. In the mornings she reached out and gathered him gently into the warm folds of her flesh, and when it was time to get up, she felt a pain in the release of his body from hers, as if in holding him, she were holding on to life itself. She felt tender towards him in a way that was beyond her past experience and present understanding. Love. She supposed.

'It must be love,' Karin said, as Sinead rang to say she was free, after all, for a drink that evening. 'Ah yeah? Using your mates to fill the gaps till you see him again,' she added playfully. 'Well, just watch yourself woman. It's only been a month – don't go rushing ahead of yourself. You've not won the Valentine bet yet y'know.'

Sinead felt faintly irritated by Karin's slagging. She had, already, elevated her and Miles's relationship to a higher level than Jack's tacky bet. But there was still a sly satisfaction fermenting at the back of her mind. How wrong Jack was. How cruel, how very wrong, and how, *how* sorry he would be when he saw how seriously, how truthfully, how very *very* deeply in love she was.

13

'No. No message.'

Valerie hung up the phone, and a slightly lost feeling came over her. Karin was out of the office again. She hadn't seen as much of Sinead and Karin lately. There was nothing too odd about that. The three friends were often too busy to meet, and would sometimes go for months at a time before one of them, usually Karin would announce an official 'Meeting of the Coven', and usually at some new restaurant or hotel where she had been offered a freebie in exchange for a feature in the mag. But since Jack's party, Valerie had the strangest feeling that they were trying to avoid her. Of course, she knew that was ridiculous, but then, she had Tinara looking at her significantly and telling her that instincts never lie. And while Valerie kind of knew, at the back of her mind, that her instincts had not only lied to her, but frequently made a wiggling nose comb and gone 'ner ner ner ner ner' at her afterwards, she didn't seem able to access Karin and Sinead for long enough to be able to discuss it with them.

The truth was that there had been a lot weighing on Valerie's mind of late, and the two friends who would, at the best of times, have to sit her down and drag her problems out of her, were busy doing their own thing. She couldn't talk to Tinara about any of this because, in a way, she was part of the problem.

It was the shop. Over the past six months, business had been slow. It had often happened over the years that her high-flying clientele would find somewhere in London and New York and defect for a season or two following some faddish craze for an exclusive salon boutique where you had to knock three times on the window and ask for Joe, and then if the owners didn't think you were aesthetically advanced enough to 'wear' their product, they wouldn't let you in. It was competition shopping in its most highly developed stage. At times like these, Valerie relied on a few homegrown regulars and passing trade. But the influx of new money in Dublin had spawned hundreds of new high-street stores and boutiques. Ireland's rich husbands were busy getting richer, and their wives were getting bored with charity work and in danger of spending their afternoons rummaging around with the landscape gardener. So hubby would set them up with a little frock-shop so they could spend their days doing what they did best, trying on clothes which they could purchase at cost. What with rent and overheads, the men figured it still worked out cheaper than a Brown Thomas charge card and their wives were generally grateful; grateful wives being a good deal easier to manage than bored ones. As a result, half of Valerie's old clientele now owned shops of their own, and had no need of her services any more. The passing trade were distracted in their droves by the new shiny UK chain stores on Grafton Street with their all-singing, all-dancing window displays and Valerie was left with a stock of last season's gear, a bevy of young designers on the breadline and a sign in the window which, despite the fact that it was elegantly fashioned out of gold-leaf, nonetheless announced a more-or-less permanent SALE.

Tinara on the other hand appeared to be doing a roaring trade. 'Roaring' being the operative word. Every half an hour another grey-faced depressive would shuffle through the shop and up the stairs to Tinara's spiritual salon, and emerge wonder-eyed having had their aura read/chakras realigned/future told/spirit-guide contacted or karma knocked back into shape, depending on which of the Goddess's gifts they seemed most likely to believe worked. At fifty quid a pop – one hundred if she felt the mystical forces of her own power had been especially drained during the session – she was raking it in. Some months ago, as a start-up gesture of goodwill Valerie had agreed to take her rent payments in treatments. Now she realized that while being in touch with the mystical powers of the universe was great, it didn't pay the bills. But broaching the subject was proving difficult. Tinara had a way of smoke-screening the grubby subject of money with talk of the great riches to be earned through renewing your spirit and creating a special celebration within to nurture the mystical orb of dancing light that glows in the heart of each of us when we begin to honour our blessings as the cherished godchildren of grandmother earth.

In other words, a deal's a deal and don't piss on my party hat by looking for cash.

The more Valerie tried to tackle Tinara on her rent, the longer and more aura-crushingly convoluted the explanations got.

As Bernard came in for his daily jogging break of doughnuts and cappuccino, Valerie was reading a letter from her accountant saying she was sliding back-the-way and it might be time to start thinking about shutting up shop.

That Valerie had managed to run a business to date was a continued source of amazement to her friends, who assumed ruthless manipulation and cunning as essential elements in any work-related venture. And, in truth, the fact that she had enjoyed a reasonable amount of success with Rouge was testament only to her covetable sense of style and generally affable nature. Because when it came to your actual book-balancing and overall business acumen, Valerie Valentine was undoubtedly a good few eggs short of the dozen. Money wasn't something she had ever thought about a great deal. Valerie had never been particularly ambitious, and knew herself to be lucky in that she had never wanted for anything that was beyond her reach. Despite her short stint as a rock wife, she had never had any yen for a helicopter pad or a holiday villa in Spain. As long as there was a roof over her head, something pretty on her back and petrol for the car, she was satisfied. In any case, all of the big stuff – house, car, set-up money for the shop, had been provided with money from her father and the settlement with Jack. Rouge had given her a reasonable salary and, with it, a sense of independence. All she had ever had to do was keep things ticking over. And now, with this letter, she realized she had failed to do even that. Although the decline of her business had been a year in the making, it was still a terrible shock.

Oblivious, Bernard bounced straight in, 'Wonderful news darling – I'm in—'

His announcement was cut short by the look on his friend's face. 'Lordy Poppet – who stuck you with the sulky-stick today?'

Valerie slid the letter across the serving pulpit to him, and while his eyes were scanning it said, 'Sorry, but I won't be able to take anything else off you this season . . .' before bursting into tears.

'*You're* sorry . . . oh sweetheart . . .' Then fifteen stone of pampering prince encased in lime-green lycra, folded around her in a huge hug.

When she had stopped crying, Bernard gently let her go, then squalled loudly, 'Why didn't you tell me? Why didn't you *sa-ay*?'

Valerie reached for an exquisite chiffon wrap to dry her face. No point worrying now – it was already en route to the Vincent de Paul charity shop.

'I didn't know until just now,' she said in a small

voice, suddenly wishing that Karin and Sinead were here. They wouldn't fuss or dramatize. They would just know what to do.

'I blame that lunatic lump of lard upstairs. She's sucking you dry darling, she's . . .'

'It's not Tinara's fault, Bernard, really it isn't.'

But Bernard wasn't listening.

'Do you want *me* to have a word with her? I'll go up there now and sort her out.' In truth, he had been dying to get his hands on the witch for months now. Ever since she had checked his chart and told him that she couldn't intuit any romance in his life, and indeed, according to Bernard's chart, intimate physical contact wasn't likely until *at least* the Autumn of 2025, and even then, she couldn't guarantee that what she was picking up wasn't something horribly intrusive like a hospital bedbath.

'No – really . . .'

Valerie decided to use the best tactic she knew to distract Bernard from pounding up the stairs and rioting through Tinara's salon. His own self-obsession.

'So what were you going to tell me before? Your big news?'

His expression of annoyance was instantly wiped with one of exuberant joy.

'I'm in love, Valerie! Truly, madly, deeply in love!'

Had Valerie possessed an ounce of cynicism in her delicate blonde head, she might have noticed, over the years, that Bernard fell in love a good deal more often than was either returned, or even consummated. Sometimes it happened with people with whom he had shared no more than a single dalliance, often with people to whom he had never even spoken, and always – *always* – with men who entered either the unsuitable or unavailable categories. However, Valerie was as naïve as this great gay bear was optimistic. She wasn't stupid. She just had an uncanny ability to refresh her innocence as she went along, and edit out other people's unpleasant and irritating character traits before they sank in. Sinead said it was how she kept her looks – by liking everyone and not noticing normal human frustrations like traffic congestion and bad service. That way the lines of aggression never got the chance to take hold in welts on her forehead.

'Bernard! That is truly wonderful.'

He raised her out of the hug with a hands-up gesture and launched into his 'this time it's *different*' speech.

'I know, I know that I have been led sideways in the past, Valerie, but this time it's *different*. All those pretty little boys in leather and lace? Not interested. Young men are shallow and fickle creatures. I've given my heart and lost too many times over that one, Valerie. I have fallen, I confess it, for men who would abuse me for the love I have to give. Well, not any more. *Not any more*, Valerie. Bernard Chequers has *had it* with the clubs and the saunas and the meaningless merry-go-round of cruising casual sex. This time it's for real. A mature man, like myself. Someone who is in it for the companionship and the comfort of a special friend to share their life with. An equal. A respectable person, with the same interests. Somebody to go to the opera with, to host dinner parties with. An intelligent, sensitive man who you wouldn't be ashamed to take home to your mother. Somebody who will stand by me through the bad times; nurture me though the sad times . . .'

Valerie was genuinely delighted for him. That was the sort of person she was. The good fortune of others always managed to cancel out her own problems. Karin often said that she'd start going back to Mass again if God swung Valerie's sainthood for her while they were all still alive to enjoy it. Soon-to-be-liquidated Ms Valentine was so excited on her friend's behalf that she let out a squeal.

'Oh this is great news . . . tell me more, tell me his name, how did you meet him?'

'Err . . . things haven't quite got to that stage yet.'

Bernard was starting to shuffle around a bit. He knew himself that under this kind of brass-tacks scrutiny it didn't hold up too well. But Valerie was a trooper when it came to keeping other people's delusions fresh, and turning a simple crush into married with two kids or – in this case – a lawnmower.

'Right well so . . . you must know *something* about him? Being in love with him and all that . . .'

Even Valerie suspected she was clutching at straws here, but Bernard was getting his second wind.

'We-eelll . . .' he began, flapping his hands in an expansive wait-till-I-tell-you gesture, 'he's five ten, five eleven and around forty, give or take. Gorgeous hair,' (being bald himself Bernard lived vicariously through other men's hair), 'and let me think what else – he's my neighbour, and most importantly, Valerie,' he paused then to give this next bit the added truth of a look weighted with integrity, 'I *know* he likes me back.'

'How *do* you know, Bernard?' She felt like maybe she was pushing him too hard but, actually, she was genuinely curious.

'Listen to this. Every morning I can see him *watching* me while I do my Jane Fonda.'

Valerie looked slightly puzzled now, as well she might – the sight of Bernard Chequers doing physical exercise was not one that brought the word lust immediately to mind.

'He lives in the flat opposite, and I've seen him, staring out of the window. Watching me. I know it's unbelievable, but it's true. And Valerie – it is *so* erotic. You know what I mean? Kind of *voyeur-iss-tic*.' He dragged the word out like he got enough pleasure out of saying it alone.

One look, however, at the innocent blue eyes gazing widely from behind their spiked mascara frame reminded him that Valerie could not possibly begin to understand that kind of pervy-peeping buzz. It came from a lifetime of being in denial about the fact that she was the object of every man's desire. If Valerie had as much as suspected the kind of frantic page-gluing that went on as a result of her career as a popular Irish undies model, she would simply be unable to survive.

'Anyway,' he continued, 'he looks highly respectable, and he definitely has a job. Leaves the house at eight thirty every morning, and in a suit. I think he might be American or Canadian or something. He has that kind of outdoorsy, healthy look,' then in a burst of girlish remembering, 'Oh, Valerie, Valerie – *he's ab-so-lutely gorgeous!*'

Valerie was naïve but she had lived. She was not so innocent that she couldn't smell trouble.

'Bernard – I don't know. I don't like the sound of this watching you business. I don't want to worry you or anything, but suppose he's a stalker?'

Even Bernard, deluded and all as he was, could not help but be charmed by the notion that, having loitered for hours around the bins on the off-chance that his handsome stranger might take his rubbish out, religiously waiting to start his exercise each morning until he thought he might have seen the curtain opposite his balcony twitching and having, out of pure desperation, purchased a pair of birdwatching binoculars when he didn't know a robin from a rabbit, Mr Flicky-Golden-Haired-Maybe-Canadian-Man was stalking *him!*

'Oh honey – you are so swee . . .' The sentence crumbled in his mouth as Bernard's eyes were diverted to the broad glass windows that led out into the arcade. He had seen something flit past the window with the speed of a scurrying mouse. It was strange but he was sure it was – *thereitwasagain* – no, it can't have been. No, he was imagining it, it was too silly, too crazy to even think for one moment that – *andagain* – the same movement – flit past then duck to the side before anyone sees. This time Bernard really was sure. 'OhmiGod! OhmiGod! OhmiGod! *Oh-My-God!*'

Valerie looked out to see what had caught his eye.

'What, Bernard?'

'Don't look, don't look, don't look! It's him, it's him, it's him!'

'Who?'

'Him, him, him-him-him-him-him! The man! The one who's been watching me. He's outside the door – out there, there, there! Ohmigod, there he is again, quick, don't look, don't look, don't look . . .' Bernard was hopping around the place now like he was barefoot on a hob.

'Your neighbour? The one you like?'

'Yes yes yes yes yes. Don't you hear what I'm telling you! He loves me! He followed me here! Ohmigod, I've got a stalker. I don't believe it! How exciting! Jesus, there he goes again! Don't look, don't look, don't look!'

Valerie was getting a bit nervous herself. She didn't like the idea of some weirdo following Bernard around. He was six foot one and wide enough that one of his shirts could tent a small family. What kind of a peculiar mind would be following a heifer like that around. It didn't make sense.

'Jesus, what do I look like? No don't tell me. How's my hair? How's my—Merciful Hour look at the state of me . . .' Bernard was bending down to get a look at himself in a mirrored jewellery podium. 'I've got to get changed – quick – I've a pair of trousers in the bag. I'll run out back and throw them on – Jesus look at the state of them! Fuckit they'll do . . .'

She had never seen the big man in such a state of heightened hysteria before. He must really like this guy.

Never one to deny any creature the benefit of the doubt, Valerie decided to take action.

'Hold on there, I'm going to get him.' And before Bernard had time to grab the corner of her skirt and drag her back, Valerie was gone out the door.

14

Karin had not wasted the few weeks leading up to her interview with Claude Moore. She had impressed herself by being doggedly persistent with regard to placing one of Ireland's Highest Minds in the pages of her celebrity mag. It was going to be an uphill struggle. She knew that. *The Black Carnage of My Soul* contained no clue whatsoever that its author might be willing to don a cheesy smile and lounge 'casually with cigar' in a gilded flocked hotel chair. That was unless she had missed the point, which, she confessed she may well have done. *Black Carnage* was heavy stuff all right; not much of a story going on but lashings of angst. But it was extremely clever. Undoubtedly. It must have been, because Karin knew she was no daw and it had gone straight over her head. She had pleaded with Sinead to try and decipher the first couple of chapters, but she couldn't make head nor tail either.

'Sounds like this guy got swallowed up his own hole.'

'Excuse me! You are talking about the man I intend to marry.'

'Oh right, yeah, sorry.'

If truth be told, Sinead was beginning to get on Karin's tits of late. This falling-in-love-with-the-midget business just smacked of attention-seeking behaviour and Karin could not, frankly, see the difference between that and the time her rock-chick chum announced at a *How'ya*-sponsored charity ball two years ago that she found Eamonn Doyle 'strangely attractive' and proceeded to make a champagne-induced show of herself by trying to lure the poor man up onto the dance floor. That was the one and only time that Karin could remember actually having 'felt' for her disfigured boss. Black Tie had the ability to turn almost any man into something approximating James Bond. But it would take more than an ill-fitting tuxedo to transform this balding gargoyle. Karin remembered noticing how hard he had tried that night. Some ambitious hairdresser, no doubt attempting to ingratiate themselves into the pages of *How'ya*, had taken Eamonn 'in hand' that afternoon, and ditched his usual oily comb-over in favour of a shampoo and set. The results were truly horrendous. Balls of backcombed curls sat atop his head like a pile of sleeping hamsters. He was inordinately proud of this 'new look', the perpe-trator of said crime having convinced him that orange curls were impressively 'this season', and had waddled over to Karin like a pantomime penguin, his face pained with the hope that she would approve. As editor, she had been hosting the affair on the magazine's behalf, and he had commented on her dress with his usual crudeness, 'We must be paying you too much.'

She had been about to snap back with a laughable easy comment on his coiffure when he added, 'Honestly, Karin, you look beautiful. A perfect hostess. I'm proud of you.'

She had felt sick with a mixture of pity and shock. The way he had said it like ... ahh – she didn't want to think about that – but anyway, she had thought it unnecessarily cruel for Sinead to lead him on like that. Pretending to fancy him like she did. And she must have been pretending. Golfing Gargoyle was hardly on her list of Male Must Haves – as could be said of any female in her right mind.

Anyway, this whole Miles affair smacked of sham. Sinead had been thoroughly nauseating about the whole thing, bleating on about true love and that certain something that (allegedly) happens when you meet someone for the first time and You Just Know. Sinead had started to sound just like that Freak Wig, Tinara. Two Become One. Soul Mates. All that kind of Significant Specialness really got Karin's goat. Sometimes she thought it was because she was jealous. But then she had a kind of built-in pragmatist button. She was too sensible and intelligent to fall for all that Hollywood bullshit. Her mother's generation had known the score. Two arms, two legs and a job. Easy on the eye and a sense of humour was a bonus, but there was no point in pushing your luck. You shopped according to your budget – not your preference. Karin felt that her own budget was reasonably high. All right, so she was borderline forty which more or less ruled out being mammy to a Walton-style family. Still, no great heartache there. She had minded her ovaries, and indeed the rest of her body, well enough over the years that she felt confident they could heave at least one kid out of her, if the hardship were deemed entirely necessary. In terms of reeling them in, she felt sure that the only reason she was still single was that she hadn't applied herself properly to the task of finding a husband; fluttering about with a mixed assortment of fellow journalists and semi-professionals whom she dumped as soon as commitment had threatened to interrupt the steady upward flow of her career path. Since the bitter turn in her fortunes, from high-flying political journalist to shallow mag hag, she knew that she had adopted a hard-bitten persona that was, frankly, frightening to most men. Except for the butt-headed ignorance of country-golfing types like Eamonn Doyle who kept banging away with their crude flirtations believing that their few bob would compensate for a complete lack of social grace and decorum. But Karin was not even going to go there. Not yet in any case. She'd not put in all those years of intricate four shades of blonde highlights and never leaving the house without the polished nails in place to settle for some bowsy in a cheap suit. Not until she had gone full throttle into landing herself something a good deal more glamorous. In her age group barristers were always an excellent option. It took them forever to qualify, and decades again to build a strong enough reputation to support a wife. They were renowned for their dapper dress sense and firm grasp of male hygiene, due to the fact that they had to spend years wooing

solicitors into giving them jobs. Any of them that managed to make it past fifty were generally ludicrously well-
off and worn out trying to keep a woman while they
scrabbled frantically towards becoming a judge. Enter
Karin Sheridan who, in the right kind of black dress had
'dinner party hostess' written all over her. Yes, if worst
came to worst, barristers were an excellent fall-back.
There was every chance that Sinead might pip her to
the post for Jack's million, if her current state of slobbery sentimentalism was anything to go by. And in any
case, both women had agreed that, if they did win, they
would throw a lump of it in Valerie's direction because,
God knows, she deserved it more than either of them.
However, it was important that they kept the whole
thing quiet, as Valerie would be not only offended but
hurt to think that either of them would get involved in
such an enterprise. Valerie's naïvety was part of what
made her so special, but at the same time, given the
cynical nature of Karin's current mission, she found all
that guilelessness and sweetness a little hard to take. She
knew she would have to sit down with both Valerie and
Sinead and sort all this stuff out. Men or no men, those
two friends were more of a lifeline than she could afford
to lose right now. But before that, and before the B-list
of barristers, Karin was going to give her all to hitting
Mr Number One on her Single Suitables' list, successful
novelist and cleverest man in Ireland, Claude Moore. As
far as she could tell, he had it all. Karin was a pragmatist,
but that did not preclude her from being a bit of a snob.
At one time she herself had been tipped to be one of the

cleverest women in Ireland, with her incisive and cutting political commentaries. Clever was better than rich or handsome or funny or great-in-bed. Rich, in her current situation was, naturally enough, important. But clever. Clever elevated all comers to the top of Karin's sex-appeal dial. And with the nail-biting four-week wait to get to him, and then his friendly approachable phone manner, Claude Moore was already dinging the jackpot bell.

Karin bit back a tinge of disappointment when she saw that Claude's bell indicated he inhabited the top floor. Fitzwilliam Square said 'elegant Georgian residence'. Top floor said 'attic garret'. For sure, *Black Carnage* was not exactly your first choice of airport novel, but Claude had been shortlisted for a couple of prestigious awards – and, besides, these well-known academic types made most of their cash on the world university circuit giving lectures and the like. She hoped she hadn't got it wrong and landed herself a penniless poet. A woman's voice said, 'Top floor, missis' through the intercom and buzzed her in. A woman's voice. God, the *Who's Who* hadn't mentioned a wife, but you couldn't be too careful. Karin was quite flustered with nerves by the time she walked up the five flights of stairs and a homely looking middle-aged woman answered the door.

'Missis Sheridan is it hugh? De h'editor off *How'ya* magaseeeen. It's my fave-reet. Is it you cum to hinterview himself? De h'editor herselfff! Oh did iss an honour –

will ya cum in. Cum in dere and don't be standin' out in de colt!'

Talk about a royal welcome. Mrs Morley had even taken the rollers out and given herself a slash of Rimmel Apricot Wonder lipstick in order to ready herself for being in the presence of such glamour. Claude had been incensed by her suggestion earlier that he 'smarten hisself upabit, pud on a nice suit dere, for d'important lady', preferring his poverty-corduroy-and-tweed ensemble, and riled by the implication that the editor of a mere populist publication was more important than him. Evidence of same betrayal came in the form of half a dozen of Mrs Morley's finest home-made scones which he had been denied with a flick of a tea-towel and a crude 'Geyaway-outatha – dere for de lady' not half an hour beforehand, after which he had sat in his leather chesterfield sulking while his excited housekeeper went flustering and muttering about the place in the manner of Mrs Bridges in *Upstairs Downstairs* preparing for a visit from the Queen Mother.

For Karin, at least, it was heartening to be greeted with such warmth. Better still, the apartment was magnificent. Wall-to-wall mahogany bookshelves, crammed with first editions no doubt, and an awe-inspiring collection of antiques. None of your repro-nonsense here. The real thing. Karin gave a quick scan around for tell-tale signs of sad no-hope bachelors or latent homosexuality, but there were no porcelain animals or extravagantly ruched curtains. By the large marble fireplace a small but lavish table was set and, by the star-struck expression on Mrs Morley's face, it was obvious that it was all she could do to contain herself from donning a French maid's uniform to serve tea. Actually what she wanted to do more than anything else in the world was to ask Karin had she *really* interviewed Neil Diamond on his last visit to Ireland and was Dickie Rock's house as magnificent as they said it was. But in the meantime she'd better not harass the poor woman, not until she had interviewed the Great Grumpy Bollocks and had a couple of scones inside her.

'Sit down dere till I getchew some tay.'

Once Mrs Bridges had made her exit, and knowing that his guest would surely be looking around the room to check for his presence, Claude rose from his chair. Then with his back still to Karin, he paused for dramatic effect to stare out the window in the manner of a man suddenly struck with the inexplicable beauty of nature, before turning, and peering at her intensely for a few seconds from beneath the fecund glory of his generous fringe.

Karin felt her stomach tighten as he made it across the room in two strides and held his hand out for her to shake it. His faux hospitality did not stretch to a verbal greeting. Neither did he smile. Geniuses don't smile. True brilliance always atrophies one's face into an expression of pained isolation.

The affliction of permanent seriousness is not attractive if one is, say, hosting a dinner party or trying to get served in a busy pub. But to the impressionable magazine journalist who desperately wants to be perceived as being cleverer than she is, it can be discombobulatingly sexy.

Karin temporarily lost her grip on the nature of her hard-bitten mission and remembered, with gusset-crumbling surety that she was in the presence of, not only one of the most coveted bachelors in Ireland, but one of the most brilliant minds this century. Allegedly.

The reality of it rendered her speechless. Claude wasn't going to speak, and so for a good few more moments than was comfortable, they both sat in silence – him peering mysteriously and she gawking openly as she desperately tried to mentally construct a sentence that would convey both her respect and admiration for him whilst disguising her almost overwhelming desire to leap across the room and tear into his trousers.

'Dere we are now wid a few of me scones, ye mus be gaspin' for a cup of tea – I bawd in a bidda dat low-fat spread for de lady dere. Sure dere's nodda pick on her, I said to mesel' dats a lady dat dussn ead budder!'

Mrs Morley's entrance demolished the instant in which Claude was wondering if agreeing to be interviewed by this female was a mistake while said female was simultaneously mistaking his look as a signal of intense sexual chemistry, temporarily distracting the author with the prospect of a warm buttered scone, and allowing Karin to gather her wits for long enough to procure her ready-typed questions and tape recorder without too much girlie handbag rummaging.

That done, she slid straight into the interview without introduction or nicety, largely as an attempt to mollify the knicker-heating that her hormones were currently waging against her better judgement. However Claude was impressed with her straightforwardness. He had chalked her down as a babbler, and more than anything else, he loathed babbling women – unless like Mrs Morley they were bearing gifts of buttered goodies.

The interview went better than either of them could ever have dreamed possible. Never, Claude thought afterwards, had he ever been asked a series of such intelligent and well-thought-out questions. Some of which the bright woman had obviously thought of asking on the hop, as it were.

'Claude. Have you *always* known that you were going to be a brilliant writer?'

'When did you first realize that you were cleverer and more brilliant than most people?'

'Claude – how does it feel to be among the best-loved Irish novelists of our time?'

'How do you feel when people compare you to Joyce and Beckett?'

'Claude – you have a beautiful home. Tell me about some of these wonderful artefacts and antiques.'

'You are obviously a keen reader. Do you love books?'

There was one small mistake.

'Claude how did you feel when *The Black Carnage of My Soul* won the Booker Prize?'

'It didn't.'

In her mortified shock and chagrin, Karin Sheridan won, if not Claude Moore's respect, for the moment at least, a little affection.

'But – well, I can hardly believe it. Didn't win! But how? Surely it is the greatest piece of modern literary work this century. I mean . . . Well, that's unbelievable. I'm no judge but, and I'm sure I wouldn't presume to know as much about literature as you, but . . .'

How charming. How lovely. She was right of course, it should have won. But there was something so – so – feminine, beguiling almost in the way she had made that mistake and then been so – well – emotional on his behalf. Emotion wasn't something that he usually responded to, but in this instance? Well, it was different somehow. The subject matter of his own undeniable greatness being at the centre of it.

But Karin Sheridan knew one thing that Claude Moore didn't. He may have been the most intelligent man in Ireland, but few people are smart enough to see through a Kiss-Arse Codder – not if they know how to do it properly. And as the editor of *How'ya*, Karin gave the best damn Celebrity Ego Wank this side of Des O'Connor.

Struck by her sincerity and obvious intelligence, Claude Moore asked her to accompany him to a special performance of arias from one of his favourite operas, *The Ring of the Nibelungs* by Wagner, at the National Concert Hall that Sunday.

Success. Bingo. He was that easy won and – *and* – she actually fancied him.

Very possibly soon to be one million pounds richer and the proud owner of a Celebrity Husband of the very best kind, Karin hit Fitzwilliam Square mobile in hand

and tapped Sinead's number for an emergency update meet that evening. Suddenly Miles didn't seem like such an interloper any more. In fact, Hey! Karin thought as she tripped lightly back towards the office to transcribe her tape, if Miles was as intelligent as Sinead said he was, perhaps they could double date?

15

It was one of those Action Man moments, where to hesitate would be to lose all.

Filling his leisure time in Dublin had proved a challenge for Barry Hooker. With the station closing up this Friday to make way for the army of carpenters and set designers to slash up Doyle TV's multicoloured living-room set, a whole extra day stretched out in front of him like a vat of bland, dribbly tapioca he somehow how to work his way through.

Barry was busy enough during the week. Busy, and frankly, somewhat overwhelmed with the breadth of his responsibilities in the run-up to the TV station's launch, which included finding and interviewing Sales Entertainers and even writing scripts for the alarming array of useless and, in Barry's opinion, quite non-saleable items that his boss Eamonn Doyle kept pushing at him. The two men had enjoyed several heated discussions that had highlighted their polar positions on the ethics of television sales. Eamonn had a stock of five thousand Mary Robinson Fine Porcelain Statuettes that he had been unable to shift to the Americans since her presidency ran out. Barry Hooker was not impressed. He was genuinely committed to enhancing the lives of his audience with products of good value and real usefulness. In Australia, he enjoyed sackloads of mail from people around the country expressing their heartfelt gratitude for his personal testimonials of such life-enhancing items as Molly Bishop's Instant Irish Brack Baker or the Pack of Five Edible Business Ties – For The Executive Who Has Everything. But his argument that only items with a 'unique usefulness' could be successfully sold in this way, was falling on deaf ears. Eamonn was insistent that his Mary Robinson statuettes would be a welcome addition to any mantelpiece, and the only thing that was standing between him and the offloading of nearly forty grand's worth of entirely pointless gee-gaws was the right kind of TV coverage.

'But they are the very best-quality hand-crafted porcelain, Barry!'

'I understand that, Eamonn,' placated the six-foot Australian, anxious not to offend the reputation of Fine Irish handicrafts, 'it's just that we need more than this . . .' He lifted the figurine from its green velveteen box and held the ex-president's likeness by the waist of her miniature red suit. 'The intricacy, the beauty . . .' (For it was true! There was surely no man alive who wouldn't be seduced by the firm yet undisputed femininity of Ireland's First Lady – even in statuette form), 'of this . . . this – ' he struggled for a word that would promote the item he held in his clumsy hand beyond mere ornament – 'this

Shelf Adornment, would be lost in the Third Eye vision that television creates.'

Eamonn was impressed that he had employed the kind of professional who was able to smokescreen issues with technical jargon. Somebody who at least sounded like they knew what they were talking about, even though they didn't. The man standing in front of him was so tall, so handsome, so bronzed, so hirsute in a blond wavy sort of way – so damn *television* that surely to God he must know what he was talking about.

'And that means, Barry?'

'It needs to *do something*, Eamonn. The statuette of Mary Robinson is not enough in itself. It needs to have a special purpose. A unique selling point. A Mission Statement.'

They both stood looking at the smiling supine figure resting in her velveteen coffin, and contemplated the injustice of her apparent uselessness. Mrs Robinson – one of the greatest political and humanitarian figures Ireland had ever known. First female president. Mother Ireland of the Nineties – she had ditched the keening and the wool shawls of old and replaced them with an educated pragmatism and a Louise Kennedy two-piece. For all she had done, she had still not achieved the iconoclastic status of the J. F. Kennedy portrait on sale in Woolworths shops worldwide.

This TV thing was a new venture for Eamonn and he wanted it to work so a compromise was reached. Mary was going back to the factory to have holes drilled in her head and a plastic plug inserted into her hollow underside so that she might grace the tables of the Irish TV Shopper as a patriotic condiment set.

On this particular Saturday, Barry had managed to fill a couple of hours of his otherwise empty morning with a wash and blow dry at a salon on Grafton Street. It had turned out to be a most unsatisfactory experience. The girl firstly appeared bemused that he didn't want a trim then failed to flick his fringe to its full potential. When he corrected her choice of styling brush and suggested she use a smaller one with tighter bristles, she pretended she hadn't heard him, leaving him feeling like he was being a fusspot – which Barry knew himself certainly not to be. As it was, he left with his parting a good centimetre to the left of where it should have been, and his normally feathered ends glued into place with some manner of sweet-smelling goo. Normally such things would not have the power to dent his general good humour, but over the past few weeks, Barry Hooker was beginning to wonder if this whole Ireland thing was going to live up to its promise. As he wandered out into the shoppers' mash on Dublin's busiest shopping street, he thought wistfully of his personal groomer, Irene, who used to come and style him every morning for his show. One coat tinted moisturiser, a light dust of powder and the hair! She was so good it stayed in place for the full three hours with only a brief brush-up in ad-break three. Didn't even need hairspray!

He was starting to miss Irene, and the plush airy Sydney studio, and, if truth be told, the weather, and the beach *and* his Shamrock Surfing chums. His washboard stomach was already starting to go a bit puréed potato on him, and the small gym he had found on George's Street, to which he had attached great hopes of perhaps meeting a nice lady who shared some of his interests, had turned out to be men only. The men there were extremely friendly, and he didn't want to put a name to it, but suffice to say Barry suspected that some of them might be interested in crossing that boundary between male chumminess and physical intimacy. Once or twice he had seen his big neighbour with the green lycra shorts leaving there, and it was that which, despite his increasing feeling of weekend loneliness, prevented him from popping around there for a cup of sugar.

And so it was that at two o'clock on this Friday afternoon, in an effort to battle the negative effects of a disappointing hairdo and banish the onset of immigrant isolation, Barry Hooker decided that he would spend the empty day that stretched ahead of him exploring Dublin city in the manner of a tourist. Clutching a freshly bought map, he marched towards St Patrick's Cathedral, trying not to allow the persistent drizzle and hoards of family shoppers to dent his determination to turn this day around into a positive experience. As he reached Patrick Street, Barry saw an opportunity that lifted his spirits instantly. The Viking Splash Dublin Tour Bus was an amphibious vehicle, which drove around all of the capital's places of interest, before easing its audaciously painted body into the River Liffey like a fat woman in a bad swimsuit. For tourists, and people so lonely as to have nothing better to do of a Friday afternoon, it looked like fun. Barry was that desperate his heart leapt at the promise of adventure in its gaudy bulk. In the shadow of the dull grey Protestant cathedral was a *Raiders of The Lost Ark* opportunity and he was going to take it.

Due to an air strike, the tour had been mercifully spared the usual influx of rowdy British stag weekenders. And so, the genuine Pillaging Viking count being low, Barry was handed a horned helmet by the guide, which he jammed down onto his newly coifed head with the requisite amount of enthusiasm that a responsible adult shows when in the company of five American children under the age of twelve.

Barry was chatting nicely with the American parents – they had won the trip as a competition prize with Shillelagh Snax, green crisps shaped like little hammers which their middle child, Brad was ambitiously cramming into an already overflowing mouth – and if things had happened differently, or rather, not happened at all, Barry might have been invited to join them for dinner in Jury's Hotel that evening.

But that's not the way fate works. Kismet waits for no man. It does not take into consideration one's dining arrangements, nor indeed the fact that one might be in a ship-shaped moving vehicle with a locked door, limited window escape options and a team of squalling American children standing between you and it.

And that was the way it was when Barry saw her. Not just *her* – you understand. As in Love At First Sight Woman Of Dreams 'Her'. Barry saw those kind of Hers all the time. Not so often that it might be said to be commonplace. But often enough to know that leaping out of a forty-seater tourist bus raised some ten feet off the ground was not a sane option in their pursuit. No – this was the Actual Her. The one in the picture. The air hostess with the golden hair and the smiling face and the teapot and the tempting scone. The one in the brochure his father had brought back on that last trip to Ireland. Barry's history. His heritage. The reason he had moved here. Until that moment when he saw her he had not realized that was the reason he was here. In Dublin. To find her. It was a fleeting thing, but when love strikes, time stands still. Like a Charlie's Angel in slow-mo she flicked back her hair as she wandered, unaware of the gathering attention of this love-struck buccaneer, past the lumbering ship and he saw her face. Full bud lips and batting blue eyes. It was her all right. He had time to neither hesitate nor think it through. Male instinct at such times does not accommodate cunning plans and ruses. It does not say, 'Think this through, man. Go and explain to the driver that you have a rare condition of the colon and must exit the bus as a matter of urgency before nature forces you to evacuate the contents of your bowels.' No. It says, 'He who dares wins! You must go to her now! Even if it means clambering out the window and down the sides of a treacherous wooden curve which offers no foothold and a speeding sea of hard tarmac underneath it.'

He held on to the window frame for a few seconds trying not to look down, as Shirley, the substantially built American mother, managed to manoeuvre her twenty-odd stone down the aisle to scream at the driver to *stop the bus*! He did so with more force than was either wise – given the busy traffic – or entirely necessary, as the jolt flung Barry to the ground. Thankfully, being a tall man and in the position from which he was hanging, his body only had a few feet to fall, and he landed, by the grace of God in a semi-run which he pointed in the direction in which he had seen his air hostess disappear around the corner. Oblivious to the puce fist-flinging ranting of the Nissan Micra driver who had totalled his bumper on the back of the Viking Ship and blind to the incredulous stares of pirates and passers-by alike, Barry sprinted back in the direction of the city centre, eyes peeled for the flutter of the chiffon scarf she was wearing and nose set for the expensive cologne trail she must surely have left in her wake.

At the corner of Stephen's and George's Street he spotted her, coming out of a sandwich bar holding two take-away coffees and a paper bag of something he suspected was buns of some description. He edged against a shop doorway and watched as a slight wind whipped the scarf around that beautiful face and she awkwardly pushed it back with the hand holding the buns. Oh how Barry longed to put himself in her path and with a gentlemanly sweep offer to carry her coffee and buns for her. But alas he could not. For the shop window revealed to him a terrible truth – he was still wearing his Viking helmet. Aside from the obvious alarm all honest souls feel when they realize that they have unwittingly acquired a piece of property which does not officially belong to them, Barry's upset was nearing completion with the head-turning looks he was getting which ranged from amusement (a group of pointing youngsters inside the shop outside which he was standing) to severe disapproval (a passing nun). He smiled sheepishly at his audience, but as he tried to remove it, he found that it was jammed onto his skull as firmly as an athlete's toupee. He pulled and tugged but the helmet was going nowhere. As the mirth of his uninvited audience grew to Titanic proportions, so did Barry's frustration – culminating in the near dislocation of an ear followed by a terrible despair as, fists still grabbing on to the reinforced plastic horns, he turned his head around and realized that he had lost her.

A lesser man would have sat on the pavement and wept. A weaker man might have entered the shop, now fizzing with merriment at his predicament and tried to find enough dignity and fortitude to ask if they had a wrench he could borrow. Unexceptional tendencies could even have led a more ordinary man to scurry straight home to his apartment to spend the afternoon making busy with a pound of butter and a prayer. But not Barry Hooker. Not today. Not with the object of his dreams made manifest wandering about Dublin somewhere in a chiffon scarf. He was not going to stop until he found her.

For almost one hour Barry peered in the window of every shop he passed. Some people tittered, others muttered, smiled, pointed – one wandering drunken cockney, a left-behind casualty from one of the previous weekend's stag parties, even tried to ask him where he got 'yer hat mate'. But Barry was neither deterred nor distracted from his task. Finally, having frightened the holy soul out of a woman in the throes of returning a kilim next door, he found himself outside Rouge. And there she was. His girl. After the excitement of actually having found her, his impulse was to just walk in and say, 'Hey darling – bin lookin' for you all afternoon. Where you bin hiding?' like he had known her all his life, which, in a way, he had. But, although Barry wore make-up as part of his job and was as in-touch with his feminine side as any man who takes inordinate pride in his magnificent flicky hair, he was, at the end of the day, a hot-blooded Australian Male. He wasn't much into pubs, but he knew what to do in them and if push came to shove, he could do an impersonation of a knock-them-back-and-watch-the wind-girls Aussie male – no problem. But a ladies' wear boutique, stocking frilly knickers and who knows what other type of female paraphernalia, was just not on his list of places where an Australian man could enter alone. Englishmen went in there and bought things for their wives and girlfriends and seemed to be able to get away with it. Frenchmen – well they practically lived in the places. But Australians? Well the culture gap was just too wide to cross. And besides, even if he could figure out a way to finger his way interestedly through racks of blouses and bras, there was the hat to consider. A well-dressed Italian in a ladies' boutique he could get his head around. An Australian in a Viking helmet? He'd be put on the first plane back to Sydney. No question. Barry decided to just stand around the corner and have a really good think about what his next move was going to be. Sooner or later she would leave the shop, and then, he felt sure, some kind of an opportunity would present itself.

And yet, she was mesmerically beautiful and he could not take his eyes off her. He walked swiftly past the window a few times when he sensed she wasn't looking. As he did he caught the eye of, amazingly, the green-legged fat neighbour of his. As he flit past the window again, just to make sure it really was him, the germ of an inspiration began to form in his mind. Clearly his girl knew this man. Perhaps there was something in that? An opportunity? He rounded the corner and as he found his hidey spot, Barry reached up one more time to have a tug of his helmet.

As if by some miracle it unplugged itself with a teasing ease, and as Barry Hooker slung it into an adjacent wheelie bin the Virgin Mary's own choir of angels themselves appeared to light down from the heavens above and sing songs of almighty and unending celebration as the figure of Valerie Valentine was suddenly standing before him.

16

Little's nightclub was *the* place to be and be seen on a Friday night in Dublin. After midnight, the capital's serious partygoers flocked there in their droves, leaving the square and the sober to make their way home to suburban beds. Crammed into the ornate opulence of its velvety interior the bald and the beautiful worked their way up and down the social ladder of its various VIP and members' rooms according to notoriety and bank balance. Ground level was for Joe Publics wearing the requisite footwear and with the £20 entrance fee, first floor was 'members only' and £5,000 a year bought you the right to wear any kind of footwear you pleased and get a bit lairy with the bar staff. At the top of the house was the Holy of Holies – celebrities and VIPs only. It was this room that ensured that Little's was always buzzing. The knowledge that Bono Himself might be looking down on you from above was enough to put the most die-hard dullard in a party mood. The crowd there was always refreshingly mixed and convivial. There were the usual teenage babes and half-cut business boyos, but if you saw somebody's mammy trying to get a drink at the bar, you didn't shove her because she was almost certainly the mammy of 'somebody'. Strange old men in jumpers were never looked at sideways because their mere presence there meant they were surely some visiting film director or famous photographer. There were girls whose lip-lined glamour meant they were there for a reason; then others, hair loose over their day suits, had obviously just got caught up in a skite after-works-drinks. There were poofs on the pull, poets on the piss, jiggers and liggers, bra-less and legless, teenage and old-age, boozers and cruisers, glittered and skittered; some of them wasted and all of them witless with the glamour and excitement of being at the very centre of the city's night-life pulse.

Karin and Sinead were flimsy with drink by the time they arrived at Little's, just before midnight. Karin had already started preparations for her date with Claude that Sunday with a facial and Sinead had spent a fruitful afternoon ringing Miles's answering machine just so she could hear the sound of his voice.

The two women met in the packed bar of the Fitzwilliam Hotel at six, successfully commandeering a comfortable corner seat as if they owned the place which, given the amount of time and money they spent in trendy hotel bars around Dublin 2, they more or less did.

Straight off, they got the niceties out of the way. Sinead was naturally 'delighted' that Karin had hit it off with Claude, and Karin, in turn was 'delighted' that Sinead's relationship was blossoming into 'something serious'. Neither of them mentioned Jack Valentine or his bet. One could say that it just never came up in conversation, but its unspoken fact nonetheless permeated a conversation they had about their impending birthdays.

'How long have you got now?' Sinead asked, as she expertly sucked the base of her Romeo and Juliet and snapped open her Zippo.

Karin hated the smell of cigar smoke, and evidence of the polite tension between them came in her saying nothing about her friend's opulent chuffing.

'Three months or thereabouts . . .' (Seventy-seven days to be exact. Plenty of time to fit tux, frock and order the flowers.) '. . . and you?'

She knew well, and Sinead knew well, as indeed she had known well exactly when Karin's birthday was. They were testing each other. Seeing which one would bring up the grubby subject first and open negotiations.

'About seven weeks or something.' Something being at last count fifty-five days. But it hardly mattered, she was that sure of Miles's affections. It would be a small but stylish affair. A bit different – themed perhaps. Snow White? Something quirky and fun. A statement nonetheless. It would be a registry office job at this stage. She'd test Miles out on the idea tomorrow.

'So while we're still in our prime, what say we ditch these old lady G&Ts and dash down a bit of the bubbly stuff?'

After that, they moved on to the general craic-chat of

gossip and reminiscing on which their relationship was built. Karin and Sinead had known each other so long that it was easy to lapse in and out of intimacy. In the years during and since their suburban schooldays they had witnessed and shared in each other's spots, first periods and romantic histrionics. Together they had lost handbags, virginity, jobs and men. They could tell each other anything because there was little about the other they didn't already know. They were fond of each other of course, but sometimes the fact of their sisterly closeness was enforced by shared history rather than choice. Like a long-time married couple who have learned the wisdom of always holding something back for yourself. Valerie was different in that way. Both women had met her when they were in their twenties and so, old enough to choose her as a friend. In any case, Valerie had an innocence that made her impossible not to love, and guilelessness that made it feel satanic to lie to her. Karin and Sinead both felt bad that they had made this secret pact with Valerie's ex-husband, and so both of them were in the throes of acting out the Cruella de Ville version of their own guilt. It was wickedness as a fashion statement, hence Sinead's cigar-smoking and Karin's higher than usual shoes. Both women sometimes saw in the other a hard-bitten wordly-wiseness that mirrored some part of themselves that they did not like – yet could not help but copy.

They left the Fitzwilliam after closing, and when they hit the sharp night air on Stephen's Green they were that hungry they could have eaten furniture. They filled up in Burger King on Grafton Street, and arrived in Little's well and truly ready for Round Two.

The place was packed, and as Sinead went to find the hostess and see if they could mosey on up to the Holies for a nose around, Karin stood half-heartedly swinging her hips wondering if another vodka cocktail might propel her onto the dance floor. She was tired of talking to Sinead and perhaps a boogie might be just the distraction they both needed. As she was just about to turn around to tell Sinead to forget about scoring them a table in the gods, Karin saw Jack. Topless and toasted, he had a gaggle of giggling taut-titted teenagers encircling him as his naked skinny limbs air-guitared to 'It's Raining Men' with a buttock-clenchingly shameless degree of pure emotion. Now, up in the Holies this kind of mortifying display was par-for-the-course. No – *expected*. In the privacy afforded by the exclusive company of your fellow famous, one could sing 'Bye Bye Blackbird' at the piano, or play 'How Far Can You Get Your Mickey Down the Neck of a Champagne Bottle' with no questions asked. Only trusted journalists, like Karin, were allowed in there because they weren't tabloid and wouldn't tell. But in a city the size of Dublin, a certain amount of dignity was expected in their appointed celebrities. It was their job to swan around in sunglasses looking glamorous. Being stoned was, under certain circumstances, tolerated as long as it was done in a Designer Drugs / Riding Supermodels type of way or tempered with a hefty dose of the tortured alcoholic but creative genius gene. Air-guitaring to 'It's Raining Men' in full view of the door-fee-paying public of Little's ground floor was simply not on the list. It was a flagrant breaking of the Cool Celebrity Code. If they all went about acting the maggot in full view of their fans then nobody would want to see pictures of them lounging about the grounds of their manors in wellingtons and Karin would be out of a job.

Panic and pity collided in her stomach – but Karin did not feel like going down there and hauling him back up to the Holies on her own. Frantically she looked around for Sinead, and found her drunkenly schmoozing the living daylights out of the club's owner, a diminutive and by now slightly irritated looking Mike Little.

'*Faaab-you-luss* new signing coming up Mike – *got* to get him membership darling. Name is Miles Fisher. Got that? *Miles Fisher.* He's going to be hu-uuuge. Massive – except of course for the fact that he's a bit smaller than the usual in that – oh what the hell, Mike, he's a midget! But hey! That's me – something a bit different, Mike. Mind you, you'd understand that not being exactly tall yours—Karin! It's my old chum – cum'n choin us! Woss juss telling Mike abou . . .'

'I think you'd better come and look at this.'

Mike was as horrified at the breach of celebrity ethics, currently advancing to full Chippendale stages to a souped-up nineties version of 'Brown Girl in the Ring' by Boney M. It was not a pretty sight, and Jack objected as mightily as he was capable to the trouser-hoisting scrum of his three rescuers who hauled him back up to the top floor where he was planted at a corner couch, and spent the rest of that night dribbling over a visiting Nobel Prize winner before Mike organized one of his own men to drive him back home to Wicklow so he wouldn't be the talk of the Dublin taxi scene.

Karin and Sinead decided to call it a night shortly after their rescue mission, heroism having sobered them both up. As they passed Burger King, Sinead saw Dizzy sitting, with her back to the window and apparently alone.

'Daft bitch,' she muttered, 'she shouldn't be sitting around in these places at this time of night on her own.'

She was about to go in and 'rescue' her silly secretary when she saw a child coming towards Dizzy's table with a tray piled with unspeakable late-night rubbish food. Sinead hesitated at the door, fascinated by this bizarre scenario. The small figure put the tray down, then hoisted themselves up to the seat next to the blonde and planted a full and unmistakably adult kiss on her lips.

Sinead staggered back.

'Fuck.'

'What – what is it?' asked Karin.

'What the fuck is going on. Some kind of a mistake here . . . or . . .'

But there was no mistake. Miles and Dizzy were together. How it happened, why, when – perhaps if Sinead had cared less these questions would have been the first thing to enter her mind. Perhaps if she had cared more, she might have gone into denial and imagined that they had bumped into each other and were in there now

184

talking about his record contract and their mutual love and respect of their girlfriend/boss.

Sinead fell off the steadying cliff of her usual anger and straight into a humiliating hole of hurt.

Karin was looking in through the flourescently lit window now, but she didn't know what she was looking at.

'What? What is it, Sinead?'

Sinead thought about saying something, but she didn't want to put words on it right now. She just wanted to get home to her bed and make a coffin duvet to curl up and die in.

'It's nothing. Really. Just thought I saw something.' And she tried to muster enough of a smile to convince Karin she wasn't lying. Karin knew there was something up, and she was stung by Sinead's reluctance to tell her, but she wasn't going to push.

'Come on, there'll be a queue for the taxis. We'd better head.'

11

Jack Valentine strained one eye open, and daylight lanced through the lashes like hot pins. A vague remembering tipped the edge of his temple as he tried again, but as soon as he did the gates to hell opened, and an army of claw-footed gnomes with red-hot hammers started to demolish the inside of his skull. He closed them immediately, trying to clamp them back into the atrophy of his drunken sleep. The decomposing hamster that was his tongue started to stir as his mouth formed around his familiar chanted hangover whisper 'Alka-Seltzer . . . Alka-Seltzer'.

It was a few seconds before Jack remembered that his medicinal request was falling onto no ears. Bridie MacFarlane had reluctantly agreed to come on and 'do' for the village's resident pop star five days a week. However, Mrs MacFarlane's general countenance and level of devotion to the Catholic Church limited the span of her duties to the basics of cooking and cleaning and did not stretch to include other required duties such as negotiating with Jack's dealer, organizing nubile female company or when it came right down to it, the administration of 'cures', especially *not* for self-induced ailments such as alcohol poisoning. In fact, the weekday mornings that she did arrive to find her employer weak with the effect of his previous night's excesses, far from approaching him with the courtesy of a sympathetic serf, she tended towards turning the *Gerry Ryan Radio Show* up to full belt whilst clattering her saucepans pointedly before turning his stomach into somersault with a stodgy fry that would keep your average racehorse fuelled for a month.

In any case, today was Saturday, her day off, so she was doubtless at home harassing her hen-pecked husband for a lift to a Hairy Heffernan concert.

Jack knew by the cut of his pounding head that getting up was probably too ambitious a project at present. It would take a few minutes before he could untangle in his mind what position his limbs were in. Although, the brief opening of his eyes and the hard prickling sensation on his cheek indicated to him that he was currently splayed in some sort of a complicated format on his library floor, and therefore wantonly wasting the feathery comfort of the seven gothic hand-carved four-posters which were only on the floor above his head – but which, at this moment in time, he felt he might need a hospital helicopter to access.

Actual physical movement being the challenge it was, Jack decided to engage in a spot of mental exercise instead – a.k.a. establishing his whereabouts last night.

Right. Here we go.

First question. Why was he sleeping on the floor?

Pause.

No, nothing. Fine. That was a hard one to start off with. Take a step back in time and try again. Now. How had he got home?

Pause.

Damn, nothing there either. This was tougher than he thought. Christ, he must have been really totalled. Slightly worrying, but try moving back a couple of hours and see how we get on with that. Ready? Jack Valentine your starter for ten points is this. Did you in fact go out at all last night?

Beeeep.

Straight on the buzzer with that one with a confident 'Yes!'

He clearly remembered splashing his chest and indeed, rinsing his mouth with a bottle of Issey Miyake For Men. Evidence enough for any jury that he was innocent of staying in on a Friday night. Aha – there it was all flooding back to him – yesterday was Friday! He was making real headway now. He liked this game now that he was winning. Memory loss? Pwa – that was for poofters who couldn't hold their drink. All right then – where had he been?

Pause.

Nothing.

OK – who was he with?

Pause.

Nothing.

Come on now you can do it, Jack. Details. What were you wearing?

Pause.

No. No good – he had lost this round. Fucksake. He'd have to go right back to the beginning and pick through the pieces before the phone started ringing.

Friday afternoon. In house all day. Bacon and cabbage in front of *Thunderbirds* at lunchtime. Paying Mrs Mac-Farlane her week's money and feeling kind of bad after she left. Shower, Issey Miyake splash, slash – now what?

Brief pause.

Ah yes – went down the library for a little drinky. Jack Daniels – not much, maybe three or four half tumblers. Feeling in the party mood – decided to ring a few friends to see who wanted to come out and play. That's where it started to go all wrong.

Other people.

Somehow, Jack Valentine philosophized, it was always their fault.

His first call was a Rolling Stone neighbour who, despite his grand old age, was still in active service. His house-keeper (full-time/live-in the bastard!) informed Jack that her boss and his entire family were in Gstaad celebrating the twenty-first birthday of his youngest daughter, and that if he was Mr Bryan Ferry she had been told to tell him to get straight on the next plane over because his suite at the Hilton had been double booked with The Edge and it was first come first served, otherwise he'd have to make do with a Double Deluxe.

Jack said that no he wasn't Bryan Ferry and hung up

before the disappointed girl could take his name. That was the last time he was including that mouldy little has-been in his plans. Bryan Ferry? Who the hell was *he* being invited to Gstaad! The Edge? Get the fuck outta here! A nobody of the highest order. Of course there must have been some mistake. Perhaps Sinead had the invite in her office, in which case she was fired!

Nonetheless, he consoled himself with his favourite double act, a whisky followed by a whisky chaser, and continued his way down the list.

The hell-raising British actor in tax-exile was away in Disneyland with his grandchildren.

The *Vogue* photographer was playing polo in France with his new wife and her family.

Two more of his pop-star peers were charity gigging for Romanian orphans and celebrating their parents' fortieth wedding anniversary in Ashford Castle respectively.

Then – the final straw. His dealer Charlie. A morose and depressing bastard, but always guaranteed as a committed hanger on, once there was free booze and birds on the menu.

'Hey Jack man! Sorry, no can do, mate – I just got engaged! Can you believe it? I'm so happy, man! And guess what else! I'm clean, man! Yeah! Forty-seven days now! Got my chit from AA and everything! It's beautiful man! And hey! Met Tommy at a meeting last night! Yeah he looks great man! He was asking if I'd seen you – said we should both come round one afternoon for tea yeah? Pop in and see the old bastard for a chat and a catch up.

Heard your new housekeeper makes a mean fruit brack man!'

Oh well, now this really was marvellous. Not only had Tommy pissed off and left him, but he had taken his dealer with him. Now they were planning to come round for a bit of do-goodery born-again bollocks. Oh Jack knew the score. Half his chums had gone over to the other side at one time or another. The whisky was fuming inside him now flambé-ing his chagrin and frying what bit of reason he had left.

He fumbled through the phone book looking for AA.

Ah yeah – Tommy, thinking he was the clever little cunt giving up drink. Big fucking deal. He'd show him with his clevery little cuntish ways. He could be clever too – fucking AA – full of look-at-me I've given up the drink cleverishness. As if there was anything to it. As if he couldn't stop any time he wanted. He'd show them he'd—

'Hullo – Dublin 4538998.'

It was a woman's voice. Jack almost hung up, then he thought of how Tommy had betrayed him. How he was plotting to reform him. About all those bastards over the years who had patronized him with their posh manor-house treatment centres, and their one-day-at-a-times, and their smug mineral-watery ways. Looking down on him like *he* was the alcoholic when, in fact, he was the only real rock star among them! The only one with the courage to take it to the limit. The only one truly committed to living the rock & roll dream. It wasn't easy – no of course it wasn't – but he had a duty, a *responsi-*

bility to keep the legend alive in the name of the Great Hell-Raisers, Jim Morrison, Hendrix, Keith Moon, Brian Jones. Although all five of his heroes had something else in common that he couldn't quite put his . . . oh yes . . . they were dead – but he didn't have time to think about that now. One thing for sure was that Jimi Hendrix would never have swapped the whisky neck for a cup of strong tea in a parish hall with a bunch of self-righteous goody-goody losers.

In any case, Jack had one of them on the end of the phone and, bird or not, he was going to wind them right up.

'Hullo – is that Alcoholics Anonymous?'

'Yes it is – can I help you?'

The fucking cheek of it! Implying that he needed help – the patronizing piece of pussy! Him? Need help? As if!

'Actually – I don't need any help at all, if that's all the same with you. I am calling on behalf of a friend.'

'Ah – a friend.'

Oh so that was her game, yeah? More clever dickery psycho-games, eh? He knew – he knew what she was getting at.

'Yes really a friend –'

'Well, you tell me what's going on with this "friend" of yours then . . . em?'

'Jack.'

'Right – Jack . . .'

'Valentine.'

'Actually, Jack, there's no need for surnames here, we . . .'

'Jack Valentine – the rock singer – lead singer with eighties chart-topping band Sell-Out.'

Let the bitch know what she was dealing with here. She'd have heard of him, of course she would. They'd all heard of him! Every last fucking one of them. His exploits were well documented in the tabloids. 'Lead Singer Sells Out Disappointed Donnington Fans.' 'Be My Valentine – Rock Singer on Charges of Lewd Behaviour in Public Bar.'

So some people might say he was out of control. So what! He was only doing his job. That didn't make him an alcoholic. Did it? *Did it?*

'Well? *Does it?*' he demanded out loud to the AA lady volunteer on the other end of the phone.

'I'm sorry?'

'Yeah – well, so you fucking should be!'

After all – she was talking to him like he was just some ordinary Joe calling up for help with a drink problem. Drink problem? Drink problem? The only problem he had was that he couldn't get enough of the stuff into his . . . whooopsadaisy . . . clattered the bottle over the sofa there . . . just go and pick . . . aha ha ha . . . dropped fag under table . . . just lean down and . . . argh . . . no – no good, have to let go phone . . .

'Holdonaminutethereluv.'

He staggered over to the cupboard and grabbed a second bottle. Look at all that in there, he thought to himself – packed with drink. Vodka, Dubonnet, sherry-fuck'ssake! Everything! Sure if he was a *real* alcoholic he'd have the lot drunk by now. What the fuck were

they talking about! All those people who thought he was
. . . he wouldn't have a pot to piss in now if he was a
real alcoholic. Whoever heard of an alcoholic with great
shitloads of money like him? He had stocks and shares
and look – a spare million to chuck away on a bet with
those daft bitches! Real alcoholics didn't have cupboards
full of drink still and financial security. They had big red
noses and shite livers and lots and lots and lots of hair
coming out of their noses and chins and everything. That
wasn't him – no – not at all. Look at him here now
lounging about on his imported Moroccan leather settee
thingy with a big mountain of drink there only a few feet
behind him and only one – *one* – little bottle in front of
him which he was more than entitled to because it was
a Friday night and everybody was allowed a little drink
on a Friday night – especially – and this was important
– *especially* if they were a really famous rock star who
hadn't been invited to Gstaad and that most certainly did
not mean that they were an alcoholic by any manner of
means, no it most certainly did *not*. And do you know
who needed to be told that more than anyone else in
the whole wide world? Well do you? *Do you?* The lady
from Alconemolics Anominous. She *needed* to be told.
She *deserved* to be told. It was urgent, imperative, essential
that she be informed in no uncertain terms about the
complete and utter non-alcoholic status of Jack Valentine.

'Imshnot an alkiholic,' he murmured down the phone,
'ashk mfren Tommy – ees one – yesseeish.'

'Hullo, Jack.'

Gaaaah! A man's voice!

'Thought it was you – Marjorie here in the phone office said there was a Jack on looking for a chat – told her I used to work for you, so she passed you on. How you doing anyway?'

Fuck! Tommy!

Click – down with the receiver.

Why the sound of his old sidekick's voice unsettled Jack to such an extent was not something he felt like sitting in and mulling over. He went straight out on the blind tear – and who could blame him. He was at the centre of some kind of a conspiracy to clean him up, he was certain of that much and the only cure for anyone in their right mind was to go out and get completely and utterly faceless. The rest of the night was a blur – and about the time that a vague vision of himself dancing to disco music on the floor of Little's cha-cha-chaed it's way across the red-mush of his brain, Jack decided that enough was enough on the library floor and if he didn't get crawling in search of a cure soon, he many never walk again. On all fours he made it as far as the drinks cupboard and grabbed the first thing he could. His hands shook as he wrenched the lid off a bottle of Bristol Cream then drank from the neck. The sticky liquid burnt down his gullet like lighter fuel. He haunched himself around so that he was sitting on the ground with his back resting against the mahogany doors, the sherry bottle still in his hand until the alcohol took enough effect that he could stop shaking and safely put it on the ground. No matter what way you looked at it, this was not a great turn of events. Not by anyone's standards – not even Jack's.

The phone machine clicked on in the kitchen, and from where he was sitting he heard the Rolling Stone saying to come on over to Gstaad – the party was only starting. A guilt call perhaps – but in any case, Jack couldn't get up off the floor, never mind get on a plane at a moment's notice.

All his friends had wives and families now. They had normal grown-up lives. They had nice wives with faded blonde looks; model babes who had earned out their years with the bad boys and were now reaping the benefits of husbands who were too old to be bold and were settling down. Maybe that's what he needed to do now. Settle down. He needed a woman to look after him. If he had a proper woman looking after him, none of this would be happening. He'd have the warm lazy breast of an old friend to lay his head on. Someone to tell him he was forgiven. Someone to make him cut down on the high life. Someone to keep him alive. Someone tender to mind him.

Valerie.

Oh Valerie, Valerie, Valerie. He should never have let her go. He should have let her stay and stick out the bad years, then he would have her now to put him back together again. To make his life normal.

Maybe it wasn't too late.

Legs crumbling with the effort of standing, Jack made it over to the phone and dialled her number.

18

It had not taken Lativa Noreen Doyle long to settle into her new life in Dublin. Within days of her arrival she had enrolled in college, found the funkiest boutiques, the best sandwich shop, the grooviest pub, and had managed to make friends with several of the Irish girls on her course. Being reared in Paris was a head start when it came to making friends among wannabe fashion designers, but she was wise enough not to milk both her obvious talent and natural style to the point of intimidation.

She was also refreshingly sensitive about the fact that every boy in the college and several besides were following her around like rats on a chain. She altruistically nudged each and every one of them in the direction of lesser females in order to (a) win brownie points with the girls (b) get them off her back and (c) keep the path clear in case she came across something truly interesting.

Which, on this particular Saturday – she did.

Digger – or Gerald Deignan as he was christened – was not your average first choice for a sophisticated, mature young woman who enjoyed the life opportunity of being able to pass herself off as 'a bit French'. His beanie hat housed a good deal more hair than could be considered attractive or, indeed, hygienic, and his anorak had the unmistakable odour of a garment which doubled as a duvet. The young man's general demeanour, while clearly not drug-induced, nonetheless had the slightly hunted and haunted look of the newly homeless. On the night when Lativa sashayed over to a corner bench where he was nursing the dregs of his last paid-for pint of the evening, Digger was just about at his wits' end.

Gerald Deignan – DJ handle 'Digger' was a poet of sorts. A rave poet. His work largely took the form of one short phrase repeated more times than one might care to listen to it. Like many great artists before him, Digger drew his inspiration from his own life and those 'everyday things' which at first may seem mundane, but in the hands of a great artist can be turned into something fascinating. His family however, did not share his enthusiasm as Gerald had taken to hiding his recording equipment around the house, then using their private musings to entertain the crowd at Busting Belly – the club he ran every Thursday at his local town hall in Bunkelly Co. Galway. His greatest success to date was 'Teacup Twister' which featured percussion courtesy of the ancient Granny Deignan banging a spoon on the side of her mug to attract her daughter's attention, while her son-in-law provided the sample lyric, 'Mary. There's a terrible smell in there. I think your mother is after breaking wind.'

Repeated some thirty-seven times before the single

track was over – almost treble that for the Extended Club Mix, and as counted by Digger's horrified fourteen-year-old sister, Shaznay (official girl gang handle – real name Bridget), who had sneaked into the club and wasn't even supposed to be there. She had confessed to her parents two weeks later, and had found that Gerald's invasion of the family's privacy had provided an excellent diversion from her own illicit night excursions – with a double bonus of her being a blameless child clearly under the influence of her older brother's shameless shenanigans.

Digger was cast out into the cold, and took the bus straight to Dublin where he imagined the capital's appreciative club-goers would take him to their hearts and lavish him with fame and fortune. Sadly, it did not work out that way, and by the time Lativa Doyle found him, his B&B budget was two days spent and it had been a toss-up between a Burger King meal or a pint. Lucky for him the pint won.

He told all of this to the clean-cut young woman that had obviously mistaken him for some 'normal' lad, and was suitably impressed when she seemed entirely unfazed. In fact, far from backing off, she was keen to know more about his music – it sounded really interesting – she would love to hear some of it.

And so it was that Eamonn Doyle returned home that Sunday morning from a particularly dull overnight golf business trip to find his daughter sitting in his living room alongside a half-naked pimply youth with one of his Landed In Laois beach towels wrapped around his skinny waist.

Over the past month, Eamonn had been adjusting to living with his daughter. He had noticed her sweet-smelling face creams appearing in the bathroom, the pinky-tan skids of make-up on his face towels, the addition of tofu and endive in his fridge and he had feigned to himself a slight irritation at having a female about the place. He had told some of his friends at the golf club that she was there, throwing his eyes to heaven in a mock gesture of 'you know yourself!' But the complaint was really a veiled boast. In reality, Eamonn was really enjoying having his daughter around. She was, despite her elegant and ladylike appearance, a fun housemate. She was laid-back about things such as egg sandwiches over the sink, and sensitive about delicate matters like laundry. Eamonn had dispensed with housekeepers after the last one had crossed the boundaries of personal intimacy when he caught her sniffing a pair of his discarded underpants to see if they were worthy of the wash-basket. Lativa never overstepped the mark by ironing his underpants or leaving her frillies up to dry in communal areas, but at the same time she had made the place seem more like home with the addition of a few scented candles and making herself at home in an easy, fleecy-pyjamas sort of way. He was inordinately proud of her, even though he still didn't know her well enough to know exactly why, but more than that, he was sort of proud of himself for having made her. He found himself trying to engage in competitive conversations about her with his business associates; wanting to explain that his daughter was prettier and cleverer than anyone else's.

More than once he had the urge to rummage in his wallet for a picture of her. But it had only been a month and they weren't at that stage yet. Eamonn had an ambition to take his daughter on a day trip to Dublin Zoo. But he knew she was too old and would hardly be interested. Besides, it would seem like a silly request and the very fact of his wanting to go there reminded Eamonn that the opportunity was coming to him some ten years too late. That aside, Lativa's charm and a maturity beyond her years had made living with a teenage daughter easy.

However, a strange half-naked youth in one's living room is, by any father's standard, a scene of teenage carnage. Even if he is sitting on the opposite side of the sofa to one's fully clothed daughter and the setting is accessorized by nothing more sinister than a pot of coffee for two and a small plate of fig rolls. By the fundamental ethics of any right-minded man walking back into his own home after a tiring golf outing, Eamonn would have been perfectly within his rights to have indulged in a spot of elbow grabbing and youth evicting.

'The cheeky strap,' he would have announced had one of his friends described a similar scenario perpetrated upon them by one of the troublesome fruits of their loins, 'I hope you turfed the gurrier out on the street and gave the little madam a good hiding into the bargain!'

But here is the funny thing.

So relaxed and happy did his daughter look as she rose from the sofa to greet her 'Papa', and with such innocent charm did she enquire as to if he would be 'joining them in a cup of tea?' and with such a perky spring in her step did she bounce through to the kitchen to reboil the kettle, that Eamonn would have felt foolish doing anything other than sitting down alongside sheepish young man and suggesting;

'You might want to put some clothes on there lad.'

When the answer came, with the requisite mortified blush; 'N-ner-ner-ner-ner noreen p-per per put them in the washing machine,' Eamonn found himself taken aback, not by the stammer or even by the fact that this stuttering young lad's smalls were currently whizzing around his Hotpoint without so much as an introduction, but by the fact that this boy had used his daughter's birth name.

'You mean Lativa?'

'Ker-ker-kept cer-cer-calling her Latvia ser-so I asked i-if she ha-had an-an-an-other one.'

That simple eh? Smart lad. From the country too by what he could gather behind the staggering syllables. He had his doubts of course. The boy was naked for a start, then there was the business of why his clothes needed to be washed. Did he not have a mammy? Certainly the shadows under his eyes and the look of acute discomfort under the current circumstances suggested that his mammy was too far away to have put him here.

Sympathy would be too strong a word for what Eamonn felt for him, in fact, felt would be too strong a word in itself also. Rather, he was curious as to when his daughter was going to explain what the hell was going on and happy enough to sit there in silence until she returned.

'Papa – this is Digger,' she said handing him a mug of really good strong tea for a French person. 'Digger, this is my father and these are your clothes.'

Gerald lighted upon the pile like a starving man and rushed gratefully from the room.

'Are you cross?' she asked straight out, holding Eamonn's good eye in the challenging way that she did.

'Well, I'm er . . .'

'Good – because I want you to give Digger some money.'

'Well now here, I mean . . .'

'Not much. Maybe a few hundred pounds. Just enough for him to get somewhere to live for a few weeks – unless you want him to move in here?'

'Well – I don't know about that . . .'

'Brilliant! You needn't worry though. He is going to be famous very, very soon. I can feel it. I know these things – and he will pay you back and so will I. That's settled then.'

And with that she walked calmly over to the sideboard and began to fumble through the DVDs.

'Digger hasn't seen *Car Wash* yet and I told him he should. He is *very* impressed with your record collection by the way. He says it is very unusual for someone of your generation to have such a historic understanding of dance music. He says he wishes his own parents were as educated as you.'

Digger walked back into the room, considerably more comfortable now that he was dressed. The three of them sat for an hour or so, and the two young people were fascinated as Eamonn told them all about his disco dancing days in Crosscarney, Aloysius Moses' trip to London in the seventies, and their formation of the Funk Masters. Noreen asked him to dance for them, but on this occasion, he said he would decline – but he promised Digger he would go to his first gig and see what this rave business was all about.

As it began to get dark, his daughter gave Eamonn the wink and began to clear away the cups. While she lingered in the kitchen, he took five hundred pounds out of his wallet (booty from a 'cash deal' he'd done on a hundred novelty T-shirts on the golf course), and gave it to the scruffy young man.

Digger didn't want to take it, and as Eamonn insisted his bottom lip began to quiver.

'Just take it son – and no funny business with my girl, eh?'

He nodded his reply and stuffed the notes into the leg pocket of his combats.

As they saw him off, Digger shook Eamonn's hand and called him 'sir', and the older man was suddenly struck with the normality of this little tableau they were making. Father, daughter and daughter's young man. They felt, for all the odd circumstances of their coming together, like a family.

After Digger was gone, Eamonn put on his favourite Barry White CD for a wind-down after all the excitement. As the horns of the orchestra's drums gave way to the slow rhythm of their lazy drums and the melting chocolate of Barry's voice slid over the words 'Now that I'm here – no more tears', Noreen walked across the room and silently wrapped her slim arms around her father's neck and pressed her lips against his cheek. It was a small gesture of thanks and Eamonn knew that. But it had been forever since he had felt anything so tender, and saying nothing he placed his hands gently on her back and father and daughter slow danced in a semi-hug as the man who had bought so many lovers together sang, 'I've got so much to give to you my dear, it's gonna take a lifetime, its gonna take years.'

Neither of them stopped to wonder how they felt so easy encased in each other's arms. Or that, in this day and age, people might find it unusual, even uncomfortable to see a father and daughter enjoying such an easy intimacy. But for both of them it felt like the most natural thing in the world to be shuffling around an Arnott's rug to Barry White in a suburban house on a warm September afternoon. Convention was in another place – out on Donnybrook golf course doing six rounds no doubt while its children got ready to leave home. He had just got his daughter back after ten years, and in the innocence of their dancing, and the eccentricity of their shared love of music, Eamonn Doyle vowed that he would never let her go again.

19

A cynical person might have said that Karin Sheridan's preparations for Sunday night were less like those of a sophisticated, educated woman going on a first date, and more like a general preparing troops for a military operation. And, ashamed though one is to admit it, they would have been right.

09.00 to 10.00: Full home body wax.

10.00 to 12 midday: Eye mask and meditation tape – *Get in Touch With Your Inner Goddess* – office freebie as yet unused gets first airing.

12.00 to 12.10: Light bran breakfast and litre water to clear body waste.

12.10 to 12.15: Body-waste clear-out.

12.15 to 12.50: Full body exfoliation with Mean Skin Mitt.

12.50 to 13.00: Exfoliation process interrupted by unaccounted for body-waste expulsion.

13.00: Facial, to include rigorous pore-check, eyebrow pluck, checking of errant nostril/chin hairs and one hour paraffin mask.

14.00 to 15.00: Wash hair, 20-minute hair mask, application of rollers.

15.00 to 16.15: Manicure and pedicure (put back fifteen minutes by additional body-waste clear-out. Jesus! How much more can possibly be in there!).

16.15: Rollers due out but nails wet.

16.45: Face beginning to crack with mask. Nails still wet.

17.00: Nails dry but cannot remove face mask as risk wetting rollers. Cannot remove rollers while mask still on. Gaah! Smudged toenail – start again.

17.30: Scrape face mask off with wet tissues.

17.35: Remove rollers. Gaaaah! Big hair! Big hair! Big hair! Tie hair back in manner of Hitler and hope will calm down.

17.50: Make-up.

18.05: Make-up too obvious, remove start again.

18.20: Still doing make-up

18.35: Still doing make-up.

18.50: Still doing make-up.

18.55: Still doing – aaaargh! Got to be there in forty minutes – what to wear!

18.55 to 19.05: Really, really annoying additional body-waste expulsion.

19.05 to 19.15: Little black dress or elegant trouser suit? Little black dress or elegant trouser suit? Little black dress – elegant trouser suit? Little black dress – elegant trouser suit? Little black – oh fuckit, where are my tights?

19.15 to 19.20: Look fine, second leg laddered. Times seven. Last hope – cheap and nasty but straight

out of packet – catch on renegade toenail. Fuck!
Elegant trouser suit. What top? What top? What
top?

19.20 to 19.22: Not again! Will not give in to Bowel
Terrorism. Will not . . . will not . . . will not . . .
oh fuckit, go once more!

19.25 to 19.30: Shit, forgot to call cab!

As a result of the best-laid plans, Karin tore out of her
flat, forgetting her pre-drawn-up List of Interesting Topics
to Discuss With Renowned Intellectual and her purse.

She threw herself in front of a cab and spent the five
minutes of her journey terrifying herself over the hur-
ried choice of a ludicrously low-cut top that was really
a glorified bra and the fact that in her panic she had
forgotten that most rudimentary of beauty routines – the
brushing of one's teeth. She toyed with the idea of getting
the driver to stop at a petrol station so she could chaw
back a packet of mints, and it was then that she realized
that she had forgotten her purse. Pulling up outside the
National Concert Hall three minutes before the orchestra
were due on stage to put their maximum all into Wagner's *Der Ring des Nibelungen*, Karin tried to negotiate
with 'Kevo' her driver. He was having none of it. 'Oim
sarry lay-the but de mayter says foive poun' fiff-the, an'
foive poun' fiff-the iss wha'iss gonna costya.'

Offers to send him a cheque for twenty pounds; to
meet him tomorrow and confer gifts on all belonging
to him; he could come around to the apartment for break-

fast – he knew where she lived – and what she wouldn't do for him if he would only, only, *please* let her off this five-pound-fifty he would be rewarded with fifty, sixty, seventy, eighty, a hundred pounds – not to mention the special treatment he could expect in God's Good Heaven for helping a damsel in distress, were all met with no more than derisive laughter and several 'No can do luff,' s.

He knew well by the cut of her that she was meeting somebody inside, and so, under Kevo's watchful eye and crippled with mortification she went inside to ask Claude for the money. He was not diffuclt to find, as he paced around the rapidly emptying lobby, slapping the pro-grammes on the leg of his moth-eaten tux, his face as agitated as an ostrich on heat. By the time he saw her, he had no time for niceties.

'Quick – they're starting,' he barked, moving in the direction of the auditorium.

'Look Claude, this is really embarrassing, but I've got a little bit of a problem. Well, it's not so much a problem as . . .'

'What? What is it for God's sake – they're closing the doors!'

'Well, you won't believe this but I've only gone and left my purse at home and . . .' She knew she was babbling but she just couldn't seem to stop herself. 'You see the taxi driver is waiting outside, and I know it's ridiculous because of course, anyone can see that I'm not the sort of person to, you know, run off, but well . . .'

Claude thrust a ten-pound note at her, without sym-pathy or ceremony and kept on up the stairs.

'Hurry up – or you'll miss the first half.'

Which she did.

A most unbelievably appalling turn of events on several counts, them being:

1. She now had a time period of over one hour to sit about and obsess about what impression she must have given Claude, sub-list containing:

(a) Flibbertigibbet unable to keep time

(b) Sad lonely person with nothing better to do than hang around a lobby waiting for him

(c) Babbler

(d) Somebody with very horrible tied-back hairstyle which she had forgotten to take down.

2. All of the programmes had been nabbed on the way in, and so there were none left for her to brush up on her Wagner with. She hadn't the first clue what *Der Ring des Nibelungen* was about – all she knew was that Wagner was very hard work indeed.

3. It was v. hot and she could not remove her jacket as was wearing lacy underwear as top.

The one small speck of hope was that she had time to 'undo' her Hitler hairdo – and it was while she was rummaging around for a brush in her bag that she found a twenty-pound note folded into a handful of old receipts. A frustrating find, under the circumstances, but she decided to invest it wisely in calming her nerves at the bar. Four swift gin and tonics later, and Karin was feeling decidedly more relaxed. Actually, she was beginning to feel rather chummy, and cosy, and truth be told, a bit *cuddly* by the time Wagner's fan-club of Dublin 4 high-brows spewed out of the auditorium to their pre-ordained interval orders. Claude was glowing with joy at the great wonder that was, apparently, this evening's performance of *Die Walküre* (The Valkyries, Act I – for those undered-ucated unfortunates who require translation) and Karin managed to feign a level of deep joy that 'the transition between the Prelude and Scene One had a gloriously playful mobility that really captured the playful teasing of the Rhine Daughters.'

'Thank God for that!' exclaimed Karin, pretending for all her life was worth that she knew what the fuck he was talking about. Perhaps she would be able to wing it after all.

He took her arm and all but skipped into the bar, where he immediately plunged the two of them into a group of crusty squidgy-faced opera buffs, uniform in the squareness of their home-cut fringes, their sex identifiable only by bow-tie or high-necked moth-eaten evening dress. One of the women was wearing earrings, and it being the only evidence of frivolity in the group, Karin stood next to her. She might have got away with it if she hadn't been half-cut and feeling slightly dippy with the misguided illusion that they were only people and that she was more than able for them. Therefore when they started to compete frantically with their enthused critiques:

'A firm and imperious Siegmund – Claude what did you think?'

'Magnificent – what longevity and if it's not too obvious a comment – a *lyrical* performance I thought. Truly in the truest sense of the word. Or perhaps I'm being sentimental . . .?'

'No, no, no, I agree – one really felt that he *possessed* the text with such . . . with such . . .'

'Verisimilitude?'

'*Exactly* – that was the word I was looking for!'

Rather than keeping the head down and busying herself at the bar getting peanuts or something, Karin decided to chance her arm and leap right in with an observation of her own.

'Don't be talking! I can't believe I missed it! And can I just say that, of all the Rings, in all the world Nibelungen's Ring is my very, very favourite. Oh yes, if anyone were to ask me, Karin? Whose ring would you prefer? Lord Of or Nibelungen's, I would have to say it would be Nibelungen's every time!'

A slightly confused company stood around and eyebrow raised for a few seconds, trying to decide if the glamorous blonde was being ironic or ghastly horror of horrors, if she was one of those nouveau mass-market opera-types who had compilation Three Tenors CDs, and thought that *Pavarotti Sings Gershwin at The Point Depot* was real opera. The troll with the earrings decided to give her a break, and came straight back with a challenging, 'So what did you make of Karajan's casting of Dietrich Fischer-Dieskau as Wotan with the Berliner Philharmoniker? I was listening to it again last night, and, while it's undoubtedly different to Hotter, I think it

nonetheless complements Veasy's Fricka with a certain –
manipulative intelligence? Don't you think?'

A sudden thwack of sobriety clouted Karin's knees.
Errr . . . out of her depth? And then some!

Eight beady eyes glittered with a vast galaxy of impos-
sibly clever facts she could not hope to answer, and none
glittered more brightly than those of Claude Moore in
his expectation of his date's forthcoming comments on
the leitmotiv nature of Wagner and the *Götterdämmerung*
in general.

'Ab-sol-utley!' she said, dragging the word out and at
the same time imbuing it with enough emphasis that this
single word might pass itself off as a sentence, before
mercy of merciful mercies, she was saved by the bell for
the second act.

She tried, Lord knows she tried to stay awake during
the performance. If only to strain her eyes studying
Claude's programme and notes. But while her date's face
was contorting to the unspeakable unimaginable indisputable power and passion that is Wagner at his most
imperiously brilliant, Karin found herself nodding off.
Perhaps if the performance had enjoyed the visual benefits
of costumes and sets instead of a selection of fat people
in bad evening wear pretending to be about five different
people each, perhaps, even if it had been in English, Karin
might have managed to maintain the clipped-wide-open
expression of acute interest she had displayed for the first
half an hour of the second act. But when, after what
seemed like an interminable amount of time passed and
she was informed by a corrective tug of her elbow that

the current tumultuous applause did not signal time to go home, but was in fact merely the end of Act II with Act III to follow, she had no option but to put the head back, set her face to a position of Listening in Appreciative Repose and let the great thundering dullness of being at *any* kind of classical concert do the rest. Had she not had that fourth G&T, she mightn't have lolled quite as obliviously and dribbled slightly onto Claude's shoulder just as Wotan was using his Runespear thus summoning Loge in his fire/elemental form to surround the sleeping Brunhilde. Not, according to the assertive poke in the ribs she got from Claude, a moment when one might be excusably lulled to sleep in a kind of melodic ecstasy.

When the performance was ended, Karin excused herself immediately and escaped to the ladies' toilets to refresh her tactical manoeuvres. She had taken her eye off the ball, big time, for the first half of this date, but she was be-damned if she was going to let a minor handbag mishap and a lack of opera appreciation stand in the way of her everlasting happiness – worse, to stand in the way of her pride. In years to come, she thought as she determinedly readjusted her lipliner where the sleep-drool had rivuleted clean through it, Claude and I will be enjoying a glass of Chianti and laughing over this disastrous date. She had not endured a full day witless with nerves to the point of squibbly shites for it to be anything but the other. I am going to get it together, then *we* are going to get it together and we will look back on this day in years to come and laugh, she mantra'd to herself. Yes we will, yes we will, yes we will.

Then finally, for luck, aloud, 'Yess we will,' Karin announced to her reflection before brushing a little blush across her décolletage and marching out for her own Act II. A dancy, tuneful little number which she had appropriately entitled – *Der Ring des Karin's Finger*.

20

'You have one new message in your mailbox.'

Sinead's heart leapt out of habit. She had only known Miles for one month, and yet the excitement of hearing his voice had already formed an emotional routine. It was Sunday morning, and she was waiting for some anger to loosen the dense fog of shame that had taken root in the pit of her stomach. She knew that Miles would ring and she dreaded what she would say. She would have to ask questions, expose herself. Submit herself to the cliché of having expected more than was on offer. Expose herself as having cared. Pretend it was her fault for getting the wrong end of the stick. Laugh it all off as if it didn't matter. Be grown up, and cynical, and one of the lads about it. She would have to continue with Miles's music deal, because that was just good business, and pretend that she wasn't crushed by his rejection. Revert to form and play the modern female warrior, impervious to the frail complexities of girlie love. A great big hard old Amazon, who rides freely across the rugged plains of Dublin manhood by night and still takes care of business during the day. She had twenty-four more hours before she had to put a brave face on it. Saturday had been spent in bed with the phone unplugged, and today she had managed to make herself breakfast and put the phone back on – although she hadn't had the courage to answer it.

The message was from Valerie.

'Hi, Sinead. Can you call me back – there's something I really need to talk to you about. It's Valerie. Bye.'

She sounded awful, and under normal circumstances Sinead would have started dialling before she had finished listening to the message. But today she just could not cope with somebody else's problems. If she could just get today over with – Monday had the ring of a new dawn. A new week. She would call her tomorrow when . . .

The phone rang again making Sinead leap with shock and spill hot coffee down the front of her chemise.

'Shit!'

This was madness being stuck in here round the clock. It was just making things worse, and the phone would be going like that all day. She needed to get out of the house – clear her head. Drive out to the sea or something. Get a bit of peace and quiet. Be on her own where nobody could find her.

She threw on a pair of jeans and an old sweater and grabbed her car keys.

It was a crispy, sunny day, and she headed automatically south towards Wicklow. Along the canal, its narrow paths scattered with Sunday couples and city dog walkers and then out past the sensible squareness of the suburbs with its shopping centres and housing estates set in uniform patches of green. The roads began to narrow; the city's hard edge giving way to a disorganized topography of mountains and fields and with it Sinead's anxiety mellowed. As she reached the heathery boglands of Sally's Gap, its stunted mountains rising up from the road in orange mounds, Sinead pulled over into a lay-by and disintegrated into tears.

Ten minutes later she was feeling better, and decided to amble on.

Fifteen minutes later, she was feeling kind of mad. She stuck on a CD.

Twenty minutes later she had her foot to the floor and was tearing round Wicklow's bendy roads like a mad thing. Who the fuck did he think he was! The smarmy little shitbag conman with his Glamorous Brazilian Mother and his Designer Architect Dad? He was probably from some ghastly English suburban estate in Milton Keynes for all she knew. Passing himself off as a fascinating piece of work when all he was was a . . . was a . . . was a . . . philandering half-pint! Frigging around with a goddess like Sinead O'Sullivan? Why how dare he! She must have been mad . . . and as for Dizzy? The treacherous little toe-rag – after all she'd done for her? Whipping wasn't good enough – she'd turn the jumped-up little slut inside out and use her as a handbag!

Sinead was fairly belting along now at this stage – stereo blaring, fag smoke fogging up the windscreen and generally boiling with indignation in her very own little road-rage pod.

It does not take long when speeding along country roads in Ireland on a Sunday before one encounters a farmer pottering along in his tractor, resentfully going about his business even though it is officially the Lord's day of rest. And it was one of these very farmers that Sinead came across, rather suddenly, and at very close range. One of the advantages of driving a tractor is, of course, that they are more or less indestructible. The same cannot be said of the Astra GTI whose advantage is speed rather than resistance to having a couple of tonnes of enforced steel rammed into its bumper. As soon as she saw him, Sinead slammed the brakes on, steered somewhat to one side, but caught the left part of her boot and bumper in a nasty crunch. She could have been dead, and she wasn't. On a sliding scale from wheelchairbound, through concussion to even severe whiplash – she came out of it unharmed. On another day, this might have struck her as something to be grateful for. But today, as far as Sinead was concerned, God was taking a day off and this was just another disaster. If she thought Almighty Forces were testing her patience, that was before she met Gubnet O'Shaunessey.

Sinead decided to wait in the car for him to come over to her. She had never crashed before, but it seemed like the protocol in these cases. Well, it must have taken him a full five minutes to disengage himself from the complicated harness of belts and ropes with which the safety-conscious farmer strapped himself into his driver's perch each day. Another three to clamber carefully down the steps, three or four to adjust his trousers, and five more at least to stand surveying the damage to Sinead's car.

By the time he came over and stood shaking his head and chewing his teeth in at Sinead's window, she was well and truly over the shock and nearly gone mental with the eternity he was taking.

He signalled at her to roll the window down, failing to notice that it was down fully already.

She figured she ought to apologize but – you know? – she *really* wasn't in the mood for apologizing today. To anyone. For anything.

'Grand day . . .' he said, scratching his head.

Grand fucking day! I could be dead! thought Sinead. No, no – just keep the head and get the fuck away from here as quickly as possible.

'If you could just give me your insurance details there, Mr . . .?'

'Sure thatwus a fair aul schpeed yeswus cumming roun' th'corner there . . .'

Sinead did not want a discussion. She wanted a mobile phone so she could call a tow truck, but she had left her own at home. She was going to have to communicate with this gom to get out of this middle-of-nowhere place. Could this day *get* any worse? She should never have left the house.

'Well now . . . d'yeh see . . . we'd want to be moving you fairly schpeedy like outta here . . .' And with that

Gubnet pulled a pristine mobile out of the front pocket of his disgracefully mucky overalls and began talking in a dialect that might have been Urdu for all Sinead recognized of it.

Within two minutes a young man with pointy teeth and scary hair arrived in an ancient Nissan bearing a rope. Between them they negotiated a price to tow this glamorous and therefore wealthy Dublin woman back home.

'Tree hundred pound,' Gubnet said carefully, his fingers loping the string braces that were holding his trousers up as if the action might add business-minded gravitas to the ludicrous price.

Sinead rustled around in her handbag, found a pen and wrote Jack Valentine's address down on an old petrol receipt.

'Take me to this address – I'll give you twenty pounds, take it or leave it.'

The younger man grudgingly agreed, and half an hour later Sinead was banging furiously on Jack's door trying to rouse him out of his usual Sunday torpor.

When he finally arrived, somewhat confused by the racket having thought it was coming from the inside of his head, Sinead fell into his hall.

'Jack – thank God. I need a stiff drink and I need one now.'

Jack was great because he never asked questions.

'Lady,' he said in his best Lord of the Manor accent, '*you* have come to the right place!'

21

Despite the letter from the bank on Friday, the early part of Valerie's weekend had been quite fun. Bernard's dream man turning up at the shop like that had been very exciting and Valerie had really enjoyed playing the matchmaker. She had invited the man into the shop, found out a bit about him while Bernard was out back tidying himself up and generally trying to find a suitable blouse. His name was Barry, he was Australian and he worked in television. He seemed like a lovely person, and just the sort of chap a girl might like her friend to get hooked up with. Gay men were so lovely really and they had a really nice chat. He admired her hair, and she admired his in turn, and he said he wasn't very happy with his hairdresser, and she gave him the name of her colourist and he seemed delighted and so on. He went a bit quiet then when Bernard came back in, but she guessed he was just shy. Perhaps he felt awkward about following Bernard like that, and she had to admit, that was a bit strange. He hadn't struck her as that sort of person at all – but then, you never know. It wasn't fair really, her being there – but she couldn't leave them alone in her shop, and neither man seemed able to make any other arrangement. So Valerie fixed them up on one of her and Bernard's 'Blind Date Specials'. Valerie would suggest they all meet up, that evening, as a group, for a drink, no romantic undertones. Then she just wouldn't show. It had worked dozens of times before for Bernard, and she felt sure, by the lovely friendly manner of this Barry person, that it would work too. So that at least two people in the world would be living happily ever after.

That evening, she tried to call Sinead and Karin, but they were both out with their mobiles switched off. She had a nasty sinking feeling that they were avoiding her, but she shrugged it off. She'd try them again tomorrow and fix something up for later in the week.

Saturday turned out to be a busier day than expected, and when she was totting up at the end of the day, she felt a little bud of optimism that perhaps she might be able to keep the shop after all. She had an appointment with her accountant later that week, so she spent a couple of hours after closing up marking down some more pieces for the sale rail. She was half-waiting for Bernard to pop in and give her the low-down on how he had got on with Barry the night before, but his no-show indicated that perhaps they were enjoying the first throes of new love with a full weekend holed up in either one's apartment. She would have liked to have caught up on the news but hey – it was obviously a job well done on her part and that was enough consolation.

Valerie got home at about eight o'clock, and that was

when it all started to get nasty. Nothing happened, as such, but sometimes, you don't need anything more than the contents of your own mind to send you spinning.

And a message from an ex-husband on your answering machine.

Not just an ordinary message either. But one leaden with the punctuation of hidden meaning, barely concealed anguish and historic regret.

'Valerie. It's me. Jack. I need to talk. To you. But – you're not there. Call me back. Please. Soon.' Click.

Just twenty words. She counted them as she replayed the message over and over. She knew that she shouldn't. That he was probably drunk. That there was no point. That she should ignore it, and just walk away as she had done over ten years ago. The problem was that she hadn't stopped walking since, and she was tired. The sound of his voice seemed to be telling her to stop, to look back. When Valerie did look back all she saw was flowers stolen from a garden and a man who was broken. She didn't see the years in between. The self-abuse, the womanizing, the excess. She couldn't. When she tried to study them, there was a reason for every line of coke, every infidelity – and each reason was the same. Her. Valerie Valentine. The fact that she had walked away. He had never blamed her outright. He didn't need to. He would drink and drink, then that one too many would flood the hurt that was always there and it would spill right out of him in a tidal wave of pain. He played the rock and roll icon, but Valerie had seen through to the other side. Waking to find his arms searching her out in the night then curling into the comfort of her body as though he were a small child. His eyes begging her to stroke his head in the morning. The overwhelming silence of his shame filling every room of their massive Tudor house, even when he wasn't there.

Valerie felt she had been the cause of it too. With the tyrannical tidiness of the life she tried to create for them. Little Miss Perfect with her matching suites of furniture and her dinner parties. She had known back then – known in the way that she felt she loved him, even though he was the way he was. But she was too young and too afraid to look. Too weak to do anything about it – so she had allowed him to send her away. She knew now that he had done it because he loved her. Because he knew what that part of him he could not control held in store for her. Jack hid himself well underneath the arrogance and the abuse. But Valerie knew that some-where inside him was the bottomless well of his sorrow. She had stood on the edge of it, and he was the one that had pulled her back.

This phone call was a cry for help by anyone's standards.

But for Valerie it was set at the terrifying angle of an invitation.

She did not know what to do.

For the rest of that night, she put all of her energy into not calling Jack back. She bleached and rebleached her bathroom. She cleaned the inside of her fridge until it looked new. She hoovered under her bed, dusted and polished her skirting boards, reorganized her crockery and alphabetically organized the food produce in her larder – decanting and labelling dried goods into jars. Anything, anything but call him back.

While she worked she thought. Thought about what Jack needed from her, and about what she was able to give him. She dragged out every bit of dingly-dangly wisdom that she had ever heard Tinara spout at her, and weeded out the bits she wanted.

By the following morning, her hands were rough with work and her mind was made up.

No. She was not going back in there. She was not able to deal with Jack. The thought of even being his friend terrified her. She was born to blind-date nice homosexuals and sell lovely clothes to appreciative customers.

She'd had enough pain in her life, and she had spent enough time and energy putting herself out for other people's.

Maybe it was the fact that a big birthday was looming, and certainly it was triggered by Jack's phone call, but in that eight-hour run of compulsive cleaning all the years of doormatting and doing for others combined with the questions she had always asked about herself brought her, for the first time in her life, to a place of certainty she never thought she would reach.

She was nearly forty, and things around here were going to change.

She would do one last thing for Jack Valentine and that was pass his plea on to someone who was better able for him.

And so she rang Sinead.

She wasn't in – again, so she left a message asking her to call back. Jack would have to wait.

And with that, Valerie, at eight a.m., on a Sunday morning, unplugged her phone and took to her bed for the most peaceful night's/day's sleep she had ever enjoyed.

22

There is only one thing worse than being in the company of a tediously boring person – and that is when, courtesy of the emotions of fear and the intense desire to impress, one finds one has become tediously boring oneself.

And this was the position Karin Sheridan found herself in about halfway through her date with Claude Moore.

It was no small task extracting Mr Moore from the group of enthused scary-fringed buffs who were obviously keen to spend the rest of that evening entwining clever critique around clever critique until they had knotted themselves into an intellectual frenzy. All very well and good in itself, but not exactly conducive to the process of romantic canoodling that Karin was still determined to set in motion.

In the end she had to resort to emergency measures to get him on his own. The fail-safe female date-tactic of 'I'm hungry', code name – Take Me to a Restaurant and Sit Noticing How Lovely I Am.

Scary Fringe Avec Earrings however, put a spanner in the works by declaring that they should *all* retire to a 'fabulous little Chinese' around the corner to continue their discussion. Quick-as-a-whip Karin was in with a hastily invented allergy to MSG.

'How about Indian then?' another suggested. Karin grimaced an apology and feigned a 'delicate stomach'.

Problem solved, according to a goateed professor of Biophysics, who had four dozen oysters, freshly delivered from Galway that morning and cooling in a bucket in his fridge.

'Perfect!' everyone chorused and began to make moves towards leaving. But Karin was not to be deterred.

'Can't touch seafood,' she declared into the business of coat gathering, 'I blow up like a balloon!'

Finally, *someone* got the message.

'Right then, Claude – you take your young lady off somewhere nice, and we'll see you at *Parsifal* next week.'

It was only then that Karin realized that Claude had not bumped into these people by accident. It was some kind of a ghastly Wagner Appreciation Network that probably met every week. She was a tag-along, an accessory. When Claude had said, 'I have a spare ticket for a concert on Sunday', he had actually meant 'I have a spare ticket for a concert on Sunday', and not 'You're a devastatingly attractive woman and this is just a subtle way of saying I wish to launch an investigation of your underwear.'

Oh dear. Karin had her work cut out for her more than she had thought. The odds were lower than she'd hoped, but she was, determinedly, still in the running.

They left and walked down Harcourt Street towards St Stephen's Green. Claude's shoulder hunched in the morose sulk of a Brilliant Mind who had just missed out on a bellyful of oysters and the opportunity to flex his intellect and establish academic superiority amongst his peers, and Karin alongside him with the hopeful skip of a schoolgirl trotting after the dishiest boy in the class hoping he'd notice her.

Somewhere approaching town Claude finally mumbled, 'So where do you want to eat then?'

Difficult. Her favourite three options, Chinese, Indian and seafood were off the list. Think. Quick. Am modern woman of impeccable taste and sophistication.

Aha – Kerrigan's! Posh new brasserie on the Green itself. Nearby, new – reputedly low-key interior, splendid food.

'Let's go in here,' she said casually as they were passing the double bay trees at its entrance, 'I've heard it's very good.'

Claude thought it looked a bit pricey, but he supposed it was as good a place as any to humour this ignorant creature. Escape was impossible, at least until after she had run the interview in that third-grade publication. That she had fawningly appreciated his talent had trapped him into her company – but Claude had felt that he had learned an important lesson tonight. Fawning appreciation was, after all, no more than he deserved. But it was not grounds for friendship unless the other party was at least approximating an intellectual par with himself. The female was, after all, little more than a shocking combination of hair and handbag – with no brains under one and no money in the other. He would drop her, naturally enough, but until the article came out, he would have to tolerate, tolerate, tolerate. A challenge, but then, a bed of his own making.

As the maître d' showed them to a candlelit side booth, Karin was starting to feel better. They were in classy, civilized surroundings – with real art on the walls. The menu arrived and was pant-restrictingly expensive, but that was all right because Karin had already decided that, whatever the cost, she was going to pay. Show him that she wasn't the sort of woman who was on the take. Prove her status as an independent millennium woman who thought nothing of whipping out her credit card and paying for . . .

Oh Merciful Hour of Jesus!

Shit!Shit!Shit!

She'd no purse. She was a purse-free zone. No money. Claude would think that . . .

'I suppose I'll be paying for this tonight,' he said, barely able to disguise his shock at the exorbitance he was holding in his paws, 'so we'll just have a starter – gravadlax' he finished, snapping the menu shut and passing it over his shoulder.

This was not a pretty turn of events, and it threw Karin into something of a panic. Normally as self-assured and confident as any woman can hope to be, the combination of intellectual insecurity and eagerness to make this man like her finally conspired to turn her into what every single woman hopes never to become. A desperate people-pleasing 'like me' bimbo – in sharp contradiction to the *Intelligent Modern Irish Woman's Guide to Dating*.

On Friday, she had come up with full marks in the ingratiating flattery module.

She had thus inaugurated herself into the creating of an opportunity.

Now she could see that opportunity slipping away, and she did what came naturally. She panicked. And when Karin panicked, she talked.

Talked shite.

Steering well clear of subjects that might take her out of her depth; opera, metaphysics, works of great philosophers, aesthetics etc., she allowed the dull not-worth-mentioning flotsam that floats around on the surface of even the most interesting of minds to take over. The traffic crisis in Dublin, parking, property prices, soap-opera plots, the abundance of UK chain stores on Grafton Street – God Bless Us and Save Us if the weather didn't even get a look in. To further perpetuate the horror of this, each dull monologue seemed entirely designed to somehow illustrate how sophisticated she was by including clumsy poorly disguised statements of her own fabulousness, and ended with a perkily phrased question to which 'yes' or 'no' were the only possible answers. Example.

'Well, it is just a disgrace the price of property in Ireland – although I am so glad I bought when I did *(am solvent home-owner)* and my friends in Paris *(am popular person – have Europewide network of friends)* are shocked –

shocked! – when I tell them how much a three-bed-roomed terrace in Donnybrook costs these days *(read Irish Times property supplement)*. Having said that you know, I think Dublin is really great – I mean – it's impossible to park, and the weather is awful but you know – I've been to New York, and London, and Paris and well – all the world's capitals actually *(am v. well travelled)* and I still choose to live here. I don't know why, I suppose it's just because we Irish have a certain 'je ne sais quoi', *(I speak French)*, don't you think?'

As the hours went on, Karin was aware of herself being dragged faster and deeper into a vortex of out-of-control, ever more obnoxious-sounding drivel. But in the face of Claude's obvious indifference and the desire to, somehow impress him into fancying her, she was unable to stop herself.

Claude was suffering too, let there be no doubt about that. But by the time Karin opened the subject of 'the diabolical nerve of Dublin taxi drivers charging £20 when you had just got off a plane from New York (Business Class)' he had consumed a full bottle of Chablis on a stomach lined only with the merest suggestion of cured fish. Being in a state of semi-inebriation, he began to worry that he mightn't have sufficient wherewithal to politely allay any intentions she might have for coming back to his apartment for a nightcap. He supposed these 'types' of women had ways of manipulating these situations to their advantage. So when Karin suggested that they 'pop down to Little's for a late-night drinky-poo' (for by now she had slipped into a pretending-to-be-posh coy Middle England role), he figured he would be able to lose her easily enough.

Which he did.

⬭

Barry was not enjoying his first date with the woman of his dreams. Largely because she was not there. Who was there was the large neighbour and friend of Valerie Valentine (for that was her name – Valentine! My pretty little Valentine as Barry had cooed to himself earlier whilst standing at his bathroom mirror preparing for this evening, flipping and flicking his fringe to perfection, joyously oblivious of the awkward horrors that the hours ahead would hold). This man called Bernard, about whom Barry's unspoken reservations were beginning to take shape. The Love That Is Afraid to Speak Its Name had whispered at first to Barry in the form of a manly arm around the shoulder in Little's members' bar, and was currently speaking its name for all and sundry to hear as it transmogrified itself slowly, and with indisputable sure-handedness into something that can only be accurately described as a 'cuddle'.

Bernard, for his part in what his grandmother had once cruelly described as 'a crime against nature' was in seventh heaven. An old-fashioned romantic, Bernard did not go in for the quick-fix cruise of the gay scene. There was none of this 'nice trousers, now let's have a quick go of the contents before I lose my place in the queue for male model in the corner.'

No. Bernard was more of the settling down 'another iced bun ducky?' school. He longed for a meeting of minds; a nice tailored type to share a mortgage; someone who'd appreciate his ability to arrange muslin round an ordinary window and transform it into 'something splendid'; someone to build the bed while he ruched the velvet; someone to talk to the guests while he basted the beef and piped the potatoes. Years living on his own had widened Bernard's interests and made him a good catch, he knew, for a certain type of discerning man. All right, he was no tight-trousered Adonis, but he was well read, travelled, and there was little he didn't know about art and music. Barry was no intellectual, but he was certainly a bit-more-like-it after Bernard's recent bad run of experimenting builders and heart-breakingly beautiful one-night stands.

So Bernard was in no rush, and the early part of the evening had gone extremely well. They had met for a drink in Cocoon. Trendy, quiet, straight. No prying eyes or cruisy queens to distract them from each other's company. Just lots of lovely 'getting to know you' chat. Barry had been really interested in Valerie – which was nice because Val was Bernard's best friend and it showed that he was a caring, family, let's-all-get-together sort of social person and not a sex-driven cock-monster who was only interested in one thing. So they had something in common already.

Barry had talked about growing up in Australia – his family, his job, that sort of thing. Bernard took the lead and talked about growing up in Ireland – his family, his job, that sort of thing. No talk of ex-boyfriends, or relationship disasters, or sexual preferences or the usual smutty nonsense. It was nice. Civilized. Bernard asked him how he was getting on in Dublin and he said fine but that he had yet to find a good hairdresser and Bernard said I know what you mean and scraped his hand across his number-two crop and Barry laughed and he laughed and it was lovely. Barry had said that he hadn't made any friends yet really and Bernard said that he was his friend now and Barry said that he was pleased and Bernard said that that was lovely. And it was. Really lovely.

Little's had been an excellent idea. Bernard was a member and had called ahead for a table, so there was a bit of special treatment at the door – which is always nice, and they were shown to a quiet couch in a nice corner. And, of course, the very *nicest* thing about Little's was that you could have a sneaky little cuddle and nobody would bat an eyelid. Bernard disapproved of public face-chewing and groin-frottage generally, but a bit of a friendly cuddle on a hideaway sofa wasn't going to offend anybody and it just sort of established where you were with a person. He was pretty certain that Barry was giving out the right vibes, but there was no harm in making sure.

Then, just as he was starting to move the arm down towards Barry's waist for a friendly-but-we-know-what-this-is-all-about-really-semi-cuddle, the Australian belted up from the sofa.

'I know her!'

It was a woman from the same office as him. He

didn't know her name or anything about her, but she was some kind of a route out of the social predicament he found himself in, which was:

1. Valerie's friend was trying to get in amongst him.
2. Bernard was Valerie's friend and, as such, Barry didn't want to upset him.

Bernard looked up and saw Karin Sheridan up at the bar with Claude Moore, author of *Illuminati Insurrection*, one of his favourite books, but nonetheless an unwelcome distraction from the task almost in hand.

'Ah, you know Karin?' said Bernard trying to sound casual.

'Karin! Karin! *Karin!*' Barry hollered across the bar, barely concealing the desperate tone in his calling.

Karin caught his eye briefly but ignored him. It was that imported bozo Australian that Eamonn was giving all his attention to these days – and bollocks, he was with Valerie's friend Bernard, the big annoying queen. If she didn't turn around, they'd leave it go. Jesus, you could go nowhere in this town.

But in Barry's frantic waving, Claude saw the dawning of an opportunity. Dump her with them and then, well, dump her. He gave Karin a sharp poke in the side. 'Look – friends of yours. Let's go over and you can introduce me.'

Karin was a bit put out by Claude's apparent rush to join her 'friends' but she consoled herself with the notion that he would get to see her 'perform' socially in circumstances which did not involve opera chit-chat with hard-core hairy clevers.

The half-wit Australian lighted down upon her like she was Liz Taylor on crutches, leaping up from his seat to make room for her then abandoning the couch altogether and settling onto a stool opposite her across the low table.

This annoying man created such a bother about the seating arrangements that it was a few minutes before Karin noticed that Claude was sitting, not next to her, but on the opposite side of Bernard – who was having a personal crisis of his own.

The gentlemanly flourish with which Barry had risen from his seat to let Karin sit down, the keen way in which he was now locking his eyes onto her could only mean one thing. The teasy little bollocks was straight.

Absent-mindedly, with all the dignity of the recently disappointed, Bernard asked Claude where they had been that evening. *Der Ring des Nibelungen* eh? He was sorry he'd missed it, (said with some conviction given the waste of time this evening had turned out to be), although, in truth, he doubted if the performance could top Janowski conducting the Staatskapelle Dresden recording. Claude assured him to the contrary with such a convincing burst of enthusiasm, that Bernard found himself becoming more and more distracted from the issue of Barry and his lovely hair.

By the time Karin managed to extract herself from the Australian's schoolboy whooping delight that they had a mutual friend in Valerie, she found that her date was deep in what seemed like a genuinely gripping conversation with Bernard, the big homo openly making a play,

'*Illuminati Insurrection*? Don't be talking to me Claude! Beckett? I tell you no word of a lie when I say he's only trotting after you!', and Claude protesting to the contrary when it didn't take a telescope to see he was literally squirming with delight.

Karin got a nasty feeling, and while Barry lashed back his fizzy orange and waved some speedy goodbyes, Karin turned her hawkeye on the two men.

Bernard's arm was resting on the back of the couch and his hand was touching – touching! – Claude's shoulder. She decided to call it a night herself and quit while she was – well, not ahead, but at least not humiliated quite to the point of no return.

Barry walked her out, but if she was half-hoping for a consolation ride, she was disappointed. He declared that any friend of Valerie Valentine was a friend of his, shook her hand and said he would see her on Monday and they could continue their chat over coffee in the Doyle Ind. canteen.

As Little's was closing up at five a.m., Bernard took his second chance that evening and slipped his arm around the Mighty Intellectual's waist. As he did, a rather drunk but, for the moment at least, intellectually sated Claude Moore rested his head gratefully on the big dress designer's shoulder.

Finally, Bernard's day had come.

23

It can't have been more than six or seven when Sinead woke up. The curtains were open, and the sky outside was still a translucent grey waiting for dawn to give way to daylight. Her stomach instantly tightened. She had been drunk but, she regretfully realized, not so drunk that she couldn't remember. Not so drunk that she could excuse herself; that she could deny that at least some part of her had wanted this to happen.

Jack had treated her like a one-woman party when she arrived unexpectedly at his door. He looked like shit – ragged and wild-eyed as usual, but frayed at the edges, like a scrapping dog who's been rescued from a fight he didn't think he was going to lose. He had been up drinking since herself and Karin had seen him on Friday, of that much Sinead was sure. But frankly, the state she was in she didn't care. All she cared about was that she was in a warm comfortable house with a friend. But Jack wasn't the sort of friend she could curl up on the sofa and tell her problems to. Not indeed that she much felt like doing that anyway. Sinead wanted, for the time being at least, to forget. And that was Jack's forte. Forgetting.

They drank a bottle of malt whisky between them, although, in fairness, Sinead's was diluted with tonic and ice on a sober stomach, and Jack's was neat and on top of a forty-eight-hour cocktail of whatever-had-come-to-hand in his latest binge.

Neither of them talked about anything significant – Jack didn't mention calling Valerie and Sinead didn't talk about Miles. Perhaps, looking back, that was significant in itself. Sinead lit a fire and they sat around it like two old rockers sharing stories of debauchery and devilment from the past. Jack scrapping with Wet Wet Wet at a *Smash Hits* party back in '89. Sinead emerging from the back of Billy Idol's tour bus and pretending to the paparazzi she was his press agent. As they got drunker the conversation got bolder; Sinead trying to get the black dye-rim off Jack's forehead before the *NME* cover shoot after he had taken a chance on dying his hair himself. The two of them rolled around the carpet laughing, remembering the camp make-up artist's face when he saw the rash caused by the nail-varnish remover Sinead had used out of desperation.

'He thought you had fucking scurvy!'

'He should have taken a look at my bollocks – they were in rag order after that Dutch hooker . . .'

In-jokes. Things that only the two of them shared. They felt close like this when they got together – like brother and sister. But it rarely happened when they were alone. And never before when they were both this vulnerable.

In retaliation he brought up the husband-bet.

'Found anyone to marry you yet, you old scrubber?'

Sinead was surprised to find that the question didn't cut her.

'No – well I thought I had but – it didn't work out.'

'Good,' Jack said.

'Ah yeah – you tight bastard!' she joked back.

'No,' he said moving across to sit next to her, 'I mean "good".'

Then he kissed her. He tasted sour, like old beer had turned to sticky vinegar inside him. The sex had felt warped with the wrongness of fraternal curiosity, and once or twice Sinead had wanted to laugh, but at the same time it was strangely comforting to be with someone she had known so long.

When it was over, she had turned away moaning like she was drunker than she was and pretending that it didn't matter. Jack leant into her back, kissed her neck and mumbled, 'Good night Babe'. Sinead lay and wondered whether he knew who she was any more or if he was just replicating his routine for an anonymous fuck. Eventually tiredness and drink had dragged her into the relief of a velvety sleep.

And now the sleep was over and Jack was gone.

She checked her watch. Nine a.m. Shit, and it was barely light outside. She'd have to ring the office. Dizzy. No, she couldn't bear to do that. She sat on the edge of the bed and tried to gather herself. She felt hung-over, but not from the drink. It was an emotional hangover from the shit her life had managed to acquire in less than three short days.

She got dressed, and went into the bathroom to throw a bit of water on her face. Clear of make-up, she was surprised at her reflection. She didn't look as old as she felt.

'Grow up,' she said snarling at herself in the mirror, 'just fucking grow up!'

Downstairs, she found Jack creating a scene of chaos in the kitchen. There were two fags burning on opposite sides of the worktop, a glass of whisky beside one, and he was struggling against a frantically spitting pan of bacon.

'Here,' she said rescuing its red-hot handle from the flames with a tea towel, 'give that to me', and she marched it outside to cool down.

'Barbecue breakfast, yeah?' Jack said when she came back in. He was already slightly tipsy and he had just woken up.

Sinead felt she should say something about last night. Ask something – establish reason, discuss cause and effect. But looking at Jack standing there, his skin mottled, his hair matted with a stripe of white at the roots, his face wrecked – wretched – yet twitching pathetically trying to make himself amused at his own joke, Sinead felt moved to tackle something else entirely.

'You know Jack – you really ought to do something about your drinking.'

Something in the calm way she said it made Jack somehow not able to react. She called a taxi from his phone, and gathered up last night's rubbish while she was waiting. Jack sat down on a chair with his whisky and watched her moving about the large kitchen, gathering up and putting away in that amazing sure-footed way that women have. Seeming always to know what needs to be done even in other people's houses, when Jack was not always certain where his own cutlery drawer was. After fifteen minutes the doorbell rang, and Sinead gathered up her things and left – waving goodbye but not kissing him or making any reference to last night. Perhaps it hadn't happened after all. And if it had, it hardly mattered anyway because Jack Valentine was, in the words of his ex-friend and drinking partner Tommy Grady, well and truly fucked.

PART THREE

AUGUST

24

It was a twenty-four-hour disco fest at Eamonn Doyle's house these days. The few hundred pounds had secured Digger a bedsit in Rathmines; a day job flipping burgers and enough confidence to start hawking his talents around the Dublin club scene. He had sent home for his mixing equipment and clothes, but he barely had room for everything in the damp six-by-nine foot hovel he was paying three hundred punts a month for. As a result, Eamonn had reluctantly agreed to let Digger keep some of his stuff in his unused but converted attic room. Noreen (for she was fully adopted back to her birth name by now) had hung curtains, painted the walls, relocated a sofabed from the conservatory and thrown together a few cushions and rugs. Before Eamonn knew it he had a 'Studio/Den' where his roof once was and, while Digger slept some nights in the bedsit, he had become more-or-less a new tenant. That the daughter Noreen had moved her boy in was no real surprise; the surprise was that Eamonn found himself not minding. He made some pretence at irritation, as was only fitting for a father to do, but his protestations to 'turn the music down' were largely unfounded as both Digger and Noreen were developing a taste for his own music collection. A fact that made him feel both proud as a father and oddly trendy.

That weekend Digger had his first gig, a one-hour slot at Out-Rave-Us which, seemingly was the 'in' place with Dublin youngsters looking for a wild night out.

Noreen and Eamonn had volunteered their judgement to help Digger prepare for his Dublin debut. Noreen was on holiday from college and had persuaded her father to take a couple of days off from work on the grounds that he was working too hard and becoming cranky. An outrageous and unheard of act for the workaholic businessman who was just three weeks into Doyle TV having gone live and well down on his projected sales of the novelty gizmos that the newly sophisticated Irish Public seemed, frankly underwhelmed by. Karin had taken her eye off the ball entirely with *How'ya*, and last month's issue with Ireland's Most Eligible Bachelors had contained a litany of man-hating digs that he felt sure was going to land the company in court. When he had tried pulling her up on it, she had been bitchier than usual and unnecessarily personal using the words 'odious' and 'repugnant' in relation to himself seeming to pitch openly for the sack. Which he would gladly have done except that Eamonn had, of late, somehow acquired a layer of humanity that he found was impeding his professional judgement.

'Is there something wrong Karin – you've seemed out of sorts lately?'

This had sent her into a kanniption of head-spinning rage that was entirely out of proportion with the matter in hand. Aside from the twinge of semi-sexual satisfaction he got out of watching her blow like that, Eamonn was worried about her.

He told Noreen about the incident when he got home, and her prognosis was simple.

'She is probably sexually frustrated. You should sleep with her.'

He was shocked by his daughter's outrageousness.

'Noreen, that's a terrible thing to say!'

'What? It's obvious . . . she wouldn't get away with that carry-on long in France, I can tell you. She'd be slammed over a desk and given a good seeing to pronto, displaying that kind of passionate emotion at work. She's asking for it.'

Eamonn really wished that his daughter didn't feel so comfortable talking to him about sex, or indeed conjuring up such graphic images of the primary object of his own frustrated sexuality with her knickers down. But he was flattered nonetheless.

'I don't think Karin would be interested in anything like that from me now. Anyway – you're my daughter. Stop it with the filthy mouth – you're scaring me!'

But Noreen wasn't letting go. He had been on about this woman since she got there. Nothing definite, just Karin this and Karin that in a regular stream of daily news from the office. She was curious. Her father was, after all, a fabulous fellow, and she wondered that he was still on his own when he so clearly deserved somebody special.

'How do you know. How do you know she doesn't secretly like you? Have you ever asked her? Have you ever tried?'

Eamonn managed a derisive 'Ha!'

'What?'

'She's not interested.'

'How do you know?'

'I asked her out – once or twice – ages ago,' he said in a tiny voice, mortified at the mere memory of the rejection.

'Where? Where did you ask her?'

'To dinner.'

'And?'

'She said "No".'

'Like *how* did she say "no"?'

'She just said no, no, no – all right leave it now, Noreen.'

'Did she say "No" like "I am busy this evening" or "No" like "No – go away! I hate you!" because . . .'

Eamonn was surprised at how upsetting he was finding this conversation.

'Noreen, she thinks I am a "repulsive little man" and an "odious creep" – she told me that this week – now will you just leave it, I am starting to get annoyed.'

'Eh bien! Now we have it – she likes you. She wants

you and you are afraid! It's so Irish! So obvious! Women are complex and Irish men do not understand. This is why you are all still at home making your own egg sandwiches!'

When she felt passionate about something, Noreen tended to come over a bit French. When talking about food, or fashion sometimes. It was an idiosyncrasy that Eamonn had really liked. But in this instance it was infuriating.

'No Noreen – this is different. When an Irish woman says she thinks you are a toad, she means that she thinks that you are a toad. There is no hidden agenda. That's it – c'est tout!'

Finishing his sentence in French was a signal that the conversation was well and truly ended. But later that evening Noreen had talked him into taking a couple of days off, tempting him with a trip to the zoo with herself and Digger – and slipping in later still that it would really help her college course if she could spend a couple of weeks' work placement in the fashion department of *How'ya* magazine. She'd get the measure of this Karin woman and see if *she* was good enough for her Papa!

Digger was testing out one of his favourite pieces of work on his captive audience of two. A catchy little number called 'Get the Feck Out of My Kitchen'. Digger was proud of this track from his *Family Secrets* collection as he felt it represented something of a political statement for the Irish Mammy, containing, as it did, a genuine statement of discontent on behalf of his own mother, whose unmistakable cry was the central lyric.

'Get the fe-fe-fe . . . fe-fe-fe-fe . . . fe-fe-fe . . . fe-fe-fe-fe . . . fe-fe-fe . . . fe-fe-fe-fe-feck out of my kitchen' Mammy Deignan bellowed over a pounding drum and bass.

Five more tracks featuring the underbelly of Irish family life meshed one into the other: 'Has Anyone Seen My Hammer?', 'My Head Is Opened', 'I'm Going For A Pint (Slam Door Remix)', 'Don't Be Bringing Muck In On My Nice Clean Carpet' and the classic and strangely romantic 'If I've Told You Once I've Told You a Thousand Times'.

When the longest forty minutes of Eamonn Doyle's life had finished, Digger looked at father and daughter with a keen look of expectation drawn across his face. Now it was Eamonn's turn to be brave and speak his mind. Noreen was fond of the boy – he didn't want to hurt him.

'It has potential,' he said.

Digger was crushed.

'You don't like it.'

By now, Mr Doyle had become something of a hero to this young man. OK – he wore stay-press slacks and had a comb-over, but Noreen had confided in him that her father's challenging appearance was about to undergo serious improvement by her own fair hand. And that aside, the baldy businessman had the finest collection of disco, soul and funk music the young lad had ever seen. If only his own parents had been such arbiters of musical style and taste.

'It's not that I don't like it . . . it's just that . . . well perhaps I'm just not in tune with today's sounds.'

Eamonn tensed as he saw the two faces of these hopeful youngsters staring at him in unison. His heart went out to them.

'Look,' he said firmly, 'I am not really one to judge. I'm a bit out of touch. Only a listener – not a player. But I do know a man who might be able to work with you on this.'

Noreen could only half hope that she knew where he was coming from.

'Not . . . not . . .?'

'Yes honey. I think this young man certainly has enough promise to bring the Legend over to his side.'

Noreen beamed and in that moment Digger knew everything was going to be all right.

'Not . . . the Devil Daddy Himself?'

'The next best thing my love – Mr Aloysius Moses – the King of the Crosscarney Disco Sound.'

Eamonn punched Al's number into the phone and after a few pertinent questions to establish any possible gaps in his executive friend's collection – 'We've Got The Funk?' 'Got that.' 'Hot Pants?' 'Got that.' 'Brick House?' 'The Commodores?' 'That's the one!' 'Better bring it with you.' He grabbed his Emergency Disco Kit and caught the first bus to Dublin.

How'ya was a mess, Doyle TV was struggling – but Eamonn Doyle still felt that this was the best day's work he had done in a long time.

25

Barry Hooker's life was not going according to plan. That is, if he had taken the trouble to think things out properly instead of following his mad notions about living in romantic Ireland and then falling in love with a woman who was the daughter of a woman in a picture he found under his father's bed three decades ago, he might at least have some class of a plan around which to judge his life.

But he didn't.

In any case, Barry Hooker had never dealt in plans. He had built his life around four simple rules. Be Irish. Work hard. Meet girl. Be happy. Back home (for already, he was starting to think of Australia as 'home'), the first three were eminently achievable and the fourth therefore inevitable.

But here, in Ireland, the foundations upon which his generally cheery outlook were built had started to crumble; his rules for life somehow twisting into a nasty, complicated version of themselves.

– Be Irish. In Australia all you needed was Irish

parents – or grandparents – and a T-shirt with a Guinness logo. Such was Barry's unshakeable belief in himself as a true Celt, he had taken his Irishness to the limit, accepting chairmanship of the Shamrock Surfing Club five years in a row and ditching the overly Australian greeting 'G'day' in favour of 'Slan'. He was deeply attached to his Irish roots, and from them enjoyed a firm sense of security and identity. It was part of who he was. Irony not being high on Barry's list of intellectual skills, he was therefore puzzled and perturbed by the fact that, now that he was actually living in his cherished homeland, people saw him only as Australian. At first he had protested, 'Actually I'm Irish' – but on more than one occasion he had found it landing him in the centre of heated political discussions about the reunification of Ireland. Did he agree with it? Was he a supporter of the IRA? Was he one of these misguided Plastic Paddys who did whip-rounds in Sydney pubs for NORAID? Barry just wanted to belong. Wanted people to like him, but he never imagined it would be this complicated or this hard. He knew the words to 'Danny Boy' and he kind of figured that would carry him through. How wrong he had been. There was a whole lot more to being Irish than he had thought, and he wasn't sure he wanted it any more. One afternoon he had heard one cameraman say to another 'Whoever heard of an Irishman called "Hooker"?' and it had cut right through him with the decapitating trauma of defeat.

– Work hard. Enough said. Barry had not realized how many unspoken conditions had been attached to that one thing. Back home he was happy to work hard because he was earning lots of money, had his own make-up artist, hairdresser, sympathetic producers, sunny assistants, inspirational sets, and thousands – millions – of happy, grateful, adoring viewers. At Doyle TV everything was make-do and cardboard and he had to work like a skivvy for less money than he had ever dreamed possible in the shiny spangly world of TV. In fact, the only ray of hope was that he had managed to secure a job there for Valerie as his co-presenter. 'She is beautiful, charming, intelligent,' he had told Eamonn Doyle, 'and I need somebody.' No four things were ever as true, and no facts had ever been turned around on their heads so thoroughly by such mean twists of fate.

If his yen for the love of this perfect woman had been panning out well, Barry might have been better able to put up with all the rest. But then, if everything else had been going well, Barry might have had more confidence to be able to push his feelings for Valerie Valentine through to some kind of a pleasurable conclusion. But where once Barry would have leapt right in there with the boldness of a dishy national hero, he found that his strong feelings for her were trapped in a tight impenetrable knot in his stomach which he was unable to unravel sufficiently to even ask her out for dinner – or tell her she had lovely hair – or eyes – or any of the basic requirements for letting a lady know that you like her in that special way that men sometimes do. Two other things were also standing in his way, and Barry was further confused and paralysed by the fact that they were possibly, also, of his own making. First, she thought he was a homosexual and secondly she liked him as a 'friend'. Concerned that she might think him unfriendly, stand-offish, or worse, homophobic, he had made a great show of telling Valerie what a thoroughly nice chap he thought her friend Bernard was. He now realized, of course, that he had gone right over the top by saying that they had had a 'lovely, *lovely* evening' and that he 'really, *really* liked him', when what he *should* have said was, 'I'm not a homosexual – you have lovely hair/eyes – please may I take you out for dinner.'

In retrospect, as always, it seemed to be too late. The damage was done. Thinking that Barry was heartbroken over Bernard's rejection of him, sweet-hearted Valerie began to console him with gifts of Karmic massages with a truly terrifying woman called Tinara (whom he was fairly sure did *not* think he was homosexual and had started to become, frankly, a little heavy handed with the Aura Oil), and lovely cheery 'boys' blouses' which he felt obliged to wear for fear of offending her, but whose puffy sleeves and diaphanous fabrics left no doubt in the mind *whatsoever* as to the sexual preferences of the wearer. As a result of his new image, and the recent on-air launch of *Shop A.M.*, he had become something of a gay cult icon and could not walk into any bar in Dublin without being subjected to all kinds of secret belt-looping, knee-pointing, eye-widening signals that he was neither equipped, nor inclined to understand. Valerie, in her new capacity as his (very) platonic best friend was only too keen to point out the ones that were interested in him and the ones that, in her capacity as his (very, very) platonic friend, she felt he should be responding to. All of this was in between her telling him about her ex-husband, a man who sounded to the clean-living Australian ingénu like the devil incarnate and a satanic force whom she seemed almost keen to get back to. Being with Valerie was not, however, completely without its emotional benefits. She said she had never had a friend like him before. He was a wonderful listener. He had wonderful hair – and eyes actually. That he need not be ashamed to wear flamboyant see-through clothes because he certainly had the body for it, given in her professional opinion as an ex-model of course. She had never felt able to talk to anyone before in the way that she talked to him. She could tell that he was a kind and 'special' person and she was grateful to him for getting her the job in television and being her friend. When Valerie said nice things to him like that, Barry felt that she liked him and, briefly, he would enjoy a glimmer of hope that things might work out. Then she would say that the whole reason she liked him so much was that he was gay. That straight men were always only after one thing from her and that she couldn't trust them. Barry would freeze then thinking about how he had the pillows arranged in his bed so that he could imagine her warm body lying next to his at night. About the picture of her mother he kept in his wallet, and about how he had told her it was just something he had found stuck into a second-hand book he had bought that day – and wasn't it a coincidence that the woman looked like her. When Valerie had seen it, she had cried a little, and asked if she could keep it. He had felt like a cheap liar – and that's what he was. What he had become. Nothing but a cheap weak liar! With his pretending to be a homosexual to keep her as a friend, and his not asking her out for dinner or telling her she had lovely hair and eyes and his pretending his pillows were her and his not exposing himself as the hot-blooded, filthy minded rampant *heterosexual* that he really was.

Barry hated himself. Hated what he was becoming. The lovely hair and the smart clothes – small things that he had always taken pride in, had taken on a sinister new meaning. Irish? He wasn't Irish at all – everyone here said so. Even Valerie said it was 'nice' to hang out with someone who was 'different from the rest'. Barry used to be sure of who he was, proud of who he was – light-hearted, honest, open – living life without shame or fear. But Ireland had changed him. Barry Hooker was beginning to think that perhaps it wasn't worth it after all. He was thinking that it was time to go home.

26

Sinead was waiting for Karin in the Horseshoe Bar in the Shelbourne Hotel on a Friday night. Both women had suggested it simultaneously as a meeting place to discuss their impending birthday plans and as Sinead sat on a leather bench guarding a seat for her friend in the packed smoky atmosphere of after-work reverie, the subconscious desperation of their choice rose through her in a wave of depression. The bar was dimly lit, but not dimly enough.

The women all wore too much make-up and matching separates in pastel colours that set Irish fashion right back to eighties Britain. The look was Brassy Classy, and their unconvincing yak-yak laughter skidded around the room with the tuneless note of trying too hard. At best, the men were Dublin's divorced and separateds. At worst, they identified themselves as separated for this one night only while their temporarily estranged wives curled up in front of *The Late Late Show* after an afternoon bawling with the au pair over their definition of 'light housework'. Status here was judged on racehorses, golf-handicaps and the all-round congratulatory smugness of the middle-class, middle-aged South County professional. Tonight the men hoped to add the fumbly grope of a bit of fresh tit to their list of triumphs. The women weren't looking for much more than that, or glory upon glory, they might get lucky and net the last live single male in Dublin. Warm and still breathing was about the strength of it. In here at least the lights were low, and they could be assured that the men had a few bob floating around. The Prince of Wales checked blazers and the BMW keys flung on the oak bar laid testament to that. Plus, you could always get a seat, and on a Friday night in Dublin, that was a valid consideration. There was always some fat sleazeball ready to unplug a barstool from the heaving cheek of his sweaty arse to make room for a 'lady'. A lady who, hopefully, would put out for half a dozen vodka martinis and the assertion that she didn't 'look a day over thirty!'

Sinead was grateful for the small mercy that at least she had not chosen to sit at the bar and was therefore a silent witness to and not an active participant in the circus of middle-aged loneliness.

With her fortieth birthday just over a month away, the terrible irony was not lost on Karin either. She signalled to Sinead as she entered and went straight to the bar. No less than three wobbling beer bellies moved aside to let this cool blonde in business suit and heels through the heaving bar-mash. As she ordered, sausage-like fingers fiddled with keys and wallets trying to come up with a suitable opening line to engage her company.

'Jesus, but you're a fine-lookin' woman,' some bloated accountant muttered after her.

'Piss off!' she unceremoniously snapped at him as she weaved her way over to Sinead. This really was the pits. What the fuck had she and Sinead been thinking coming to this place. When you started cruising the Horseshoe on a Friday night you really were five miles clear of the last gas station; the stuff of modern women's fiction; a desperado hitching a ride in the hope that they might take you somewhere safe.

A less glamorous and more pathetic collection of golfing hogs Karin had never seen before in her life. She had never found the Horseshoe more offensive than she found it tonight, and it was undoubtedly because she was nearing the age-bracket for this market. This was hopeless. There were no men in Dublin. God knows she had spent the last few weeks looking. To find those that were left you had to come *here* – to their swirling beer trough – and pick them out like abandoned pets at the dog pound.

How'ya's Eligible Bachelor List had been Karin's last-ditch attempt to find somebody before her fortieth and cash in on Jack's offer. Three closet homos and an octogenarian trying to pass himself off as fifty-nine later she had finally given up. The whole project, she now realized, had been a pathetic attempt to keep the impending bitterness of her middle age at bay. A last little ray of hope that perhaps this side road might lead her back onto the big successful highway of life she had set out on. She realized that it was pointless now. Soon, she would be forty, single, living in a shoebox and in a shallow ridiculous job she would be obliged to stay in until she was dead. It was only a matter of time before she became a mad-lipsticked powdery parody of herself and had to be pensioned off for wearing hats to work and calling herself 'The Grande Dame of Irish Society'.

Where were the pretty boys? The chiselled entrepreneurs, the tweedy academics, the barristers she thought she'd be able to reel in when the lights came up on her thirty-something party and it was time to find someone to go home with?

Sinead cut in on her thoughts.

'They're elsewhere – being gay.'

'You think I don't know that?' Karin snapped back.

'Oh yeah. Sorry.'

Karin looked down mournfully at her G&T and wished she had ordered five more to save her going back up to the bar.

'I should have moved to New York years ago.'

'I should never have left London,' Sinead joined in.

'I'd be editing *Vanity Fair* by now.'

'Head of Sony for sure.'

'Living in the Hamptons in a Fuck-Off Greystone.'

'Pad in Chelsea – co-hosting benefits with Elton.'

'Wardrobe of designer samples from my best mate Donna.'

Sinead joined in this game with Karin, but she didn't have the conviction for regrets. Not really. But then she had her own house and business. She wasn't as desperate as Karin. She regretted having slept with Jack Valentine, but she had not been able to find a way of telling anyone about it, not even Karin. She was kind of waiting until things had settled down although, again, she wasn't quite sure why or how that worked. That was the thing about Jack. He was chaos – always had been. His pleasure-seeking ego was so big that he never even saw all the mess he left behind. That was why Sinead had never slept with him before. Because she knew that somehow it would become complicated. Perhaps that was why it had taken all these years for the inevitable accident of a drunken tumble to happen. It had taken the abandonment of a recently broken heart for Sinead to be careless enough to let it happen. Immediately afterwards she had felt strangely strong and assertive. As soon as she had got back to Dublin she had found Tommy's parents' number in the phone book, and contacted him. They had briefly discussed Jack's drinking, and she had suggested the time might be right for him to step in. A week later, Tommy rang her and said that Jack was in a treatment centre in the South of England, and would be in there for at least five weeks. Sinead was pleased something was being done, but she was also relieved. That was the end of it for the time being. Something crazy that had happened through drink, and while he was locked away over there, nobody need know it ever happened, although he'd be out any day now. Sinead knew she was just putting things of. That the story wasn't fully ended yet.

Karin was only getting started.

'The thing about New York is, it's a Cosmopolitan City. Dublin? This shit kip's only a fucking Provincial

Town. Look at this place – crawling with fucking cul-
chies. Where's the sophistication? Where's the excitement? Where's the glamour?'

Sinead nodded in agreement, although she knew it
was entirely arbitrary whether she did or not. Karin was
on a roll. She had seen her like this before. Tinara labelled
such behaviour as 'victim' mode, and so would Sinead
have done if she thought she would have survived such
a comment. At times like this, however, Sinead and Karin
pretended to be the same for the other's sake. Karin
leched alongside Sinead over young lads in tight trousers
even though the idea of their boyish hairless bodies made
her feel slightly sick, and Sinead joined in with the bitter
mag-hag diatribes as if they were her own. They both
needed someone to partner their insecurities about themselves as women who had managed to get to forty
without acquiring, accidentally or otherwise, a husband.

In one such conversation some years ago that had
taken place during a dry patch in the three friends'
thirties, Sinead and Karin had declared Valerie exempt
from the failure of true singledom. From the position
of still having enough hope to sit around and discuss
their romantic prospects openly, talk had come around
to that 'hope I die 'fore I get old' topic – at what age
must a single woman put her hands up to the poverty of
spinsterhood.

'Forty,' Sinead and Karin agreed, but Valerie was not
so quick to set targets.

'Age is all a state of mind,' she had offered, 'I don't
think you should expect less love as you get older.'

Sometimes when Karin and Sinead got onto their power-of-negative thinking, I'm-a-tough-bitch, self-deprecation program, Valerie's little pearls of loveliness seemed irritatingly trite.

'Yeah well, that's coming from the luxurious standpoint of a teenage bride/divorcee,' Karin had snapped.

'That's right – having been married and failed is a whole different thing to having never even been asked.'

Valerie was deeply ashamed of the fact that her marriage hadn't worked out. And while there was some comfort in her friends presenting it as a positive thing that she had been married at all, the memory of it always made her feel small and worried. This tough talk seemed to shock the innocent Valerie, but somewhere underneath the batting eyelashes and the 'oh-deary-me' coyness, she hung out with these two women because they said the things she didn't dare think, but deep down hoped were true.

'So how many times have you been asked for your hand Karin?' asked Sinead with biting affected curiosity.

'Oooh – I don't know – let me see – ' she held up her hand to count – 'ah yes – none! And you Sinead?'

'Ooh well now that's a tricky one – pass me the calculator there Karin till I tot them all up and hey! what do you know? A sum total of Nil!'

Then the two women turned on the deliciously strawberry blonde.

'Valerie?'

She was smiling now – lapping it up. They used to make her feel so good, building her up while they put themselves down. It was a game. She envied their swagger and their intelligence, and they envied her beauty. All the insecurities and hang-ups out on the table so they could play around with each other – knowing nothing they said could ever really hurt.

'Six times,' she finally said with reluctance.

'Seven, you bitch! Don't discount the Arab horse dealer just because he had a few wives already. He still counts.'

But Valerie wasn't here tonight in the Horseshoe. Sinead felt awkward about having slept with Jack, especially after Valerie had called asking her to step in as his friend the very morning after she had been with him. She had felt a twinge of jealousy too that Jack had been onto Valerie beforehand. She had always known that Jack had never really let go of Valerie and it irritated her now that she seemed involuntarily bothered by that fact. She had only slept with him, and it felt petty to care that he was in love with somebody else. Especially somebody whom she considered a friend. And as for Karin? Well Karin was so utterly absorbed in herself these days that the phone conversations with Valerie about her losing the business had kind of grated. She knew it was bad, but somehow no one was allowed to be having a worse time than her at the moment, and by the time she had found a little window in her self-pity to make room for Valerie's problems, the vulnerable blonde had already got herself a job at Doyle TV, was knocking around with that Aussie Nancy – Eamonn's new golden boy, and was very possibly earning more money than her. It didn't bear thinking about at the moment, so Karin didn't – think about it or Valerie, or anything much except for how hard-done-by she was and what a thoroughly hateful and insufferably shite life lay ahead for her forties and fifties and sixties and . . . Forty! Forty! Forty! How was it fucking possible she had got to this age and was still . . . still . . . still . . . oh everything and fucking nothing! That she was still having to *try*. That she wasn't there – *there* – wherever it was she should be there by now and she wasn't.

If Valerie was shouldering Karin virtually ignoring her at work with her usual forgiving generosity, and Sinead was humouring her dark moods, Karin was getting bored listening to herself complaining. It was like she had a nagging mother living rent-free in her head these days. Telling her she was a failure. Telling her she was a nasty hard-nosed person. Telling her she wasn't good enough. Telling her there were plenty of perfectly nice middle-aged men out there if only she would cut her coat according to her cloth instead of rushing about looking for someone that was, frankly, beyond her means and tying them down to an unrealistic date. In the past few days the brain-tenant Mammy had been going on at her twenty-four-seven, coming up with all manner of new criticisms that made Karin feel like perhaps she was bordering on the psychotic. Look at the state of your draining board – when was the last time that scrap of metal saw a sprinkling of Ajax? Another bottle of wine in here on your own is it? Friends sick of listening to you are they? I'm not surprised – you were always a boring whingey little bitch. Man? You? Oh – excuse me – a *husband* no less is it? The way you're carrying on you'd be lucky to get mounted by the neighbour's dog!

On and on and on – moaning and complaining and giving out stink to herself. The only relief she had from it was sitting here and giving out to Sinead about how she should have moved to New York and how it had all gone horribly wrong for her until – the final straw. A happening so deadly, so humiliating; an ego-crushing truism the irony of which was impossible to escape.

Across the smoky bar of the Shelbourne was Eamonn Doyle. That he raised his glass and threw her a big friendly wink was in itself, given the mood she was in, insufferable. But the irritation that Karin felt by her boss's mere existence on the planet, and therefore the inevitability of his turning up after hours, was not insurmountable. No – what totally threw the cat in the mangle was the fact that he was not alone. By his side – in fact clinging to his side – was a young and extremely attractive young woman who, even in this dimly lit pit Karin could clearly see was looking at him with an expression of undisguised admiration and devotion.

Sinead misunderstood her friend's silence and temporary closure of 'The Complaints Department' to mean that she was ready to talk about their joint birthday plans.

'Right – now where are we going to go out in style and have a great big bash then?'

But Karin had had enough. She had gone beyond it now. Into the realms of so enormously annoyed, that she really did not have the resources to accommodate actual expression of same. Eamonn Doyle and a beautiful young girl. It was too much. So too much that it shocked her into a kind of clear-mindedness.

'You know what?' she said to Sinead, gathering up her coat and bag, 'I'm going to just leave it for tonight. This whole business about turning forty and the husband thing, it's kind of . . . My head is fucked, I've got to go.'

Sinead walked out with her and they went their separate ways at the door. As she watched her friend's frail body press against the wind, her high heels perilously clipping along the wet pavement, Sinead felt a wave of pity for the unhappiness that she had seen in Karin tonight. Under all the vicious mouthy nonsense, she knew she was having a really hard time – fighting something big inside her. What Sinead did not know was that Karin was done losing. As she trotted towards her Ballsbridge shoebox, the feisty mag hag had gathered her troops for the final conclave. The war for Mr Wonderful was lost, but a whole new infantry of deadly paramilitary forces had formed in its wake. The conquering careerist was emerging and her target was suddenly blindingly obvious. One Mr Eamonn Doyle.

27

'Good Morning Ireland – no . . . *cough* . . . G'day . . . *ehem* . . . G'Day Ireland – and have we got lots of treats in store for you this . . . Jimmy? Is this OK? My tie? Is it buzzing on screen?'

It was sixty seconds to air and Barry was just warming up. Doyle TV budgets did not stretch to a wardrobe department and so Valerie had volunteered herself as Barry's dresser as well as co-host. This morning he was wearing a pink shot-silk shirt and a boldly patterned monochrome op-art tie which he was, correctly, concerned would appear on screen like a moving hologram. By the time the sleepy floor-manager realized that Barry's loud accoutrement had taken on a life of its own, they were already on air and the tie's pattern was wriggling up and down and across the patch of chest it occupied in a way that would make the hardiest of viewer sea-sick – never mind at eight o'clock in the morning!

'Six-five-four-' three, two, one were mouthed silently to accompanying fingers and the camera panned across the DTV/sunshine logo and over to Barry and Valerie sitting across from each other on the *Shop A.M.* sofa.

'Good morning Ireland – welcome to *Shop A.M.* – and boy what a wonderful morning it is out there today, Valerie?'

'Certainly is a beautiful morning, Barry.'

They had both risen at six a.m. to persistent drizzle from the night before, but Barry was killing time as the studio runner seemed to have forgotten that he had to sneak the first product of the day onto the *Shop A.M.* coffee table while the camera wasn't looking.

Close, up, Barry.

'Still – every morning is a sunshine morning with *Shop A.M.* and here in the studio we certainly have some fantastic items lined up for our lucky viewers, eh Valerie?'

The autocue had already started rolling on Valerie's first item – but the item itself, a revolutionary unwanted hair removal system – was nowhere to be seen. Instead a pot of coffee and a plate of croissants had been hurriedly plonked in front of them.

'Wow – you can say that again Barry. I know I am certainly looking forward to presenting to our viewers some of the wonderful things we have on offer today and I believe you have some wonderful things too . . . em . . . to present to our viewers? Barry?'

Valerie was lost without the autocue to guide her. Once she had the product in front of her, she could ramble on about it ad nauseum, driven along by the vocational zest she had for each of the beauty/fashion based nonsenses she was selling. But when it came to pure personality-telly, Valerie was no match for her old-pro co-presenter.

Without taking his eyes off the camera for a second, Barry could sense Valerie's bottom lip quivering and the coffee and croissants still sitting on the table in front of him. It was his job to rescue his damsel from the distress of an autocue breakdown babble-ogue, and save the show.

'Valerie – before we start the show – may I just say how lovely you are looking this morning?'

Valerie loved when he did this. Engaged her in no-pressure TV chit-chat. He was such a professional – the way he could switch like that, and she always knew it was leading to him somehow bringing the whole thing together.

'Why thank you, Barry.'

'And I know our viewers will be asking themselves the same question that I am asking myself right now – Valerie? Have you done something to your hair?'

'Actually no, Barry – it is just the same as usual.'

'Well it must be just the miracle of you managing to look lovelier each day.'

Valerie allowed herself a little head-cocking laugh and a brief 'Well thank you, Barry'. Then he was straight in for the kill.

'But while we're on the subject of hair, Valerie, I know that you women sometimes have problems with your hair – and I'm not talking about the hair on your head!'

There he was! Saving the day! All Valerie had to do was follow his lead.

'That's right, Barry. This morning we are going to be tackling the very serious problem of unwanted hair.'

Still the croissants and coffee were stagnant on the table at his knees. If Valerie could take a hint, the floor manager was obviously still half asleep. Barry had to get his attention.

'And there's a *very special product*, isn't there Valerie – a revolutionary new system designed to help people get rid of their unwanted hair. So viewers can I invite you to *finish* your breakfast,' – no sign of runner – 'your *coffee and croissants* or whatever you start your day with,' – a bit of hand waving from the floor manager – 'while Valerie introduces *Zap-O-Fluff*' – frantic scurrying across studio of runner – 'a revolutionary new system' – runner desperately rummaging through pile of products to identify correct one – 'in a beautiful *aqua-green* presentation box that is about the size of *a computer screen*,' – runner grabs box and careers across floor towards set – 'and that, once *you've finished your breakfast*,' – floor manager rugby slides floor and removes breakfast tray out of shot – 'the really lovely Valerie, who really, can I just say again, is looking particularly lovely this morning in her beautiful lilac two-piece,' – tray gone product in place – 'will be delighted to tell you *all* about.'

Despite the false-start, the show went reasonably well after that. Several people rang in about the hallucinogenic effects of Barry's tie on screen, and he changed it during the first commercial break, even alluding to it briefly in a little joke when they came back. A woman from Kerry also rang in to ask where Valerie had purchased her lilac two-piece, also commenting that in fact, her hair did look particularly lovely today. They sold a respectable number of the Zap-O-Fluff units, several Wakey Wakey teasmakers, five sock darning units which looked rather like something a Dutch family-planning tutor might use to teach teenagers how to apply condoms, and the switchboard was still jammed with orders for 'The Scientifically Approved Skin Transmogrification System' which promised over a ten day period to turn the most hoary old hag into a teenage Top of the Popster in just 'twelve easy steps'.

Given that the last few weeks since they had been on air had been, in Eamonn Doyle's unmitigated opinion 'a fucking disaster' sales-wise – all in all it had been a good morning's work.

Valerie and Barry were enjoying a mutual admiration moment in the café next door to the studio.

'No, Valerie, the highlight for me was the way you handled that sock – you really let the viewers see close up how accurate the darning was. I mean it, Valerie – you have the nicest hands of any woman presenter I have ever worked with. Really. It's a crime we're not doing jewellery. I'm having a chat with Eamonn next week. With hands like those 9-Carat Gold-Plated Six-Piece Claddagh Sets would be flying out the door!'

'Barry – you are so sweet. I really thought I was going

to lose it earlier on when the Zap-O-Fluff didn't show, but you are such an experienced host, you just turned the whole thing around without taking your eyes off camera – I don't know how you do it!'

During moments like these, when he saw Valerie looking up at him with those batting blue eyes of her, Barry almost believed that things would work out. Then he would catch hold of himself – remember that he was wearing a pink shirt whose shiny fabric could comfortably be recycled as a Barbara Cartland chihuahua cushion, and that the platonic nature of their friendship was the very thing that allowed Valerie to say inflammatory things to him like how he had lovely hair and the like. Oh, how Barry Hooker longed for Valerie to say he had lovely hair in a 'please may I run my fingers through it and give you a big kiss to boot' kind-of-a-way rather than a 'you have lovely hair, what shampoo did you use this morning' way. In his pocket Barry could feel the wallet that held his ticket back to Australia in four weeks' time burn against his breast. He had bought it in a fit of depression after Valerie had tried to set him up with an interior designer who was, rather disturbingly, called Nylon and who had approached her before Rouge closed looking for a job.

'Oh don't be like that Barry . . .' she had pleaded with him after he groaned at the invitation, 'Nylon may be a bit of a run-around but that's only for the want of the love of a good man.'

'Let me be the good man who loves *you* then!' he longed to cry. But such a rousing declaration would not, he knew be convincing from a man who had been emasculated to the point of wearing neck-kerchiefs fashioned from expensive ladies' scarves. In her willingness to please him as a friend, with each new gift Valerie was pushing him further away towards Australia where a flicky hairstyle, a clean appearance and an open friendly manner were merely components of a successful TV persona as opposed to an open invitation for homosexual activity. Barry knew that as the months went on, the friendship between Valerie and himself would grow and deepen, and with it the lie that went with it. He knew that he should, of course, be more of a man about it all. Cast aside the flimsy blouses and the appliquéd jackets, declare his love for her openly – throw caution to the wind and gather her into his arms; a he-man trouser pressing clinch leaving her in no doubt whatsoever as to his intention and sexuality. But the truth was, every time he was in her company Barry was as weak as a kitten. This friendship, this dressing him up as a pansy and fixing him up with her lonely male friends was what she wanted. What she needed. She had more or less told him so. So powerless was Barry in the face of his truest love, that all he wanted was for Valerie to be happy. In his capacity as her new best gay friend he was able to do that. But he knew, as his very trouser content was telling him as he watched her full, glossy lips suck back the last strawful of her frozen cappuccino, that this game could not go on forever. If he didn't move away soon, the forces of nature would take over, and who knows what hideous masculine wrath he might be driven to subject this delicately feminine flower to. He had four more weeks, then he would go home to Sydney. It was for the best.

Valerie's mobile rang, and mouthing 'excuse me' she went outside to get a better signal. Barry spotted that nice little Noreen from the *How'ya* office whom he'd shared a coffee with last week. She was in their offices doing some work on the magazine's fashion pages, and had come over to the studio to ask if he would participate in a spread they were doing on menswear for Autumn/Winter. She said that she had picked him out as one of the most stylishly dressed men she had seen since she moved to Ireland from Paris. 'It is so refreshing to see a man who has the courage to wear pink!' she had said, and by now adept at reading when people were taking the mickey out of his clothes (his wardrobe was the source of some amusement for the DTV cameramen), he was relieved to see that she actually meant it. Anxious not to be made even more of an experimental exhibition of by yet another fashion-obsessed female, Barry had politely explained that he was more of a Spring/Summer man himself, but they had had a lovely chat anyway – and he had been, frankly, relieved not to be in the company of a woman who did not talk about other men in terms of their being a potential love interest for him. He had just asked Noreen to join him for coffee when Valerie came back in. Barry knew instantly that something terrible had happened. He also had little doubt as to the source of her distress, although she had relayed to him, with some delight, that her ex-husband was currently residing in an alcohol rehabilitation centre in the UK. He had been pleased for Valerie as she had seemed so happy that Jack was 'getting his act together', but also miserable at the prospect of his coming home 'a new man' and winning her back. A turn of events that was sure to happen. Not having Valerie was bad enough, but seeing her walk into the arms of another was something he wanted to be on the other side of the world for.

'That was Jack,' she said.

'Is he all right?' asked Barry, secretly praying that the answer was 'No – he's dead.'

'Oh, he's fine, due out in a few days. Part of his treatment is to face up to bad things that he's done and he put me first on the list.'

Barry couldn't understand why she hadn't been on the phone longer. By the sounds of it, the man had plenty to apologize for.

'What did he say?'

'Blah blah blah – sorry for being a bad husband etc . . .' That didn't sound too bad, 'Oh and that five weeks ago, he slept with my best friend Sinead.'

Barry knew how much her friends meant to Valerie.

'Valerie, I'm sorry . . .'

'You've nothing to be sorry for, Barry.' And her eyes started to fill up and she grabbed her jacket and bag saying, 'I've got to go now – I'll see you tomorrow.'

Barry wanted to follow her and somehow help her make it all right. But the truth was, he wasn't enough of a friend to know what to say. He wasn't a lover and, when push came to shove, he couldn't really rally on the tougher issues like an old friend would. So he just sat there, looking at his coffee and trying out an apologetic smile on the young stranger Noreen.

Alone, awkward and Australian. Things couldn't get much worse than this.

28

Karin had not been one bit impressed with Eamonn foisting his under-age girlfriend on her for a few weeks' work experience on *How'ya* magazine. Aside from the generic irritation that women of a 'certain age' feel when men in their own market-place (even the scraggy leftover ones which they don't want) get snapped up by the younger generation, there were a number of other reasons why Noreen's presence in her office was unwanted.

Noreen was uncommonly pretty and quite bright. Had she been some class of a tragic throwback with pimples and the ungainly demeanour of a needy, abused child in desperate need of a bit of affection, Karin might have found the fact of her relationship with Eamonn easier to stomach. As it was, she was confident and charming.

Eamonn had introduced her appointment as a fait accompli, saying nothing about the fact that he was obviously riding her. In fairness, there was no way Karin would have known this if she had not seen them mooning over each other together in the Horseshoe that time – but still, he might have at least acknowledged that

Karin was doing *him* a favour rather than implying it was the other way around by saying he knew that this inexperienced young woman would be 'an invaluable help'.

It turned out that, by the end of Morning One, Noreen had already proved herself to be 'an invaluable help'. She had reorganized the filing system, set up an interview and events diary – and done all of it with a cheery pragmatism that appeared sensibly oblivious to Karin's snappy tactics.

Since the night of the last hopers experience with Sinead, Karin had decided that she was going to take her career in hand. She had taken the verve with which she had approached her recent husband-hunting endeavours and was using it to formulate some sort of a new publishing venture that would rival Doyle's miserable publications and secure a decent future for herself. This plan for world-domination however was still very much at the germinating stage, and a perky Doyle spy looking enthusiastically over her shoulder at every turn was not helping its progression.

All of the above were culminating in a nasty suspicion in Karin's mind that perhaps – only *perhaps* mind you – she had underestimated Eamonn Doyle's intelligence. Worse again was the niggling fear that perhaps there was some modicum of attractiveness there that she had missed? The mere suggestion that the one-eyed-imp whom she had so often, and so thoroughly, reviled might have some kind of albeit well-hidden depth in the attractiveness-to-females department was both distracting and extremely annoying.

It was therefore with a substantial measure of begrudgery that, at the end of Noreen's first week Karin was forced to growl her approval at the young girl's performance, and ask if she was free to come in the following week. Karin had double-booked herself and needed somebody to oversee one of Ronnie's photoshoots. Noreen was astonished and delighted to be given such a challenge so early on, but Karin was quick to bring her back down to earth.

'This is Ireland, honey – and we are not operating on a fucking *Hello* budget. Doyle is as tight as a fly's hole – it's either you or the cleaning lady who gets a crack at it, so don't get above yourself and go thinking I'm giving you a big opportunity or anything.'

It would be safe to say that Karin's behaviour towards Noreen that week had not screamed 'lovable step mom', but nonetheless, Eamonn's determined daughter was not going to be deterred. Karin was obviously under a great deal of pressure to get this magazine out, virtually single-handed – aside from which she was stylish, intelligent and her father liked her. Quite why, Noreen had yet to find out. But she felt confident enough that, in time, she could be won round. As she had recently discovered with her own estranged parent – things were not always as cut and dried as they seemed. Perhaps getting Karin out of the office environment might be a start.

'Do you fancy going out for a quick drink?'

Karin was utterly taken aback by the front of the child. She was sitting at her desk while Noreen stood behind her in a trim, fitted black coat that was frankly, irritatingly covetous and expensive looking. No doubt a gift from her sugar daddy.

'What do you mean?' Karin swivelled around and looked her up and down rudely.

'Well – it's Friday. That's what people do here, isn't it. Go out for a drink after work?'

Such was the innocent look of keen willingness on her new assistant's face that Karin felt she had to turn her head back to her computer screen before uttering a reserved.

'No thank you.'

Weird kid – go home.

'Oh – I just thought it would be nice to go and get to know each other a bit better. You've seemed a little, well, tense this week.'

Tense? *Tense?* She'd give the cheeky bitch tense!

Karin swivelled again, and anchored herself with a precisely placed stiletto before standing up to eye-ball Noreen with the icy stare she normally reserved for late motorcycle couriers and incompetent subordinates in general.

'Oh really?'

Noreen was infuriatingly undeterred.

'Yes – and actually, I was wondering if you had some sort of a problem with my being here?'

Given the circumstances, this understatement was delivered with such steady authenticity that Karin was temporarily discombobulated.

'A problem?' Being met with the steady gaze of this child suddenly brought it all to a head. The fucking unimaginable nerve of the little slut.

'Well – yes, actually you could say that I do have just a little bit of problem.'

It was head to head now. Ding for Round One of Ego Cat Fight.

'Oh really? Well, perhaps if you tell me what it is we can clear the air.'

'Well, how about this for starters. Your relationship with my boss. Contrary to what you might think – it does not exactly serve as a reference!'

Thwack – Noreen falls – temporary wound lick – up again.

'Well, I'm not exactly getting paid a fortune to work for you and I think I've put in more than my money's worth . . .'

Thwack – Karin staggers but only temporarily stunned.

'Paid? *Paid!* You're getting *paid* for this. I was told you were on work experience. Work experience do not get fucking paid! How much are you getting?'

Noreen backed into corner. Must tactic her way out.

'Eamonn asked me not to say that . . .'

Karin steams in for victory.

'The conniving cunt! How dare he show such blatant

fucking nepotism – the ugly baldy one-eyed fuck – I'll tell you something but I'll be straight into his office on Monday . . .'

But Karin's last final blow proves clumsy and ill-advised. It riles her adversary no end, and turns this into something personal. Noreen with truly balletic skill slides out of corner and in a crafted defensive/offensive move throws her final, winning punch.

'Actually Karin – given my relationship with Mr Doyle, I really don't think it's a very good idea to talk about him with such disrespect. At the end of the day – he *is* your boss.'

Noreen was the victor. Karin slayed into silence. This little cow was not worth losing her job over. When she had her plan for international publishing domination complete; when she had moved to New York and become editor of *Vanity Fair* – then she could put the boot in. In the meantime, however, she had a mortgage to pay – fuck, damn and blast it – and this manipulative strap was smart enough to get her fired.

'So how about that drink then?' Noreen said with a sunny smile that made Karin smart with defeat.

It is astonishing how the arduous battle for seats in an ordinary city-centre Dublin pub, coupled with the feisty fobbing off of a few drunken advances and several vodka and tonics can bond two arguing women.

Less than an hour after they had locked horns, Karin and Noreen had mellowed into each other's company in a way that they both found slightly elevating. Karin figured the young wan was shifting Doyle for all he was worth and, if she could stomach him, well then fair play to her. Noreen was impressed with the way Karin held herself. The older woman was exactly the kind of tough-talking fashion-bitch she had always admired, and if she thought that her father was revolting, well, at least she had the courage to say it and, in all fairness, there was little denying that he *was* a bit of a holy show in the looks department. However, she was not about to let go of her plan to fix the two of them up.

Noreen had begun to pick up signs that Karin had assumed the two of them were a romantic item as opposed to father and daughter, and decided to use this to her advantage. Bit of competition never hurt anyone.

'So why do you hate Eamonn so much?'

Karin looked at her sideways as if she might be starting again, but Noreen immediately put any thoughts of that aside by adding, 'You know I have my own reservations about him. It's not what you think.'

Karin thought about it for a few seconds then said: 'Nyaaah – you know I don't really *hate* him Noreen. You know, he's done a lot for me really – gave me a job when I really needed one – and he's put up with a lot of shit from me over the years . . .'

'I bet!'

Karin flumped out a relaxed wry laugh. 'It's just that he's a bit . . .'

'Coarse?'

'Yes.'

'Badly dressed?'

'Yes.'

'Horrendously ugly?'

'That too.'

For a split second, Karin felt kind of concerned that Eamonn's new girlfriend was talking about him in such disparaging terms – like she kind of gave a shit that he wasn't taken for a ride. But then, each insult was strangely infused with an affection that made her think Noreen might genuinely love the man.

'I know he's kind of awful, Karin – but we all have our reasons.'

'Ah no, don't get me wrong – he's not a bad aul stick.' And then before it turned into an Eamonn Doyle Admiration Society Karin added, 'Look I'm sorry about before. You've been really great this week – it's just I've got a lot on my mind at the moment. To be honest, it wouldn't be a bad idea for you to step in now and get to know the magazine. I might be leaving soon.'

Disaster! Karin could not leave. Not now. Not before she had fixed the two of them up.

Noreen wheedled Karin's job plan out of her in exactly ten seconds. That was all it took because it did not amount to much. A c.v. to a whole bunch of unspeakably out-of-her-league *Vogue* type publications and a half-baked idea of starting her own highbrow political magazine financed 'somehow' by 'somebody'. Not exactly a military campaign and the whole thing smacked of desperation and unhappiness.

'Would you not stay where you are for a while?' she asked. 'Is *How'ya* not enough of a challenge for you?'

Karin's own words came as much as a surprise to herself as anything she had ever said. It had the unpleasant tang of a truth that had been festering away in a closet at the back of her mind too long.

'I need to be successful at something again, Noreen. I have to start living up to my age.'

Karin lit another cigarette and as she dragged in the smoke she looked at the fresh young face looking over at her and knew that she didn't understand. She had the same bright intelligent hopefulness that she had enjoyed twenty years ago. A confidence that tells you that life is going to be an exciting adventure. That hard work and talent will be rewarded. That if you carry your beauty with grace and gratitude, it will always pay out dividends of happiness and success. Karin wanted to explain to this young girl that it wasn't the case, but the devilish streak of cynicism seemed to have gone, so instead she said, 'You're a bright woman, Noreen. I think you'll go a long way.'

But Noreen wasn't interested in Karin's patronizing little statements about how bright she was. Tell me something I don't know, would have been the reply, had her mind not already started whirring around plots and plans of her own.

'The problem is Karin – the TV station is where Da . . . Doyle is at the moment. That's all he's really into making work right now. If we – you – us – whatever, could come up with a way of expanding his broadcasting interests, I think we – you – whatever might be on to something. I mean think about it for a second . . .'

Karin did.

'Do you know – I think you could be onto something here? He's got that shitty morning programme going out with that big homo and Valerie and what else?'

'Nothing – and he's under huge pressure with it by the way. The stock's not shifting . . .'

'Not surprised – have you seen the garbage they're selling?' said Karin.

'I mean – I know it's not state-of-the-art or anything, but hell the licence is in place and the basic equipment and staff are there . . .'

'They're only broadcasting a couple of hours each day – it's crazy! For a few quid more he . . .'

'We!'

'Sorry – *we* could get a few more programmes up and running . . .'

'For a price . . .'

'Of course . . .'

'I've loads of ideas . . . how about a dance music programme? Or fashion?' said Noreen.

'How about I get us another drink and you have a rummage around in my bag for a notebook. We've got some serious planning to do, girl!'

●

By the time the barman rousted them out after closing, Noreen and Karin had the bones of a half-a-week's TV schedule scrawled down on paper. Noreen was going into the office to type it up the following day, and Karin had to trawl through her address book looking for outgoing egotistical chums who might work for a pittance for the glory of being on TV.

They hugged at a taxi rank – destroyed with drink and excitement – and before they parted Noreen said, 'Oh – by the way, Barry is not gay – he just likes wearing pink and he's in love with your friend Valerie,' and Karin thought what an extraordinary piece of work her new young friend was.

By the time she got home, Karin was buzzing – on a real high. More excited than she had been fifteen years ago when she broke her first big political scandal. She wouldn't shaft Eamonn outright, but she felt sure that with Noreen's help, they could clinch this thing. If this worked, she felt sure she could secure a cut of the profits, and if she had to blow the directors of every big ad agent in town – surely that was better than mincing around a golf club after some sweaty husband, or knowing that your success was somehow built on a hand-out from some sick gamey rock star. In one evening Karin had got back that thing that she had worked so hard as a young woman to earn. Her independence.

It was five to midnight when she got in, and she went straight to the phone to call Sinead, when it rang as she was picking up the receiver.

'I've been trying to call you for hours – where've you been . . .'

The voice on the other end was weepy and hysterical. So distressed she hardly recognized it.

'Valerie?'

More weeping. Karin spoke gently until she got her to calm down. She had never heard her like this before.

'I have to see you, Karin. Can you come over?'

'Of course, honey – of course – but what is it – what's happened?'

'It's Jack.'

The bastard. Perhaps he'd finally overdosed and put them all out of their misery.

'He's slept with Sinead.'

29

A couple of days later Valerie had calmed right down. She didn't know why she had been so upset about Sinead sleeping with her ex-husband. It wasn't as though Jack was some kind of a sacred cow. He was, after all, a revolving door of sexual activity – paying little heed to details like who and where, and keeping the emphasis firmly rooted in self-gratification. He might have slept with Sinead several times over the years – or Karin – or anyone she knew for that matter, and Valerie, head-in-the-sand ingénue Valerie, would never have known. But the way he had called her like that; the beep-beep of the payphone making him sound like he was in a prison; the serious tone with which he had confessed his crime: 'I've something terrible to tell you'; the way she had to drag it out of him as if it was a murder or something, 'I slept with one of your friends . . .' Pausing then, allowing the suspense to grow before he revealed the person's identity, the depth of the betrayal. 'Sinead. I slept with Sinead. I am so sorry, Valerie.' He said it as if he really meant it. As if it was something so terrible that he should be really sorry about it. He almost said it like Sinead had gone down on her hands and knees and begged him for it.

It was the first time Jack had ever apologized to Valerie. For anything. And it gave the event a special significance. If sleeping with Sinead was worth apologizing for then, somehow, it must have been a more terrible thing to have done than, for instance, storing his cocaine in her vanity case and letting her travel with it; deciding to not turn up at the last minute to her mother's anniversary mass because he found 'death a bit depressing'; coming home drunk at twelve noon after spending the night in an orgy of cheap women and designer drugs.

In fairness, Valerie had long since let go of any expectations of basic decent behaviour from Jack. But Sinead? Why hadn't she told her? Not that she would have expected either explanation or apology. She was officially entitled to neither. But to be told like that – to have been kept in the dark. It seemed somehow deliberate and deceptive. That was why she had phoned Karin first. To see if she had known about it too. To see if she was part of the conspiracy. She had seemed as surprised as Valerie, but the relief that she felt as Karin exclaimed, 'Sinead and Jack – Jesus I don't fucking believe it!' only served to highlight that fact that, of late, Valerie had felt somewhat estranged from her two closest friends. It was nothing as severe as a rejection – they still met up as they had always done. But Valerie had an instinct that they were holding out on her. The conversation between them often appeared stilted, and while the other two appeared to know every detail about each other's lives –

Sinead's broken heart over Miles, Karin's disastrous date with the recent closet escapee and Bernard's new flame Claude Moore – Valerie was hearing about these things in snatches after the event. This had made her not want to confide everything about her own life to them, and so the close circle the three women had once formed, had seemed to widen and the chains that bound them loosen in parts. Valerie's life mentor Tinara had proven to be small comfort, seeming more concerned about the fact that, with Valerie leaving the shop, her rent might go up – and while her friendship with Barry was nice, it wasn't the same. Wasn't the same as the lounge-about-in-your-nightie girl-gang intimacy she had enjoyed with Sinead and Karin. Valerie's beauty had isolated her from making close women friends, although she had always assumed their standoffishness was because she wasn't so bright, in reality it was more often that they were jealous and couldn't handle the competition. Sinead and Karin had proved themselves exceptions to this and the fact that they loved her had, over the years, meant more to her than the attention of any man. Now they seemed to be moving away. Valerie supposed that this was what maturity was about. That perhaps it was time to let go of the 'best friend' mentality – the schoolgirl crushes she had had on both of them. Perhaps they were all at an age where it was time to look after themselves. Move on.

Valerie was sitting at her kitchen table when the doorbell rang, playing with a small candle-holder that Sinead had brought back from a trip to Morocco years ago. Each of the women's homes were filled with trinkets and gifts they had bought for each other; romantic relics to illustrate that each meant more to each other than any man ever could.

Valerie gathered her silk robe around her slim body and half opened the door. It was Sinead. She was carrying a huge bunch of lilies wrapped in flower seller's white paper.

Valerie's stomach lurched, but she held it together and opened the door silently, walking back down to the kitchen where she busied herself putting on coffee and getting cups out of cupboards. She could not handle confrontation and was afraid that if she stood still she might combust.

'I'm so sorry,' Sinead.

'Forget it,' Valerie replied – still with her back turned. And she meant it, cursing herself for having opened the door. She filled a tall vase with water.

'Thanks – they're beautiful,' she said peeling the paper back from the trunk of flower stems and carefully separating them into the vase as she had been taught in the finishing school. She was time-wasting, distracting herself by studying each flower before snipping each stem so the height of the arrangement was graded.

Sinead knew what she was doing and it made her crawl inside. She wanted this to be over – to do what she had come here for.

'Valerie sit down.'

'No – I'm fine,' she said, her voice pitched high with a forced joviality.

'Valerie – sit down, will you, and talk to me.'

'I'll just get the coffee.'

'Fuck the coffee, Val – just sit down.'

Valerie snapped then. Who did this woman think she was? Betraying her then arriving with flowers, thinking a little chat would make everything all right! Valerie was sick of this. Sick of people telling her what to do; telling her how she felt and who she was. Treating her like she was some kind of a benign doll that could be manoeuvred and manipulated. Never getting upset, never getting angry; a lifetime of beauty and good-natured serenity guaranteed. She turned around to face Sinead and sent the rest of the lilies crashing off the table.

'How fucking *dare* you come into my house and tell me what to do! No I will *not* sit down! I am fed up sitting down. Nice little Valerie, good little Valerie, take-it-lying-down-while-we-tramp-all-over-her-Valerie. Well no more. I've had enough. In the last month I have lost my business, cleaned out my inheritance to pay off tax debts, started a new job – which by the way thanks for asking is *terrifying* – and where have you my oldest and supposed best friend been? Calling me up and seeing if there is anything you can do? Around the shop helping me pack up the last seven years of my life? Taking me out to try and cheer me up? Oh no – sorry I forgot! You were too busy *having sex* with my ex-husband!'

Valerie was standing in the middle of her kitchen floor now as if it were a stage. She was dishevelled with fury, her hair normally a smooth carpet of blonde was streaking down her shoulders in messy clumps; her chest trembling under the flimsy robe with the shock of her shallow breathing. Mascara had carved her sockets into hollow caves from which her eyes glittered with anger. She was almost unrecognizable; like some emotionally deranged version of herself. Julie Christie doing Lady Macbeth. Sinead had never known Valerie to lose the rag like this before, and while she was shocked at the outburst, she was also kind of pleased that her saintly friend was finally losing the run of herself and letting it all hang out. Of course, she felt bad – but not so bad that part of her didn't want to grab Valerie and say 'G'wan girl and give it some more whasky there!' In other words, Sinead found that the content of Valerie's speech was somewhat overshadowed by the feisty realism of her demeanour. As a result the delivery of her statement, 'I'm sorry, Valerie', lacked both conviction and authenticity – coming out, as it did, as rather shallow and not aided in the least by a nervous smile. If she was expecting instant forgiveness, she was very much mistaken.

'That's the whole point, Sinead – you are not in the least bit sorry. I expect that kind of selfish thoughtless behaviour from Jack – but not from one of my friends. I mean that is just Jack all over, deliberately seducing you to get at me. He knew I would find out, and then when you didn't have the decency to tell me – he has to ring and tell me himself . . .'

Sinead started to feel uncomfortable. 'It wasn't like that Valerie . . .'

'Oh really?' Valerie's face curled into a cold expression

of sarcasm which didn't suit her to such an extent that for an instant she looked like somebody else.

'So what was it like then? He bought you flowers? Took you out for dinner? Told you he loved you? Give me a break, Sinead – he is a manipulative lying scumbag and you tumbled into bed with him without thinking. Without thinking about me. I thought you would have more respect for me, Sinead. More respect for yourself. But I was wrong. The pair of you are as shallow and messed up as each other.'

'I *said* it wasn't like that, Valerie.'

Far from being cowed into guilt by Valerie's harsh words, Sinead's heart was pounding nineteen to the dozen with some other, as yet unnamed emotion. Something in the tone of her voice made Valerie sit down at the kitchen table beside her.

'Jack's in trouble, Valerie. I know that he's an awful bollocks but he isn't a bad man. He's just messed up. I'm his friend and I care about him.'

'So that's why you slept with him. Because you care about him?'

The question was slightly tinged with cynicism, but not so much so that Sinead didn't feel able to give a genuine reply.

'Maybe.'

They sat in silence for a few minutes, both absorbing the tragedy of what it was to care about a man like Jack Valentine. Caring about him as a friend was a grim day's work. Loving him was another notch down on the

Women Who Love Too Much ladder, and if Sinead had bought a ticket for that train Valerie knew only too well that she was to be pitied, not reprimanded. In fairness, Sinead was no idiot and knew that the less said the better. Not for Valerie's sake this time, but for her own. Putting words on her feelings around that night would be tantamount to commitment; an admission that her heart was about to carry her off on a disastrous, dysfunctional journey that was more fitting for a seventeen-year-old star-struck groupie than a woman of her age and experience. She loved Jack Valentine and there was no excuse in the world big enough to carry that foolishness. The best she could hope for was to ignore it and hope it went away. She shifted her attention back to the matter in hand.

'Valerie, I really am genuinely very sorry.'

No smile this time. Valerie nodded.

'No really – there's no excuse. I've been selfish and shitty over the last few months, I know it.'

Valerie started to fill up. The translucent blue eyes disappearing behind great blobbery whelps of tears.

'I've just felt cut out of your life, Sinead, and Karin's too. Why? Why have you both been ignoring me? Is it because I'm boring? Is it because I'm too needy, wanting to be best friends all the time? Is it time to move on? Why?'

Sinead reached over and took her friend's hand.

'Oh – none of the above honey. There is one really simple reason and Karin and I kept it from you because we are stupid and immature and we thought you couldn't handle it.'

Then Sinead came right out and told her all about Jack's bet. Valerie listened to her talk about the fallout of the challenge. The serendipity of meeting Miles when she did, and then the ensuing heartbreak. About Karin's desperate attempts to secure the money via Ireland's 'Most Eligible Bachelor' lists. As Sinead talked the whole thing through she was aware of how ridiculous and trite the whole thing sounded. Ludicrous. As if anyone could take such a thing seriously. A tacky scheme built entirely on the mad ego of one man and the insecurities of two foolish women.

Much to her surprise however, innocent Valerie whom they had been protecting from all these seedy shenanigans was drinking it all in.

'And did Jack really mean it?'

'I think so. He had legal documents drawn up anyway.'

'Well he has the money – but would he have followed through?'

'Assuming one of us got married? I think so – but it's a long sho—'

'And I suppose neither of you thought to include me in this?'

'Well, we both said that if you got married well then of course, but I mean . . .'

'Hullo? How many times have you and Karin been asked for your hand? None! How many times have I been asked for mine? Seven! Who do you think has the best handicap for this race? Do the maths!'

'Yes, but we didn't think you . . .'

'Exactly. You didn't think! What's my deadline?'

'Your birthday.'

'Of course. Two weeks. I'll have to act fast.'

'You mean . . .?'

'And then some, but you'll have to help. Jesus, Sinead, I can't believe you didn't tell me about this before.'

'Well, you're such a romantic, Valerie, we thought it wouldn't be your thing.'

'Yeah right. And who is the one who has been running about falling in love before and behind her in the last few months while yours truly has been winding down a business and paying off the tax-man? I'm sorry Sinead, this isn't about romance, this is about money. Jack has it and we don't. I'll split the fee with the pair of you if you come on side.'

'But who are you going to get at this short notice?'

'Actually, somebody already springs to mind. He's gay – and *obviously* gay if you know what I mean – but I'm sure we can turn him around. He's a good friend, but I'm sure he'll . . .'

The phone rang and Valerie picked it up mid-sentence. It was Karin.

'Valerie, I think you had better get down here. I'm in Pearce Street Garda Station. It's your friend Barry. He's been arrested.'

30

Aloysius Moses Tuffy had extended his stay in Dublin. His given reason was of course the pure altruism of the continued disco-appreciating development of his young charge, Gerald 'Digger' Deignan. But it would have to be said that the freedom with which he was able to down-tools in Crosscarney and set up an increasingly perma-nent-looking camp of clothes and CD collections in one of Eamonn Doyle's (ever decreasing number of) spare bedrooms was due in no small part to the fact that business on the Tuffy Mobile Disco – Karaoke Specialist Extraordinaire front had been a bit quiet of late. While Al had voluntarily relinquished his regular Tuesday night spot in Crosscarney's emporium of love – Candelabra's Nite-Club – he could not but help feeling that his position as Funk Master of the West was being somewhat over-shadowed by the youthful appetite for 'rave' that seemed to be creeping across even the most remote outposts of Rural Ireland.

'Dhere takin' dhrugs to bate the band down dere in Candle's on a Sahur-dhay night,' complained bachelor

Frenchie Merrion, one of Al's staunchest followers since the sympathetic DJ had accommodated a long-awaited clinch with Bridie Mahon by extending Lionel Ritchie's 'I Just Called', her favourite song by a full three minutes, in order that Frenchie might maximize his chances with the sultry schoolteacher;

'Gob Al but ye'd hardly believe what's goin' an down dhere dhese days sure hardly ye wouldn't did-n I see Matty Nolan's young wan sure she's onny a bairn hersel' got up insome class'o a bikini she was and chawin' the face off of a gutty from Galway, annot a daycent bit-o-a-tune to be heard dhere now onny the bang-bang-bang an' dhe kids wavin' dhere hans in dhe hair like mad things entirely.'

'The world's gone mad,' Aloysius would concede, although, despite the sorrowful chagrin of his old clientele, he could never really be drawn to openly denigrate this new bang-bang culture on the honest countryman's ears. As far as Al was concerned the jury was still out on rave and all its cousins – house, jungle, techno – that he had struggled these past few years to keep up with. He was not, he would have to admit, immediately drawn to this harsh, pumping sound. Naturally, he lamented the old days; the mellow crooning of Mr Vandross, the universal danceability of a perky Billy Ocean groove – thirty farmers up jigging about joyfully to 'Love Really Hurts', its lyrics – 'You run around town like a fool and you think that it's groovy' becoming a rousing war cry for every Crosscarney bachelor farmer who'd been let down in love. In his eighties hey-day, it seemed that the tunes that Al Tuffy played on his Saturday night gigs had become a soundtrack for the townsfolk of Crosscarney, the spangly rhythm seeming to add colour to their everyday lives. When the first big supermarket had opened in the Market Square, Al had hosted a street party from a marquee supplied and paid for by the new proprietors. As a snake numbering some two hundred locals had sat on the damp ground to participate in the Ooops Upside Your Head rowing dance, Al had felt that he had reached the zenith of his dream to 'hep' the ordinary Irish joe to his 'groove'. All the early days of ridicule, the hard slog of retraining the ears of the jigging and jiving set to the funky strains of Edwin Starr and his ilk, had seemed, in that glorious moment, to be worth it.

But now he had to put his hands up and admit that those days were in the past. 2001 in Crosscarney was a different kettle of fish entirely. All Red Bull and Hoodies and gutties up from Galway pushing E.

When Al had got Eamonn's call from Dublin about this young DJ needing his tutelage, he had known himself that perhaps it was as much an opportunity for him to update his own repertoire as offer up the value of his extensive experience.

He could not have been more right.

It was a mere matter of hours before Digger and Al had joined Gilbert and Sullivan, Bonnie and Clyde, Dolce and Gabbana in forming an alliance which both man and boy felt certain would lead to great things. Of course when two great creative minds such as these meet, there is always the problem of artistic differences; the Disco

King of Crosscarney and the Bangin' Boy from Bunkelly being no exception. There were moments when their endeavours to mix 'old' and 'new' came unstuck, Al responded with acute alarm to Digger's suggestion that they download and fiddle about with the drumbeat on 'The Trouble With Me', the Barry White track being a work of such colossal genius that he declared it, in no uncertain terms untouchable. The young philistine was then punished accordingly when Al suggested that some of his sampled lyrics, specifically a tune featuring Granny Deignan's repeated cry of 'Gerraway outta tha' ye little fecker!' were too negative in spirit for a successful dance record, and that furthermore there was no call for 'language' of that kind, and to humiliate his poor dear grandmother into the bargain. Digger had taken um, stating that the samples were meant to be 'ironic' and had then sulked to such an extent that Al had finally conceded to go through the entire library of Deignan family quotes until he found one upbeat enough to justify the kind of life-affirming tempo of a true disco great.

On this Saturday morning therefore, the two of them were mixing up the strutting guitar riff of Stevie Wonder's 'Very Superstitious (Writing's On The Wall)' to Digger's Dad declaring 'Mam – This Soup's Delicious (Any Chance of More?)'. If the hokey-cokey hot-trotting of their landlord as he went about his usual Saturday fried-egg-sandwich-over-the-sink routine was anything to go by, they were making rather a good job of it.

Eamonn Doyle was not a man who was given to sitting around thinking about how lonely he was living on his own. Rather, it took for the house to be full of daughters and DJs and fellow disco veterans for him to realize that things were, perhaps, better this way than they had been when he had the house all to himself. He made a show of complaining about the accidental infiltration of his sock drawer by the odd G-string, and Al was not a great man for wiping the bristle ring off the bathroom sink, but nonetheless their host was aware that the house felt somehow alive these days. If there had been a true sacrifice in opening his home to others, it had been the unpleasant matter of Digger's feet. Encased as they were from dawn to dusk in a pair of ancient trainers they were, not to put too fine a point on it, thoroughly odious. Eamonn's own golfing shoes were nothing to write home about, but such was the vigorous toxicity of said items of rotting padded nylon, that the smell had resulted in floorboards being lifted in search of a nest of dead mice before Eamonn and Noreen had finally identified the real source of the problem. Negotiations for the disposal of Digger's 'lucky' trainers had involved a shopping trip to town to purchase suitable replacements, at the end of which Eamonn himself had been talked into a pair of flashy Nikes. While he lacked the courage to christen either outdoor pavement or the carpets of the Doyle Ind. offices with his new look in springy footwear, Eamonn had to confess that, when it came to rug-cutting in the privacy of his own home, they were surely the business. Of course, Noreen had tried to get him into all manner of way-out togs and costumes that day – but he was having none of it. The cheeky little mare was all into her fashion course and constantly trying to get him up in all manner of daft outfits – tailored suits that cost a fortune when, as he repeatedly told her, he had plenty of perfectly good clothes at home in hard-wearing fabrics like Teflon which hardly ever needed pressing or cleaning. She was a good-natured child, but all of this whinging about his golfing slacks and lemon V-neck sweaters was beginning to get on his nerves. Wasn't he grand as he was – although, if truth be told he did feel like a bit of a demon disco prince with the trendy new trainers on him and the mad music blaring down the stairs. Something about the air pockets underfoot and the thrum of the base from overhead made him want to . . . want to . . . well, there was only one word he knew for it and that was 'boogie!'

Eamonn put the egg to one side, took the pan off the heat and pottered in a step-half-step up the attic conversion stairs to the source of the irresistible beat.

He knew he was distracting the men from their important work, but sometimes, well, you just had to dance. For Al to whip off his headphones was but the work of a moment, and the two old buddies launched straight into a skanking, air-pointing, hip-jiggling version of the funky chicken which, frankly, would take the sight out of any eye.

When Digger saw the old men dance that way he was weak with admiration. He was a simple head-nodder himself. Bend knees and nod head in time to the music was all was required these days. If you could heap in the odd shoulder-shrugging shuffle, you were away on a hike in terms of being a cool raver. But these old boys did steps. Steps! And the dances had names. Names! For dances! There was the Hustle, the Slide, the Funky Chicken – and as for the James Brown, well the grand-duke of cool himself was only trotting after them. Make no mistake, there was no laughing at these boys – although Digger could well imagine there were people ignorant enough to do it. 'Such a shame they're not black,' he would say privately to Noreen, 'and they'd be able to get away with it.' Noreen would agree, but she said, she had other plans in mind for her Dad. 'You wait and see,' she would say when Digger pressed her, 'I've plans to transform Dad's life. You'll find out soon enough.' Digger trusted her like that. She was a strange, serious girl full of secrets and surprises. But he didn't think too much about it. He liked the mystery of her. She knew everything about him and managed, although he was living in her father's house and sleeping with her every night, to keep the most important part of herself back. He busied himself just loving her and never pushing for any more than just being around. In his wildest dreams Digger had ordered the prawn cocktail in love and somebody had brought him the lobster by mistake. He knew Noreen loving him must be some kind of a cosmic error, but he wasn't going to risk drawing atten-tion to it by asking too many questions.

When he went downstairs to use the bathroom, he found Noreen in the hall weighed down with dozens of shopping bags. Lofty logos: Brown Thomas, Alias Tom, Arnott's, suggested that the contents of same were to do with her new job styling at the magazine.

'Is Dad upstairs,' she asked?

'Yeah,' Digger said, 'he's dancing.'

'Can you tell him to come down straight away. I want to see him in the living room. Alone.'

When he came out of the bathroom and was heading back up the stairs, he found Noreen dragging a full-length mirror out of the bedroom.

'Here – let me give you a hand with that,' he said taking it from her.

'Thanks. In the living room – by the window please,' she instructed. The bags were gathered in an empty pile by the door, and men's clothes were draped on the back of the sofas and hanging from the curtain rail. She was saying nothing about what she was up to, but her face was as stern and set and determined as he had ever seen it. Best not to interfere. All would come clear in the end.

As he headed up the stairs again she said, 'Could you and Al leave me and Dad on our own for a while?'

'No problemo,' Digger said trying to keep the curiosity out of his voice.

When Eamonn entered the living room, Noreen was arranging an orange tie around the neck of a blue-black shirt.

'What the hell is going on here?' he said at the sight

of his living room having been transformed into some class of a shop concession.

'Shut the door please, Dad.'

'I will not shut the door until you tell me what the hell all of this stuff is . . .'

Noreen marched over and shut it herself.

'I,' she said drawing herself up to her full height, 'am giving *you* a make-over.'

Eammon's face collapsed with eyes-to-heaven irritation.

'Noreen – we've been through this before. There is *no need* . . .'

'Oh, but that's where you are wrong, Dad – you see there *is* a need. A *very great* need. You just don't know it yet.'

'Noreen, now lookit – enough's enough – will you get it into your head . . .'

Eammon's daughter was blocking the door so that he couldn't escape.

'Will you get out of my way and stop this nonsense, girl!'

'I am not a girl, I am a young woman. And as a young woman I am telling you that if you do not allow me to make some serious wardrobe choices on your behalf you will never – and I mean *never* – find the key to everlasting happiness.'

There was no talking to her. He knew that by the tone in her voice. He had a rave DJ living in his attic who was living proof of his daughter's determination to succeed in whatever daft goals she set herself.

'How long will it take?'

'Forty-five minutes max. All the clothes are on loan for a shoot and any you don't like I can take back.'

'I don't like any of them.'

'You won't know that until you try.'

'Jesus, Noreen – is it that important?'

With an emphatic nod of her head which belied the frivolous nature of simply trying on clothes she announced; 'Yes Dad, it is. *Very* important!'

'All right then so,' said Eamonn Doyle, taking off his T-shirt, 'let's get this over and done with.'

Noreen grabbed a Paul Smith single-breasted suit and handed it to him.

'I'll be back in a minute,' then she crept out into the hall to let him change, and gave out a silent celebratory air punch.

Her transmogrification plans were under way.

31

Barry Hooker had never been arrested before.

If he had found the past few months living in Ireland a challenge, the disappointment and disorientation he had experienced to date was as nothing in comparison to his current ordeal. Residing not four foot away from him was a gentleman who had introduced himself as 'Brigadier Chief Lieutenant Cornelius Clegg', whose current outfit featuring a profusion of ill-matched trousers and ladies' cardigans, topped off with a poncho fashioned from a car-seat cover which he flipped at intervals over his deranged hairy head, suggested that the title was either well and truly defunct, or had only ever existed in a parallel universe. The brigadier's real name was Turbot Madigan, a fact which Barry had ascertained when the booking sergeant had announced to the constable gripping his arm, 'Trow him in dere wit Turbot til he cools off.' Some forty-five minutes later, as he heard one guard explain his presence to another, the awful realization hit that himself and 'Misder Madigan' were both in there on the same charge – 'Causing a public nuisance.'

If Turbot hadn't been cruising him threateningly from an eye-hole in his car-seat cover, Barry might have been lain right down there against his cell wall and died of shame. Causing a public nuisance. That's what he was. A nuisance. That's what he had become. He used to work in the service of the community – being a nation's breakfast host. Finding them things they wanted and needed. He had been an important guy. A pillar. Now – here he was. Locked in a cell with a nutter. A nuisance. A public nuisance. A public nuisance in a pink blouse.

It was all the blouse's fault, of course. He hadn't even been seeing Valerie that day. It had just been the closest thing to hand when he had run out of the flat not two hours ago to get a pint of milk to dash through his muesli. He had been up most of the night before, ruminating on his own misfortunes. At least five hours had been devoted to standing in front of his bathroom mirror practising saying 'I am not a homosexual' in a way that might convince Valerie into looking at him in a different light. He had been unable to even convince himself. Perhaps if he hadn't been feeling so desperate and tired, he wouldn't have snapped like he did. On his way to the shop he had noticed two lads lurking in a shop doorway looking like they were planning to get up to no good. As he walked past, he thought he heard one of them mutter 'homo'. He said nothing, but his shackles rose to a sharpened point. On his way back, with the pint of milk in his hand, the boys were still there. He heard, clearly this time, one say to the other, 'Look – it's that big Aussie homo off the telly.' Again, a surge of testosterone almost crippled him into stopping, but sense some- how prevailed and Barry kept walking. When he was outside the launderette next to his apartment block, he felt someone grab him from behind. The milk went flying as the youths tackled him saying, 'Give us yer money ya big poof!' while at the same time somewhat nervously brandishing an army knife which looked like it was straight out of the box and probably belonged to one of their fathers.

It felt like Barry had been waiting months for this moment. All the pent-up frustration, the distortion of his God-given good nature into this sinister, twisted version of himself had been festering into a toxic fuel tank. Now these little bastards had lit the match and the fire injected through him in a mighty backdraft of anger.

Before they, or he, knew what was really happening, all three were in the launderette with Youth One halfway into a still-spinning tumble dryer which contained the sheets and smalls belonging to one Tess Malone for whom it was the work of a moment to call the gardai. Youth Two and his incriminating flick knife were long gone, and by the time the constabulary arrived on the scene all they found in Sudsy Soapworx was a whole bunch of hysterical women, a very shaken young man half swallowing a pair of ladies' drawers and an enormous Australian in a suspect pink shirt hollering 'I AM NOT GAY!!!!!'

He had calmed down considerably by the time they got him to the station, but they figured an hour with Turbot would put relevant manners on him and remind him that it was one thing wearing car-seat covers and wandering down Grafton Street announcing you were the Virgin Mary when you were a bona-fide home-grown lunatic, but when you were a guest in this country, stuffing locals into launderette dryers was just not on. Even if it was clear to the most inexperienced guard that, judging by the slobbery defensiveness and threats to sue from the streetwise youth, Barry's actions had, in all probability, been at least partly justified.

However, Barry was not privy to such subtleties and had not been filled in on the finer points of the Irish judicial system. Perhaps, he thought at this moment, they would sling him in jail. Furthermore, such was the depth of his despair, he honestly believed it was probably, no, definitely what he deserved. He'd sold seven Mary Robinson Condiment Sets this week – that was surely grounds in itself. Then there was masquerading as a homosexual in order to inveigle the affections of an innocent woman, add to that his current record and he was bound for a stint in pokey for sure. He'd never see the sun rise over Sydney Harbour again. He'd never see the sun again at all if he stayed in this county anyway. Valerie would visit him for the first few months, then she would forget him. She would get back together with the newly transmogrified and apologetic Jack and . . .

'GOT MYSELF A CRYIN', TALKIN', SLEEPING', WALKIN', LIVIN' DOLL . . .'

Turbot, who after his initial introduction had confined all communications to the body language of slumped, staring and poncho-flipping, had decided that it was time to sing a song. Although singing was perhaps too gentle a word for the murderous volume and tone of his voice as he fairly belted it out at full blast, scattering droplets of spit before and behind him.

'GOTTA DO MY BEST TO PLEASE HER, JUST COS SHE'S A LI-HIV–IING DA-HOLL . . .'

Barry, quite understandably taken aback, tried on a weak smile as Turbot pointed and winked at him as if the lyrics held some special meaning for the two of them. Barry's smile petrified into a pained grimace.

'GOTTA ROAMIN' EYE AND THAT IS WHY SHE SATIS-FIES MY SA-HOOLE . . .'

Such was the level of the crooner's conviction at this stage that had circumstances been different, one might have almost believed that he were Cliff himself and Barry the mini-skirted dolly of his affections.

Turbot was a small man, a good couple of feet shorter than Barry, a fact that he became aware of as his cell-mate slipped out of his flip-flops and began dancing barefoot around the alarmingly restricted floor space. But despite this, and perhaps because of the trauma of the day that had been in it thus far, Barry found himself terrified of this psychiatric pixie and more especially frightened, for some reason, at the choice of his song. He curled himself up into as small a space as possible in the corner of his bed by the wall and thought he might be in very great danger of weeping.

'TAKE A LOOK AT HER HAIR, IT'S REAL – IF YOU DON'T BELIEVE WHAT I SAY JUST FEEL . . .

'I'M GONNA LOCK HER UP IN A TRUNK – SO NO BIG HUNK CAN STEAL HER AWAY FROM ME.'

At mention of these last words, Turbot poked Barry in the chest with a bony finger and his meaning was clear. Barry was the 'big hunk' who had stolen his 'living doll' – or worse – much worse, he intended to have a feel of his hair to see if it was real.

Barry leapt up from the bed and banged on the cell door to be let out.

By the time the guard arrived, Turbot was back on his bed pretending to be asleep with the car-seat cover over his head and it was Barry who got ticked off for the singing.

Irish justice. There was no fighting back.

<hr />

'So what did he do?' asked Valerie as she hopped out of her taxi and found Karin standing outside the station.

'I'm not sure,' said Karin, 'I was just in paying a parking fine and I saw a couple of guards drag him out the back. He was in a bit of a state all right – didn't even see me. I didn't say anything to the guards. Just came straight out and rang you. I hardly know the guy – thought I'd leave it to you.'

Barry arrested? What in the name of God could he have done? Valerie thought to herself. Mild, gentle Barry? Jesus – not some unpleasant public-toilet-type activity? No, surely not. He wasn't the type. But then – arrested? Maybe she didn't know the guy at all.

'Valerie,' Karin asked just as they were going in the door, 'is there something going on with you and Barry?'

'Well – how do you mean? We're friends like . . .'

'No I mean, something *romantic*.'

'Don't be daft, he's gay.' Valerie swung her bag over the shoulder and had one foot in the door ready to go rescue her chum.

'Er, Valerie – no he isn't.'

'Karin, for God's sake – what is this? Of course he's gay . . .'

'Ahem – I know for a fact he isn't. Also know for a fact he's got the serious lap tremors for you.'

Valerie stopped in her tracks.

'What the hell are you talking about?'

'He fancies you – oh sorry – I forgot. Men don't go around just fancying Valerie Valentine – that would be too easy. He's *in love* with you by all accounts.'

'By whose accounts?'

'A little birdie. What does it matter? Did you not know?'

It all began to fall into place. Her not turning up for that drink with Bernard. His complete lack of interest in the men she set him up with. The polite, but slightly joyless way he accepted her gifts. Mother of Divine Jesus, yes! The doe-eyed way he looked at her! The constant willingness to be at her beck and call! The above and beyond the call of duty support he gave her at work! The getting her the job! How could she have been so stupid? She had *assumed* he was gay because . . . because . . .

because she felt so safe, so protected by his company that she believed it could be the only explanation. Perhaps her immediate instinct to marry him was not about Jack's money after all. Perhaps it was something else entirely – something that she had been let down in so often that she had stopped daring to hope for it years ago. A genuine partnership based on mutual love and respect.

'Only,' said Karin, sheepishly, 'if there is something going on I think you should tell me and Sinead because . . .'

'Jack's bet – yes I know. Sinead told me this morning.'

'Oh – ah – em – sorry.'

Valerie had neither time nor inclination for another girlfriend showdown.

'Forget it,' she said, 'let's go in there and get my fiancé out of jail.'

32

There was a great deal of teamwork involved in setting up the wedding in under three weeks, but with the three women's network pulling power it was easily done.

Karin, whose plans with Noreen over Doyle TV expansion were taking shape in an impressive document, declared the nuptials of 'Ireland's favourite TV personalities' a *How'ya* Wedding Special and called in sponsorship on everything from food to flowers. Sinead was put in charge of finding a venue, and having scoured the length and breadth of the country came right back to basics and chose the TV studios themselves. With Tinara's help, some class of a dingly-dangly pretend-priest was secured to marry the couple on the actual *Shop A.M.* set. Valerie's young designers were queuing up to design the dress, and Karin and Sinead having blankly refused to be got up like bridesmaids, both agreed to wear matching trouser suits and assume the title Best Women in Waiting. Barry eventually agreed to accept Bernard as Best Man, who was beside himself with relief that Barry was straight after all, allowing him to flesh out the fantasy that *had* he been gay, Bernard would have been first on his list. Barry was more than happy to let Bernard take on all groom-type responsibilities – aside from the 'I Do' bit and the choosing of his outfit, which was something resolutely macho in blue serge. In fact, he made rather a point of showing no interest whatsoever in things like canapés and flowers, although he secretly hoped that lilies would feature. He also took the precaution of secretly booking himself in for the subtlest of subtle highlights a week in advance of the day itself. Sinead was somewhat taken aback when she was informed by Karin that her boss, Eamonn Doyle, had been rather insistent that, as they were holding the wedding on his premises, he be allowed to employ the DJ who was an old friend of his. The fact that the Golfing Troll knew anybody remotely connected with the music business came as something of a surprise to both of them but, frankly, they were so busy cramming for the big day, that neither had time to stop and either comment or argue with him.

On the morning of the wedding itself, Karin and Sinead gathered in Valerie's family home in Dalkey.

'Can you even bear to go into the house?' Karin asked Sinead at the door.

'Valerie's old man will be as vile as usual, the snooty old bollocks,' Sinead agreed. 'I don't know why the hell she wanted to spend the night before her wedding here?'

'Tradition I suppose.'

'Karin – she is getting married for the *second* time on a television set by an expelled bogus priest who calls himself Wicca Merlin. I hardly think tradition comes into it. Christ knows what the cranky old fuck of a father of hers is going to make of it all . . . Hullo George!'

Sinead and Karin had only met George Barton a few times before, but it was certainly a few too many as far as both parties were concerned. How in the name of God he had managed to produce as sweet-hearted and genuine a daughter as Valerie was a mystery to them both, as was his daughter managing to fall so far from the disciplined grace of her childhood to be in free association with such a heinous couple of sluts to the old man. Sinead, always up for a bit of antagonism sensed his disapproval and, when the opportunity presented itself always laid on plenty of chirpy paddy-chat just to annoy him.

'Sure isn't it a grand day in itself there Mr Barton? You must be beside yourself entirely with excitement over the event that's in it?'

Karin followed her lead and joined in.

'Stop the lights but there'll be mighty craic altogether once the wedding gets started. Book a dance in there for me Mr Barton like a good man yourself – the bridesmaids always get first crack at the bride's father isn't that right, Sinead?'

'Oh that's right surely, musha . . .'

'I'm not going,' snapped the old man, heading both women off at the pass before they whipped woollen shawls out of their handbags and started keening in his hall. 'Valerie is upstairs in her room – you know where it is.'

They found her sitting at the old mahogany dressing-table. Her make-up was done and she was gently peeling Velcro rollers out of her hair. The light from the long Georgian windows was bouncing off the three rose-tinted mirrors in front of her. She was still wearing her dressing-gown, but even in that Valerie seemed to be glittering like an angel. She looked like a million dollars – literally. Both women felt a pang, somewhere between pride and shame, as they realized that she deserved this day, and all that it meant, more than any of them. At almost forty, she could have been a nineteen-year-old virgin again. Valerie had the innocence and the natural glow of a born bride.

'You look beautiful,' Sinead said.

'Your father's not giving you away then?' Karin blurted out.

'He gave me away years ago,' said Valerie, in a slightly mournful tone. 'I just wanted to get ready here in memory of my mother. I found her wedding dress last night in the attic when I was looking through some of her old things. It smells a bit moth-bally but I was half thinking of wearing it?'

The dress was lying across the bed. Layers of delicate net lace gently stretched to form the shape of the woman who once wore it, arms folded carefully across the empty chest. It looked beautiful as it was, but also fragile with the indignity of having been ignored all of these years. Sinead reached down and picked up the hem, fanning it across the edge of the eiderdown.

'Let's try it and see. Karin can bring the new dress

along in the car and you can change into it later for the party.'

As the three women came down the stairs, bride first, George Barton was crossing the hall. He got one helluva shock, as something in the manner of this uniquely feminine procession had known that he would. None of the friends had openly thought about what the effect of his daughter wearing her mother's wedding dress might have on the old man, but there was nonetheless a powerful knowing that had passed between them in the age-old tradition of women preparing women for their wedding day. They walked down the stairs silently, in reverential awe at their own joint beauty, each having been silently passed an ancient secret by Veronica Mullins in the wearing and holding of her magnificent dress. Which was: you can fight a man, and strive to better him, but at the end of the day, nothing whacks them harder or disarms them more thoroughly than being in the presence of perfect female beauty.

George muttered a frosty 'goodbye' and in a cowardly back-turn scuttled back from whence he came. Valerie's back paralysed briefly into a set hurt, but she quickly moved her cortège out the front door of the house with a chirpy 'Ready girls?' before Sinead and Karin had time to openly despise her father's rejection.

George Junior, Valerie's banker brother who had travelled the day before from London was waiting outside in his hired Mercedes. The three women piled into the back.

'Blimey, Val,' he announced in his pretend cockney

accent – quite the fashion for boys educated at Harrow these days it seemed – 'you look smashing!' Sinead and Karin both breathed a sigh of relief that Valerie had at least one decent male in her family to give her away.

On the way across town to the TV studios, a question occurred to Karin that she had been meaning to ask since this whole business of Valerie getting married had begun. Something that had troubled her since she had found out about Valerie knowing about Jack's bet. Now might be her last chance to say anything, so she did.

'Valerie – do you love Barry?'

'What kind of a question is that!' snapped Sinead, 'of course she bloody loves him – Jesus woman, a time like this!'

Karin felt, rather hard-heartedly, that Sinead was a bit too focused on the 'Day Out' aspect not to mention the three-way million-pound split. But she said nothing, only repeated the question.

'Are you,' she asked gently, 'in love with him?'

'You mean am I just doing it for the money?'

Nobody was expecting such a blunt reply coming, especially coming from such an ethereally beautiful-looking creature as Valerie was at that moment. George Junior's ears pricked up in the front of the car, but he was not in the habit of interfering in women's conversations. Another smart little trick he picked up courtesy of the British Public School system.

'Well – no – I mean yes – sort of – I suppose so – I just wanted to make sure that . . .'

Sinead glowered horribly at Karin but she was not to be deterred.

'I just want to be sure you are not making a mistake – I mean – I just want you to be happy that's all.'

'Here it is,' said Valerie, taking the hand of each of her friend's, 'I'm not sure.' Then, before they had time to cut in, 'But what I am sure of is this. Barry loves me – he is a good friend and I trust him. He is good-looking and heterosexual and I have, believe it or not, tested him for problems in that department and am happy to report there are none . . .'

'Easy girl – more information than I need!' called George from the front seat.

'Am I in love with him? No probably not. But I am extremely fond of him and I know he will make me happy. In other words, he'll do!'

The two other women squirmed in their seats. Despite all they had been through in the past few months, something in the manner of Valerie's pragmatism was upsetting them both.

'It's not worth it, Valerie,' said Karin, squeezing her hand.

Valerie was starting to get a bit irritated herself now.

'Not worth what?'

'Settling for . . . settling for . . .'

'Settling for what? Second best?'

'Yes!' the two women said in unison.

'Second to whom?' she challenged them. 'Jack Valentine?'

'George – what do you think of Barry? You were out with him last night.'

'Fucking fine fellow – thoroughly decent chap!'

'And Jack?'

George said nothing but took a turn rather sharply.

'Sorry girls – I fell in love once. With the wrong man. For me,' and she gave Sinead's hand a secret squeeze.

'What I need now is a strong man, a good person – someone to love and cherish me. I respect him and I love him in a peaceful happy way – a way I could never have loved Jack. He is the best I believe I am ever going to find, and I'm sorry but I'm just not prepared to hang on for another ten/twenty years holding out for some indefinable special something that I'm not sure I have in me any more. In other words, I'm going for the happy Hollywood ending, rather than the dramatic Hollywood opening.'

There was a stunned silence after her speech which Sinead broke by saying, 'Actually, being arrested and declaring his love for you in Pearce Street Garda Station is a pretty dramatic beginning if you ask me.'

'Worthy of Hollywood's best,' agreed Karin, as George pulled the Merc into Doyle TV car park.

The three friends emerged from the car and marched arm in arm through the studio's door, fully prepared for the happiest day of their lives.

33

Jack Valentine did not feel much like a new man. What he felt like, actually, was a whisky and soda. Or a gin and tonic. Or a vodka martini. Or a pernod on ice. Or a pint. Or a little glass of sherry even. A line of coke – would that be out of the question he wondered? Or a spliff? A little one – a tiny weeny puff on a little spliffarooni – surely to God there'd be no harm in—

'Cup of tea, Jack?'

No! Not another fucking cup of tea! He'd had six weeks in that hole in the Cotswolds doing nothing, only drinking tea twenty-four-seven and talking about his 'feelings'. He was fed up to the back teeth doing both. The treatment centre had been extremely expensive and, as far as he could tell, the main indication of that was in the variety of herbal and 'healing' teas on offer as supplement to the usual PG Tips variety. Of course, he had nothing to compare it with because he had never 'guested' in a rehabilitation centre before but if service in such places was to be judged on beardyness of counsellors (men and women alike), tears shed in group therapy sessions (buckets) and choice of quality teas available – Humility House certainly earned its five-star status.

However he was now two days back home, and Tommy had moved back in for 'moral support' (his altruistic fellow-recovering-alcoholic motives tainted slightly by his having had a spectacularly unsuccessful run as an independent caterer and the fact that Jack's roof over his head was considerably more pleasant than the bedsit in Phibsborough where he had ended up), and to 'keep a watchful eye on my old friend-ha-ha-ha.' Ha-ha-fucking-ha my hole, thought Jack. He was turning the house into a prison with his cups of tea and his AA meeting schedules and his relentless one-day-at-a-time chirpiness. Right now all Jack wanted was to belt down to Little's and get totally off his face before lashing four underage dollies into the back of a taxi and taking them home for one of his special rock-star seeing-tos. And indeed he could not see any reason why on earth not? He was fine now. A six-week break off the booze and he was feeling as right as rain now. Perfectly normal. Ready to start again. In moderation of course.

What stopped Jack from cracking open the JD which he had secretly stashed in the back of his larder, and telling Tommy to go take his tea-bags and wave them elsewhere was a complex series of such conflicting thought processes that he could not even hope to unravel them. Years of careless drinking, drug-taking and general misbehaviour of all kinds had become enmeshed with the six-week brain-bashing rehab message that he was a bollocks of the highest order and had better get his act together. The 'It's a disease' business was given very short shrift when Jack announced in 'group' that he intended to get T-shirts printed saying 'Unstoppable alcoholic – you are obliged to forgive me'. But what was totally stunting Jack's God-given desire to go out and get totally blitzed in celebration of his heroic stint as a sober person, was the question of choice. It had his head opened. He could go out and get trolleyed – he knew he was something of an expert at that. But he had never, in the past actually chosen to do so in cold blood, so to speak. It was just something that happened. Not entirely always by accident it would have to be said, but certainly never before by actual choice.

When the hairy-scary counsellors had asked him to describe his 'rock bottom' in group, he had regaled them with fabulous stories of debauchery and excess, throwing in plenty of fellow celebrity gags to impress the smack-addicts from Watford who were in there on National Health assisted beds. But sitting here now in his kitchen, all he could think of was the flat tone of Sinead's voice as she had said to him when she was standing right where Tommy was standing now, *'You know Jack – you really ought to do something about your drinking.'* It had been like she was close to not really giving a fuck any more. Like she said it – but if he didn't do anything about it and died – well then, that was just too bad. It had hurt him. He had rung Tommy and said he'd go do it, just to prove to them all that he could. That it was no big deal. Yeah – Super Rock Star Jack Valentine getting on the great sobriety bandwagon, show the fuckers he could do the whole abstinence gig. There were girls doing it now fuck's sake. Supermodels. Maybe, he had thought, there might be a couple of tasty anorexics in there to amuse himself on. But it hadn't been like that. Without the benefit of drink, and with the bit of denial he'd had left knocked out of him, the picture of Sinead walking away from him like that, dismissing the night before for the sad, lonely event that it was – it was enough to make a man want . . .

'A Chocolate Kimberly? G'waa-an. Got to keep those sugar levels up Jack.'

Jack looked up at his friend with such a joyless glare that Tommy thought he'd mention the eight o'clock meeting in the village a bit nearer the time.

'It's tough, mate, I know.'

Tommy thought if he could just get Jack to talk about things, he'd feel better.

'I know my first few months were really hard. I remember my old sponsor Cruisy Conor used to say to me, Tommy? he used to say, you've just got to take it one-day-at-a . . .'

Blah, blah, blah – another fucking AA anecdote. Was this it? Two men sitting in a huge house like a couple of leather-clad monks? Endless cups of tea and once a day go mad and treat yourself to a Chocolate Kimberly? He couldn't drink, he couldn't do drugs, he couldn't ride strange women – he was sure of that – without the former two inside him but he couldn't – could *not* – sit through another hour and a half of Tommy's 'How I Got Sober' story.

'Did the paper arrive yet?' he interrupted.

'Oh sure,' Tommy wisely sensed this was not the time for wisdom, 'here' and he threw it across the table and said; 'I'm going out for a bit of fresh air. Gorgeous day. Hey maybe we should both get into a bit of gardening one of these days, I believe it's a great way to . . .'

Jack was already flicking through the paper and pointedly not listening.

'. . . right then so – I'll just go out then – for a walk . . . bye.'

He flicked through the Saturday *Independent* trying to find something to distract him, perhaps something about himself coming out of treatment in the gossip pages. But instead of a sympathetic piece about his recent ordeal, Jack found something else altogether.

VALERIE VALENTINE TO MARRY
TV SWEETHEART TODAY

We saw love blossom over our breakfast tables, and now TV personalities Valerie Valentine and Barry Hooker are to wed at midday today in the Doyle studios. Patron of the new TV station Eamonn Doyle said last night . . . blah . . . blah . . . blah.

He couldn't read any further. Suddenly, it all came tumbling in around him. It wasn't just Valerie getting married. It was everything. Everyone. They were all out there living lives. Getting married, having children, doing jobs. The world kept turning. Sinead was probably at the wedding wearing a hat or something. They weren't all at home sitting around thinking about how Jack Valentine was getting on since he came out of treatment. How he was getting on and what a great man he was. Jack, in that terrible moment, realized that he was not, in fact, as he had always so firmly believed, the centre of the universe. He knew it was stupid to be upset but – well – it just wasn't fair!

He sat curled up in his leather armchair, the Kimberly crumbs melting into his scrawny fingers and he cried like a baby for ten whole minutes. When the ten minutes were up and Tommy hadn't come back to make a fuss of him, he decided enough was enough. Hey! He didn't need drink to be the centre of the universe. He could be the centre of the universe very well without it thank you very much. Jack Valentine? Did he need mind-altering drugs or babes to be at the revolving epicentre of the very cosmos itself? Did he hell! He was a star! A hell-raiser! An internationally renowned rock star of Titanic proportions.

Fuelled with the vim of nothing more than his own brilliance, Jack Valentine bounded up the stairs and selected a gold velvet frock coat from his on-stage ward-robe. With it he matched a frilly white shirt with – fuck-it, it was a wedding after all – solid gold cufflinks. He went to the bathroom, gave himself a quick sluice of Moschino and brushed his hair back into a slick ponytail. Then he ran out of the house and got behind the wheel of the new Alpha Romeo he had just had delivered as a coming home gift.

This was one party he was *not* going to miss!

34

Eamonn did not know why he was getting himself so all
in a heap about this wedding. OK, so it was a golden PR
opportunity. His two presenters getting married. The
newspapers would cover it in their society pages, Karin
was going to be pushing it big time in *How'ya*, and God
knows Doyle TV needed all the positive publicity it could
get. Since its launch the station had taken something of a
pasting from the viewers and press alike. Various reviews
had described it as 'drivel' and 'dross' and in a recent
influential *Irish Times* piece on the 'Deconstruction of
Irish Culture' had held Eamonn Doyle almost single-
handedly responsible for the '. . . *tacky Americanization of
the Irish media generally and the cheapening of Irish broadcasting specifically.*' Eamonn was more than able to take
such criticisms on the chin, as long as he was making the
few bob. But the truth was he was losing money hand
over fist on this new project. The broadcasting authority
had already threatened to revoke his licence and did not
seem to think that selling toilet-brush holders inscribed
with the works of great Irish poets was sufficient to

justify the clause that he provided programming of cultural and artistic merit. It was also apparent from the lack of sales that the Irish viewers themselves did not consider he was providing them with 'a valuable and beneficial broadcasting service', as their complete lack of interest in the Mary Robinson Condiment Sets laid testament to. His original investment had been long devoured by cranky unionized technicians, and Eamonn Doyle was worried that perhaps he had bitten off more than he could chew.

All of this had really come to light only in the past few days, and on the Saturday morning of the wedding Eamonn was musing miserably on his bad fortune. After a few hours of same, unable to find solace in the simple pleasure of his usual breakfast treat, miserable musing gave way to a dark despondency, and it was in his darkest moment – an unforeseen battle with a disobedient comb-over – that his perky daughter bounded into the bathroom to inform him that his shoes did not go with his trousers.

Now, as any important businessman will tell you, the very last thing one needs when the rose-tinted scales of a risky entrepreneurial venture have fallen, plunging one into the depths of abject fear of both failure and poverty, the very last thing that one needs is fashion advice. No matter how fond one is of one's daughter, no matter how much one might have taken her point in the past about the naffness of one's trousers or the dodginess of one's haircut, one is inclined, at such a time, to snap back.

'Fuck's sake, girl, get the hell out of here and give me some peace.'

Noreen backed out of the room, but she was not backing down.

When her father emerged, his sullenly drooping head topped off with a set of flattened stripes and an old vest mournfully half-tucked into a pair of limp Teflon slacks, Noreen was ready for him.

'You are not going to the wedding dressed like that.'

'Noreen – for God's sake will you just . . .'

'No! I have put a lot of work into making this day special, and I am not having you turn up looking like that.'

He shuffled past her into the kitchen and turned his back.

'Will you just leave it today now, girl . . .'

'I most certainly will not leave it at anything. I went out of my way to get you a whole new wardrobe and . . .'

'NOREEN!' he yelled, banging the kettle on the kitchen counter.

It was the first time he had shouted at her and in that instant there was silence, but before he had the chance to feel bad, she started up again.

'Dad – I know you think this isn't important, but it *is*. I just don't want you turning up today not looking your very best. You deserve better Dad, you deserve . . .'

Now this really was too much. Here he was standing half-naked in his kitchen, *again*, being forced into another conversation about clothing and hairstyles and the like when there were altogether more important issues at hand – like for instance, the imminent crumbling of his empire. Perhaps this had been the problem all along. In fact – yes! Now he thought about it, he could trace the beginnings of this downturn to the distraction of Noreen coming back and her relentless demands that he lodge DJs and start wearing different trousers.

'What I deserve is a daughter who shows me some respect – and leaves me alone from time to time to concentrate on my business!'

'Well, what about my coming into the office and helping you out?'

Eamonn closed his eyes and breathed in. Really, he didn't want to hurt her, but he was getting frustrated now. As much with himself as with her. How in the name of God he had allowed this young woman to come in and take over his life, put that kind of trust in her when she was clearly, still just a child?

'Noreen – it's been great having you help out at *How'ya*, but it hardly constitutes a turnaround in the business. There are problems there that you cannot possibly understand and I need the time to concentrate on getting them sort—'

'You mean *Shop A.M.*.'

Jesus, even she had noticed there was a problem. Was it that obvious?

'Well, we are running into problems – but what I really mean is that I think it is time we both had a bit more space to ourselves. Next week I'm going to put the deposit down on an apartment in that new development in—'

'You mean you want me to move out?'

'Well, yes but . . .'

'And Digger too?'

'Yes – you can both . . .'

'Fine!'

And she stomped down the hall.

Eamonn felt bad that it had come out like it had, but really, it was for the best. The girl needed to learn to stand on her own two feet, start managing her own life. It was all very well and good her living here under his wing, but sooner or later she was going to have to fly the coop and learn how to look after herself. Digger seemed like a nice lad, and he felt sure that . . .

'Here!' Noreen suddenly appeared in the kitchen door-way again, and all but flung something at him, which he caught.

'I was saving this for Monday, but seeing as how you are chucking me out because I am, apparently *useless*, I thought you might as well have it now!' And she stormed off again. No doubt to start packing her bags.

Eamonn looked down and in his hands was a heavy document, beautifully bound with an official-looking grey cover. He leaned against the counter and began to flick through it. It was entitled, 'DTV: A New National Television Station For A New Ireland.'

The index featured everything from Why Ireland 2001 Needs A New Entertainment TV Channel to Financing DTV – An Investment Opportunity.

In between were programme ideas and budgets for each. The whole thing was about sixty pages in length and beautifully laid out. Professionally put together to a point that was actually kind of intimidating. The fact that it had been put together by his barely over teenage daughter was positively frightening. Eamonn was suitably gobsmacked. Right away he could see a few changes and alterations that needed to be made, but all the same . . . it was good. No, he had to admit it – even his daughter's involvement excepting – it was brilliant. So brilliant in fact that he had to sit down. Which he did, on the kitchen floor, and went through it page by page in a kind of open-mouthed awe, which took about an hour. It would be expensive, but it was doable. Maybe. Possible. And if it did happen, well then, hell . . .

When he had finished, and the idea that this might actually work had begun to swim through his veins in heavy blobs of excitement, he called out her name.

'Noreen? Noreen! Come in here.'

No reply. The house was quiet. Digger and Al were above at the studios getting ready for the reception, so she must have heard him. Oh Jesus, he'd pissed her off. In all the excitement he had forgotten.

He raised himself up from the floor and went to her room, gently tapping on her door.

'Noreen? Noreen can I come in?'

'I suppose so,' she mumbled as he was already halfway in the door.

'I don't know what to say.'

Noreen was sitting on the bed and looked up at him

from under a curtain of hair. Suddenly she looked very young.

'How about thanks?'

'Did you do it by yourself?'

She arched an eyebrow and the little girl was gone again.

'No – myself and Karin did it together.'

'Karin Sheridan?'

'Do we know another one?'

Eamonn groaned inwardly – and then outwardly.

'I suppose she didn't do it for the good of her health?'

'I suppose not. Promotion, a cut of the profits and general world domination would be my guess.'

'Jesus – she's one manipulative cow, pulling my daughter in on her schemes.'

'Actually it was *my* idea, and she still doesn't know I'm your daughter. You told me not to tell her.'

'Well then, what does she think? She's not the type to go about . . .'

'Never mind what she thinks – will it work do you think?'

'I don't know but – ' he gave her a big smile – 'you're a bloody smart little cookie all the same there, Noreen Doyle.'

'My father's daughter, eh?'

'And then some.'

'Will you let me cut your hair then? And dress you for the wedding?'

'Ah now Noreen, will you give it a break. Amn't I all right as I am?'

Noreen was getting frustrated now. What the hell did she need to do to effect this make-over?

'No you are not all right. You are a hideous Golf Troll!'

Eamonn was slightly shocked at the smart mouth on her. Not like his daughter to be so bitchy.

'Where the hell did you come up with an expression like that?'

Noreen felt bad when she saw her father's cheeks redden – but then hey! You've got to be cruel to be kind.

'Karin.'

'Is that what she thinks of me?'

'Yes, Dad.'

Deep in his heart of hearts, Eamonn knew it was true. The sleepy eye, the comb-over, the practical stain-proof, permo-crease trousers. He told himself he was trying, but he knew in himself he was not trying hard enough. Perhaps his resistance to Noreen's makeover attempts ran deeper than just parental churlishness. Perhaps they were his way of keeping women at bay. The freedom of the fried-egg sandwich, the Saturday-morning scratcher sessions, the life of a country bachelor replicated in posh Donnybrook with a stack load of money, no woman to bog him down. But the house was full now, he was used to having a woman about the place with Noreen here. For the first time Eamonn saw that perhaps his daughter had been right. He was not being true to himself after all. Inside him was a suave, smooth disco prince just wanting to break out. He decided to give it a go.

'Right, well then young lady – perhaps it's time to

prove all those Karin Sheridans of the world wrong. What do you have in mind?'

Noreen beamed and reached under the bed for a pair of clippers.

'Let's start with the hamster hairstyle!'

35

This was the happiest day of Barry Hooker's life. Certainly. Without a shadow of a doubt. Definitely it was. The happiest day of his life.

Except . . .

Except that as our hero stood at the especially constructed studio altar, with its multicoloured and slightly chaotic flower arrangements, and a large banner hand-painted by Tinara proclaiming 'Souls of the Universe Unite in Love', the Wicca Merlin standing in front of it, poe-faced with the seriousness of the task ahead of him despite the comic frivolity of his purple robes, Barry could not help but sense a feeling of . . . what? Not dread exactly – no that was the wrong thing entirely. He loved this woman. He wanted to marry this woman. He was far from dreading the day ahead. Fear? No – not exactly fear either. What was there to be afraid of? Marrying Valerie? Certainly not! Being the centre of attention? He was well used to that. No it was something else. Something unfamiliar. Something he couldn't put a name to . . . something . . .

'Eeeuew! Look what just walked in – the day is *doo-oomed* to hell!' Bernard, his best man, grabbed his arm in a dramatic pinch.

Doom. That was it, a sense of doom. Like something terrible was going to happen to ruin it all. It had all been so perfect the way it had worked out these past few weeks. Valerie finding out he wasn't a homosexual, and being pleased about that and even asking *him* to marry *her* and saving him all that trouble. And even the way that her thinking that he had been homosexual for all that time had kind of brought them closer together in a funny sort of a way. And now, here he was, on the brink of living his dream, and he just had this feeling of, well – *doom* – like it was all going to go wrong. How silly was that! As if. He was here. Valerie was on her way. He was wearing his blue-serge Shamrock Surfers' Captain's blazer looking like a proper big blokey bloke make-no-mistake-about-that, and well, the highlights had worked out lovely. Totally natural. Nobody – not even Valerie – need ever know. No. Nothing could possibly go wrong. Feeling of doom misguided. Gone. No need for doom or any of his cousins to visit here again thank you very—

'Look at that fucker walking in here like butter wouldn't melt? Might have known he'd turn up to spoil things ... look ... there he is ... smiling over...' Bernard nodded and smiled to the mysterious guest whom Barry had his back to, and continued hissing through his teeth, 'Yesssss ... hullo ... Jack ... Mr Fucking fucker Jack Valentine ... Jesus when Valerie sees him here she'll flip – or worse. I *told* Sinead – I said girl, check and double-check that reptile is still locked up in England before we set the date but oh no! It'll be fine, Bernard, she said. Don't worry, Bernard, she said. He'll not come, Bernard, she said. And well then who is that over there, would you mind telling me – Prince Fucking Charles? There'll be dramaszzzz . . . there'll be war, oh yeszzzzz – WAR I tell you!'

In Bernard's defence, his behaviour as best man up to this had been exemplary. Buttonholes: on time, low-key and pinned to perfection. He had admired Barry's mono-grammed blazer, even though he thought it was terribly inappropriate and common. He had even (and this was no small feat), protected his charge from Tinara dousing him with a special Nuptial Love Blend which Bernard announced would have left the groom smelling like a 'tart's fart'!

On these counts – ten out of ten.

On the count of allaying the groom's waiting-time-at-altar nerves however, he had just lost some serious ground.

Barry started to shake.

This was it. This was the doom he had been feeling all morning. It was real. It was happening. Jack had come to steal his beloved Valerie away from him. On his wedding day. On the happiest day of his life. In front of all these people in this strange country. How could he have been so stupid? How could he have thought that it would all work out so wonderfully so quickly after it had all been so bad up to this? Why had he worn this silly blazer?

Barry tried to keep it all in, but before long his chin started to quiver with the pressure of containing his panic. His tear ducts, fit to burst, started to suck the water upwards like cola through a thirsty child's straw. He didn't even want to look around and get a look at his adversary, so afraid and certain was he that he had lost the game. He felt certain he could sense the congregation, all friends of Valerie and people from the studio, glaring hotly at his back, willing him to step aside and let the reunion with the satanic rock star begin. Barry concentrated all of his energy into not crying and getting his legs to move.

'I'm just going to the toilet,' he croaked at Bernard, who was still muttering about Jack, and he walked around the false wall of the set in front of them. There was, of course, no toilet back there. Only wires and cables and an English sound technician called Eric who was organizing the music for the wedding tape which the producer had decided snippets of might be used for the opening sequence of the show to boost ratings.

Eric was having a quick fag, a highly illegal activity given the electrical cable situation. He figured he would blame it on the smoke machine which the Wicca Merlin had requested to herald his entrance into the Wedding Tableau.

The groom suddenly appearing almost caused him to swallow his butt. Although a second glance suggested that this new arrival had other things on his mind than snitching on sneaky smokers.

'Nervous, mate?' he asked in a whisper, so they couldn't

be heard. In fairness, Barry's shivering demeanour did not warrant a verbal reply. But he answered anyway.

'Yes.'

'Having second thoughts then?'

Barry felt trapped suddenly – like there was no way out. Although he knew it was not the case, he nonetheless felt like Eric had been planted there, possibly by God, to ensure there was no escape from the humiliation that was sure to follow.

'No.'

'Well then, what are you doing back here mate?'

A pertinent question.

'There's no back door here you know.'

An all too obvious statement.

'I was not trying to escape.'

A bare-faced lie.

Eric stubbed the fag out carefully under his foot and took a look at his watch.

'Less than three minutes to go mate. You'd better make your mind up quick.'

Barry had gone into a kind of terrified trance, and now Eric started to panic. If this bloke didn't get back out front, he might be charged with something worse than smoking on set. Leading him astray or something. He tried to think of something to say, and his mind whizzed through all the Hollywood films he had ever seen searching for the correct cliché.

'Do you love her, mate?'

Barry remained rooted. More dramatic measures were called for.

Eric grabbed both his arms and shook the big Australian by the serge blazer, bringing the epic moment through to its climax.

'Dammit man! Do you love her?'

That did the trick. Barry awoke and all the things he had ever wanted became condensed into this moment.

'All my life – and more than anything or anyone else . . .'

Eric was getting into his stride now. He should have been an actor.

'Then what's stopping you, man!'

'I'm afraid . . .?'

'. . . Eric'

'. . . Eric – I'm afraid she'll never be able to love me the way I love her.'

'You will never know unless you try. Is she worth trying for . . .?'

'. . . Barry.'

'Is she worth taking the risk for, Barry? Is she worth trying for?'

'Yes!' Barry all but howled.

'Then go! Be a man! Go to her now, Barry – before it's too late!'

'I will! I will go to the woman I love! I will risk the years ahead to . . .'

Eric checked his watch again and cut him off.

'No time for speeches, Baz – you've got thirty seconds mate, so piss off out there and get on with it, eh?'

When Barry came back onto the set, he arrived to a standing ovation and a curtain of hankies and tears. Eric had stood on a mike switch stubbing out his fag and their whole conversation had been broadcast throughout the studio. Of course, Barry didn't know this – not right away. As far as he was concerned, he was just in front of a studio audience for the most important performance of his life. Except this time it was for real. He wasn't Barry Hooker, TV personality with lovely hair and benefactor of time-saving novelty items. He was Barry Hooker, Irish-Australian and would-be husband of the most beautiful woman in the whole wide world. This crowd were cheering him on, not for what he could do for them – but for what he was about to do for himself. For the very first time in his TV career he felt genuinely, unconditionally loved.

The wedding march started up, and the crowd turned to look at the bride coming down the audience-seating aisle.

From his position on the stage, Barry could see straight out the door of the studio to the front of the building where there was a revolving door. Valerie came through the glass circle with her brother – a thoroughly decent bloke whom he had met last night and who was giving her away in the absence of her father. Barry had been looking forward to meeting her old man and doing the whole asking for her hand formally thing, maybe throwing back a few scoops and all that bonding bloke stuff – but by all accounts he sounded like a nasty old sod and it wasn't to be.

Then there was a bit of shuffling about with the two

bridesmaids frantically waving and calling at them from outside. Valerie turned around just as Sinead was coming through the revolving door, and wrenched bride and brother back outside again. Barry's stomach lurched, but he stood firm. The crowd started shuffling as the wedding march was well and truly under way but there was no sign of bride and frock.

Just under a minute later, Valerie emerged through the door again. She was holding the arm of a stern old man got up in the stiffest, most formal outfit Barry had ever seen. His eyes were looking resolutely straight ahead, and glowering at the groom with the unmistakable threat of a protective father. Barry kept his head and greeted his glare with an assertive nod, as if to say, 'You can pass her over to me mate – no problem.'

Valerie, he was afraid to look at at first. She just appeared like a streak of glimmering light. His eyes passed across the old man's shoulder onto her face. There were tears rolling down her face and she seemed to be smiling and laughing at the same time.

And then Barry remembered why he was marrying her after all. Not because it was what he wanted, or because he had seen a picture of her mother when he was ten and had fallen in love with her, or because he had followed her around Dublin in a Viking helmet and nearly broken his neck into the bargain. He was marrying her because she was delicate and vulnerable and he wanted to cherish and protect her. It wasn't about him any more – about his passions and his needs. It was about

Valerie, and the fact that he was the best man in the world to look after her in a way that her father wasn't able and Jack Valentine never could.

She belonged to him. She always had, and, a few short moments from now – she always would.

36

'Well – I thought that passed off very civil . . .' said Karin as Sinead and herself came out of the ladies after a twenty-minute face-recycling session to put right the streaking from their tearful hour in the 'Chapel of Eternal Love'. Tinara's high priest had put on a fairly good show, despite the robes and the incense burning exercise – doubtless stopping short of stripping off and doing a fertility dance when he saw the stern disapproving expression on George Barton's face as he walked his daughter up the aisle.

'Could have done without the reptilian rock star showing up though.'

Sinead bristled but Karin didn't seem to notice.

'Did you see the ponytail and the gold jacket? Very "attention seeking" I thought, turning up uninvited like that, and done up like he was going on stage or something. Very tasteless turn of events, but then, what else would you expect from . . .'

Sinead cracked.

'What the hell is it with everyone and Jack? Just what is your problem?'

Karin pulled an 'excuse-I' face.

'Er . . . well let me see now? Could it be that he shit all over our best friend? That he is a sneak-around womanizing coke-quaffing out-of-control alco? That he takes his shirt off on the dance floor of Little's and struts around to 'It's Raining Men' like he is Mick Jagger? Or could it be . . . oh yes . . . that he turns up uninvited to the wedding of his ex-wife for no other reason than to spook the shit out of her?'

'Well he didn't, did he? Scare the shit out of her . . .'

'No – but then hey – not for the want of trying.'

Sinead shook her head and half-laughed.

'You know – you just won't give the guy a break will you?'

'Dur – and he deserves one – why?'

'Maybe he came here to wish Valerie and Barry all the best.'

'Muryaa. Don't buy that one. Try again.'

'Or to give her the million quid . . .'

'Ah now Sinead – in all fairness – do you really believe that?'

Karin was standing now with the eyebrow arched and a look somewhere between patronizing and pity wiped across her face.

'Well – I don't know is all,' Sinead knew she didn't have much of an argument but she kept going anyway.

'None of us know, is all I'm saying. I know he's had his problems in the past, but Jack Valentine is not a bad man. He seems to be trying to get the drink and drugs thing sorted out and I'm just saying that perhaps we should all give him a chance that's all. Not be so judgemental, people can change, people can . . .'

'Whatever,' Karin butted in. 'The point is he didn't make a scene – *yet* – and we should be grateful for that I suppose. Anyway, what the hell are we doing standing around talking about him when there is a party to be thrown and weeee – ' she flicked back the tips of her hair as they stood at the doorway into the reception – 'are in charge of throwing it!'

'Yeah – you're right,' Sinead conceded but without the same level of enthusiasm. As they went to sit down at a table, she heard Karin say half under her breath, 'Jesus – it was only the one ride . . .'

Sinead felt hurt at the obvious reference, but she let it go. She didn't want to be fighting with her friends today and besides, she still wasn't one-hundred-per-cent sure that Karin wasn't right about Jack.

Eamonn Doyle was feeling like an egg. Not like eating one soft fried between two buttered slices you understand, but like he was the actual egg itself.

He was sitting alone at his table while Noreen went up to the buffet to get them two plates of food.

'I don't want you walking around with plates in your hand. It doesn't look elegant for a man.'

'Elegant', and permutations of same, 'sophisticated', 'debonair', 'dignified', 'charming', 'tasteful' and 'refined', were adjectives that his daughter had been using liberally in the past few hours since he had allowed her carte blanche over his appearance.

He felt like a stuffed turkey. A bald stuffed turkey, for the tidy-up trim she had promised him had turned into a total scalping or in Noreen's words, a 'trendy' crop.

'You look like Dennis Hopper,' she had said.

'I look like an egg,' he had wailed, 'and who is Dennis Hopper?'

The suit she had chosen was a dark grey double-breasted pinstripe which he wouldn't have worn to his own funeral. The trousers were too tight, and frankly, restricting – and as for the shirt? Black! And a dark grey tie! The whole ensemble made him feel like his father circa 1947 done up to have tea with the bishop.

'Is it not very depressing?' he had asked miserably. 'It's a party after all and I've a lovely Hawaiian shirt I bought in Marbella a few years ago. It's not a formal wedding, I believe, and well, am I not a bit old-fashioned looking?'

'You look very debonair,' Noreen had assured him. The pretty young thing had looked so happy and pleased with herself, and what with time running out Eamonn didn't have the heart to put up a fight.

On their way to the studios, Noreen handed him a little box, gift-wrapped. He was moved that she had bought him a present, and started, 'Ah – you shouldn't have', although he was puzzled as to what the occasion was.

Inside was a pair of sunglasses.

The sun was not shining.

In the sky, Eamonn Doyle's heart or otherwise.

'They're Armani,' she squealed, not seeming to notice his disappointment, 'the very latest thing. Try them on . . . try them on . . .'

The world went orange.

'Wow! They look *fantastic*! So *sophisticated*! You *must* wear them!'

Again, this daughterly enthusiasm which was impossible to refuse.

So he had shuffled into the chapel, and then to the reception, unrecognized by even his staff, in the old-man's suit and the daft glasses and the whole chilly no-hair scenario. He wished he had a hat. He didn't like this feeling of total nakedness upstairs. It felt unnatural, exposed. In fact, now that he thought of it, he felt sure he had a red and green 'I swing for Mayo!' novelty golf-cap left over from an old batch he'd had made up for a tournament somewhere in his office. He'd run upstairs and get it after Noreen came back with the food. If she'd let him. Which she probably wouldn't.

Al and Digger were setting up in the corner, and they both winked over at him. They seemed to be the only two people in the place that actually recognized him. Even Florrie, his secretary of some fifteen years, had passed by the table giving him no more than a cursory glance. Eamonn was feeling so self-conscious about his 'new look' that he had no desire to speak to anyone, fearing that they would ask him questions about his sudden change of image that he would be unable to answer. He also sensed that several people, many of whom he did not even know, were looking at him strangely, which didn't make him feel any the more comfortable. Several women, in particular, had cruised past his table slowly, giving him very odd looks. The hefty red-head who had been helping that daft priest with the ceremony had wafted past him several times, her voluminous Indian-print skirt brushing the edge of his leg at one point. There was certainly something very peculiar going on here that Eamonn was not privy to. Like there was some kind of a plot afoot that was somehow tied up with Noreen's long-term plan to getting him up like a kipper. Being inadvertently in disguise, as he surely was, at an event which he was effectively supposed to be hosting was a very odd experience indeed. In truth, it was making him feel a little paranoid.

Eamonn looked over at Al enviously as he was attired in his comfortable working gear. A pair of shellsuit bottoms and a T-shirt emblazoned with 'I'M THE DEVIL DADDY' across his chest, then, '. . . AND I'M GONNA FUNK YOU UP' on its back. Digger in deference to his master had a similar one printed with 'DISCO COWBOY', and when he turned, 'I'LL LASSO YOU TO THE GROOVE'.

In under an hour the music would start, and Eamonn would be able to throw off this strait-jacket and get down to throwing a few serious moves.

Noreen came back to the table and put a plate of food down in front of him.

Seeing him look longingly over at the DJ station she said, 'I hope you are not even *thinking* about dancing.'

'I feel a right idiot done up like this Noreen,' he said

shifting about in the seat, 'these trousers are riding right up my . . .'

'Never mind about that – you are to sit still and look sophisticated.'

'Pass us over the cutlery there then so I can eat my dinner.'

'There isn't any.'

'What do you mean, there isn't any?'

'I didn't bring you any.'

He moved to get up from the seat.

'Don't move you . . .' she snarled out the side of her mouth, 'Jesus Christ do you know *nothing*?'

She said it like the idea of bringing food to a table and then not eating it was the most elementary of social protocols, and answered her father's incredulous expression with a swift explanation as if she were explaining something for the umpteenth time to an irritating child.

'The plate of food is just to be polite. A truly dignified man never actually eats in public, it's uncool. I am not having you guzzling back a big dinner like a country farmer . . .'

Eamonn moved the chair back. 'Ah now here, Noreen, you've gone too far this time. The hair was one thing, but this now is ridiculo—'

'Da – haaad . . .' she hissed out of the side of her mouth with the pleading urgency of an embarrassed teenager, 'there are people – watching.'

Eamonn followed her eyes across the room, and she was right. There, standing at the door was Karin Sheridan and her friend Sinead whom he'd danced with at that do a year ago. They were clearly looking directly at him and they were doing that dreadful thing that had put the fear of God into him since the days of his youth when he was the ugly boy in the corner of the dancehall that nobody wanted to go near. They were whispering.

The combination of the hair-loss shock, the stiff suit, the not being allowed to eat and all the bizarre circumstances that appeared to have been inflicted on him by his bossy daughter this day combined to root him to the spot. Eamonn Doyle didn't feel like eating any more, or dancing, or even taking the risk of standing up and walking across the room to make his escape. All he felt capable of doing was sitting stock-still and staring morosely into the middle distance until it was time to go home.

'That's more like it,' thought Noreen, as she tucked heartily into her plate of food, 'there'll be results yet before this day is through.'

37

'Spank me Daddy,' said Sinead as soon as they walked into the room, 'who's the hunk in the slick suit and the shades?' Her snit over Karin's diatribe having been instantly dissipated by the sophisticated vision in dark grey across the room.

'Where?' said Karin.

'Over there – *there* – sitting with that kid from your office.'

'Oooh yes – he's not bad. She must have traded in Eamonn for . . .'

The words crumbled in Karin's mouth as she took a closer look.

'Ah Jesus, it's the old scrote himself. Christ, she must have given him a going-over with the fashion manual.'

'Care I not,' Sinead snapped back, 'he looks pretty good to me. Do you remember last year and the two of us had great craic dancing at that dinner? I'm steaming over there for a few how-are-ya's.'

Karin grabbed her arm.

'You are not!' Sinead did not conceal her amusement, especially after Karin's hurtful comments about Jack.

'Ah yeah? Want him for yourself, do you?'

'Actually,' Karin drew her face back into a snooty snarl, 'I wouldn't go near him in a fit and well you know it. Besides, that "kid" from the office, Noreen, is his girlfriend.'

'That little teenage slip sitting next to him?'

'Yes.'

'Ha! Ya big fecking lug – she is in my hole! He's not the type to go chasing around after teenage skirt.'

'Excuse me? And how the hell do *you* know?'

'Oh for God's sake, Karin, I can just *tell* he's not the type.'

'Ha – you don't know him. I've been working with him for seven years, and I'm telling you he's her sugar daddy.'

'Well – if you say so, but I reckon you've got it wrong.'

Karin was getting irritated now. She hated to be contradicted at the best of times, but especially on something that she *knew* for a *fact* to be true.

'And how, would you mind telling me, is it possible that you know all this when I work with them *both*?'

'Well, I don't know. All I know is I've met Eamonn a couple of times and he doesn't seem the type. You know – he's intelligent, a good laugh, a fantastic dancer, from what I can remember – I was a bit jarred – anyway he just strikes me as one of those guys who'd be happy enough with someone his own age. Nothing to prove and besides . . .' She seemed reluctant to finish the sentence, which made Karin all the more curious.

'*Besides* what?'

'Well . . . em . . .,' ah feck it, rather out than in, 'you're not exactly Einstein when it comes to judging men.'

'And what the fuck do you mean by that?'

'Ah come on, Karin. The homosexual novelist? Picking off all the single men in Ireland from the *Who's Who* when any eejit would be able to tell if they've slipped the net this long there had to be something wrong with them?'

Karin went puce with rage. 'Well – I seem to remember your record of late hasn't exactly been . . .'

Sinead was kind of enjoying getting Karin's goat. She was so easy to goad. And anyway, it was true.

'Look I'm not criticizing you, honey. It's just that you've never really worked on your instincts – not just with men either. Remember the three-bedroomed kip in the Liberties you fell in love with, then you went the sensible route at the time and bought the shoebox? You're just one of those really logical, pragmatic people who puts all of their energy into things like work, getting results. You just never really give things time to develop and when it comes to men . . .?'

'And who are you – fucking Barbara Cartland?'

'Ah come on, Karin – I know I'm not exactly . . .'

'The pot calling the kettle black is what you fecking well are. Anyway, Eamonn and Noreen are an item and I don't want either of them pissed off at the moment for my own reasons – so watch my lips – *leave him alone.*'

'Whatever . . .' Sinead said with a casual shrug but barely concealing the mischievous glint in her eye.

'I'm going up to get a drink,' growled Karin and headed off for the bar, 'so *be-have* or be warned!'

For the next hour or so the two women got on with the niceties of being hostesses on the radiant Valerie's behalf. Occasionally they both looked over at her as she moved around the room, iridescent in her floating lace dress, gloriously happy with her new husband by her side. Both women were happy for her, and yet neither could help a small twinge of regret. Not so much at their own missing out, but at the gap between how perfect Valerie fell into the fairytale ethos of this day, and how far away both of them felt from experiencing that same kind of innocent joy.

Sinead looked around for Jack, but he was nowhere to be seen. She had noticed Tommy appearing at some stage after the service, but had not had the chance to go and talk to him between arranging trains and holding Karin back from crucifying the photographer. She expected he had spirited Valentine back from whence he came, and while it would have been the perfect opportunity to see how the old dog was, she thought that his absence was probably for the best.

Karin was not in good form after the exchange with Sinead about Eamonn. A number of swiftly downed glasses of wine had not improved her mood any, and in fact had swelled her initial irritation into a kind of crimped paranoia. The contradiction of symptoms she was experiencing were, by turn, an inability to take her eyes from the new-look debonair figure of Eamonn Doyle as he sat firmly staring straight out at nothing in particular and a boiling rage at the *nerve* of the man turning up here in a suit with a Dennis Hopper crop looking like a big dish when the world and his mother knew that he was a boil on the arse of Irish manhood and had no right to be going around fooling people into thinking he was a hunk when he was anything *but*! This emotion was further complicated by a head-banging annoyance at herself for even wasting mental energy thinking about same, and a nagging little doubt poking the edge of her conscience that perhaps Sinead had been right – sort of – about something.

As the lights went down, and the horrendous couple of mismatched nyuks that Doyle had appointed to do the music started up their barrage of disco, Karin decided that enough was enough. She was going over to talk to him. She waited until Noreen was loo-bound and plonked herself down next to her boss.

'You had your haircut,' she raised her glass drunkenly in a faux toast laced with sarcasm.

'It's a bit short all right.'

The big prick. Despite the trendy gear he had nothing smart to say for himself as usual.

'You've a big lump on the back of your head,' she said for the want of anything better. He looked crestfallen. Devastated actually. This was more like it. Although actually, the better part of her announced through the descending fog of drink, that perhaps she'd better try to be a bit nice. Noreen and herself were planning to present the document to him on Monday.

'Noreen looks well today.'

'Ah – she's a grand girl alright.'

Eurk! Grand girl! What a way to describe your girlfriend!

'Yeah – I like her. She's a great worker too,' and then although it stuck her to say it, 'you're well-matched the pair of you.'

'Ah sure, why wouldn't we be?'

Well how about you are a hideous culchie gremlin and she is a gorgeous urbane chick! She could not help herself. 'Well – you know, the age thing.'

'How do you mean?' he looked genuinely confused. He didn't even *know*. He didn't even think it was weird. Jesus – the arrogance of him! Who the fuck did he think he was! She decided to 'borrow' from Sinead in the interest of keeping her job.

'It's just that I never had you pegged as the type. To go with younger women, I mean.'

He was looking at her very oddly now – as far as she could tell with the sleepy eye tucked away there behind the glasses. Before he had the chance to reply, Noreen came back. She ran her hand quickly along his newly velvet head and said, 'You all right there, Daddy?'

Argh! This was too much! 'Daddy'! How revolting! The little girl act – and he didn't look too unhappy about it either! Karin couldn't stick it another minute. She was disgusted, frankly, with the pair of them. Eurk –

they were welcome to each other. She didn't want him anyway. Wait a minute. She really *didn't* want him – where the fuck had that come out of?

'I'm back off to the bar – *Daddy* . . .' Karin announced with as heavy a dose of sarcastic dignity that she could manage under the cloudy circumstances of her current thought pattern. Then she criss-crossed the five-inch mules across the floor, shaking her head at intervals with the horror of the nauseating scene she had just witnessed.

'Why did Karin call me Daddy?' Eamonn asked Noreen when she'd gone.

'Maybe she likes you?' his daughter replied.

'What's that got to do with anything?' he asked.

'You'll see,' she said mysteriously.

⬭

Al and Digger were taking it easy. Playing it safe for the first half. Eamonn had told them there was a big music agent in the wedding party, and Digger had got himself all worked up into a lather of excitement wanting to throw the remix of 'Mary – what did ye do with me trousers?' right from the word go. Al, the old hand was having none of it. 'We'll warm them up first, lad, with a few golden oldies. None of your rock rubbish mind, just ease them in with a bit of Barry – turn up the heat with Disco Inferno – make sure they're sizzling hot with a few drinks inside them before we whack them with the real thing!'

A few reluctant bodies were jigging along half-heartedly to George McCrae's 'Rock Your Baby'.

'Sexsee,' Al crooned along into the karaoke mike, trying to whip up the crowd, 'Woe-man, take me in th'harms en' rock-ya-bay-bay – come on there and good evening laydeez and gennelmen, let's get up there on th' dance floor now and throw it all up now for th' luffly Valerie and her new husban' Barry there now on their big day – Cum-hone a' said – woe-man, take me in th'harms en' rock-ya-bay-bay – ah-haaaaaaaaaaaaaai – there's plenty more where that came from laydeez and gennelman, let's get in the mood there now with the great George McCrae – take me in th'harms en' rock-may . . . a classic hit with 'Rock Your Baby' there and I want you all up now for the next track – another classic disco hit . . .'

Digger didn't know where Al was going with all the blather, but, fair play, a few more bodies appeared on the designated studio square. Newcomers included two skinny aul lads, their wild grins saying more about drink taken to date than the bit of foot hobbling said about their affinity to Original Disco. They were joined by ladies in hats ranging from fifty to seventy who struggled to replicate moves learned in a recent Loosen Your Limbs This Winter in a Telly Aerobics slot on afternoon television. It amounted to hand jiving accompanied by perpetual knee bending broken by the occasional low kick. Digger was starting to feel desperate. It was not exactly Out-Rave-Us, and Al's continuous use of the mike was not, he believed, helping.

'. . . and I know you'll all love this one, go gerrup here and shake your booties for Van McCoy and his legendary

Soul City Symphony for that most merciful of hip-spankin' tracks – "The Hus-tle"!!!'

The old ladies hadn't a clue what he was playing but, feck it, they were delighted with themselves for still being able to stand, never mind having their jiggling bottoms described as 'booties' which made at least two of them squeal with delight.

What Al knew that Digger didn't, was that if you can get a few enthusiastic pensioners up warming the dance floor, it liberates the rest of the crowd. Shy bods would figure if their granny could make an exhibition of herself, well then hey, they might as well join in. Besides that, there is nothing more uplifting than seeing pensioners party, and all experienced on the wedding scene knew how infectious it could be.

So the older DJ had devoted an hour of his meal-time to working the room, flirting with ladies in lilac suits who thought he was the epitome of all that was fashionable in his risqué T-shirt and his back-to-front baseball cap, and flattering the shite out of them.

'I'd say now a fine lookin' woman like you will be getting this party started and no mistake.'

'Gerraway outta tha', I'm sixty-six.'

'Sure never mind that, isn't experience in a woman a great thing.'

'I've two new hips since last October.'

'Well let's seem them wiggle and put them to work.'

To which they would howl with laughter and slap his arm and call him a cheeky pup. 'You'll not let me down there, Mam – I want to see you up there showing us all what you're made of.'

When 'The Hustle' came on, the old ladies were enjoying themselves, but there were others there for whom the freedom of dance seemed an unattainable ambition.

Eamonn Doyle was tortured with the desire to dance.

'The Hustle' was his forte. But what with being strait-jacketed in the suit, and Noreen's assertion that he was to live up to his sophisticated new image and not be making a Holy Show of himself, the lyrics seemed to be simply torturing him with their sweet temptations.

'Oooooooooooooh – ooh – ooh – ooh – oooooh . . .' the seductress sang – and then like a plea to his very soul, 'Dooo it!'

Despite all instructions to the contrary, Eamonn found his feet were tapping out the rhythmic long-learned steps under the table. When she finally called, 'Do The Hustle!' he thought he could stand it no longer.

He was to be finally saved, as is so often the way with such cases of unexpressed emotion, by a series of karmic coincidences.

First was Digger's mimed demand for a pint to calm his nerves from the DJ station, which sent his warden Noreen to queue at a crowded bar.

Secondly was the fact that a woman present that day had once, not a year before that date, allowed herself to be swept away by the delights of dancing disco. At the moment that Mr Van McCoy with the assistance of his Soul City Symphony was sending his 'ooh-ooohs' and his maracas pulsing through the innards of the tortured, inert body of one Mr Eamonn Doyle, Sinead O'Sullivan was squealing to herself, 'Eeeek – I remember this one – where's Eamonn!'

It was but the work of a moment for her to land her long legs across from bar to dance floor, grabbing her erstwhile dance partner on the way.

They were magnificent, gliding across a designated small section of the floor in an understated salsa. Eamonn slid his foot backwards and forwards in perfect time and when he put his hand around her waist and gently pushed she found herself progressing into a perfect demi-turn without hardly having to think. Together, they were everything Noreen feared her father would never be on a dance floor. They were elegant and distinguished. They could have been French, they were that cool. Or Brazilian diplomats, they had that much natural rhythm between them.

But if Noreen was quietly pleased with her father's show-stopping display, there was another woman who was not impressed. That person was Ms Karin Sheridan. The last few minutes had taken something of an unnatural turn. Firstly, was a conversation she had had with Sinead immediately prior to the Amazonian dance-queen kidnapping her boss.

'She calls him Daddy! Can you *believe* it?'

'What's so strange about that?' Sinead had teased.

'Well – it's disgusting, don't you think? Calling your partner "Daddy"? Especially with that age gap . . . eugh!'

'Well, he is her daddy.'

'Ah now, there's no need to be facetious.'

'No – I mean he really *is* her daddy. Barry's after telling me. Noreen is Eamonn's daughter. Told you you'd got it wrong . . . Eeeeek, I remember this one . . .' Etc.

OK. So first up was a few seconds' shock. To be expected. Then of course, there was the all-falling-into-place stuff. Noreen never actually saying right out what her relationship with Eamonn was, the fact that they were living together so early on in their apparent 'relationship', her ability to slag him off for his appearance – blah-blah-blah. On an' on until it seemed like the most obvious thing in the world and Karin the most stupid half-wit to have not copped on earlier. Then, of course, there was the question of how she could have been stupid enough to have thought them lovers in the first place. She had a third-level education and so was, obviously, not *actually* stupid. The answer to that question then was obvious. She was a bad, horrible, mean, nasty, churlish, resentful, filthy-minded individual who was incapable of forming a relationship not because there weren't any good men out there, but because she was a loathsomely unattractive sample of humanity. Despite all of this being obviously true to Karin at that moment in time, some hardy corner of her spirit instructed her not to close the case just yet. Hanging herself from the central toilet light-fitting on Valerie's wedding day was an obvious gesture of martyrdom that could possibly help ablute the depth of her crimes against self and society. But then, perhaps there was an alternative. Perhaps all was not lost after all.

Sometimes you don't know that you know things that you know until you actually know them. And such was the case with Karin Sheridan at this apocalyptic turning point. It took her two seconds to decide that Eamonn Doyle was not only not such a bad stick after all, but that in fact he was kind of great. *Actually* great, actually. He had never said a cross word to her in work, never without being actively driven to it by her in any case. He had been good humoured about her constant slagging off of him over the years, and in fact the worst that could be said of him was that he was a bit – well – sad. But by God, he didn't look sad today. Not at all. Not up there on the dance floor, the suit jacket slung to one side as he caressed and hip-ground with her friend Sinead. Far from being his usual picture of stunted pathos, he looked kind of smooth. Sexy. So did Sinead, as a matter of fact. Look sexy. In fact, grinding their hips and slithering in and out of each other's steps they looked very sexy indeed. The pair of them. Up there together. Looking sexy.

And this is where part two of Karin's unnatural turn took place.

New-Look Eamonn Doyle out there looking sexy with someone else? Oh no. This would not do at all. Where he should be, at this moment in time, thought Karin, is over here looking sexy with me. This was most certainly not the natural way of things. In fact, so not right did it feel that Karin started to feel not a little put out with Sinead. Look at the cut of her, she thought, the big lanky hulk giving it loads all over him like she was in ownership of same. Salsa-ing to save her friggin' life, a big meaty grin on her face. The cow.

Despite the recent transmogrification from heartless to humble, it was nonetheless not within Karin Sheridan's social repertoire to go steaming in there mid-Hustle and lashing Sinead out of it. Too coarse. Too obvious. No. What Karin needed was a partner of her own to illustrate to Eamonn and indeed all present what a disco-diva *ought* to really look like.

And so, inhibitions loosened with the skite of gin swilling around inside her, and senses honed in pursuit of her man, Karin Sheridan searched quickly around the room for a suitable foil partner.

38

There were two men for whom the wedding day of Valerie Valentine and Barry Hooker had turned into something of a reflective experience.

The first of these was Claude Moore.

While his recent ejection from the closet straight into the arms of Bernard Chequers had not been as traumatic as he might have once thought (Oscar Wilde, plenty of perfectly adequate war poets etc., no shame in the love that dares not speak—etc.), their relationship had been, while not quite kept 'under wraps' so to speak, not of a publicly cuddly nature. There was an unspoken suggestion, for instance, when they were seen regularly together at functions that there might be 'something' going on, but to date there had been no hand-holding 'oh-he's-my-gay-lover' displays. The opera/recital/lecture/poetry reading itself had always taken precedence over the whole 'togetherness on a date' aspect.

This was different. A wedding. Weddings were things you brought partners to. Claude had begged not to come but Bernard had insisted, openly threatening to cut off all scone supplies and insisting he would fashion a full-length ball gown from the purple velvet drapes he had recently purchased on their trip to Florence and wear it with earrings to the next formal meeeting of the Wagner Appreciation Society if Claude did not attend to support him on his big day as best man. Bernard could be a cantankerous old queen when he wanted to be, and Claude was able to comfort himself that the crowd would doubtless be wall-to-wall commoners, hence there would be nobody there he need worry about.

Aside from that, weddings were simply not Claude's 'thing'. He had an intellectual's dread of mindless phenomena like women-in-hats and discos, both of which were here in abundance, and the cynical disgust with which he was surveying the reception scene from a safe corner of the bar was further compounded when he spotted that truly dreadful woman he had been out with on the night be met Bernard, moving assertively in his direction.

Sneering disdain turned to blind dread as he noticed that she was not only moving in his direction, but actually *dancing* across the floor towards him. And not only was she dancing, but she was writhing her hips in a manner which he assumed was meant to be erotic. Beads of sweat broke out on his brow. He turned quickly – but there was no escape. Before he could say 'Go away woman and don't be annoying me', Karin Sheridan had thrown what must have been, and certainly felt like, an industrial-strength pashmina around his waist and was dragging him with more physical force than he could ever remember having been exerted on him in the past, in the direction of the dance floor.

For her part, Karin had illogically assumed that if she could get Claude Moore, Dublin's driest shite, to dance, she would prove to all and sundry that she was a seductress of the highest order. It was the toughest challenge she could think of, but even at that she could not have imagined the snooty goat would prove as intransigent as he did. Maintaining her fun-girl aplomb while her heels were all but digging a trough with the effort of yanking him away from the bar was not easy. But driven with the insane urge to prove a point she somehow managed it, and before long Claude found he was centre stage in what can only be described as his own personal corner of hell.

A seething mass of jiggling women in peach and lilac suits parted to make way for them. 'The Hustle' had finished and for one glorious moment Claude thought he was off the hook. But it was not to be. Right away Al slapped on another record whose farting bass and speeding drum made Claude feel slightly dizzy. Not a sliver of sense could Claude make of it all, as the lyrics blasted out on top of him.

'*Burn baby burn . . . to ma surprise – one huun-dred storeys hai . . .*'

To be in such immediate proximity to a noise of such astronomical dreadfulness was, in itself, a trauma that Claude thought he would never get over. But that was only the start of it. The woman – Karin – was circling around him like a mating turkey, strutting and spinning in turn in time to the music. He would have happily left her to it, only for two things. One, the length of her pashmina was still wrapped around his waist and she was maintaining as firm a grip on it as she had earlier, except now she was wriggling it across his hips in some class of a Dance-of-the-Seven-Veils effort. And two – everybody in the whole room was watching them. Or rather, as Claude felt it – they were watching *him*. Mortified to the very hem of his being, Claude began to shuffle his feet with a reluctance befitting a man of his intellectual stature.

'*Burn baby burn – Disco Inferno – burn baby burn – burn the mother down ya'll . . .*'

As the voice belted out of the speaker Claude thought it would never end, until he noticed something else. Another voice – and clapping. Claude took his eyes from the floor where they had been rooted in his embarrassment and there, at the edge of the dance floor, not three feet away from him was Bernard. He was jiggling those great big lovely legs of his in time to the music, and wiped across his face, pointed in the exact spot where Claude was standing, was an expression of such undisguised joy and pride that, for a moment Ireland's most renowned academic was taken aback. Could it be that Bernard was egging him on in this ludicrous display? A one-hand wave followed by a series of claps and 'G'wan ya's Claude' confirmed same. Surrounding his loved one, the crowd, far from being convulsed in fits of hysterical laughter at the sight of a Great Literary Novelist 'shaking his booty', were also clapping him on.

378

Then it happened.

If one had ever asked Claude Moore if he had seen the film *Saturday Night Fever* in his youth – or indeed if he could name the actor, one Mr John Travolta, who had starred in the film – our genius would have had to answer in the negative. However, such is the way of popular media culture that, no matter how much a young man might hide themselves away in genuine pursuit of higher intellectual planes, somehow the image of the man in the white suit and the black shirt will wangle itself into their consciousness.

Driven on by the love of his man (and, he was to admit on a subsequent Saturday night sojurn to Little's, the indefinable force of the funky beat that, despite one's prejudices, is inclined to, at some time or another, smack it to one nonetheless), Claude flung one pointed hand in the air in a gesture of defiant disco. Up and down, up and down that pointed finger went until he found that, despite himself, the knees began to bounce. Before he knew what was happening to him at all, the pointing finger and the bouncing knees had fallen in with the beat of the music (how had he missed it before!) and it would do nothing but for Claude to grind his hips in a full circle just to break it up a bit. As a natural progression of same, the arms flung themselves out in front of him in fists and he was mixing up that boiling vat of disco boogie to beat the band!

Karin Sheridan, as the catalyst for the best fun he had had in ages (and later he was to reflect, probably the *first* bit of fun he had ever had – Bernard's brand of affection excepting), was rewarded for her efforts by total inclusion in his version of the buttock-lunging bump before the Disco Inferno was extinguished.

Claude could not be moved from the floor after that, and Bernard strutted over to join him with an immeasurable dose of enthusiasm.

Karin's work done, she sauntered over to a quiet corner and waited.

She had looked good out there and she knew it. Claude Moore up dancing? Don't be talking! She was something special in the seduction party-girl department and make no mistake.

She did not have to wait long.

Eamonn had a second glass of champagne in his hand as an excuse.

'They're about to cut the cake.'

'I'm not hungry,' she said smartly, but without malice.

She liked him, but by God she wasn't going to work for it. Let him have another go. He'd been trying with her long enough. All she needed for him was to try one more time.

Eamonn wasn't sure if he could stomach another put-down. God knows, what with the haircut and all, she had enough rope. Although he had to admit, there was something slimming about the cut of that suit that had made him feel unnaturally cool out there dancing with Sinead, and the glasses over the eye were giving him a weird kind of confidence.

On top of that, Karin was radiating something different today. She had always been a good-looking woman, but in the white suit, and her colour heightened with the dancing, she looked – well – magnificent. Far too magnificent for him of course, and that fact rendered him, for a moment, speechless. Best play it safe and bring up work.

'I read the report you did with Noreen.'

'Oh yes?' Karin was surprised to find herself slightly disappointed.

'Very good.'

'Thanks.'

'Excellent in fact.'

'She wasn't supposed to show it to you until Monday.'

'Oh.'

'Yeah well – no harm I suppose.'

The moment had turned a bit dry. Both of them wanted to break it, but neither really knew how. Eamonn handed her the glass, and turned to go.

'You're a good dancer,' she blurted out just to keep him there. It sounded highly teenage, but it was the best she found she could manage.

'Are you slagging me?'

There was something different in the way that he said it. An assertion in his voice that she had never heard before; the suggestion that there might be an actual consequence to her having perpetually taken the mickey out of him over the years. Sacking perhaps? But she sensed it might be more along the lines of putting her across his knee and giving her a good spanking. With the glasses masking his face, she couldn't tell.

Karin put her drink down and reached over to remove them. Eamonn blinked, somewhat taken aback, then opened his eyes and, for the first time since they had known each other he looked her straight in the face.

It wasn't as if Karin did not notice his deformation, but in that moment it did not seem to matter. Beyond it, and perhaps because of it, Eamonn's eye's were challenging her with a hard confidence that felt unfamiliar and peculiarly attractive. He was staring her down. Karin felt slightly weak under this obvious display of domination, but it wasn't in her nature to concede.

'I might be.'

Eamonn let on a wry smile.

'Well then, Karin – that was some show you put on out there yourself.'

Touché. She raised an eyebrow and nodded through a smile.

He wasn't going to run away and hide in his office. Not today.

'I thought we might go out to dinner next week – to discuss your future position in the company.'

'And anything else?' she said, excited by this sudden flirtation.

'Not for the time being . . .' He looked away briefly before suggesting, 'Unless . . .?'

'Unless what?' Karin leapt straight back.

'Unless you fancy skipping out of here and going on somewhere else?'

'Why, what on *earth* could you be suggesting, Mr Doyle?'

He could have been halfway on the road to the biggest put-down of his life – but Eamonn Doyle didn't care any more. Finally, he had got wise to the firm hand required by this woman and, oddly enough part of what was driving him along was the new suit. It made him feel a bit like a Bond villain which what with the bald head and the nasty eye and all, was a fantasy he didn't mind at all pursuing.

'I'm suggesting nothing, Miss Sheridan. I think I'll leave all suggestions up to you, if you don't mind.'

'Well then how about dinner at the Merrion?'

'Sounds good to me.'

'Room service?'

Eamonn nearly swallowed his own teeth, but managed to keep it together.

'Better still,' he said. Then he offered Karin his Armani-clad arm and the two of them wandered off into the night just as Al slipped a spot of Mr B. White onto the turntable to play them out.

While Claude Moore was being freed from the shackles of his intellectual prison, Jack Valentine was still smarting from the painful fact that, even though he was indisputably Mr Centre of the Universe, even though he had got himself done up like a knight and made a big entrance at his ex-wife's wedding, even though he had suffered through six weeks of rehab clean and sober – nobody appeared to give a shit.

As the ceremony progressed, he felt sure that everyone must have been looking at him *really*. That while they were all clapping and sobbing and hugging the bride and groom, *really* what was going on in their heads was, 'Look over there at Jack Valentine. Isn't he a marvellous man altogether to have pulled himself together like that and in the gorgeous gold jacket. Didn't he wear that outfit at his farewell concert in '94?'

Reality began to dawn when, outside the chapel, he found himself utterly unapproached by adoring hoards of autograph-seeking fans. Even that fat fag dress-designer who had been giving him dirty looks in the church before the wedding took place, appeared to have forgotten about him altogether. Everyone, including Sinead, seemed swept up in the whole drama of the event as they gathered around Valerie and her goon of a groom taking pictures and chucking confetti and the like. Jack, and his own little inner dramas were dwarfed and left standing alone in a corner.

Tommy turned up to save the day. Mr AA on his white fucking charger, thought Jack as he saw him anxiously looking around. But at the same time he was grudgingly grateful that someone cared enough to notice he was there.

'Read the paper after you'd gone and figured you'd come here.'

'Fat lot of fucking good it did me.'

'Well – why did you come?'

Jack didn't like this line of questioning. Too hard.

'Oh never fucking mind. Let's get the hell out of here.'

They walked to the car and Tommy asked, 'Home? Will I drive?'

'No,' said Jack, fully aware that Tommy was just gagging to get behind the wheel of his flash Alpha. 'I fancy a walk.'

Jack walked in silence while Tommy annoyed him with stupid questions and platitudes which were supposed to make him feel better – but didn't.

'Do you fancy going to a meeting?'

'No.'

'There's an excellent one on at eight o'clock in . . .'

'No!'

'My sponsor always says that—'

'Will you shut the fuck up, Tommy!'

Finally his hapless, only-trying-to-help friend snapped. He'd done everything in his power possible to help this arrogant bollocks and all he was getting in return was shit.

He stopped dead in his tracks and grabbed the centre-of-the-universe by the arms.

'Listen here, you ungrateful cunt. I have tried – God knows I have tried to help you out here – but if you want to piss all over your own life well then that's up to you. I would like to see you get your act together, but if you want to go back out there and fuck it all up again, then by Christ there's nothing I can do to stop you. It's up to you Jack . . . do you fucking understand me? It's up to *you*!'

Jack looked at him, incredulous that somebody was putting it to him like this. As Tommy started to walk away Jack called out.

'No-ho-ho-ho-body cares about me-hee-heeee . . .' he wailed.

But Tommy had seen it all before.

'Oh yes they do, Jack Valentine. There is at least one person that I know of who cares about you very, very much.'

Jack's face brightened with curiosity.

'Valerie?'

'No.'

'You?'

'Oh, for fuck's sake. YOU – you selfish prick. You care

so much about your fucking self, or rather, you are so bothered, so *obsessed* with yourself that, frankly, everyone else is bored – B.O.R.E.D. with you.'

Jack was gob-smacked but he wasn't arguing.

'You didn't go there today to wish Valerie the best did you?'

For once, Jack decided to tell the truth.

'No,' he said in a tiny voice.

'Well then, *why* did you go Jack?'

'Dunno.' Jack felt as small as a pea. He'd fought against the counsellors like a dog in Humility House. Now he was getting the hang of it, a week after he'd come out. Typical. All that money wasted.

'You went because you wanted to cause trouble – you ignorant fuck. You put that woman through hell, Jack. HELL! Now she gets a crack at a new life, a second chance and all you can think about is turning up on her big day and causing trouble. And you can't even do *that* properly. Look at you, you self-pitying pathetic little prick. You'd be better off getting yourself plastered than going back to cause a riot. Do the job *right* Jack – or don't do it at all!'

Tommy was right. Jack was far better at drinking than at not drinking – that was clear enough. He should go out and get himself trolleyed. Except? Except for ... something strange occurred to Jack and the words were out before he really knew he had said them.

'Except I don't want to drink.'

Tommy shook his head and walked over to him, resting his hand gently on this impossible gobshite's arm.

'Well, then why don't you just get on with that then, mate? Why don't you just get on with being sober?'

Jack nodded.

'One Day At a Time – Jack. You know my sponsor used to say to me, 'Humility', he used to say . . .'

'Don't push it, Tommy.'

Tommy laughed.

'All right then so. There's a meeting at eight o'clock in Molesworth. I'll be there and I'd be grateful for the lift back, if you fancy turning up.'

Jack shrugged, but somehow Tommy knew that he'd make it.

'You walking back into town?'

'Naaah,' Jack replied, 'think I'll just hang out on my own for a while. Few bits and pieces to think about, yeah?'

Tommy left him to it.

Sinead was having a fantastic time altogether. The two lads doing the music, despite the worrying start, were totally brilliant and now that the party was under way they had started playing this pure mental stuff that was like a cross between disco and rave. Sinead, who had, Miles excepting, never liked this kind of music found herself stuck to the dance floor in a homosexual sandwich between Claude and Bernard. She had not given Jack Valentine a second thought, until she saw him suddenly appear at the doorway. Her stomach lurched. A kind of automatic reaction since that night they had spent together. Whether it was because she feared he might cause a scene or something else, she didn't really know. In any case, she felt somehow responsible. As if she should be the first to approach him.

As he saw her come over Jack tried smiling. The result was a kind of lopsided half-hearted effort laced with a sadness that seemed to take the bottom out of Sinead's heart.

'Hey Jack – you're back.'

The rhyme was delivered with less brightness than it deserved.

'Yeah. I probably shouldn't have come.'

There was no answer to that, and none was attempted.

'How's the bride?'

Sinead turned her head around and Jack followed her eyes to where Valerie was standing by the DJ booth, her head thrown back in laughter while Al told her some joke. Barry was close by gazing at her with abandoned adoration.

'See for yourself,' Sinead said, aware that Jack must be finding this painful, and wondering if that was the reason he had left after the chapel.

'She looks a million dollars,' he said, and there was no reply to that either. It was not often that Sinead felt stumped for words. Jack was one of her oldest friends, and yet she didn't know what to say to him any more. Without the brash edge that drink gave him, Sinead didn't know who she was dealing with any more.

They stood for a few minutes in silence, then Jack said, 'I'm going to give it to her, you know?'

Sinead looked slightly puzzled.

'The million.'

'Yeah?' Sinead was surprised, and even more surprised that she believed him.

'Anonymously.'

'She'll know it's from you.'

'Yeah well – that too. Ultru . . .? '

'Altruism?'

'Yeah that – s'never really been my bag.'

'You can say that again.'

Sinead felt better for the bit of repartee. Perhaps there was no need to feel so awkward after all.

'Sinead, I . . .' The tone of his voice suggested that there was major awkwardness coming back. 'Sinead, I'm er . . .'

This was the hardest thing that Jack had ever done. He had never said sorry once in his life. Or rather, never once when accompanied by a feeling of actually *being* sorry. The business on the phone with Valerie had only been bluff. He knew he'd have to go back and do it again, but he also knew that today was not the time to do it. He'd practise on Sinead, and in all honesty, he did feel very sorry for the way he had behaved towards her. Looking at her standing there in front of him, the Amazon Agent, as he called her, he knew that she had always felt something for him. No friend had ever been as loyal to him over such a long period of time. It may not have meant that she was in love with him – but he knew that she loved him in some way nonetheless. Jack suddenly felt towards her a kind of trust. As if, of all the people he had ever had and lost in his life, this was the one relationship he could not afford to destroy.

'Sinead – I'm sorry about the other week. You know the . . .'

'The sleeping with me?'

'Yeah. That.'

'Was it that bad?'

Jack started to squirm.

'No, that's not what I meant, I . . .'

'Because I had a great time.'

'Really?'

'Yeah. No regrets.'

'Really?'

'None. But if you didn't enjoy it, well then . . .'

'No – I did.'

'What?'

'Enjoy it.'

'Really?'

'Really.'

'Well then – good then. That's over and done with so.'

Both of them stood for a moment, not really knowing what to do next. The natural thing was to go to the bar and start up the business of getting hammered. But that wasn't on the agenda. Neither was doing the whole 'Congrats' to the bride and groom under the cirumstances.

Jack looked lost, and so Sinead decided to step in.

'What are you doing now?' she asked him.

'Oh – I don't know, I'm meeting Tommy later but . . .'

'You've got the afternoon to kill?'

'That's it.'

'So how was Humility House?'

'All right – no, pretty grim.'

'Well it worked, you look pretty damn humble to me . . .'

Throwing in a slag was a risk, but she had to know if there was anything of the old Jack Valentine left.

'. . . apart from the get-up. What in the name of God induced you to turn up today in the gold velvet. Have you lost your mind?'

Jack looked a little crestfallen, but only for a second.

'Ah, fuck off, Sinead – can you not be nice for a change?'

'Sorry, Jack. I don't do nice. You should know me well enough by now to know *that*.'

And, in fairness, he did.

'Well then how about "nasty"?'

'Very – and *always*.'

She said it with a glint in her eye that let Jack know exactly what she was driving at. And to his utter astonishment, and it would have to be said, extreme pride, Jack Valentine noticed that he was experiencing the first full-blown hard-on he had had since he gave up the drink.

'And are you feeling a bit nasty now I wonder?'

'Well, you'll have to take me somewhere and find out,' Sinead cooed straight back.

'I've a meeting at eight.'

'Better hurry up then or you'll miss the deadline.'

Hardly 'happily ever after', thought Sinead. But it's a start.

ACKNOWLEDGEMENTS

In my last book I was laughed at for writing the most long-winded gushing string of acknowledgements ever. I hope one day to be cool and clever enough to just say 'Here I come there's nobody like me – am spectacular all by myself', but alas, that day has not yet arrived. So thank you to my family for consistently being on side instead of taking me down a peg or two, which was doubtless tempting. Especially to my brother Tom for making me appear more erudite than I am by giving me expert info on Wagner. To fellow writers Suzanne Power, Marian Keyes and Ailish Connelly for their encouragement. Thanks especially to Gai Griffin for sourcing the words to 'Living Doll' at a moment's notice. To fabulous mine of information rock journalist Tony Clayton Lea for letting me pick his brains and reminding me of the existence of Chesney Hawkes and Climie Fisher. The nightmares continue. To Pat McCabe for treating me like a fellow writer even though he is a literary giant and should be too busy bagging Bookers than bothering with the likes of me. Thanks to yourself and Margot for being such supportive friends in my first year as a writer. To Renee for 'letting me get on with it' and providing big roast dinners on demand. To my agent Marianne Gunn O'Connor for flitting around the globe on my behalf. Thanks also to Vicky Satlow over there being glam deal-doer in Milan. To Imogen Taylor at Macmillan for nudging me along and being on the other end of endless 'Am I good?' e-mails. To the Macmillan gang en mass. Aside from the professionalism etc., I've had great fun, and thank you for all the wardrobe-expansion opportunities. Special thanks to Lucy Henson for the 'minding'.

Lastly, to my husband Niall. For keeping our life going as 'normal' – even though, at times, it has been far from that. For managing that line between freedom and security and for your quiet trusting support.